ARKANE
THRILLERS
BOOKS 4-6

J.F. PENN

ARKANE Thrillers Books 4-6
Copyright © Joanna Penn 2017. All rights reserved.

One Day in Budapest
Copyright © J.F.Penn (2013, 2015). All rights reserved.
Second edition.

Day of the Vikings
Copyright © J.F.Penn (2014). All rights reserved.
First edition. Printed 2014.

Gates of Hell
Copyright © J.F.Penn (2015). All rights reserved.
First edition. Printed 2015.

ISBN: 978-1-912105-91-5

www.JFPenn.com

This book is a work of fiction. The characters, incidents and dialogue are drawn from the author's imagination and are not to be construed as real. Any resemblance to actual events or persons, living or dead, is fictionalized or coincidental.

The right of Joanna Penn to be identified as the author of this work has been asserted by the author in accordance with the Copyright, Designs and Patents Act,1988. All rights reserved. No part of this publication may be reproduced, stored in a retrieval system, or transmitted, in any form, or by any means, electronic,mechanical, photocopying, recording or otherwise, without the prior permission of the publishers.

This book is sold subject to the condition that it shall not, by way of trade or otherwise, be lent, resold, hired out, or otherwise circulated without the author's prior consent in any form of binding or cover other than that in which it is published and without a similar condition being imposed on the subsequent purchaser.

Requests to publish work from this book should be sent to:
joanna@CurlUpPress.com

Cover and Interior Design: JD Smith Design
Printed by Lightning Source UK

www.CurlUpPress.com

CONTENTS

One Day in Budapest   1

Day of the Vikings   103

Gates of Hell   185

ONE DAY IN BUDAPEST

A THRILLER
J.F. PENN

"All murderers are punished unless they kill in large numbers and to the sound of trumpets."

Voltaire

Dedicated to the memory of those buried in the mass grave of Dohany Street Synagogue, Budapest

PROLOGUE

THE GUN-METAL DAWN ended another bleak night of Hungarian winter. The sky lightened from pitch black to the colors of bullets and armor, the military might of Hungary's past resonant even in nature, a landscape unable to forget its violent past.

Father Zoli Kovács pulled his vestments closer about him and hurried across the square towards the Basilica of St Stephen, looking up at the grandeur against the backdrop of rain clouds. Although physically chilled, he felt the spiritual warmth of ownership, a pride that came from working at the heart of Hungary's faith. The grand Neo-Classical facade was flanked by two bell towers that stretched into the brightening sky, beacons of faith in a country that had suffered so much. Over the gigantic entranceway were carved the words of Christ, *ego sum veritas et vita*, I am the truth and the life. Father Zoli murmured as he crossed himself, his fingers crippled with arthritis now, but still able to perform his most treasured of gestures.

As he slowly mounted the Basilica steps, he thought that he heard a footfall echo in the square behind him. He turned, but it was empty, with only a few desultory pigeons pecking at the litter left by yesterday's tourists. There were homeless around here, of course, but he felt a shiver up his spine as he sensed something different. After a moment, he shook his head, dismissing his feelings as the wandering of an old man's mind.

Entering the Basilica, Father Zoli paused and breathed in the cool air, the scent of incense hanging like a prayer. Every morning he went through this same ritual, for he felt closer to God in the dark. When he turned on the lights, the splendor of gold seemed to push the vault of heaven far from him, so he savored this quiet moment as a special blessing before he started his day. Sometimes he imagined that the angels guarding the church were watching, that his gentle presence allowed them to drift into the ornate dome and find a place to rest, knowing that he would protect the church during the day. Father Zoli was at peace as he began to light candles around the church, making his way deeper into the nave as the day began to seep in through the stained glass. He stopped to light a special candle in front of the altar dominated by a huge statue of St Stephen, known as St Istvan in Hungarian.

Stephen had been the first King of Hungary, reigning in the early eleventh century, conquering the lands of Transylvania and the Black Magyars, extending his realm and power through battle. As he lay dying with no living heir to succeed him, Stephen had raised his right hand and implored the Blessed Virgin Mary to take the Hungarian people as her subjects and to reign as their Queen. After his death, miracles occurred at his tomb and King Stephen was canonized as the first confessor king of the Catholic church, venerated as the patron saint of Hungary as well as of all kings and dying children.

Reflecting on Stephen's devotion, Father Zoli crossed himself again and headed into the side chapel to check on the holy relic that lay at the heart of the Basilica. As he turned, the candles flickered and he heard a door bang, but the entrance to the church was too far away now to see clearly. Father Zoli debated whether to go and greet the early morning faithful, but he was a man of routine and his duty called.

He unlocked the door to the side chapel from a bundle of keys at his waist and walked through the wooden doors to the shrine. The Holy Right was St Stephen's mummified and incorruptible right hand, the very hand that had given Hungary into the keeping of the Virgin Mary. The brown, shriveled flesh was bunched into a fist and lay upon a bed of scarlet velvet, studded with pearls and rubies. The relic was surrounded by a glass case with a vaulted roof, decorated with gold and silver filigree and protected on all sides by angels and winged beasts. Crossing himself once more, Father Zoli approached with reverence and placed his fingertips gently against the glass. This was the closest anyone could get to the most holy relic of Hungary, a representation of the State itself, precious as both a religious treasure and a national symbol. World War I had seen the decimation of the Austro-Hungarian Empire, and subsequent regimes had oppressed the people, but this hand was a sign that one day Hungary would rise again.

Taking a clean white handkerchief from his pocket, Father Zoli polished the glass, wiping it clean of his prints and making it new again. Tourists paid for the privilege of lighting the shrine in order to take photographs, so he felt that they deserved a clear view.

He heard footsteps and then the creak of the door opening into the shrine. He turned to see a man enter, clean cut, well dressed, with the air of the privileged. His nose was like a beak, his hair waxed to a perfect shine.

"The shrine isn't open to the public yet, my son," Father Zoli said as the man stepped further into the chapel, his hands in his pockets. His eyes darted around the room, but as he confirmed that they were alone, they were drawn irresistibly to the shrine. Father Zoli felt a sudden stab of alarm and moved in front of the Holy Right, to shield it from the voracious eyes.

"I only come to worship, Father," the man said, stepping closer, but in his voice Father Zoli heard an echo of the past, a whisper from the dungeons of the Secret Police where the screams of the tortured drowned out all other sound. Cold fear crept over his skin as two more men stepped into the room behind the first, and closed the door behind them.

"What do you want?" Father Zoli said, his voice breaking as his heart pounded with fear.

"You protect the Holy Right," the first man said. "But what you give to us now, Father, will take the cause of Hungarian nationalism to new heights. St Istvan will be waiting for you with all the treasures of Heaven. You believe that, don't you?"

Father Zoli heard the intent and turned, desperate for a way out. He wasn't ready to go to God yet, and despite his aged body, he clung to life.

The man stepped to the side of the altar and picked up one of the ornate candlesticks, hefting its weight in his hand. Behind him, the other two men fanned out, one taking up a heavy Bible and the other pulling a knife.

"Please, no," Father Zoli fell to his knees, knowing that he couldn't outrun them. "I can get you money, my sons. I can get you help. I'm no threat to you." His voice was hysterical, sobs choking his throat as his desperate fingers clutched at the shrine for divine help.

"Sorry, Father. We need this symbol more than you need your life."

The man stepped in and swung the candlestick like a baseball bat, smashing it against the side of Father Zoli's head. The priest crumpled to the floor, pain exploding, vision clouding. He called out to St Istvan, the mummified hand now obscured by spots of his own blood. It was the last thing he saw as blows rained down and his old body became a sacrifice in that holy place.

CHAPTER 1

Dr Morgan Sierra stared out of the window as the taxi from Budapest airport sped towards the city. It was raining and the grey light served to emphasize the monotone of passing streets, punctuated only by the bright neon signs of fast food outlets and sex shops. She noticed banners advertising candidates for the upcoming elections, faces she didn't recognize and words in a language that was alien to her. Morgan smiled, for it was one of the aspects that thrilled her about European travel. Within a short plane ride, or even just a train journey, you could be in a different culture with unpronounceable words, making an adventure of even the shortest business trip.

Morgan had volunteered for the short assignment to Budapest, desperate to get out of the ARKANE headquarters and renew the boundaries of her independence. She had joined the Arcane Religious Knowledge And Numinous Experience Institute with the understanding that she could focus on her own research, but there had been little opportunity for that so far. The last few missions had taken their toll on her body and emotions, so Director Elias Marietti had asked her to remain close to base, and let time heal the scars. But Morgan was restless if she spent too much time thinking, and while her partner Jake was still in recovery, she wanted to get out of the office. She smiled to herself, because that office just happened to be an astounding complex under Trafalgar Square in London, with access to the secret knowledge of the world. Still, it felt good to be somewhere different, even for such a short time.

Her hand rested on a thick briefcase, a discreet handcuff attaching it to her wrist. Morgan touched the leather, warm from her skin, as she had held it on her lap for the short plane flight from London. The briefcase contained two precious artifacts: an early painting by the Jewish-Hungarian artist Béla Czóbel and an antique Torah. Both had been stolen from the Gold Train during the Second World War and now they were finally being returned to the Jewish synagogue in Budapest. Their provenance had been determined beyond question by the ARKANE Institute, and Morgan had volunteered to return them personally.

Morgan was brought up in Israel, her father Jewish and her mother a Welsh Christian. Although she had never converted to Judaism, Morgan knew the pain of European Jewry and wanted to honor her father's memory by being the courier who restored just a tiny part of the plunder. She had read of the history of the Gold Train, one of the many scandals of the aftermath of the war. The Nazi-operated train had been carrying valuables stolen from Hungarian Jews when it was intercepted by American forces in 1945. Many of the owners, nearly 600,000 Hungarian Jews, had been shipped off to Auschwitz-Birkenau to be murdered in the gas chambers, so the treasures had not been returned. After 1946, much of the valuable property was sold and the proceeds given to the International Refugee Organization, but two hundred paintings disappeared into personal collections. In 1998, the Hungarian Gold Train records finally became public and in 2005, the US government had settled with the Hungarian Holocaust survivors, with the money allocated to Holocaust charities.

ONE DAY IN BUDAPEST

The taxi pulled up in front of the Dohany Street synagogue and Morgan paid the fare, exiting into pouring rain. The smell of baking and fresh coffee made her stomach rumble, and she glanced at her watch. There was just enough time to grab a bite before her appointment with the Curator of the Museum at the Synagogue.

A few minutes later, Morgan was sitting in the window seat of a small cafe with a strong black coffee and a slice of poppyseed roulade in front of her. As she sipped her dark addiction, the rain eased and through a break in the clouds, the sun illuminated the stunning facade of Europe's largest synagogue. Built in Moorish style, the architecture reminded her of the Alhambra in Spain, with minarets topped with onion domes and striped bands of red, gold and patterned brick. The facade was dominated by a large rose window with the Hebrew script from Exodus 25:8: "And let them make me a sanctuary that I may dwell among them." Morgan had read that Adolf Eichmann had set up his office behind that rose window in 1944, directing the establishment of the Ghetto as he orchestrated the horror of the Final Solution. She shook her head. This area had seen such suffering, but perhaps these objects could at least bring a touch of restitution.

As Morgan finished her coffee and the last crumbs of roulade, the door opened and she heard a faint chanting and shouting in the distance, sirens wailing. A man came in and spoke with the cafe owner in a hushed voice, before going back outside and starting to pull down shutters over the front of the windows.

"So sorry, Madam," the woman who had served her said, with a rueful smile. "We close now. Would you mind … outside?"

"Of course," said Morgan. "I was just leaving anyway. Has something happened?"

The woman glanced out of the window towards the

synagogue, her gaze full of concern, fingers clutching the edges of her skirt.

"It's difficult …" The woman searched for the words in English. "Today, murder at Basilica, there may be trouble …"

Her voice trailed off but her eyes were fearful. Morgan knew that look, for she had seen it many times in Israel as the sirens warned of an imminent attack. In her years of growing up there, and later as a military psychologist, that expression had blossomed dark on the faces of Jews and Palestinians alike, both sides locked into a Sisyphean conflict. Fear, she had discovered, had no nationality.

Morgan left the cafe as the woman bolted the door behind her and folded inner shutters over the glass windows. On the street outside, a stiff breeze made the election banners wave and crackle. Opposite the shop was a huge signboard advertising the Eröszak party where the handsome face of their leader, László Vay, stared out, his clean-shaven politician's face portraying both strength and charisma. His dark curls were tousled perfectly, his mouth was a sensuous cupid's bow and his eyes, the color of the Caribbean, offered depths of implied pleasure. But the beauty of the man obscured the dark politics of his right-wing political party, Morgan thought. Eröszak was calling for a national registry of Jews and their possessions, a hideous reflection of what had happened here within living memory.

Walking over to the synagogue entrance, Morgan lined up with the other early tourists at the gate for the security check. As the uniformed guards protecting the entrance searched bags, she noticed that they kept looking nervously towards the main road, where the noise of shouting was getting louder.

"I'm here to meet with Anna Bogányi," Morgan said to the security guard when she reached the front of the queue. She was careful to keep her hands where he could see them, used to the rigors of security in Israel. She didn't want to take the handcuff off until the briefcase was safe within the grounds of the synagogue, but she opened the case so that the guard could see inside. The man was distracted, his gaze flitting to the street where it met the main road of Karoly Krt, leading to the city. He glanced in at the contents, the rolled up canvas in the specially constructed box and the Torah.

"Wait," he said, his voice curt. He turned briefly to call to one of the guards inside the metal gates in Hungarian and after a moment, he nodded.

"You can go through."

Morgan walked through the gates into a narrow area that ran across the front of the main synagogue entrance. A thin woman with cropped red hair came forward to greet her, wrapped in a multi-colored patchwork shawl against the pervasive cold. Behind her legs, a dark-haired little girl peeped out, bright eyes shining with curiosity. Morgan was reminded of her own niece, Gemma, for whom she would do anything.

"Dr Sierra. Welcome and thank you for coming all this way. I'm Anna, the Museum Curator."

Her eyes dropped to the briefcase.

"It's my pleasure to be here," Morgan smiled, noting her eagerness. "I'm thrilled to be the courier for this piece of history. And who's this?"

Morgan squatted down so that her face was level with the little girl, who hid her own face in the folds of her mother's skirts.

Anna laughed. "Don't be shy, sweetie … this is Ilona, my daughter. She helps out in the Museum sometimes." A shadow passed over Anna's face. "Today, it's safer for her to be here than at school."

Morgan noticed that behind her the security guards

were shutting the gates and instructing the remaining tourists to leave since the synagogue was closing for the day.

"Has something happened?" Morgan asked. "The lady in the cafe across the road said something about a murder."

Anna turned and indicated that Morgan should follow her into the shelter of the museum staircase. There was an undercurrent of tension as Anna glanced behind her, out towards the main street. Ilona ran in front of them up the stairs, her little footsteps echoing in the marble hallway.

As they followed her, Anna explained.

"The news has been on the radio in the last hour. The custodian priest of St Stephen's Basilica was brutally murdered there this morning, and not only that, but the Holy Hand of St Istvan, the symbol of the Hungarian nation, has been stolen. The shrine has been smashed and the relic taken."

"But why close the synagogue? What has that to do with the Jewish community?" Morgan asked.

"There was a star of David painted in the priest's blood on the wall of the chapel." Anna's eyes were hollow as she spoke, as if she saw back into the ashes of the Ghetto. "The Hebrew word *nekama*, meaning revenge, was scrawled next to it."

Morgan frowned. "But surely that's not enough for people to blame the Jewish population before a proper investigation can be carried out?"

"It could be enough to spark the anti-Semitic violence that constantly simmers beneath this city," Anna said. "But there's nothing we can do, and right now I'd rather focus on the joy of the return. The items you bring are finally back where they belong, even though there is no one left of the family they were taken from. Come."

She walked on through the gallery and Morgan followed, their footsteps echoing in the deserted space. The museum was a small collection of religious relics, mainly ritual items for the Shabbat. Morgan glanced into one case at an ornate silver Torah crown, placed on top of the scroll to symbolize its royalty and prestige. She paused to look in at the matching *rimmonim*, or decorative finials, that were etched with tiny pomegranates, reminiscent of the ruby fruit carved into the pillars of Solomon's Temple in Jerusalem. There were also a number of Kiddush cups, embossed with petals and tiny images of the tablets of the Law, used to drink the cup of wine on Shabbat.

"They're beautiful," Morgan said to Anna, feeling a thrill of recognition at the objects, for they were similar to the items that her father had taught her about, reciting scripture as the nights drew in. He would throw his prayer shawl around his shoulders and draw her under it, so that she could settle into the crook of his arm as the Hebrew words thrummed inside her, resonating in his deep voice. She had watched him read from the Torah in the synagogue, using a similar *yad* to this one, the tiny hand with pointed finger tracing the words on the page so that the sacred text was never touched. She couldn't help but smile at the memory.

"That set was saved and kept hidden in the basement of one of the houses designated as Swedish territory in 1944," Anna commented. Seeing the question in Morgan's gaze, she explained further. "The Swedish diplomat and architect Raoul Wallenberg rescued tens of thousands of Hungarian Jews when he was Sweden's special envoy in Budapest. He issued protective passports and sheltered Jews in buildings he claimed as Swedish."

"Did he survive the war?" Morgan asked.

Anna shook her head. "He was detained by the Soviets during the Siege of Budapest in 1945 and is thought to have died at the Moscow Lubyanka at the hands of the Secret Police. He is honored as one of the Righteous Among the

Nations, a non-Jew who gave everything for the persecuted Jewish people. We honor him here within the synagogue grounds with the Wallenberg Holocaust Memorial. I'll show you once we've secured these items."

Morgan looked into another display case nearby, containing a silver breastplate decorated with birds, fruit and leaves in an ornate pattern. Worn by the High Priest in the Temple, it hung around the neck of the Torah, protecting the holy words. If only it could have protected Raoul and those who died during that time, Morgan thought, clutching tightly at the handle of the case she carried. It contained so little, but was still important as a symbol of restitution, and she knew that her father would be proud that she was part of this.

"I've got a place for them here," Anna called from further down the museum's long hallway where she was putting on a pair of white gloves. Morgan rested the briefcase on a corner table nearby, finally unlocking the wrist-cuff and opening the case. Anna lifted the Torah carefully and laid it into the padded display case. Her eyes grew wider as she took out the painting and unrolled it, revealing a portrait of a young girl.

"I just wanted to see it," Anna whispered. "But I'm planning an official unveiling and a special exhibition about the Gold Train, so for now, they will just rest here, secure and safe, back where they belong." Anna closed the case gently. "Thank you." She turned and grasped Morgan's hand. "Now let me give you a tour of the grounds. At least it will be quiet now the tourists have gone. Come Ilona."

The little girl skipped ahead of them as Morgan and Anna walked back out of the museum and along a covered stone walkway towards the back of the synagogue precinct. On their left was a garden, mature trees with graceful branches hanging down towards gravestones propped against rectangular bases.

"Of course, it's not customary to have graves within the grounds of a synagogue," Anna explained. "But this area is a mass grave for over two thousand Jewish people who died from hunger and cold within the Ghetto. Perhaps they were lucky to die here, close to home, with those who loved them." Anna continued in a soft voice. "My grandfather was sent to the camps and never seen again, along with so many other Hungarian Jews."

Morgan felt the overwhelming sadness of the place seep into her as they stood in silence for a moment. Where the massive numbers of dead in the concentration camps were difficult to visualize, this intimate graveyard brought home the reality of that time. The names of the dead were engraved in marble and she silently read some of them, the Hungarian pronunciation hard in her mouth, a long way from her father's Spanish ancestry.

The grave backed onto one of the roads at the side of the synagogue grounds and as Morgan and Anna stood there, a rattle and a shout interrupted them. A group of young men loitered outside, their hands on the bars protecting the synagogue's land. A couple of others dragged metal pipes across the fencing, the hollow metallic clang a barely concealed threat, their eyes a challenge of violence.

CHAPTER 2

"Ilona, come now," Anna said, stepping away and walking quickly into the shelter of the stone corridor, out of sight. But Morgan remained, watching the youths as they began chanting something in Hungarian, no doubt some kind of racial slur. She stepped closer to the bars, smiling at them.

"What do you want here, boys?" she asked, her voice unthreatening, her posture open. They looked confused by her advance, obviously expecting her to be cowed and frightened by their threats. "Should I come out there and see if you want to play up close?"

Perhaps they didn't understand her words but Morgan knew they could sense that she was unafraid. She felt a rising outrage and a need to challenge their behavior. Although she wasn't Hungarian, these were her people and this was her land, even though she had never been here before. She would fight, even in a country that wasn't her own, because of the shared history of suffering. This group of boys probably didn't even know what they were chanting about. They were merely repeating slogans heard at the football pitch, or spouted by their parents, racial slurs that were indoctrinated without thought.

Morgan stood close to the fence. They could strike

her from where they stood, but she felt strongly that they wouldn't, that as yet their actions were just bravado. One of the boys looked at her, and she saw fear in his eyes, not of her, but of what the group might do. She tried to send him some strength, for it was individuals like him who could sometimes halt the violence of a group.

The cacophony of a police siren broke the moment and the boys looked around, then scattered. Some turned and shouted back as they ran off, making obscene gestures as they disappeared down the street.

"You have a way with these vandals," a deep voice said, and Morgan turned to see a man in a tight brown leather jacket approaching her. He wasn't tall, perhaps the same height as her, but he was stocky, and she recognized the power of a trained fighter packed into his taut muscles. Morgan sensed in him a reflection of her own tendency to favor action over retreat and she smiled in welcome.

"I'm Morgan Sierra," she said, extending a hand. "I'm here returning some of the artifacts from the Gold Train."

The man returned the smile, flashing white teeth, his jawline emphasized by a line of close-cropped facial hair. He wore a silver star of David as an earring in his left ear and his right cheek up towards his temple was scarred, a pitted surface of puckered flesh. Morgan had seen enough wounds in the Israeli Defense Force to know it was a grenade injury, and she wondered what his story was.

"I'm Zoltan Fischer. You could call me a security consultant for the Jewish community." Zoltan's grip was just a second longer than was necessary, flirtation in his gaze.

The sound of shouting and sirens suddenly intensified and drew their attention back to the entrance.

"You've picked a hell of a day to visit. But come," Zoltan said, "I'll finish the tour with you and let Anna take Ilona inside."

Anna waved to Morgan and hurried with her little girl

back towards the Museum. She was clearly grateful to retreat from the noise and stress of what could touch them out here, preferring to conserve the treasures of the past than face the potential conflict of the present. But that had been the attitude of the community back in the 1940s, Morgan thought, before the Nazis shut them into the Ghetto. She thought of recent news reports in Eastern Europe, the rise of right-wing parties fueled by anti-Semitic slander. There was even a poll in Austria showing that the Nazi party could be re-elected if the ban against it was lifted. Worrying times indeed, and while Israel focused on the threat from Muslim fundamentalists, it seemed that European Jews had as much to fear from their own countrymen.

Zoltan led the way into a courtyard behind the main synagogue. A tree made of metal in the shape of a weeping willow shone silver in the sun, metallic leaves reflecting the light. Around the tree were small piles of stones, placed there in memory of the dead.

"Each leaf on this tree is inscribed with a name," Zoltan explained. "In remembrance of the Hungarian Jewish martyrs. This park is a memorial to all who died in the Shoah, the Holocaust."

"Are any of your family here?" Morgan asked. Zoltan's eyes darkened and he reached forward to touch a leaf with gentle fingers, caressing the inscribed name. He nodded.

"You can read some of their names on the plaque by the mass grave, and there are many more in the lists of those who died at the camps." He turned back to her. "This will always be my fight, Morgan, but what about you? Why did you choose to return our memories to us?"

Morgan closed her eyes for a second, but the light from the tree had seared the names of the victims onto her eyelids, and she opened them again to meet his intense gaze.

"My father was Jewish and I was brought up in Israel. He was Sephardi, from Spain originally, and secular for much of my childhood, but he found his God later in life. I never converted, but when I defend Judaism, as I did in the Israeli Defense Force, I defend him and the right to exist and believe as he did."

Zoltan's eyes were piercing. "So you are a warrior, then?"

Morgan felt the pulsing of her blood against the scars on her body, sustained in fighting against evil. The demon in the bone chapel of Sedlec, the assassins that hunted the Ark of the Covenant, these were battles she would carry forever.

"I thought I could be just a scholar," she replied, "but it seems that I am still called to fight."

The chanting outside was growing louder and more cohesive now, increasing in volume as if the crowd had become a mob. The edge of the harsh words cut through the air, and even though Morgan didn't understand the language, she could discern hatred and destruction in their tone.

"Then I may need your help today," Zoltan said quietly. "I fear that the rabble will bring violence before the truth of the Basilica murder is uncovered."

At that moment, two security guards ran into the square, shouting to Zoltan. He spun and conversed with them quickly, then beckoned for her to follow.

"We are gathering everyone into the main synagogue building. The gates are barred and locked and we've called the police but I fear there will be bloodshed if any Jews are caught outside."

Morgan raced with Zoltan back towards the front of the building in the wake of the security guards. The noise of shouting became deafening as they reached the metal gates that only a little while earlier had opened to a line of interested tourists. Now a mob of around fifty people jeered and roared their anger, faces contorted by hate, shouting for revenge in the wake of the Basilica crimes, rattling the gates as they tried to force their way in.

CHAPTER 3

Zoltan pulled Morgan back against the wall as a glass bottle exploded on the ground in front of them.

"Our community has been preparing for this day," he said. "We knew it would come. We just need to get inside the synagogue and we'll be safe there."

"What about the other people in this area?" Morgan asked, worried for the community.

"They will have locked their doors and pulled down their shutters as soon as the news came out this morning," Zoltan said. "Now we must run across the front to the entrance. Stay close to me."

Morgan smiled at his chivalry, and together they ran the few meters across the front of the synagogue. Bottles and cans were hurled over the fence, and the screaming of the crowd tore the air around them. Morgan could smell rubbish and the stink of feces as offensive projectiles burst on the ground. The doors of the synagogue opened as they approached and then shut firmly behind them. The shouting became a dull roar, but still, Morgan thought with a shudder, the sound of an angry mob intent on violence was enough to make even a veteran soldier afraid.

Zoltan strode into the nave, where a small group of people huddled, some already swaying in prayer. He had a compelling air of authority, clearly ex-military, although he was younger than most of those present. While he gave instructions to those within, Morgan's heart rate began to calm and she became more aware of her surroundings.

The synagogue was immense and fashioned almost like a Christian basilica, with a mix of Byzantine and Gothic elements. Richly colored frescoes of geometric shapes were picked out in gold and red, dominating the ceiling, and tall arches framed the upper balconies. The Torah ark was surrounded by a towering white structure topped with a crown and, unusually for a synagogue, an organ continued the design upwards. It was a beautiful space, strangely decorative for a Jewish place of worship but, Morgan thought to herself, the people here had tried their best to fit in, even with their architecture.

Morgan watched Zoltan as he organized the group, offering words of comfort along with his authority. One old woman sat to the side on a bench, her face expressionless, lips unmoving, staring into the distance. In the blankness of her eyes, Morgan saw that she had been through this experience before, that she was reliving some earlier terror.

She caught Zoltan's eye and moved to join him, speaking in a hushed tone so as not to alarm those present.

"We have to get out of here," she said. "We need to find the Holy Right and return it to the Basilica, because if this continues into the night, I fear for these people."

Zoltan's eyes were hard. "And who are you, Morgan Sierra, to be of any use to me in this place?"

Morgan met his gaze without flinching. "I know you must have a way out, and you need a partner who can operate in the field. You have to leave your security guards on duty here to protect these people and I can be useful, so put me to work." She paused, laying her hand on his arm. "This is what I do, Zoltan. I find religious objects and I fight bad guys."

A glimmer of humor shone in his eyes. "And today, Budapest harbors these bad guys?"

Morgan nodded. "Do you have weapons here?"

Zoltan hesitated, looking back at the group. They were mainly academics and older people who volunteered at the synagogue. Morgan saw Anna comforting one woman, rocking her in her arms and stroking her hair as Ilona sat close by, eyes wide with fear.

He shook his head slowly, and Morgan saw resignation in his eyes.

"Follow me."

In one corner of the synagogue was an ornate screen. Zoltan stepped behind it and tapped into a keypad on the wall. The heavy door clicked and he pushed it open to reveal a smaller courtyard outside protected by high walls but still open to the sky. A large metal storage container loomed in the shadows.

"This area is just outside the holy ground of the synagogue," Zoltan explained. "But we keep the store close just in case."

He tapped in another code and pulled open the door, gesturing for Morgan to enter. There were several racks of guns, old but clean, and clearly well serviced. Morgan picked up a Glock 17 handgun.

"Austrian," Zoltan said. "Military issue."

"Thinking about it, I'm not sure that we should take weapons," Morgan said. "We need to stay out of sight as much as possible. If we get stopped, carrying guns will get us arrested, which won't help anyone here."

"Agreed," Zoltan said, picking up a tire iron from a pile of tools, hefting its weight in his hand. "This will have to do." He put it into a backpack with a couple of torches and some other basic equipment. "Our only chance to stop a riot tonight is to find the Hand." He picked up a protective vest. "But will you wear this, just in case? It's a spare."

Morgan nodded, reaching for it. Zoltan stripped off his own jacket and shirt, revealing a trim, muscled torso clad in a tight, white t-shirt, a criss-cross of white scars emerging from his right sleeve and continuing down his arm. Morgan watched for a second, resisting the urge to touch him, before pulling off her own coat and sweater, feeling the tension in her muscles. It felt good to move, the adrenalin pulsing through her. She claimed to be an academic, but this life of action suited her. By his eyes on her toned body, it was clear Zoltan thought so too. Their eyes met, danger sparking an attraction, then Zoltan broke the gaze as he zipped up the small backpack and they stepped from the lock-up.

"There's a tunnel we can use to get out of here," he said, re-entering the code to secure the container. "It emerges a few streets away in the basement of a bar where we have friends."

A wailing scream came from the main synagogue and Zoltan dashed back inside. Morgan followed after him to find that the old woman who had sat in catatonic silence had broken down in hysterical weeping.

"We must go now," Zoltan said, his face stony, fists clenched. "I will not allow my people to go through this again."

He led Morgan to a corridor that ran behind the *aron ha-kodesh*, the Holy Ark that held the Torah scrolls, and then into a small square room lined with books.

"Now we go down," Zoltan said, pulling aside a rug that concealed a trapdoor. He tugged it up revealing a dark and narrow hole. Morgan's thoughts flashed to the mass grave outside, the bodies of those starved to death lowered into pits like this. Zoltan stepped down onto the ladder and then passed her up a head torch. "It's not too far. My men have orders to bring the others this way if the synagogue wall is breached, but I fear that the elderly would struggle to escape down here."

He disappeared into the hole and Morgan watched him descend. She took a deep breath and followed him, climbing down about six feet. Zoltan was waiting at the bottom in a low tunnel, and as soon as Morgan's feet touched the ground, he set off into the darkness, the light from his head torch illuminating dank earth reinforced with wooden planks. With barely enough room to stand upright, Morgan had to bend to walk quickly behind him.

It must have been built after the Ghetto, Morgan thought, as back then these blocks would have been surrounded by a high fence and stone wall. No food had been allowed in, and rubbish, waste and dead bodies had lain on the streets unable to be collected. She walked faster, specters of the past chasing her through the dark tunnel, the bony fingers of the dead crying out for justice while the living wailed in the synagogue behind her. She felt claustrophobic, as if the very earth wanted to crush her. There was a light touch on her cheek and she let out a little noise of alarm.

"Are you OK?" Zoltan's whisper came back and he shone his torch at her feet.

Morgan touched her face, wiping away a crumbling flake of earth.

"Yes, sorry, just a bit jumpy."

"Only a little further." He turned and they walked on until they reached another ladder, which Zoltan quickly climbed, pushing open the hatch above. Light flooded down into the pit as Zoltan reached down to help Morgan up. They emerged into a beer cellar in the basement of a local pub, with metal barrels piled up in one corner, the smell of hops in the air.

"We need to find out more about the ultra right-wing Nationalist groups," Zoltan said. "The relic theft is not the work of Jewish groups, but of a faction trying to stir up violence for their own agenda. With the elections only a few days away, there are those who would benefit greatly from a backlash against the Jews and a resurgence of Hungarian nationalism. I know someone who can help us … but you're not going to like where he works."

CHAPTER 4

IN ANOTHER AREA OF Budapest, the Jewish delicatessen of Erzsébetváros was busy, full of people gossiping about the murder at the Basilica, their voices a hubbub of interest tinged with fear. Alma Kadosa served a customer with fresh bread, wrapping it quickly with fast hands, unconscious of the actions she had performed so many times before. She heard snippets of conversation, rumors of a mob calling for blood and vengeance and she felt a dart of concern for her parents, who were at the synagogue. She would call them as soon as the shop quietened down. They were still faithful to a religion into which she had been born but didn't really identify with. Alma was proudly Hungarian first, embracing all the opportunities the country offered hardworking young people. She only had to save a few hundred more forints and then she could afford her dream holiday, visiting the famous art galleries of Italy and France that she studied at night school.

Suddenly, the sound of revving engines interrupted Alma's thoughts and stilled the conversation around her. Brakes squealed to a halt and Alma could see men jumping out of a white van. There was shouting and the atmosphere in the shop shifted. Alma watched the old people shrink into themselves, some sinking silently behind display units as if they instinctively knew what was coming.

"Quickly," hissed Ferenc, the portly owner of the store, as he pushed open the back door of the shop and urged some of the customers to flee. Those closest to the door ran, leaving shopping bags full on the ground. Alma was trapped behind the bread counter and, although she felt fearful, she also didn't understand what was going on. How could there be a threat to their little shop?

She remained standing as the door banged open and, one after another, five men entered, their faces set in a sneer of malevolence, eyes shining with a lust for violence. Two carried baseball bats that they thumped from one hand to another and the others held guns in a relaxed grip.

Their leader strode in behind them, his eyes obscured by sunglasses. His nose was sharp, like a beak, and his dark hair shone with wax styling. He was closely shaven and Alma could smell the spicy cologne that he exuded along with an air of sophisticated violence. His eyes fell on her and Alma felt her heart pound in fear and her muscles tighten.

He walked forward, his eyes fixed on hers, while his men stood silently to one side as if waiting for a signal.

"What are you looking at, Jew-bitch?" he asked, his voice almost an obscene caress and his mouth curving into a smile. Alma could read his intent, and her hand gripped the bread-knife in front of her. She thought of her grandparents, survivors of the camps, and her parents who had suffered under the Soviets. This was her fight now, and suddenly she felt proud of her heritage. She would not deny who she was, even though she had spent her lifetime avoiding the synagogue and her parents' religious fervor.

"Can I help you, gentlemen?" Alma asked, her voice shaky. Out of the corner of her eye, she could see the customers frozen with fear. Nearest was old Mrs Karolyi with her gnarled hands who came in every day for fresh poppyseed cake. Her eyes were closed and her chest was heaving, as if she was having a panic attack. Behind her was a mother, clutching her young son to her chest, hiding his eyes and looking away, hoping that by not seeing what was happening, they would avoid the oncoming threat.

"You Jews have helped yourselves for far too long," the man snarled at Alma. "And now you have stolen the symbol of our country, the Holy Right, no doubt for some disgusting ritual." He came close to the counter and leaned over it towards Alma. Everything in her wanted to thrust the bread knife at him, but she knew that his jacket would stop the blade and then she feared he would use the knife on her. Her heart pounded.

"We don't know anything about the Holy Right. We are Hungarian, just like you." Alma's voice trembled and the man smiled, his grin wolfish. He raised a hand and slapped her face hard, the crack resounding in the shop. Anna felt the pain a split second after the noise, her hand flying to her cheek and tears springing to her eyes.

"Don't you dare claim to be Magyar," he snarled. "You are nothing, and we will show you what you are worth."

He signaled behind him and the other men started laying into the shelving and displays with their bats, smashing glass cases and bottles. The smell of pickled vegetables filled the air and the screams of the frightened customers were lost amongst the violent outburst. Alma heard Ferenc moaning from behind his till, shaking his head as his livelihood was destroyed, the perfect little shop with everything in its place smashed to pieces. Glass shards rained down on the customers, but although the men heaved their bats down right next to the people huddled on the floor, they didn't hit anyone. Alma was shaking with shock and fear now. Could this really be happening in twenty-first century Hungary?

"Today we are taking vengeance for the stolen Holy Right," the man said. "But beating you to death doesn't give the correct signal to the Jewish community. We want to cast a longer shadow into the past today." He grinned and cupped Alma's chin roughly in his bony hand. "You're pretty, little Jewess. I'll take you for sure, but we need several more for our little enactment. Will you choose, or shall I?"

Alma stared into his eyes, dark pools showing no acknowledgment of her humanity. "You can't do this," she said. "The police will be here any minute. They'll stop you."

He laughed. "Haven't you noticed, idiot Jews?" He spun and addressed the cowering shop customers. "The police aren't interested in you, they only care about defending Hungary. And today, we're doing their job for them."

He barked a command and each of the men grabbed one of the customers.

"Now, Jewess, will you come quietly or shall I take someone else?"

The man turned and his eyes fixed on the mother with her young son, and old Mrs Karolyi. He moved towards them and the old woman opened her eyes, a piercing blue that fixed on his.

"Shame on you," she whispered. "You bring dishonor to Hungary. This brutality should have died with the generation that started it."

The man laughed at her and then his face transformed.

"It is you who bring shame." He spat at the old woman. "We bring glory, for we are ridding this country of the unwanted Jews, Roma and dirty foreigners. Soon, we Magyar will be great again."

He reached for a tin of pickled gherkins from the shelf and used it to smash Mrs Karolyi in the face. There was a sickening crunch as her nose broke and a weak cry as she sagged in agony back against the young mother, who clutched desperately at her son and shuffled backwards from the violence.

As the man leaned forward to hit Mrs Karolyi again,

Alma stepped out from behind the counter.

"Please, leave her," she said. "I'll go with you."

He turned back, his hand still raised with the pickle jar stained with blood. Alma knew she could never look at one of the green containers again without seeing the red specks. He flung the jar carelessly to the floor where it rolled under a display case.

"So be it." He shouted a command to the men and they thrust the five captives through the door, guns trained on the remaining customers.

Alma was the last to be hustled into the van, all of them crammed into the back to sit on the floor, surrounded by the men with guns. As one of the women began sobbing quietly, Alma felt as if her brain was processing the situation on a totally removed level. She could see the tiny details of the scene as if time moved more slowly. A fly buzzed around the head of one man, landing on his ear as he flicked at it. There was a mole on his cheek shaped like the island of Crete, where she had spent one lazy summer. She noticed the broken zip of another man's jacket, the thin material a cheap imitation of an upmarket brand. She saw the broken veins in the outstretched legs of one older woman, her skirt riding up as she tried to stay upright in the lurching van.

As she took in her surroundings, Alma felt the cool aftermath of the adrenalin rush, the sag of exhaustion and a sense that she couldn't fight whatever was going to happen. She thought of her parents at the synagogue and hoped that they were safe, but she felt a sense that she would never see them again. She wanted to rage at the men, appeal to some kind of human decency, but they wouldn't even look at the little group. Was this how people had felt on the way to the camps? Powerless, clinging to a faint hope of reprieve?

The van finally lurched to a halt and the men readied themselves. A panel opened from the front seat and Alma saw the leader's leering face.

"Hungary appreciates your sacrifice," he said, and barked a command. The doors were thrust open and Alma saw that they were at the banks of the Danube, on the promenade south of the Hungarian Parliament building. She could see the grand lines of the Széchenyi Chain Bridge as they were forced out onto the pavement. Cars drove past on the main road, and a tram pulled up only meters from their position. Concerned faces looked out, but Alma knew that they would do nothing. The more witnesses to a crime, the less likely it was that anyone would act. That was just human nature, it was someone else's problem. Don't get involved, pretend that you didn't see anything, that was the easiest way.

"Take your shoes off," one of the men said, pointing his gun at their feet. "Quickly now."

Then Alma knew what was about to happen and her heart seemed to burst in her chest. She couldn't help a sob escaping her throat as she turned to see exactly where they were. Sixty pairs of shoes cast in iron were lined up in pairs along the banks of the Danube, created as a memorial to the Jews shot by the fascist Arrow Cross militia in World War II. She sank to her knees, sobbing, screaming "Help" at passing cars. But one man pushed her to the ground and another held her down, pulling off her shoes with rough hands. Alma scrambled forward on her knees, thinking that she could escape into the water. The man grabbed her hair and pulled her back and up.

"It's got to be done this way," he whispered. "It is a signal."

Alma felt pain blossom in her back as she heard a sound, a muted gunshot mingled with her own breath and then she was falling forward into the Danube. The freezing water made her gasp but at the same time, she was overheated, her mind fuzzy. She couldn't turn over, she couldn't breathe, she was sinking. In her last moments, she called out to the God of her ancestors for vengeance.

CHAPTER 5

BLENDING INTO THE CROWD of pedestrians, Morgan and Zoltan walked quickly along the boulevard of grand mansions and luxury boutiques in the center of Budapest. They passed the State Opera House, with its tiers of ornate sculpture, but Morgan was too tense to enjoy its beauty.

"Where are we going?" she asked.

"To see an archivist," Zoltan replied, "but his location is less than pleasant. I'm sorry that you have to witness the darker side of Budapest on this trip."

A few minutes later, they arrived at the House of Terror, 60 Andrássy Way, the address feared by Hungarians as the headquarters first of the Fascist Arrow Cross Party and then the ÁVH, the Communist Secret Police. A metal awning over the side of the top story had the word TERROR cut into it with the communist star, so that the sky could only be seen through the lettering. It was now a museum and Morgan thought it brave to acknowledge history with such a statement of fact. For even after the Fascist regime had ended, those of the Communist era had imprisoned, purged and murdered their own people. It seemed incredible that the terrors of the past had not ended with that generation and that now the rise of the right-wing witnessed it beginning again. It seemed impossible that the atrocities of the past could be repeated, yet here they were, seeking to stop violence from escalating as it had done all these years ago.

Pictures of men and women who had disappeared into the building, never to emerge, were displayed on the outside, haunting images of long-gone loved ones, with candles still burning and fresh flowers left in remembrance. Morgan glanced at the faces as she walked past, the stiff portraits in sepia representing brave individuals who had only wished for democracy. Many of them were taken in the wake of the 1956 revolution, when Hungarians had risen up against the Soviets, pulling down the statue of Stalin. The protestors had been quickly and brutally quashed by the Red Army, who killed 20,000 people in the process, arresting and imprisoning many more.

"Georg is a friend from the Army," Zoltan said. "He works within the museum now, cataloging horrors from the past, but he's also a skilled hacker and he knows the Budapest underground scene."

Zoltan spoke to the museum security official, who waved them through the queue of people waiting to enter the macabre memorial. The main entrance hall led into a wide light well, reminiscent of a prison, with walkways around the levels and doors leading off into various departments. A Soviet tank was parked at the bottom of a wall that stretched three floors to the ceiling, covered in black and white photos of victims who had died here.

Morgan was struck by the grey atmosphere that seemed to suck the light out of the air, giving the space a negative energy. Pictures of myriad faces on the walls communicated hopelessness and a complete lack of power, mugshots with obscured features, the shapes in lines of dark black. These people didn't look like the archetypes of revolution. A dumpy woman in a floral print dress. A boy with fine bone structure. A proud businessman in a suit.

As she examined them, Morgan found the features running together, until the lines of human faces became a repeating pattern on a wall of the past, de-individuation even in death. What must it have been like to be brought here, she thought, knowing that you would never leave?

"Come," Zoltan said, walking through the main gallery towards the shop and administration area. He put his hand gently on Morgan's arm, guiding her away from the vast display of the dead. "We must focus on the present, not the past."

They entered an office suite behind the gift shop, its ceilings low and oppressive. The employees worked on the paperwork of a functioning museum these days, but these rooms had once processed the bureaucracy of intimidation and death. A tall, pale man stood to greet Zoltan, his pallid skin emphasized by his completely black clothing. His features were fine, his eyes a pale brown and Morgan noticed that he wore kohl around them, highlighting the lines in a subtle manner. She could imagine him in more bold makeup, a Goth by night, perhaps, and an academic by day. Morgan found herself intrigued by this man already.

Zoltan spoke a few words in Hungarian, while Georg's eyes rested on her with a questioning gaze. Morgan met his eyes. After a moment, Georg nodded and Zoltan beckoned her forward.

Georg extended his hand and Morgan shook it. His hand was cold and firm, testing her grip as if somehow he could discern through her skin whether she was trustworthy.

"I'm sorry that you couldn't have come at a better time," Georg said, his voice deeper than Morgan had expected, his English slightly accented. "We are fiercely proud of our Hungary, but sometimes she bares her teeth."

"I want to help however I can," Morgan said. Georg nodded and let her hand drop. He looked around at the other workers in the office and nodded to Zoltan.

"Perhaps I can give you a small tour so that you can fully appreciate this part of our history," he said. "Follow me."

They walked out of the office and down a short corridor, stepping past a line of tourists to claim the next lift. As the doors closed behind them, Georg explained.

"There's another room downstairs that will be more private for our discussions. It's not a nice place to work, the shadows of history are dense down here, but we need privacy for what we seek."

The lift moved slowly down into the depths of the complex. A short video played, featuring an old man who had once cleaned the torture and execution chambers. He described death by garroting, trapping lift occupants into a forceful confrontation with the past. Despite the things she had seen, his matter of fact tone made Morgan feel slightly queasy and claustrophobic as they descended.

"All of this is portrayed as history," Zoltan said. "But many survivors are still alive, and plenty of perpetrators have been left unpunished. The scars of this terror are still raw and the wounds easily reopened." He shook his head. "Sometimes I think that our country is so steeped in blood that the ground has become viscous with it, and one wrong step will suck us all into the maw of the earth."

Georg chuckled. "So poetic, my friend."

Morgan expected Zoltan to be offended at the sarcastic tone, but he merely smiled and shook his head.

"Georg here is a gamer and hacker, and he associates with those who stand for anarchy and revolution."

"What he means is that I know the truth," Georg replied, his kohl-rimmed eyes suddenly serious. "I hack to remain anti-establishment, to keep an eye on those in power and to hold them to account. I don't believe in the innate goodness of mankind, so I seek to ensure that there are balances in place to prevent the rise of such sickness again."

"Why do you work here, then?" Morgan asked. "Surely this place represents everything that you hate?"

Georg nodded. "True, but I would have been one of the first to be thrown to these butchers, just for being different. Every day I confront the bullies of the past and I claim my right to be who I am. As you see, there are still people who want to return to the past, slam people like me and Zoltan into cells and leave us to rot." The lift jerked to a halt. "Come, I will show you why working down here keeps me motivated."

The lift opened into the dungeon of the museum and Morgan followed Georg into the stone corridors as Zoltan trailed behind.

"These are where the prisoners were kept," Georg pointed left and right as they walked indicating where thick doors opened onto cramped cells. Each contained only a dirty wooden pallet and pictures of faces on the walls. Morgan peered into one and saw scratches in the plaster, the marks of desperation an attempt to cling to life for just a little longer. She closed her eyes, the echoes of torture reverberating in her mind. For a moment she felt utterly bereft, with a realization that humanity had always tortured and murdered and always would. Was there was no stopping that darkness, despite how many fought against it?

She clutched at the wall.

"Are you alright?" Zoltan's hand was on her elbow. Morgan opened her eyes to look into his concerned face. Behind him she saw Georg watching her, and she knew that he understood. These men stood against the dark, and she would stand with them. ARKANE usually fought in the realms at the edge of the supernatural, but the violence in Budapest was altogether human.

Morgan nodded. "I'm fine. Let's continue."

"It's just a little further," Georg said, turning and walking deeper into the dungeon labyrinth. "I find it best to work in places that others prefer to avoid."

As she followed, Morgan paused again to look into a stark stone room. Although the ceiling was low, there was still space for a tall wooden pole with a few steps leading up to it on either side. A simple rope noose hung there, its knot silhouetted on the wood by the bare bulb that lit the pale space. The cell was made somehow more obscene by its emptiness and Morgan felt that the air still held imprints of the murders carried out there. For it was certainly murder, even though it had been justified by a government as a fitting punishment for enemies of the state.

Georg unlocked a door at the end of the long corridor and the three of them squeezed into another cell, barely big enough for a desk and a couple of chairs. On the desk sat a huge, clunky computer from the 1980s.

"It doesn't look like much," Georg said with a cheeky smile. "But this is Budapest hacker central. Now let's take a look at these right-wing lunatics."

He pulled out the chair and sat down at the desk, lifting the old computer to reveal a slim laptop underneath, hidden in plain sight. Georg opened the laptop and his fingers flashed over the keyboard. Morgan was reminded of the ARKANE librarian Martin Klein, whose genius skills were harnessed in the pursuit of esoteric truth. But where Martin was often physically awkward, Georg's presence seemed to intensify as he worked, exuding energy and passion for his quest. Morgan could see that this was a kind of game to him, albeit with serious consequences, a battle of good vs evil in a parallel world where he could work his magic undetected.

"Can you check the chatter on the Erőszak forums?" Zoltan asked. "See if there's any mention of who was involved in the Basilica theft and murder?"

Georg's eyes were fixed on the screen and he didn't reply, just typed faster, his brow furrowing as he read. Morgan could almost see him processing, sifting the information and weighing its importance. The Secret Police would have certainly killed him for being different, she thought, but he would have made a hell of an informant.

Minutes went past before Georg spoke, and Morgan could almost feel Zoltan's impatience beside her. She understood his need for action, it was mostly her own preference, but they needed at least some indication of where to start searching.

Georg's eyes widened and his already pale face blanched.

"What is it?" Zoltan asked.

"There's chatter about a revenge attack," Georg's eyes were hollow, a corridor of time that reflected the massacres of the past. "No specific details but it sounds like a group of Jews have been shot on the banks of the Danube."

Zoltan pushed back his chair with a violent shove, his face contorted, fists tight. His rage seemed to fill the tiny space but just as Morgan thought he would punch the wall, he laid his forehead on the cool plaster and breathed a long exhalation.

"Surely there can be no doubt that this is the work of ultra right-wing nationalists?" Morgan asked, her voice tinged with horror. "Won't the police be investigating this as a matter of urgency?"

"But they're only Jews," Zoltan growled, his voice low. "Just recently, Eröszak supporters marched near a hotel where the World Jewish Congress was meeting. The protestors wore military uniforms, forbidden and outlawed in Hungary, but the police let them march."

Georg nodded.

"Eröszak currently has one third of the Parliament, but across the country the support is much more widespread. And you can see why. Their 'Movement for a Better Hungary' has been embraced as a way to combat unemployment, crime, immigration, and the dependence of welfare cases like the Roma. Jews are again seen as too powerful, a useful scapegoat in a country where we have been murdered and driven out before. These murders will be investigated, but they won't search too hard for those responsible and it won't help us today."

While he spoke, Georg's fingers flashed over the keyboard. "The incident has brought out the big-mouths on the forums. The boasters, the braggers." His face twisted into a sneer. "Idiots." His eyes scanned the pages, while Zoltan still stood against the wall, finally turning to lean against it, his body taut with restrained power. Finally, Georg spun the laptop around for them to look.

"This man was seen in the delicatessen from where they took the victims. He didn't even hide his face, which just shows you the confidence the bastards have."

Morgan and Zoltan leaned closer to the screen. The man was elegant, his features finely chiseled and his nose long and sharp, his black hair slicked into a stylish wave.

"Hollo Berényi, known as the Raven," Georg said. "He's linked to many anti-Semitic attacks as well as to violence against Roma. There's no clear evidence that he's part of Eröszak and, of course, their leader, that slime-ball László Vay, always condemns the violence, but they must be linked somehow. Everything Berényi does furthers the Eröszak cause."

Zoltan grunted. "A few days before the election? Of course it's them. Who else has so much to gain?"

Georg continued. "Some of the chatter indicates that Berényi was also seen around the Basilica early this morning." He clicked another key and more blurred images of the man filled the screen. "Under another name, he spent several years with the Russian Spetsnaz GRU elite military force before disappearing off the radar, surfacing occasionally as a mercenary in various wars. It seems that he offers military strategy for hire, so I think it best to focus on him and what he has been doing."

"Or consider what he might do next?" Morgan said.

Both men looked at her, waiting for more.

"It seems to me that the murder in the Basilica and the theft of the Holy Right has enraged the nation," she continued. "So much so that almost anything would be considered acceptable today, even these murders by the Danube. While the Hand is missing and the Jews blamed, this Berényi can do his worst and be considered a folk hero. From what you've said, I don't think he's finished yet."

"Of course." Georg spun the laptop around again and resumed his tapping. "The police will have to investigate all this, but while there is chaos, they'll just let it ride."

"So if you were going to target Jews in retaliation," Morgan said, "but also escalate the situation by tapping into Hungary's past and attacking symbols of nationalism, what would you do next?"

In the moment's silence that followed, a siren rang out in the building, a deafening 'nee-naw' cacophony. Morgan and Zoltan pressed their hands over their ears while Georg's face froze, as if that sound conjured up a history that he thought lay only in the past.

CHAPTER 6

"It must be just the fire alarm," Georg shouted over the din, "but it can't be a coincidence that you're here." He pressed a key combination and the laptop shut down, encrypting his work. He replaced the ancient machine over the top, then grabbed a small padded case as he indicated the door. "Come on, we must get out of here."

As they ran through the winding corridors of the basement level, Morgan caught glimpses into the rooms they passed. One was stacked with the clothing of those long dead and another filled with crosses illuminated only by candlelight. Eventually the three came to an exit and Georg led them up a tiny staircase. He pushed open the door at the top carefully, inching it open to check the suburban street beyond.

"You must go," he said. "If the police are pulling in people for questioning, you can't be caught or they'll keep you in cells while the Raven rampages out there. I'll go back down to join the evacuation."

"Köszönöm," Zoltan said. "Thank you, my friend."

"Take this," Georg handed Zoltan the padded case. "It's a video camera that will upload via wireless or phone networks to my account. If you can get evidence of what's really going on, I can get it to the press. It's the only way to stop this madness. Words will no longer be enough."

As Zoltan put the camera in his pack, Morgan leaned in and kissed Georg's cheek. "We'll stop this, Georg and it will be thanks to you."

They walked quickly away from the building along Andrassy Boulevard, blending into the crowds who were ogling the scene and snapping photos in their eagerness to be a part of the day's drama. On the other side of the road, Zoltan hailed a taxi, telling the driver to take them towards Buda Castle. As they sped off, a news bulletin came on the radio and the driver turned it up to listen.

***

"Breaking news from the centre of Budapest with reports of violence on the banks of the Danube. Five bodies have been retrieved from the river with gunshot wounds, and the shoes of the victims have been found amongst the iron replica Shoes on the Danube memorial.

An anonymous phone call to the Magyar Hirlap news desk has claimed the murders in retaliation for the theft of the Holy Right, stolen this morning from St Stephen's Basilica, and the brutal murder of Father Zoli Kovács. The anonymous caller threatened further violence until the Holy Right is returned. There are reports of running battles throughout the city as Jewish groups and right-wing nationalists clash. The authorities are struggling to respond to so many concurrent incidents and the police are calling for calm as they proceed with their investigations.

László Vay, leader of the Eröszak party, has just released the following statement.

'Fellow Hungarians, we are all struggling to deal with the terrible theft of the Holy Right, but violence against the people who did this is not the answer. So I ask you for calm today in this beautiful city of ours and let the police do their job."

Even as László Vay calls for calm, there are reports coming in of a man climbing the Széchenyi Chain Bridge overlooking the Danube. There are no indications of what he's doing up there but we'll bring you updated news as we receive it."

***

The news bulletin finished and the radio segued into a pop song.

"Bastard," Zoltan said. "Vay stokes the fires even with his careful words. I bet whatever's happening on the bridge is down to him as well." He leaned forward to speak to the driver. "Széchenyi Bridge."

The taciturn driver nodded and pulled into another lane.

"Why is the bridge so important?" Morgan asked, her eyes fixed on Zoltan's face, which was creased with worry.

"There are few things that symbolize nationalism for Budapest better than the Széchenyi Bridge," he said. "Designed by an English engineer and opened in 1849, it was the first permanent bridge across the Danube, joining the two halves of Buda and Pest. It was considered an engineering wonder of the world at the time, a symbol of the strength and might of our Empire. In those days, we were kings." Zoltan smiled as if in reminiscence, but then his eyes clouded with shadow. "You know some of Hungary's suffering during the Second World War, but in 1944 we tried to withdraw, even though we were allied with Germany. Hitler wouldn't stand for it and sent German troops here, installing the far-right Arrow Cross party. But Stalin was determined to make an example of Budapest and the Red Army advanced with over a million men."

Morgan imagined these streets filled with soldiers and frightened people preparing for the impending inevitability of war. Zoltan continued the story.

"With Germans and Hungarians trapped within, Hitler nevertheless declared Budapest a fortress city, to be defended to the last breath of every man. The Siege of Budapest began, just as winter ravaged the city with cold so extreme that the Danube froze."

The taxi was now speeding along by the side of the river, and as they rounded the corner Morgan saw the bridge. Two classical stone arches stood triumphant near the banks and, slung between them, elegant iron suspension cables seemed to hold the structure weightless above the water.

"In January 1945, the Germans couldn't hold the Soviets back and retreated across the river into Buda, destroying all of the bridges as they went, including this one. Only the pillars were left." Zoltan sighed, as if recalling those dark times. "But it didn't stop the destruction. In February 1945 the German and Hungarian forces surrendered. Hundreds of thousands of people were killed or taken to the Soviet labor camps and eighty percent of the city was destroyed or damaged."

Zoltan fell silent and gazed at the bridge as their taxi slowed. Morgan put her hand on his.

"I can see why the bridge means so much," she said. "But I guess it also symbolizes that Budapest can rise again from disaster."

Zoltan nodded. "And if today is about desecrating symbols of nationalism in order to enrage a nation, the bridge is an obvious target."

The taxi pulled to a halt on the Pest side of the bridge and Zoltan paid the driver. Morgan took in the view across the mighty Danube to Castle Hill beyond, the Royal Palace dominating the skyline with its imposing facade. Her eyes dropped to the bridge itself as Zoltan joined her on the side of the main road that ran onto it.

"It's unlikely that this group would expect to destroy the bridge," she said. "They just want something symbolic to blame on the Jewish population and further stoke the fires of unrest."

Zoltan nodded. "I think that they might be saving the finale for the synagogue tonight, and the main aim today is to fire up the mob." He shook his head. "Sometimes there are days when I look to the sky and see only deep blue, a hope of happiness in a world where we have learned to live together in peace. But the storm clouds are never far from this city."

He pointed towards the Parliament building where a swarm of police and media were gathered at the Shoes on the Danube memorial. "We cannot seem to escape the wheel of history that brings violence over and over again."

"But we have today," Morgan said, turning to him. "If we can find the Holy Right, we may be able to stop the escalation. The synagogue would be safe."

Zoltan smiled, his scarred cheek furrowing.

"I'm glad to have you here, Morgan. An outside view helps when the melancholy grows too dark. Come then, let's see what we can find."

Together they began to walk across the bridge as cars accelerated past, their occupants oblivious to the possibility of disaster. Morgan scanned the walkway, her eyes narrowing as she studied each of the people approaching. In Israel, it had been a core part of military training to spot possible bombers and to be vigilant of danger in a new environment. That kind of awareness never leaves you, she thought, even though she had tried to escape that aspect of her past.

Morgan felt the ghost of her father by her side as she walked. Even though he was Sephardi, he had lived amongst Ashkenazi, Jews of Eastern European ancestry, and some of his friends had escaped this very city. Morgan's thoughts flashed to Elian, her husband, who had died in a hail of bullets on the Golan Heights. Defending the community here felt like a tribute to his memory.

As she looked out to the Danube, Morgan saw one of the many open-topped boat tours coming down the river. Tourists leaned out over the water, wrapped in scarves and gloves, but determined to take pictures of the majestic city. Her gaze shifted to the suspension cables, thick and stable, easy enough to scale quickly. Her eyes followed the cable up to where it met the towering classical arch and then widened in surprise. She grabbed Zoltan's arm.

"Look, up there. Is that a man on the top of the arch?"

Zoltan looked up, squinting to see further. Then something moved and they clearly saw a figure crawl across the top of the stone tower.

"What's he doing?" Zoltan said, as the man leaned over the edge, holding something in his hand. Blue spray paint started to etch its way across the stone as the man carefully began his graffiti.

"Oh no," Morgan said. "He's spraying a blue star of David, so whatever happens here next will be blamed on Jews."

"And it's not likely to be just graffiti," Zoltan said, as he swung himself up over the railing and onto the cable. "I'm going up to get him."

Cars began to slow on the bridge as rubberneckers stopped to watch, and Morgan held her breath as Zoltan climbed higher. The man sprayed faster, his lines more shaky as he completed the fourth line. The star was almost finished as Zoltan reached the platform high above the bridge, pulling his body up and holding his arms out to steady himself. Morgan clenched her fists with the tension of watching them as Zoltan rushed the man and threw a punch. The man ducked and then ran to the end of the tower platform. He glanced down towards the Danube, gave a cheeky salute and jumped.

Morgan gasped as the man leapt into space, his legs cycling in the air and then a mini parachute extended from his backpack, slowing his fall. He drifted down onto the boat below as the tourists exclaimed and snapped photos. Morgan saw Zoltan freeze at the top of the arch, looking down at them and then bend to something at his feet. Whatever he had found, she was going after the man who had left it. She clambered onto the ledge of the bridge, assessing the fall to the tourist boat below. She saw the summer awning still hanging above the top deck of the boat. If she could just land on that, it would cushion her fall, but she had only seconds left to decide.

She could see the man from the bridge stripping off his parachute, laughing with the tourists, and posing for photographs, seemingly unconcerned about being identified. The moment slowed in Morgan's mind. Part of her hesitated, a physical brake applied by the ancient lizard brain that protected the body from harm. That part didn't jump from great heights or take physical risks. But then she glanced to her right and saw the people gathered at the Shoes memorial. She imagined the bodies of those murdered earlier that day floating in the freezing river and their echo sixty years ago, a reflection of the atrocities of the past. Morgan thought of the people trapped by the mob in the synagogue, the potential for violence that hung over the city. She jumped.

CHAPTER 7

THE RUSH OF COLD air on her face was bracing as Morgan jumped off the edge of the bridge, looking out to Margaret Island so that she didn't pitch forward as gravity pulled her downward. She knew how to fall from her Krav Maga martial arts experience but also from the years that she had spent rock climbing and canyoning in the hills of Israel. Her muscles remembered the sensation of jumping from the top of waterfalls into icy dark water beneath. She breathed out heavily to try and stem the flood of adrenalin, glancing down to see the canopy of the tourist boat rushing up to meet her. She heard the shouts of the people below, and just before she landed she saw the man turn and spot her. His eyes narrowed and then she lost sight of him as she landed heavily on the canvas.

Morgan felt the air whoosh out of her as she slid towards the deck, turning and grabbing for a hold on the cloth. There was shrieking from the tourists below as she landed with a thump onto the wooden boards, her fall slowed and cushioned by the canopy. It took her a second to reorient herself, and then she heard the revving of a powerful motor. She stood quickly, brushing off the concerned comments of the tourists, pushing through the throng. She hopped up onto the side of the boat and looked towards the source of the noise. At the stern, the man ditched his parachute and was standing, waiting to jump onto a fast-approaching speedboat.

"Hey," Morgan shouted. "Stop him."

But the tourist crowd was more interested in taking photos of this strange incursion than joining in. The man turned at her shout and she saw his hawk-like profile. It was the Raven himself, his mouth twisted into a mocking smile, as Morgan began to fight her way to the back of the boat.

The speedboat pulled alongside, and the Raven leapt deftly in, his step light. Morgan reached the stern just as the boat pulled away, the sound of his laughter just audible above the engine's roar.

***

High above the Danube, Zoltan examined the large package that the man had left. The explosives were encased in clear solid plastic and a prominent timer counted down from five minutes. It was a taunt for anyone who discovered it, for there was no way into the package to stop the bomb going off. Zoltan felt a cold calm descend as he analyzed his options. The bomb wasn't big enough to cause severe damage or destroy the bridge, but it would be a symbolic attack on a nationalist icon, and the media would infer responsibility from the almost complete blue star graffiti. He had to do something, and fast.

The timer ticked into four minutes remaining.

CHAPTER 8

THE SZÉCHENYI SPA BATHS had always been a realm of magic for Elena, a place that transformed her mother from tyrant to soporific princess. During the summers of her childhood, while her mother lay relaxing in one of the hot pools, Elena would play in the shallows, her mind weaving stories of bath nymphs and fairies. She would sink under the water, eyes open, gazing at the hazy figures beneath. Legs loomed like sea monsters and the giants of legend while she fought battles, waiting for the reward from the Bath King who would let her sink down into the blue forever. These moments helped her to forget the packages passed in the changing rooms, and how her mother would duck into the toilets afterwards, her daughter forgotten. She would emerge smiling, rubbing her nose, her body riper somehow.

As Elena walked into the baths today, her body heavy with the false pregnancy stomach she wore, she thought back to those times and how so much had changed. The fairytale of earlier days had been but a dream before the nightmare of her real life had begun. But today, she hoped to escape.

As a child she had discovered that the goodwill from the baths only ever lasted for a short time and then Elena found herself backhanded into silence as she tried to tell her mother of the nymphs. After a while, she didn't mention them anymore. When her breasts had begun to show just before her thirteenth birthday, it was her mother who noticed first.

"Come, Elena," she had said. "We're going shopping."

Elena remembered how excited she had been, for her clothes had been the subject of ridicule at school, hand-me-downs that ill suited her. Now it seemed that her mother would dress her like one of the popular girls. Elena had been confused when the only shop they had entered sold swimwear and her mother had picked out a tiny bikini. Elena was embarrassed but her mother just adjusted it around her newly formed curves and whispered, "Good, you'll do just fine."

On the next trip to the baths, her mother had kept a tight grip on her hand, making sure that Elena changed into the bikini. In the changing cubicle, her mother had clutched her arm tight, fingernails digging into her arm.

"Now, Elena," she had whispered, her eyes dull. "We need money and you have to earn it. You'll go with someone today and you'll do whatever they want. Don't make a sound or you won't be coming home with me. But be a good girl and there will be money for nice things."

Elena had felt confused, but she would do anything to avoid the beatings her mother doled out. So when the attendant lady had come to fetch her, she had walked behind carefully, following her to the door of one of the private spa rooms.

"I'll get you in thirty minutes," the woman said, her eyes flicking over Elena, dismissing her with one glance. "Go in, then." She pushed open the door and shooed the girl inside the darkened space.

Elena barely remembered what had happened that first time, she had been so terrified. But by the end, her new bikini lay discarded on the floor and her insides felt bruised. The baths had always been a place to get clean, so why did she now feel so dirty?

After the third time, Elena had spoken up, telling her mother she wouldn't go again, that she wouldn't let the men do what they did, that she would scream and tell the police. Her mother had twisted her arm in a Chinese burn, making her listen as she told her daughter that she was a whore, she was ruined and she was nothing. This was her only life choice, this or be sold to the sex trade, and even that would be too good for a little bitch like her. Elena still wondered why her mother hated her so much.

Then, one day, she had entered the spa room and there was a new man in there, his hair a gleaming black. He had wrapped her in a towel and said he only wanted to talk, that he would pay the same amount but he just wanted to speak with her. As he had asked about her school and what she enjoyed doing, Elena had been surprised, but after a few sessions, she began to trust the man and to look forward to time with him. Her mother was none the wiser. A few weeks ago, he had asked her if she wanted to escape the life she led, that if she did one thing for him, he would get her out. She would have money to leave Budapest, to change her life. Did she want that?

Elena wanted that very much, which was why now, nearing her sixteenth birthday, she found herself wearing a false pregnancy stomach, heading into the baths for an antenatal pool session. Earlier, she had gone to an address the man had provided and listened as he told her what to do. "You must wait, stay with the package until it's collected," he had told her. He had made up her face, giving her a wig so that no one would recognize her. It was kind of exciting, like the movies and Elena wanted to do a good job for him. As she left, he had kissed her forehead and she had felt his love. Perhaps he would look after her, rescue her like she had wished the King of the Baths would do in her childhood fairytale.

Wrapping her hands around the pendulous belly, Elena leaned back and looked up at the grand Neo-Baroque entrance. Its pillars and domes were so familiar and yet today, it was as if she saw them with new eyes. The daily stream of visitors was heading through the gates, into one of the largest spa complexes in Europe, with eighteen pools and myriad saunas, steam chambers and corners to relax in. She went through the ritual of entry, her feet following a well-trodden path. The mustard yellow walls dripped with condensation from the steam that billowed through the changing area and Elena felt sweat pool beneath the false stomach. She wondered again what was inside it, knowing not to ask, only hoping that its delivery would secure her freedom.

Inside the baths, she went to her locker and then to the spa room where she had met the man, right next to the pool where the antenatal class was starting. Elena shrugged off the false stomach and placed it beside her on the bench. It looked like a grotesque sack of flesh. Would it hurt to have a look inside it?

She heard the chimes of the clock as her hand reached for the zipper on the side. Elena heard a click and there was a flash of light, a burst of pain and she thought no more as the bomb exploded her young body into a million pieces.

CHAPTER 9

Aware of the seconds ticking away, Zoltan peered down at the cars streaming over the bridge and assessed the danger from falling masonry. He looked further out at the boats on the Danube, suddenly noticing that Morgan was now on one of the tourist barges, staring out after a motorboat that was speeding away. He didn't know how she had got down so fast, but he half smiled. She certainly knew how to look after herself, and it was damn attractive.

He glanced down again, feeling a little vertigo. The Danube seemed the only option, for the package wasn't held in place on the bridge. Zoltan picked it up, as gently as he might a precious child, careful not to dislodge any parts. He walked slowly, barely breathing, to the side of the arched tower. Looking down, he inched his way closer to the edge. His heart thumped in fear, for he didn't know the power of the bomb, only sure it would be better off at the bottom of the Danube.

Peering over, he saw a gap in the boat traffic on the river. With a gasp of effort, he threw the package out and away from the bridge. It turned end over end in the air and Zoltan flinched, his muscles tight, expecting an explosion. But the package plopped into the river, floating for a moment and then sinking as the water leaked into the casing. Zoltan looked at his watch, reckoning that there would be just over two minutes remaining.

He stood for a moment looking out over the city, his anger welling up, for he would defend this country he loved to the death. He was a Jew but he was also Hungarian, like he was a son and a brother. A man could be many things, and one aspect did not define him. He would not deny any part of himself to conform to some crazy definition of who was considered a 'real' Hungarian. So he would fight those who tried to divide this glorious city. Zoltan clenched his fists as the time ticked into its final seconds and then he waited, holding his breath.

But nothing came, only the bellowing horns of the boats below, and the hum of the traffic across the bridge. Zoltan exhaled in a long rush as the seconds continued to tick by. He watched the boat that Morgan was on dock at the Vigadó tér pier and turned, heading for the pylon and the tricky climb down. He felt relief flood his body that they had managed to stop at least one of the plans laid for this chaotic day.

Just as Zoltan started his descent, he heard a muffled explosion. His head jerked towards where he had thrown the bomb, but there was nothing there. No plume of water, no ruined boats. The sound had come from the East and he looked in that direction, suddenly seeing a plume of smoke rising above the skyline as the police sirens began to sound.

***

A short distance down Vigadó tér, Zoltan could see the final passengers emerging from the tourist boat. He ran hard towards the pier, pounding the street like he wanted to thump the terrorists who had set off the bomb. Had the bridge just been a decoy? Or was it meant to be a symbolic attack, drawing attention while innocents were targeted at the same time? Zoltan felt a surge of frustrated anger that he channeled into a burst of speed. How dare these people attack his country, his culture, which had already suffered so much?

He slowed on the approach to the ferry pier and stood getting his breath back, waiting for Morgan to disembark. Tourists gabbled away in various languages, some pointing to the plume of smoke evident in the sky to the East. Some were taking photos with a frisson of excitement at being so close to something significant, as if they were somehow immune to the vagaries of attack. Zoltan shook his head, for they didn't realize how arbitrary terror had now become. They should be thanking God that it wasn't their city at the mercy of madmen.

Morgan walked briskly up the metal walkway, having finally extricated herself from the interrogation of the boat's captain. Her face was serious, her eyes fixed on the dark smoky clouds blooming in the sky. As she drew closer, Zoltan noticed the slash of violet in her right eye, almost a burn across the cobalt blue. Her dark curls were tied back and she moved with economy, the grace of a woman who knew how to fight, and how to dance. Who was she really, Zoltan wondered. He had heard of ARKANE, the name mentioned in a whisper when the Jewish elders met to discuss evacuation plans. He knew that the group had an academic side, well represented at conferences, but it was this secret militant arena that he was interested in. Because Dr Morgan Sierra was clearly not just an academic. He hadn't seen her jump, but he didn't know if he could have done the same thing.

"It was the Raven, and the bastard got away," Morgan said, as she joined Zoltan at street level. "I'm sorry."

Zoltan shook his head, dismissing her concern.

"You jumped from the bridge to go after him. I don't think anyone could fault your dedication. What were you thinking?"

Morgan gazed back towards the water.

"I thought I saw the bodies in the Danube, floating there in the water, calling for justice. Those who died today, as well as the ones from seventy years ago." She paused, looking into the eddies of the fast-flowing river. "Did you find anything up there on the arch?"

"There was a bomb, but I threw it in the Danube before it timed out. It was encased in plastic, tamper-proof." He gestured upwards to the smoke dissipating in the sky above. "But seeing that, I suspect it was a decoy anyway."

Morgan nodded.

"They were playing the local news on the boat. The bomb was at the Széchenyi Baths. Twelve dead." She paused. "It was during an antenatal class, so there were pregnant women amongst the casualties."

Zoltan clenched his fists, willing his rage to a simmer, but there was nothing he could do to help those people now. He and Morgan had to focus on what must surely come next.

"There was an anonymous call to the TV station," continued Morgan. "The bombing has been claimed by a previously unknown Jewish group, in retribution for the Danube murders."

Zoltan snorted, shaking his head. "As if it could have been organized so quickly. They've set this up so well. Whoever is behind this must have been planning it for months."

"That guy from Eröszak is calling on the government to boycott Jewish businesses until the perpetrators are brought to justice. Of course, he's not advocating violence officially but his supporters are calling for a march tonight, in solidarity with the victims." Morgan put her hand on

Zoltan's arm, her voice urgent. "We need to find the Holy Right, it's the only way to stop a bloodbath after dark."

Zoltan gazed across the water at the Palace, a dominant presence that loomed above the city. On the edge of the battlements, he could just make out the giant statue of the Turul, the divine messenger bird of Magyar origin. In the myths of the beginning, it had perched on the top of the Tree of Life, along with the spirits of unborn children in the shape of birds. It was a symbol of power, strength and nobility, a bird of prey with a beak that could rip the hearts from the chests of men, sacrificed on its blood-spattered altar.

As he considered the symbol, trying to discern a pattern in the chaos, Zoltan thought about Castle Hill itself. It was the centre of the nation, a symbol of the might of Hungary as it had once been and how some wanted it to be again. While Pest was the realm of the past, the Ghetto, the Basilica and a Parliament that had become too left wing for many, Buda was the proud fortress of might, the dominion of the future. Surely a nationalist cause would want that symbol to be at the heart of their strategy, and something niggled at the back of Zoltan's mind about the tunnels beneath the hill.

He took out his mobile and dialed Georg, who answered quickly.

"I need you to go back on the right-wing chat boards," Zoltan said. "Can you see what you can find from 2011?"

While he waited for Georg to search, Zoltan turned back to Morgan.

"There's an ancient labyrinth beneath Castle Hill. It was shut down a few years ago under suspicious circumstances, around the time when Erőszak was on the rise."

His attention returned to the phone. "Great, we'll check it out."

Zoltan pointed to Castle Hill. "Let's head up there, it's the only lead I can think of right now."

He led the way up the wide boulevard away from the ferry port. Stopping in front of a giant billboard advertising the elections, Zoltan looked up into the face of László Vay. His scar contorted as his mouth twisted with anger.

"This man knows nothing of honor, and he will do anything to further his pursuit of power. None of what has happened today is beyond him, for he wants to win this election, and I think he aims to waltz in on the back of a nationalist uprising. I knew him once, you know, we were friends … but then one day I discovered the true man behind that perfect smile."

As Zoltan spoke, he remembered that dark day in Bosnia, when his friendship with Vay was obliterated.

***

Srebenica, Bosnia and Herzegovina. Spring 1995.

"Come on, Zol. Seriously, you're always so slow. You can't do anything for it now, let's just leave."

Zoltan didn't look up from the body he was examining, this one just a boy with a gunshot through his forehead. He was used to the taunts of his friend, the dismissive attitude to the people they were there to protect. The child's arms were curled around himself as if he had tried to find comfort in the moments before death. Zoltan found himself silently reciting the opening words of the Kaddish, the Jewish prayers for the dead, even though the boy was probably Muslim in this part of town. Finally he rose.

László was smoking a cigarette, his body relaxed. He lifted his face to the sun, caught in a brief sunbeam, and reveled in its warmth. There were no dark shadows under his indigo eyes, only the movie star looks that made him the envy of the other soldiers. Zoltan didn't know how

László managed to shrug off the deadening weight of sadness that he found engulfed him every day.

They both worked as part of the peacekeeping force, seconded from the Magyar Honvédség, the Hungarian army, to help the Dutch United Nations team. But Zoltan knew that there was no way of keeping the brittle peace for long and he felt the palpable tension in the air. These people hated each other and there had always been violence in this region. It was a tribal place, united only by the fake lines drawn on maps that were as fragile as the paper they were inked on. Thousands of Christian Serbs, Jews and Gypsies had been sent to camps from here under the Nazis and after the war, Yugoslavia had been created. Now, it had broken down, as Muslim nationalists demanded a centralized independent Bosnia, Serbian nationalists wanted to stay near Belgrade-dominated Yugoslavia, and Croats wanted an independent Croatian state.

"Do you even give a shit about this place, Laz?" Zoltan asked as he stole the cigarette from his friend's fingers.

"Of course not," László said. "This land should be ours anyway. After all, Bosnia-Herzegovina was part of the Austro-Hungarian Empire a hundred years ago. Maybe if they all kill each other, it will be ours again."

Seeing the fanatical look in László's eyes, Zoltan sighed and shook his head. His friend had always been an extreme patriot, harking back to the old days of Hungarian glory. They had been the best of friends once, when their fathers had been business partners in a chain of Jewish shops in Budapest and they had played war games amongst the sacks of goods while the adults talked and drank together. László's mother wasn't Jewish, which technically meant that he wasn't either, but that hadn't been important to the boys back then.

A rattle of bullets startled the men and they flattened themselves against a wall. This area was known to be raided by Serb incursions and the sound had been close. Behind a nearby fence, Zoltan could hear the harsh laughter of a group of men, and then a woman's cry. He instinctively raised his gun and stepped forward quietly. László reached out to hold his arm.

"Don't," he said quietly. "It's not your fight."

"Then what the fuck are we doing here?" Zoltan whispered, his rage rising at the impotence of the peacekeepers to stop any kind of violence. It didn't matter to him which group was inflicting the pain, only that the suffering of the innocents would stop. This dirty war was marked by systematic rape as a weapon, mainly by the Serbs against the Bosniaks. Zoltan had heard them boasting of the 'little Chetniks' they would leave behind in the wake of abused women.

The woman screamed again, but the noise was cut short by shouting voices and the sound of a fist slamming into flesh. Zoltan pulled his arm away from László, stepping forward through the rubble of the streets to peer around the edge of the fence. There were six men, wearing the uniform of Serb nationalists, surrounding a woman who was sprawled, weeping, across the body of a dead man. One of the men said something, nodding at the woman and began to unbuckle his belt.

Zoltan felt his heart beating hard in his chest. In some way, this tiny scene represented a microcosm of this conflict, and of every injustice against the vulnerable. Zoltan had heard the stories of Budapest under the fascists, then the Communists, how friends had given each other up in exchange for another day of freedom. He couldn't alter his own country's past, but perhaps he could change this woman's future.

He stepped out from behind the fence, his gun relaxed by his side. Knowing that he and László were outnumbered, it would be better to reason with them.

"You're a long way from your camp, guys," Zoltan said as the men swung round to look at him. Their faces were hostile, and they raised their guns as they formed a phalanx around the woman, claiming their prize. Her sobs filled the air before one of the men spoke, his English halting.

"You … go. This," he gestured at the woman. "Ours."

Zoltan stepped forward, his left hand outstretched in a gesture of placation. His heart was hammering, but he knew that if he walked away now, the woman would be brutally violated. He still had a chance to stop it.

"This woman is under UN protection," he said. "So I think you had better leave."

One of the group laughed and turned away, saying a few words and reaching down to pull the woman off the body of her husband by her hair. She screamed again. Zoltan raised his gun and immediately, the other men had their weapons readied. Zoltan's senses were heightened, the metallic smell of weapons overlaid with the stink of the soldiers' sweat thick in his nostrils.

He felt rather than heard László emerge from behind. A surge of gratitude washed over him at his friend's belated backup. But then he heard a click near his ear, and realized that Laszlo's gun was pointed at his own head. A flush of betrayal rocked him.

"We're sorry for the intrusion," László said, his voice smooth, as if they were at a gentlemen's club, not on the broken streets of Srebenica. "My friend here was just leaving."

The Serbs laughed and lowered their weapons. Zoltan felt László pulling him backwards as the six men turned to their prize, two men of them now unbuckling their pants, as the woman wept at their feet.

Zoltan felt as if the world slowed in that moment, his brain frantically searching for a solution. His eyes fell on a pile of weaponry that the Serbs had left discarded to one side.

A grenade. It was the only way.

He felt almost manic, desperate to get to the woman and stop the soldiers. László wouldn't shoot him, he knew that, but he also knew that his friend would always choose the easy way out. There would be no back up.

The Serbs had their backs turned and as two men held the woman down, another bent to pull off her lower garments as she sobbed in desperation.

"Just walk away, Zol. You can't help her." László's voice was honey, tempting him with the easy path, but the words of Simon Wiesenthal, the persecutor of Nazi criminals, echoed in Zoltan's mind. *For evil to flourish, it only requires good men to do nothing.*

Zoltan broke away from László's grip, running for the pile of weaponry, his eyes fixed on a grenade. He heard swearing and then a gunshot but didn't flinch, steeling his body and flinging himself down behind the pile as he grabbed a grenade from the top. Looking back briefly, he could see Laz ducking back behind the wall, his face turned away. Zoltan knew that he had mere seconds before the men advanced to kill him, so he pulled the pin from the grenade and launched it, throwing it far enough away that it would explode against a nearby building.

The soldiers shouted and ducked as the grenade landed and then exploded, raining debris down from the scarred and shattered tenement block. They turned towards the weapons pile just as Zoltan pulled the pin and lobbed another grenade. This time the soldiers scattered, firing behind themselves at him and the weapons pile. The last soldier pointed a gun at the woman's head as he turned away. Zoltan leapt from his hiding place and charged the man as the gun went off. His eyes had flicked up at the movement so the bullet just missed the woman's head as she curled into a fetal position.

An explosion rocked the little square and as masonry

began to fall, Zoltan threw his body over the woman, trying to protect her from the rain of hell. As the other soldiers ran from the scene, he felt a slicing pain in his cheek and a burning on the side of his face as he lay there, hoping that he could just save this one innocent.

***

Zoltan touched the scars on his cheek as he looked up into László's face on the billboard, remembering that day. After the incident, their friendship had finally ruptured and split. László had inveigled himself into an officer's position, allying himself with nationalist interests and eventually pursuing a political career. He was the embodiment of what most would consider success, becoming wealthy and influential in the public arena. Zoltan had followed his moral compass, giving up the pursuit of power to stand up for those who could not defend themselves.

He felt a light touch on his arm, and turned to see Morgan's face, a question in her eyes. Zoltan knew that he could trust her, their fast friendship built on a shared belief in humanity that men like László would never understand or honor.

"Sorry," he said, glancing at his watch. "Let's go. The march will start early and as dusk falls, I fear that evil will stalk this city again."

CHAPTER 10

When they reached the tourist-ridden precinct of Castle Hill, Zoltan led Morgan away from the throng down a dogleg alleyway.

"There's an old entrance for the labyrinth workers back here," he said. "Tourists used the official gateway but that's been closed since 2011."

"Why did they shut it down?" Morgan asked.

Zoltan shrugged. "There are many conspiracy theories, because it was stormed by the police and the Inspectorate for the Environment one July day. The tourists and workers inside just had to leave, with no reason given. Some say that the company running the place didn't have the right permits, but others hint at something darker here, criminal activity or the occult. From what Georg found in the chat rooms, this could well be a secret Eröszak meeting place." He stopped in front of a nondescript wooden door. "This is it."

Pulling the tire iron from his bag, Zoltan levered the door open, cracking the lock mechanism as it splintered in the frame. A metal staircase led down into the earth, and already Morgan could feel cool air flowing up from below. Pulling torches from the pack, they trod lightly, but their footsteps still made a soft clang as they descended into the dark.

At the bottom, a tunnel carved from the rock stretched into the heart of the hill. They stood silently for a moment, the sound of dripping permeating the damp atmosphere. Water welling from the depths of the earth under Budapest had brought with it healing properties, feeding the rejuvenating hot spring spas, and over millennia, the waters had also carved out a complex of subterranean tunnels and caves. Now Zoltan and Morgan followed one of these tunnels into the labyrinth, and in the chill air, it felt as deserted as it would have been when it was created.

They walked quietly, listening for any hint of what might lie before them. Morgan reached out a finger to touch the cool wall of stone, remembering the catacombs of Paris where she had run from Milan Noble's men. But those corridors were walls of bone arranged in tribute to the millions of plague dead, whereas this place was ancient, perhaps already here when humanity was born. It would still be here when the span of human existence ended, when the wars exhausted themselves and the earth could rest again.

"The company that ran this place created a bizarre tourist trail in the labyrinth," Zoltan said, his voice low. "It was meant to be a journey into the history of Budapest and also a kind of spiral path into the self."

"I can see the attraction of the symbolism." Morgan whispered back. "In Jungian psychology, the labyrinth is a powerful symbol of the unconscious. We protect our secrets even from ourselves by winding them in deep, hidden mazes. In myth, the labyrinth held the Minotaur, the beast we must all slay to reconcile our true selves."

Zoltan grunted softly. "Enough of stories. There may be real beasts down here."

Their torch beams flickered around the tunnels running off to the side. A shadow of a figure loomed suddenly from the dark, and Morgan started suddenly, her hand moving instinctively to where she would normally carry a weapon,

"It's OK," Zoltan reassured her. "It's just one of the statues they have down here, called the Guides of the Soul. The weird red figures are everywhere. It's an odd place, with different galleries according to the time period and even a cafe, deserted now of course, which makes it perfect for a ready-made bunker in the heart of the city."

They continued down a long corridor with carved stone heads atop life-size pillars on either side, their faces featureless, similar to the giant statues of Easter Island.

"This is known as the Axis of the Earth," Zoltan said. "People would come alone to spend the night here, considering their lives."

They rounded another corner into a cavernous room, the stone walls bare of decoration. Dominating the room was a stone pillar carved with two faces, one leonine and the other like some mythical dark elk.

"This is the double faced shaman, the táltos," Zoltan whispered, and Morgan heard a touch of reverence in his tone. "The ancient Hungarians believed in soul dualism, a bodily soul for this physical realm, and another that roamed free in the world. The shaman had a watcher spirit that guarded his physical body as his powerful soul traveled."

Morgan played the torch over the figure, dual faces with harsh lines, a powerful embodiment of the shaman, while leaves and branches curled down the pillar. Zoltan saw the movement of her light and explained.

"The tree of life connects the worlds of Magyar myth, the upper home of the gods, this middle world where we dwell and the underworld entwined in its roots, where Ördög dwells, creator of all evil."

Morgan felt her skin crawl at the pronunciation of the name of the Hungarian devil, for in Zoltan's mouth, the myth seemed to live, and they were down in his dark realm now. There was a palpable sense of menace, as if the walls themselves exhaled a poison. She almost expected to see dark shapes oozing from the stone, shapes that demanded another soul to gorge on.

"The souls of the táltos could travel between the realms, drenching the ghosts and interceding for humanity with the gods, some say preventing the destruction of all by the ravaging of demons." Zoltan paused, running his fingers down one branch of the tree. "But their strength has disappeared along with the people's faith in them. And where were they in the dark days of the ghetto?" he murmured.

Rounding a corner, Morgan saw a massive head emerging from the earth, his crown a grotesque bulk that pushed out of the ground. It was a giant buried by the mountain, a fallen king, perhaps representing the fall of Austro-Hungary, Morgan thought, a once-mighty empire that struggled to rise from the dirt of history. In her mind, she saw the figure shake itself free to rule again. At first he would be noble and just, dealing fairly with his faithful subjects. But this king had twisted plans, and soon after he emerged, he would bring his giant club down upon the people.

Zoltan stopped suddenly, putting his hand on Morgan's arm, his fingers clutching it with a tight grip. He flicked his torch off and she followed suit. They stood in the dark, barely breathing. Then Morgan heard it too, a pair of voices raised in argument ahead of them. Zoltan slipped off the backpack and pulled out the camera case Georg had given them. Carefully, he inched the zipper down and freed the device, pressing a button so that a tiny red light glowed in the dark.

Morgan felt the cool stone on her back, her breath ragged in the air. She strained to hear the words, but they were muffled in the angular acoustics of the cave, deadened by the tons of stone above them. She felt Zoltan squeeze her arm and pull her forward, moving his hand down to hers so that they could inch along the wall together towards the sound.

There was light up ahead, the warm glow of candles. As they paused at a bend, hidden in the shadows, Morgan could see two figures, hands raised as they argued with each other. A warped stone cross with stumped ancient limbs stood at the end of the corridor and the walls were flanked with stone pillars topped with spiked metal roundels. It seemed like an altar to a pagan hybrid of Christianity and the ancient Magyar faith.

The voices were clearer now, an argument in fast Hungarian and a sub-text of gesticulation. One man grabbed at the other and his face angled towards the candlelight. With the sharp nose and shining black hair, Morgan recognized Hollo Berényi, the Raven, the man she had chased from the bridge. She felt Zoltan tense beside her, bracing himself for action, but they had no weapons and a frontal assault up this thin corridor would be suicidal. Recording the encounter would be far more valuable for their cause and Zoltan silently held up the camera, his hand obscuring the red light.

"They're arguing about when to reveal the relic," Zoltan whispered by her ear. "Berényi wants to take it to the rally, claiming that it will escalate the violence tonight if they announce its recovery from the Jews who stole it. He wants to leave now, but the other man talks of using it for some kind of ceremony first."

A third man stepped from the shadows behind the altar, his voice halting the argument with authority. Morgan recognized László Vay from the political posters and felt Zoltan draw in a sharp breath at seeing his former friend in this dark place.

Berényi seemed placated by the words, shrugging as László spoke, but clearly uncomfortable with losing the argument. He made a final comment, then spun on his heel and stalked away down a tunnel away from the altar cavern.

"He's going ahead to make sure everything is ready at the rally," Zoltan whispered, and in his words, Morgan could hear his indecision as to whether to go after the man. Berényi was the blunt instrument of neo-nationalist wrath, a Turul with hooked claws and a beak that could disembowel its victims, a mythical creature of violence and blood. He had to be stopped, but they both knew that László Vay was the more dangerous in the long run.

László placed something reverently on the ancient altar, wrapped in a white cloth. Zoltan was transfixed by the object and he raised the camera again. Morgan dared to hope that it would capture the detail of the scene in the semi-darkness.

The other man started to chant, his hands raised to heaven in supplication as he moved behind the altar. The intonation was strange: not just the words but even the rhythm of his prayers was off-beat somehow. The words rolled through the caves, echoing in the long corridor, as if he was calling the ancient spirits to bear witness. In the flickering candlelight, Morgan suddenly saw his face, tattooed with intricate patterns of leaves that seemed to morph into demonic visages as his mouth twisted with entreaties to the spirit world. She saw that he had missing teeth and those remaining had been blackened and sharpened, like a maw of Hell. This man made her flesh crawl, and Morgan itched for a gun.

"Those are Magyar ritual prayers," Zoltan whispered. "He's a táltos, a shaman." Morgan heard the undertone of shock in his voice. "I've heard of this tattooed man. He channels dark magic back to this country, allying himself with the Far Right who can give him the blood sacrifice he needs."

László leaned forward and, with reverence, unfolded the cloth, as the prayers of the táltos grew more frenzied. Inside was a brown, leathery object that reflected the candlelight in dull hues, its patina like a horse chestnut at the end of autumn. It was the size of a clenched fist, and in that second, Morgan realized that it was the Holy Right Hand of St Stephen.

László fell to his knees in front of the altar, like a king waiting to be anointed. He sang out resonant words, pausing as the táltos echoed each phrase.

"He claims the Right as his own," Zoltan whispered. "He claims Hungary as a new Empire under his rule. He entreats the Gods to accept the blood sacrifice offered today in their name."

As the táltos chanted louder, he picked the relic up with both hands and began to wave it in a figure of eight in the air, the symbol of eternity. Morgan could see that László's eyes were shining with fanaticism as he watched it circle, as if this Hand bestowed on him the right to rule. The táltos touched László's face with it, stroking the living flesh with the thousand year old relic in a grotesque blessing. A shudder ran through László, but Morgan could see that it was ecstasy, not revulsion, that shook him.

Placing the Hand back on the altar, the táltos took up a ceremonial knife. Strange symbols were carved on the handle, evoking the myths of the Magyar war gods. With his chants growing more guttural and violent, the táltos cut a sliver of flesh from the mummified hand. He placed the slice into a chalice and filled it with dark liquid from a flask, swirling it around as he intoned ancient words.

László opened his mouth for the tainted host, closing his eyes in prayer as the táltos tipped the chalice.

CHAPTER 11

Morgan watched László swallow, chewing a little on the long dead flesh, and she felt a rush of nausea at his cannibalism. The camera light still glowed under Zoltan's hand, and she realized that this footage would show the politician as a madman. Where people would tolerate racist violence, bigotry and hatred, they would not accept superstition and desecration. Eröszak was standing for economic revival in a greater Hungarian Empire, not the resurrection of myth and dictatorship.

"Enough," Zoltan whispered, pressing a button on the camera. They slipped back around the corner and he handed it to Morgan. "You need to get this out of here so that it can transmit above ground to Georg. It's the evidence we need to stop the rally. I'll deal with these two and then I'll bring out the relic."

The look in Zoltan's eyes was that of a man defending his family from invasion. Morgan knew that he wouldn't stop until Hungary was free from these fanatics, when it was a country where all Hungarians could live together, whatever their beliefs. She nodded and touched his hand, leaning in close.

"Be careful," she whispered. "Your people need you

alive." Then on light feet, she ran through the cave, back the way they had come.

***

Zoltan watched Morgan go, sending up a prayer that she would make it in time to stop further escalation. He pulled the tire iron from his pack, rounding the corner as the prayers of the táltos reached a crescendo. László knelt in front of the altar facing the twisted cross. As his mouth opened again to receive the final libation, Zoltan stepped from the shadows, crashing the weapon against one of the metal roundels as he ran towards them. The noise resounded through the cave and the táltos fell silent as both men spun to face the sound.

"No," László bellowed with rage, leaping up, his ritual of power interrupted. His hand fell to his belt for a weapon but as his fingers closed around the butt of a gun, Zoltan was upon him, swinging the tire iron. László rolled away and the blow glanced off his shoulder as Zoltan swung back for another strike. The táltos backed away, his tattooed face showing no fear, only a curiosity at this development. His prayers changed again and Zoltan heard the beginnings of a curse, words that had echoed down the centuries as a harbinger of desperate suffering.

László pulled his gun and turned, firing just as Zoltan slammed the tire iron down on his arm. The shot went wide, ricocheting off the stone walls and the gun fell clattering to the ground. As László clutched at his arm, Zoltan shoved the metal back into his stomach, driving the wind from him as he fell to his knees, coughing. After all the years of politics, the man was soft, relying on others to fight his battles. Zoltan stood over him with the metal bar raised, muscles tense.

"It's finished, Laz. I'm taking the relic back to the Basilica."

László laughed through his wheezing attempts to draw breath, looking up at Zoltan from the ground as he clutched his damaged arm.

"You just don't get it, do you? Always the brawn, never the brains, eh, Zoltan. Even your father knew that I was the better man."

Zoltan gripped the tire iron harder, wanting to slam it down and destroy this man, responsible for so much violence and capable of so much more.

"You can't stop the march of progress," László continued. "This country wants change, it wants the fucking Jews and Roma out. We will finish what Hitler started and the Soviets continued."

Zoltan felt a strange sensation possess him. It was as if he stood at the pivotal point of a chain of history, violence repeating itself throughout generations. He was alone, standing against the tide of hate, but he felt the weight of history buoy him up. The Jews had survived unceasing waves of brutality against them, and he would survive this. To bring the tire iron down and finish László would make him a martyr, killed by a Jew, sparking further cycles of retribution. Zoltan stepped back towards the gun. He needed to get László out of there to face some kind of public reckoning. But then the prayers of the táltos stopped and Zoltan heard the rasp of the gun, and a faint click.

He dived for the shelter of the nearest stone pillar just as the tattooed man fired. Zoltan felt a burning sensation in his arm and heard László laugh as he clutched at the wound, feeling warm blood pulsing out.

"You see, Zoltan, even the Magyar ancestors reject you. But I will be a hero today, wounded in action while killing the Jew who stole the relic and returning it to the people myself." László looked briefly at his watch. "I will produce you at the rally, the perfect scapegoat, a Jew with a personal grudge against me."

Zoltan heard László get up and walk across the cave towards the táltos, knowing that if László got the gun, he was finished. What did he have to lose anymore, he thought, and launched himself back out of the shelter of the rock, hurling himself at his old friend. Zoltan slammed into László, using his bulk to smash his body against the altar and knock them both into the táltos, who dropped the gun in his haste to back away. They ended up on the floor, a tangle of bodies, each scrambling to grab hold of the other, a snarling mass of aggression, reduced from men to beasts.

Zoltan landed a blow to the tattooed nose of the táltos, and blood gushed immediately. Zoltan saw the hatred in his eyes as the man scrabbled away on hands and knees, before standing and running off down the corridor.

His attention momentarily diverted, Zoltan felt László roll out of the grip of his damaged arm and lurch for the tire iron lying close by. He spun quickly and grabbed the man, slamming his head against the hard ground, pinning the searching fingers with a tight grip. László groaned and Zoltan felt his blood lust rise, aware that he had only to carry on smashing the man's head and it would be over. He thought of Srebenica, the moment he had seen the truth of his friend's heart. He slammed once more and then stopped, lying panting against László's prone body, trying to catch his breath. He spotted the gun a little way from them and stood, shaking with the effort.

Zoltan fell to his knees by the gun, wanting to rest now, to lean against the wall and just close his eyes. He reached for the weapon, and as he did so a sound came from behind him, a scream of rage, almost inhuman in its ferocity.

CHAPTER 12

ZOLTAN REACTED QUICKLY, GRABBING the gun and spinning towards the shriek. László held the tire iron high, its arc heading straight for Zoltan's head, his eyes a berserker's, crazed with savagery. There was no choice in that moment and Zoltan fired the gun, almost reflexively, as if he were under fire in enemy territory. It was kill or be killed, and here, under his great city, it had finally come to this most basic of human drives to stay alive.

The bullet hit László in the chest and the look on his face was pure disbelief. He dropped the tire iron and turned, clutching at the altar. The Holy Right still lay there and as he toppled, László grabbed it, pulling it to his chest like a talisman. His blood pumped out, soaking the mummified hand and Zoltan could only watch as his once friend died, his eyes going blank as his spirit joined the ancestors that haunted the cave system.

Zoltan heard footsteps in the stone corridor. He gripped the gun again, aware that there were only a few bullets left. He tried to rise, but was so weakened by the blood loss and the aftershock of the fight that he sank to the floor again. A figure rounded the corner and he saw it was Morgan, her eyes alight with concern. She ran to him.

"I heard the shots," she said. "I had to come back.

We have to finish this together, Zoltan. But first, I need to get you to a hospital." Morgan pressed her hands over the wound in Zoltan's arm, blood oozing out around her fingers. She looked over at László's corpse, with his blood forming a pool around him before the altar. Zoltan clutched at her hand, his eyes searching hers for judgment.

"I didn't mean to kill him, Morgan, but now I have to wonder … Would you have killed Hitler in 1933, given a chance? Before he gained the kind of power that led to the camps? Before Eichmann slaughtered the Jews of Budapest?"

"It's impossible to say." She shook her head. "Of course we would have in hindsight, but no one knew what kind of man Hitler would become in the beginning."

"Or no one would have believed it of him." Zoltan's eyes closed for a moment. "Except his closest friends, perhaps. Those who knew him before he became powerful, when he let down his guard and showed his true lack of empathy. László could have gone that way, Morgan. I know it. He could have even been worse in an age of media devotion to the beautiful, where his perfect face could hide his rotten soul."

"I can't believe that the people of this country would allow genocide again, that Europe could let something like that happen."

Zoltan smiled bitterly, his scar twisting into a grimace. "Srebenica was only 1995, and Rwanda the year before. We let it happen, and history repeats itself because people remain the same underneath. Brutal, tribal, violent."

Morgan shook her head. "Not all of them."

"Enough of them to call for the secret police to create a register of Jews. Enough of them to burn a synagogue with innocents inside if we don't stop that rally," Zoltan said. "Berényi is still out there, stirring up a hornet's nest of neo-nationalist hate. The city is dry kindling waiting for the spark and we have to dampen it."

He struggled to push himself up from the floor, but his face whitened with the effort and he sank back.

"I don't think you'll be much use against Berényi," Morgan said. "I need to get you some help."

"There's no time," Zoltan said, his eyes pleading with her. "You have to stop him without me." He looked round at László's body. "And I need to deal with the body and get far away from here, because if it's discovered that a Jew killed the nation's favorite son, albeit in self-defense, we'll have more than a day of terror." He pulled his cellphone from his pocket. "Call Georg from outside and tell him where I am. He'll be able to find out where the rally is, too." He pushed at her arm weakly. "Now, go."

***

As Morgan ran back through the cave system, she felt a rising sense of fatigue, for despite the death of one man who had incited racial hatred, there were many more ever-ready to take his place. The caverns seemed oppressive, their unyielding walls a reminder that the nature of humanity doesn't change. But there were furrows in the rock and trickles of water that ran down the walls, carving their way over centuries. Perhaps that was the only way, she thought as she ran, the gentle, insistent push of water reflecting the slow progress of equality. She remembered little Ilona at the synagogue, her eyes wide with terror, fearful of something that she didn't understand and a world where already some hated her for no reason. Enough, Morgan thought, the time for gentle insistence was over.

Emerging through the battered door into the light, Morgan checked the cellphone coverage and finally managed to get a signal. She switched on the camera as she dialed Georg and watched the bars on the screen as the files were transmitted. He answered within two rings.

"Zoltan, are you OK?" he asked, his voice blurred as he covered the mouthpiece to disguise his words.

"It's Morgan," she said quickly. "We've got video footage but Zoltan's hurt. He needs help but it has to be secret. He needs evacuation from the labyrinth under Castle Hill." She heard Georg's shocked intake of breath as she recounted the events.

"We're still outside the Andrassy offices," he said. "Many employees are drifting home so I can slip away too. I know those caves and I'll get Zoltan out of there." Morgan gave him the directions to the back entrance where she stood.

"Do you know a doctor?" she asked. "He needs urgent medical attention but it needs to be discreet."

Georg laughed, a harsh bark. "We're Jews, Morgan. Doctors are something we have a lot of. Don't worry, Zoltan will be fine, and we'll keep him safe. I'll need time to process the video before we can release it to the media. Shall I meet you near the labyrinth entrance?"

Morgan hesitated a moment, a part of her longing to wait for him and then fly home as she had meant to hours ago. But then she thought of the bodies in the Danube, imagining her own father's face amongst the dead. It could have been him, she thought. It could have been Elian, or any of those I love.

"No," she said. "I need to go after Berényi. He's heading for some kind of rally, a gathering of nationalists. If he succeeds in enraging the crowd, there could be a bloodbath before we can get the media to release the video."

"Thank you, Morgan," Georg said, and she heard unspoken layers of meaning in his words. Some were called to fight and others to work behind the scenes, and Georg knew that they were both important today. "Just a minute, I'll check the chatter and call you right back."

He cut the line and Morgan stood for a moment. She didn't want time to think about what she was doing, and she knew Director Marietti would have told her to get out of town hours ago, for this wasn't a fight that ARKANE should be involved in. There were no religious mysteries here, only a deep-rooted hatred embedded in the DNA of the region, startled into life again by economic crisis and spiraling unemployment. But Morgan knew that she couldn't leave knowing she might have prevented violence.

The phone rang, and she answered it quickly. Georg's voice was rushed, and there were street sounds in the background now as he spoke.

"I'm in my car now, heading for the labyrinth. The video is processing and I'm editing it to remove your voice and Zoltan's in the corridor." The sound of horns made Morgan move the phone from her ear, then he continued. "I'm also monitoring the neo-nationalist forums and there's chatter about a large gathering at Memento Park, just outside the city center. One right-wing fundamentalist blogger has been tweeting about the atmosphere building there, how they're waiting for something huge to kick off, how the Jews will pay, that kind of thing."

"Sounds like it might be the place." Morgan said, as she headed back towards the main road of Castle Hill. "What are the police doing? Surely that's got trouble written all over it."

"They're strung out all over the city, trying to quell the unrest evident in a spate of revenge attacks on both sides. The Jewish community isn't entirely innocent in this anymore, Morgan. Some groups are taking steps to retaliate for the Danube murders."

Morgan closed her eyes, willing frustration from her.

"Of course, this escalation is exactly what Eröszak intended. I'll get to the rally and see what I can do."

"There will be a lot of media there on a day like this.

With so much potential for conflict, it's a broadcaster's dream and we can use that." Georg paused and Morgan could almost hear his brain whirring. "There's a USB key in the side of the camera, do you see it?"

She turned the camera over in her hands, finding the tiny device embedded in the base.

"Yes, got it."

"If you can plug that into a media device, I can hack in and send the edited video. It will be more effective if you can do it at the rally rather than me posting it on the net."

Morgan thought of the potential danger of walking into a neo-nationalist rally and trying to share the explosive video. It would be hard enough to get that close and even if she could, the crowd wouldn't exactly be receptive to the dark unveiling of their favorite son.

"I'll try," she said. "Keep your phone handy."

She thrust her hand out, waving at an oncoming taxi.

CHAPTER 13

THE TAXI DROPPED MORGAN a little way from the entrance to Memento Park because the roads were so busy. It seemed that all of Budapest was gathering, or at least those who supported the nationalist cause. And what good Hungarian wouldn't want to, she thought, as the red, white and green flags fluttered in the breeze. There were families holding hands and groups of young people laughing and drinking. It was a scene that resonated with pride, and Morgan certainly understood the attraction of nationalism. After all, who didn't want to be proud of their own country?

She looked around for Berényi but the crowd was thick, moving through the park slowly, and there was no sign of him. Around the edges, Morgan could see groups of men with hard faces and fists that clenched plastic tumblers of beer. They wore the uniform of the civilian militia, officially dissolved by the Hungarian courts, but tolerated, and even encouraged, by many who supported their cause. The black uniform and caps evoked pictures that Morgan had seen in Yad Vashem, the Holocaust Museum, in Jerusalem. She knew that psychological research had shown that a uniform cloaked the individual in collective responsibility, and it was the best way to get people to obey authority figures and overcome their natural reticence to hurt others. She had read reports of the militia's torch-lit marches around Roma communities, creating terror in the persecuted group and even causing some to be evacuated for fear of explosive violence. It wouldn't take much to encourage this lot to attack the synagogue in revenge for the outrage of the Holy Right.

Morgan entered the gates and moved with the crowd into the park. It was a strange throwback to the Communist era, with huge statues of famous figures like Lenin, Marx and Engels as well as the boots of Stalin, all that remained of the dictator's statue, torn down in the 1956 revolution. Nearby, the Liberation Army Soldier stood six meters tall, striding with fists raised towards the enemy, shouting for revolution. The park was meant to be a reminder of the fall of Communism, but Morgan felt it somehow glorified those dark days, its propaganda now serving a modern purpose.

The open plan park was designed in six circles surrounding a central seventh, with the Communist star in the very middle. A dais had been set up there, but the focus of the crowd was on a large stage near the back of the park where a band was playing folk rock. As Morgan slid through the throng, she could see that some of those massed in front of the band had their right arms raised in a Fascist salute. No one seemed to care, and again, Morgan felt that she was witnessing a flashback, or an alternate universe where the last seventy years had been but a dream.

Behind the band, large screens projected visions of Hungary's greatness, images of propaganda that the Communist regime would have been proud to call their own. The handsome face of László Vay smiled while he greeted housewives and kissed babies, as strong men shook his hand and pledged allegiance. The video switched to footage of the militia marching underneath the banner of the

Turul, the mythical bird, representing power, strength and nobility. Morgan noticed that many in the crowd watched the images even if they ignored the music, and the press were gathered around the edges, interviewing people. She had to get the footage of the labyrinth up onto that screen.

Weaving through the crowd, Morgan smiled up at the leering men so they would let her pass. Women eyed her suspiciously and Morgan suspected that any violence here would be equal opportunity. The smell of sweat and beer intensified as she made it to the front of the crowd, who were now swaying and singing along to what must be a popular song.

Peering into the shadows at the side of the stage, Morgan tried to see where the video was controlled. There was a guy hunched over a several laptops and a mixing desk, earphones on his head. Next to the technician, she spotted Hollo Berényi, compulsively looking at his watch, clearly expecting László to arrive for his big speech any moment. He pulled out his smartphone and dialed, appearing to be swearing silently as it failed to be answered. He must assume that László was still underground, but he would be more concerned soon enough.

Morgan noticed the lead singer glance to the side of the stage and Berényi made a gesture to carry on, keep playing. So László was already late, and that meant she didn't have much time. If Berényi couldn't fire up this crowd, he might take his militia and attack the synagogue anyway. Morgan thought of little Ilona, and of the old woman, screaming as she relived past horrors.

Her phone buzzed in her pocket.

"We're out of the labyrinth," Georg's voice was halting as he tried to catch his breath. "We've dealt with the ... package ... and I've got Zoltan out and we're at a local doctor's. Where are you?"

"On location," Morgan said briefly. "I should have

something for you in the next ten minutes. Will you be able to monitor when the feed goes active even if I can't call you?"

"Yes, if you can plug the USB in, I'll get a ping on my phone and I can send the video. I'll be waiting."

Morgan considered her options. Berényi had seen her briefly on the boat but would he place her face on this day of chaos? She made her decision and ducked back out through the crowd towards the busy bar. She adjusted her clothes, pulling down her T-shirt to reveal a little more cleavage. Grabbing two beers, she headed back to the screen control desk, evading the attentions of several inebriated men along the way.

When she returned, Berényi had his back to her and was talking to three other men, their bulk barely covered by the tight-fitting black uniforms. A couple of them glanced at her as she approached and she raised the beers in fake inebriation, giving a cheeky smile before she bent to the man at the desk. After a second, they carried on their conversation, clearly thinking she was a groupie for the band, but Morgan knew that Berényi's eyes could fall on her any minute. She hoped that Georg was ready to initiate whatever he needed to do if she managed to get the USB key into the computer, because she was on the edge of potential trouble here.

The technician turned at her approach and said something in Hungarian. His tone indicated that she shouldn't be there, that he was busy, but Morgan saw his eyes take in her curves with barely concealed interest. He was fat and his skin was pockmarked, clearly not the most attractive member of the band's team. Perhaps he would take any chance of attention. She stepped in close and gave him the beer, smiling and turning with her back to Berényi, shielding the view of the mixing desk and hiding her face.

"I love the music," she said, mouthing the words, as the

band segued into something more thrash metal than folk.
"You must be so clever to work with the band."

"Oh, English," the man said, smiling in a way that made Morgan suspect that he had enjoyed the attentions of British groupies before. He patted his lap, pulling out the chair to make room for her. She swallowed her disgust and sat on his knee, using the chance to get a look at his setup. She felt a hot hand on her thigh as he indicated the computer system with pride.

"This ... most important for band," he said. She smiled and nodded, seemingly enthusiastic as he explained the setup in Hungarian, pleased to have someone share his passion. Morgan noticed a USB port on the side farthest from her, but she would need to stretch across him to plug it in. She felt his hand move up from her thigh, towards her breast, his breath hot on her neck.

Morgan fought the desire to get up and run, instead pressing forward into his hand. As he took the chance to feel her soft curves, she retrieved the USB key from her pocket. Palming it, she turned towards him, trying to glaze her eyes in a parody of drunken lust. She could hear the band winding up their song, the chorus on its third repetition. She bent her head, her lips meeting his and as he closed his eyes, she felt behind her for the USB port.

The man's thick tongue plundered Morgan's mouth, all sense of his job forgotten as he groped her breast with one hand and with the other pulled her firmly onto his stiffening crotch. Just one more second, Morgan thought, her body desperate to pull away as she tried to dock the USB key. She felt the click and she leaned away from the man, smiling coquettishly. He said something in Hungarian, no doubt some version of "let's go somewhere more private later," his hand never leaving her breast. Everything in Morgan screamed at her to use her Krav Maga close combat skills and get out of there, but she had to stay and make sure that the video was delivered.

She smiled again, nodding as if in agreement, glancing over his shoulder at the screen. Nothing had changed and the band played on, with the video of militant propaganda still playing in the background. Had something gone wrong?

"What are you doing here?" The voice was rough and heavily accented. Morgan felt a hand on her arm pull her away from the technician's lap. She found herself staring into the dark eyes of Hollo Berényi, his black hair shining, like an oil slick hiding the lifeless depths beneath.

CHAPTER 14

"I'm on holiday," Morgan said. "And I wanted to meet the band." She smiled at Berényi, forcing flirtation into her gaze, fully aware of what this man was capable of. "Are you part of the band?"

Morgan's senses were in overdrive. As Berényi's eyes assessed her, she could feel his men drawing in closer behind, their interest sparked by her lewd behavior with the technician. She needed to get out of there, but so far, there was no change on the screen. Had the USB stick not been pushed in far enough?

"I've seen you before," Berényi said, suspicion growing in his eyes and an edge of menace creeping into his voice. "What are you really doing here?"

The crowd started chanting as the band led them in another popular song, the chorus some kind of repetitive rant. But then the sound faltered, tailing off into silence as the giant screens flickered from the nationalist symbols to the view of a cavern lit by candlelight.

Berényi noticed the change of mood and turned from Morgan towards the screen, his eyes widening as he saw the táltos cutting a piece of the Holy Right, and the face of László Vay rapt with wonder as he knelt to receive the dark Mass.

Morgan took her chance to slip towards the barrier, but as she moved away, Berényi spun and caught her arm.

"You," he hissed. "Jew bitch."

He barked something in Hungarian and two of his men rushed forward to hold her as Morgan struggled to escape. She slipped from one grip, defending herself, but the other man caught her from behind. One meaty hand covered her mouth to quiet her, and her heart raced as she knew it was only a matter of time until Berényi would deal with her himself. She was pulled tight against the hard body of one of the guards, waiting for the order. She gathered her strength, focusing on the weak points of the man behind, her mind recalling her training in the Israeli Defense Force.

The technician was frantically tapping at the computer, clearly unable to gain control of the screens again. He spotted the USB stick and pulled it from the side but the video kept on playing, a loop clearly focused on the Holy Right and Vay drinking the tainted wine. From her pinioned position, Morgan could see disgust dawning on the face of the crowd as Hungary's golden boy showed his true colors. The press were filming and Morgan had no doubt that this was going out on national television, that the radio waves would be alive with gossip, and social media would be spreading the word. Some in the crowd held up their phones, recording the images and in this age of connectivity, there would be nowhere to hide from this scandal. Vay's disappearance would be taken as a response to public shame, and he would be forgotten.

Berényi spun from the technician's desk, and Morgan could see indecision in his eyes. Should he go on stage now and take control for his party? Or should he disappear before he was tainted with the same disgrace? He walked toward her, and she could see in his eyes that he would make her pay for this outrage. He nodded at the men and they started pulling her backwards towards the curtained area behind the stage. It had to be now.

Morgan bit the man's hand, tearing at his flesh as she bent forward hard, shifting her centre of gravity so that the man was pulled over her. At the same time, she stomped back with her boot, raking the side of his calf. That opened up enough space for her arm to swing back and hit him once, twice, in the groin, all in a matter of a second. He grunted and let her go, clearly not expecting such resistance. Morgan spun away, arms raised in the open palm Krav Maga stance. She saw the other men pull batons from their waist pouches, flicking them to full length. Morgan knew that she couldn't hold off this many, but she was determined not to go easily.

The men advanced and then, suddenly, Berényi barked an order and they stopped. Morgan looked around to see two news crews filming them from the crowd, now focused on the drama unfolding around her. It was as if the real world had suddenly flooded into Hollo Berényi's consciousness. He knew that there were too many witnesses to what he wanted to do and he wasn't going down like his boss.

The reporters called out to him, wanting a statement, but he spun away, walking quickly behind the stage followed by his men. The technician ran out after them, followed by the tenacious media, and soon Morgan was left alone at the side of the stage. The band members left sheepishly and the crowd began to disperse, the energy of the day sucked dry by the revelations of the video feed. There was an air of anti-climax, as the tension dissipated into gossip and the planned riot was forgotten. Morgan knew that the danger was over, at least for today.

CHAPTER 15

MORGAN SAT ON THE steps of the synagogue, watching as a team from the local community swept up the broken glass and picked up the piles of rubbish. The Erőszak party was in disarray and the relic returned to the Basilica, so a tentative calm had descended on the city. A woman sang softly as she worked, a melody that Morgan recognized as a tune her father used to hum. It was a song of hope and resurrection that Jews had sung as they recovered from disaster in their long history. There was great pride in the woman's cleaning, an attitude of prayer in her work, as if God saw her service.

Zoltan came out from the doors behind her, his body stiff and arm in a sling.

"Many Hungarian Jews have fled the country, but these people won't leave," he said. "This is their home and mine, despite its dangers. And I will stay to help them, because it's not over, Morgan. It will never be over while the mob is only one degree away from violence."

Morgan knew that his words were true, for she had seen it for herself in the eyes of the people at Memento Park as well as all over the world on her travels.

"You know where I stand, Zoltan," she said, reaching for his hand and squeezing it. "Your people are my people and that is my truth, regardless of what others might say. I wasn't born Jewish, but a part of my heart lies in Jerusalem, and now a part lies here."

Zoltan looked at her, and she saw past the scars to the man within. One day he would die in defense of justice. She knew that, and he probably did too, but his loyalty was to the downtrodden, to those who could not defend themselves. Morgan felt a spark of recognition, as she knew that there was a part of her that felt the same, but the ARKANE team was fast becoming her family, and she needed to get back to join them.

She stood up, brushing the dust from her jeans. Zoltan held out his hand to shake hers.

"You always have a place here, Morgan. And if you ever need me, I'll come."

She ignored his hand, leaning forward to kiss his scarred cheek. His fingertips briefly touched her back, and as she hugged him, she felt his stiffness relent and he embraced her in return. At last, she pulled away, smiling.

"I'll see you again, Zoltan. I'm sure of it."

Morgan walked out of the Dohany Street synagogue and into the waiting taxi, heading back to the airport and ARKANE.

***

As the car sped along, Morgan sat quietly for a moment, staring out at the same streets that she had passed so early this morning. Could it really have only been one day? It seemed that so much had happened.

She sighed, finally turning her ARKANE cellphone back on, ready to return to her real world. There were several text messages from Martin Klein, the genius head archivist. The first text contained her updated flight information, but the second made her heart race. *There's a strange package waiting for you. The writing is faded and the sender is noted as Leon Sierra.* But how could that be, she wondered. It was her father's name and he had died several years ago, blown apart by a suicide bomber in Beersheba. Morgan was suddenly keen to get back and find out what was in the impossible package.

AUTHOR'S NOTE

This novella is a work of fiction, but the inspiration for it comes from actual events and real places.

I visited Budapest in November 2012 and was deeply affected by the horrific layers of history that the city has endured. The Dohany Street Synagogue and the House of Terror were devastating, and once I saw the Holy Hand of St Istvan in the Basilica, I knew what the crux of my story would be. I wanted to give a taste of the grand city in the book but also evoke visions of a day that seemed all too possible given the political situation. Here are some of my sources if you want to investigate further.

Rise of right-wing nationalism in Hungary

We like to think that the horrors of World War II couldn't happen again, that we are too educated to succumb to ultra-nationalism or the persecution of minorities, that those things happen in other countries, to other people. But that belief is fiction.

In December 2012, Hungary's far-right Jobbik party called for lists of prominent Jews to be drawn up to "protect national security" bit.ly/14zRbCL . Anti-Semitic violence is growing in Eastern Europe reut.rs/SARA1x and in the wake of the European financial crisis and austerity measures, far right-wing parties are gaining popularity. European genocide happened as recently as the Bosnian War in the 1990s, so we can't believe that such violence remains in the past or just in 'other' areas of the world. With this novella, I wanted to highlight the disturbing political situation, as well as the dark history of Budapest, whose people who have suffered so much.

For more, see the following resources:

'My week with Hungary's Far Right' by Brian Whelan: bit.ly/12TivWS

You can watch part of the video documentary here: bit.ly/13PmB1u

Official terror for Hungary's Roma: bit.ly/AAHJLT

Jewish community in Budapest

The Gold Train and settlement are true bit.ly/177Shl8 but of course the involvement of ARKANE and the return of the painting is fictional.
    You can read more about the Dohany Street Synagogue, the mass grave and the ghetto here: www.greatsynagogue.hu
    The Shoes of the Danube memorial: bit.ly/8hTopj

Other Budapest City Landmarks

All of the landmarks described in the city of Budapest do exist, although the events described in the book are of course fiction.

You can see some of my photos and other pictures here: www.pinterest.com/jfpenn/budapest/

The House of Terror is an incredible museum now, with the cells as described and rooms full of secret police memorabilia, as well as stories of those lost. www.terrorhaza.hu

There really is a labyrinth under Castle Hill that was closed to the public in 2011 under strange circumstances. I have taken liberties with the internal geography, as I couldn't visit, but you can watch a video on their website that gives you a sense of the place: www.labirintus.com/en/1003/gallery

The Memento Park is full of large statues, a memorial to Communism www.mementopark.hu

DAY OF THE VIKINGS

A THRILLER
J.F. PENN

> "*Sól tér sortna, sígr fold í mar,*
> *hverfa af himni heiðar stjörnur.*"

> "The sun turns black, earth sinks in the sea.
> The hot stars down from heaven are whirled."
>
> *Völuspá*, Prophecy of the Seeress,
> from the Icelandic Poetic Edda

PROLOGUE

THE NIGHT SKY FLICKERED with shades of green, at first jade and then cerulean, winking through chameleon colors and morphing into pink. Spears of silver lanced from the heavens, as if stars rained down onto the earth. The aurora borealis filled the expanse of the sky with unnatural hues illuminating the faces below.

"The armor of the Valkyries blesses this sacrifice," a woman's voice called out, low and commanding. "The gods have sent the solar winds to herald our new dawn."

Shades of indigo and turquoise enlivened the Merry Dancers, as the aurora was known on the Orkney Islands in the far north of Scotland, closer to Norway than London. Here the people still lived close to the ocean and the sky, understanding the power of the wind to sweep away the past and bring renewal again.

The lights touched the face of the man bound to one of the standing stones, his eyes glazed. He smiled with rapture as he saw the spirits leap and caper in the vault of heaven.

The Ring of Brodgar, a Neolithic stone circle thousands of years old, stood at the center of a natural cauldron shaped by the surrounding hills. The prehistoric ritual complex was the focal point for the energies that lay beneath this ancient land. On this night, it bore witness to the renewal of vows not spoken for hundreds of years.

There were seven men in the ring, dressed in furs, who knelt before one woman. Her hair was long and gray with one bright blue streak, blowing in the high winds to fly up around her like a nimbus of power. She was the Crone, embodiment of wisdom, though none dare call her that to her face. Her fingers clutched a wooden staff carved with runes. She stamped it onto the earth as she approached the bound man.

"A storm is coming," she proclaimed.

"A storm is coming," the men around her echoed, falling to their knees. They began to chant, a low rumbling repetition more animal than human, a tongue not spoken for centuries in these parts, and feared when it was.

The woman pulled a knife from her leather belt as she called to the skies.

"Odin, All-Father, give me your wisdom, lend me your prophecy, that tonight we can see the path to restoration." She touched the tip of the knife to the man's chest, gentle at first, but then she pressed into his skin, drawing rune lines across his flesh as blood rose in the path of the blade. "*Fylliz fiorvi feigra manna, rýðr ragna siot rauðom dreyra.*" The man uttered a moan, flinging his head back against the stone. The woman kept the blade moving, tracing the rune lines that emerged like a dread tattoo on his skin. "It sates itself on the life-blood of fated men, paints red the powers' homes with crimson gore."

Her voice echoed with the voices of those who had worshipped under the same skies for millennia. On the last word, the woman reversed the knife so the hooked part of the blade was uppermost. With strength that seemed beyond her, she thrust the knife into the man's lower belly, wrenching it up and around. The man howled, a sound of wolves and wild things that once had stalked this land. The stink of entrails filled the air as intestines oozed out, dripping with blood, and the man's cries resounded amongst the stones.

"Accept this sacrifice, Odin, god of Death." The woman's voice was husky now, as if she spoke to a lover. "Take this life as our payment for your hidden knowledge."

She turned to one of the kneeling men and he handed her a simple iron cup. Holding the knife, the woman slashed at the throat of the victim, opening his neck and silencing his howls. Blood spurted out over her and she leaned in to receive the blessing of the giver. She held the cup to the open wound, letting blood pulse into the chalice as the life force left the man and he sagged against his bonds.

"Give us your wisdom," the woman whispered as she mixed in the juice of the deadly mushrooms from a vial. Only the right measure would bring the visions, a glimpse of the other side. Too much and they would die here in shaking fits and voided bodies. She took a long sip, blood staining her mouth, and then passed it to the first man kneeling before her.

The woman's eyes flickered as the warm blood trickled down her throat and the drug began to work in her. She looked up at the aurora above the standing stones, the glory of the heavens. Surely it was Asgard, home of the gods, revealed through the portal of the firmament above. The branches of Yggdrasil, the world tree, entwined their realms together, its leaves made from the sinews of warriors who perished with the name of Odin on their lips. Too long had she waited, her patience tested by the gods, but now it was finally time.

The cawing of ravens began as a far-off sound but then a host of them flew across the sky, highlighted by the colors of the aurora. They circled the group below, their shrieking filling the stone circle, almost blocking the eerie light. It seemed like a thousand thousand of them thronged the skies, their cries a paean to the All-Father, a blessing on their acts in His name. The men on their knees were transfixed by the whirling birds, their black feathers shining with the hues of the bright sky, at once emerald green and then slashed with bright vermilion.

"Odin the Raven God is come to us," the woman cried out, her hands raised toward the winged messengers, blood still staining her flesh. "Here are Huginn and Muninn, thought and mind, the ravens that Odin sends out to search for knowledge. Here is our sign, and now is the time. We will go south and retrieve that which will bring us power again."

CHAPTER 1

MORGAN SIERRA WALKED THROUGH the grand Neo-Classical entrance of the British Museum into the Great Court. The early morning sun filtered through the paneled glass ceiling high above, casting lined shadows onto the cool stone beneath her feet. Morgan couldn't help but smile to be here again, a place of magic for anyone as obsessed with seeking knowledge as she was. Part of her wanted to turn right toward the Enlightenment Gallery, where every object was a gateway to another rabbit hole of research. Coming here had once been for pleasure only, but now this kind of research was part of her job at the Arcane Religious Knowledge And Numinous Experience Institute, known as ARKANE – the world's most advanced and secret research center for investigating supernatural mysteries.

For a moment, a shadow crossed her face. The last time she had been here, the main exhibition had been religious relics, the blood and bone of saints, sponsored by a man she had later seen turn into a demon in the bone church of Sedlec. Morgan's hand rose to her left side, where the scar he had carved still throbbed in the cold of morning. She shook her head, casting aside the memories. Every mission with ARKANE had its own blend of violence and mystery, and Morgan had accepted both as part of her new life.

After Budapest, she had asked for some time to investigate a book that had been sent to her from Spain, the address label in her father's handwriting although he had been killed by suicide bombers years ago. The impossible package was on her mind now, but Director Marietti had deemed this more urgent, and she had been sent to investigate an artifact on loan to the museum from a private collection of Viking ritual objects. With Morgan's background in the psychology of religion, Marietti thought she would be ideally placed to assess whether ARKANE should send a replica back to the exhibition so they could study the actual artifact privately in the secret vaults below Trafalgar Square.

"Dr. Sierra?"

Morgan turned toward the voice.

"Good morning. The curator sends his apologies, but he's preparing for a big tour. I'm Blake Daniel, another researcher here. He's briefed me on your request, so I'll be taking you through to see it."

Morgan hid her surprise at his appearance with a smile of welcome. With coffee skin and piercing blue eyes, a number-one buzz cut and designer stubble, Blake looked as if he had just come from the set of a music video, not the dusty corridors of the museum. A fleeting thought crossed her mind that she wouldn't say no to a drink with him either. Blake held out a hand and Morgan noticed his gloves, a light coffee color that ensured they didn't stand out too much against his darker skin. It struck her as strange nonetheless to be wearing them indoors on a day that was already warming up. She shook his hand, wondering why he wore them.

"So, tell me about the ARKANE Institute," Blake said, as he led the way around the Great Court toward the Sainsbury Wing where the special Viking exhibition was being held. "It must have some clout considering how fast your request to see the exhibit was processed."

"The Institute is mainly a group of academics working as a collective. We publish academic articles and run seminars, primarily around religious artifacts and unusual findings."

And then there's the rest of it, Morgan thought. The secret side of ARKANE, with agents working on supernatural mysteries around the world, generally at the flash points of religion and the occult. The ARKANE that held relics and sacred objects of power in the vaults deep under Trafalgar Square. The ARKANE where agents died to keep the rest of the world safe from things that most wouldn't even believe possible. The ARKANE that had threatened her family, and still woke Morgan with nightmares of flames and blood.

Blake turned into the Egyptian hall, where they walked past the Rosetta Stone and gigantic heads of the pharaohs. Every step within the British Museum was packed with treasures that alone would be wondrous, but here were dwarfed by the sheer volume of history. It was a place to be lost in wonder for days, and Morgan was fleetingly jealous of Blake for working here.

"So, what's your particular interest in the staff of Skara Brae?" Blake asked. "It's not exactly the focal point of the exhibition. In fact, it's more of a sideshow."

Morgan smiled, for the rabbit hole of intellectual curiosity was her own addiction and anyone who worked in the museum would understand her fascinations.

"I found an obscure reference in the Icelandic *Konungsbók*," she said. "It tells of a year in which floods would rise and the aurora borealis would be seen in southern lands; when the blood of a *völva*, a shamanic seeress skilled in illusion, would awaken the demons of old and they would usher in the final winters, heralding Ragnarok."

"That's the Viking apocalypse myth, right?" Blake asked, as he led the way through the galleries. "The fabled fall of the gods, when the final battle between all races will bring the giant sea serpent from the ocean and would lead to the world being submerged in water."

Morgan nodded, pleased to find someone so well-versed in the lore. "Of course, Britain has experienced record flooding this year and the aurora was seen in the most southerly parts of the country. Very unusual. As I delved further into the prophecy, I discovered the staff of Skara Brae which has an unusual rune. I wanted to see it for myself, rather than just in photographs, and this seemed like a good chance to examine it."

Blake pulled open a double door, waving his hand to indicate she should enter first.

"This is the back door to the exhibition, as I presume you want to skip the preliminaries. The coins, gold and jewelry are nothing to what's in the main hall, and I've put the staff in a side room so we won't be disturbed when the exhibition opens up to the public." He checked his watch. "We'd better get moving actually, as the first visitors will be in soon. The Vikings seem to be quite the popular thing these days. We're sold out daily."

The main exhibition hall was huge, dominated by the remains of a Viking longship found in Roskilde, Denmark. Ancient spars formed part of the vessel, held in shape by a metal frame with open ribs to see inside. Even with its skeletal appearance, the sheer magnitude of the ship was impressive. Glass cases and information boards surrounded the central focus on all sides, but the boat was clearly the highlight of the exhibition.

"I think more people are coming to see this than your staff," Blake said. "Although we do have some rather good swords, as well." He gestured to a glass case containing longswords and metal axe heads. The clinical display didn't do much for the imagination, but Morgan knew the damage a blade could do on a human body. Her scar throbbed at the memory. "We even have a Neo-Viking group coming today," Blake continued.

"Neo-Viking?" Morgan asked, turning away from the sword case.

"Yes, apparently it's all the rage at the moment. Something to do with the popularity of *Game of Thrones* and how much it's influenced by Norse mythology. Of course, we Brits have always liked dressing up and doing pitched battles for tourists at castles." Blake grinned. "This is just another iteration on the theme. The group will be in later, so we might catch a glimpse of them. The curator is excited by their enthusiasm – there are some impressive beards, according to their website."

Blake raised an eyebrow, and Morgan couldn't help but smile at the thought of what a band of Neo-Vikings might look like. She turned to look into another display case. At sight of what it contained, the smile died on her lips. A metal conical helmet sat above a Viking jawbone, the teeth still intact in a macabre grimace. These men were not to be ridiculed.

"They filed their teeth," Blake said. "And colored the grooves between them, as well as tattooing their skin to intimidate those they set to plunder."

Morgan imagined a longboat the size of this hall filled with warriors of this ferocity, and her hands itched for a weapon. She had once vowed to leave physical violence aside, after the death of her husband Elian in a hail of bullets on the Golan Heights. She left the Israeli Defense Force for academia, but ARKANE had thrown her back into the fray. These days she understood that the adrenalin rush of the fight was just as much a part of her as her intellectual curiosity, and she was slowly beginning to accept her shadow self.

Blake pushed open a door at the back of the exhibition hall and led Morgan into a small room.

"Here it is: the staff of Skara Brae. There are two other staffs, as well, which we've left in the case out in the main exhibition hall."

The staff lay on a white table with a pair of white gloves next to it for careful handling. Not that she'd be able to do any damage to it, Morgan thought, for the staff was iron and well made. The top was thicker than the rest, designed with a woven pattern, representing the threads of fate that could be controlled through spinning or entwining, or cutting and burning.

"You can see the inscription here," Morgan said, pointing at the rune carved in the middle of the staff. It was a geometric pattern of lines and curves and cross-hatches. "It's called ægishjálmr, the helm of awe, which Vikings believed had the power to invoke illusions and fear through incantation and inscription. This staff is the only example of its kind found in the world with this rune. The *völva*, or seeress, who held this would have been considered powerful enough to span the nine worlds of the Viking Yggdrasil."

The word *völva* meant 'staff bearer,' and they practiced *seidh*, a sorcery that bound the natural world to that of the gods. These women were powerful, with the ability to read and write runes, casting their will upon the world. Morgan had discovered that most of the staffs and swords found in graves had been bent or rolled, ritually 'killed' when the owner died. It was said that this made the powers disappear, that they were lost into the earth. But this staff hadn't been bent, or rolled. It was pristine. Did that mean it could still be wielded by those who knew the rites? Once, Morgan would have laughed at the idea, but the things she had seen in the fires of Pentecost, the bone church of Sedlec and the Egyptian temple of Abu Simbel had opened her eyes. This physical world was not all there was, and only those with eyes that could see beyond knew the truth.

Morgan put on the gloves and picked up the staff, its iron weight heavy in her hands. It had the heft of a poker kept by an open fire to prod the coals, a practical object, not something ethereal like an imagined fantasy wand. In her years of practicing Krav Maga, the Israeli martial art, Morgan had used pieces of metal like this as weapons many times. Used as a club, this could surely kill, but was it more than a lump of metal? Were its properties even something that could be empirically studied in the ARKANE labs? She laid the staff down again and bent closer to examine the rune.

CHAPTER 2

Blake watched as Morgan leaned closer to the staff, brushing a long dark curl from around her face. Her eyes were cobalt blue with a slash of violet in the right eye that made Blake want to learn what else was unusual about Dr. Sierra. He had read up on the official side of ARKANE, but Morgan was not what he had expected from a purely academic research institute, and he had his suspicions about what else they might be involved in. Morgan was toned muscle under her slight curves, and she moved with the grace of someone acutely aware of her surroundings – the type of vigilance he would expect of someone in the military. There was some kind of accent in her words, a hint of Israeli perhaps, and she looked to be Mediterranean in origin. With a name like Sierra, Spain would be the obvious choice.

His own mixed heritage made the cultural guessing game a regular pastime for Blake. His blue eyes were from his Swedish father, and his darker skin tone from his Nigerian mother. He would have an Afro if he let his hair grow any longer, but he preferred the razor buzz cut. London was the perfect place to people watch and guess where they had traveled from, or perhaps where their great grandparents had originated. This was a true multicultural city, and one that embraced the stranger, since all were outsiders in some form. This was the Britain he loved and belonged to, the endless meshing of culture in the river of city life.

"Do you have any more information on the grave it came from?" Morgan asked, standing up straight. "Or if other grave objects were found with it?"

Blake shook his head. "The curator said that little is known about the staff, which is why he was happy for me to show it to you. Believe me, if he had known anymore, he would have scheduled several hours to talk to you himself."

A flicker of dangerous thought surfaced in Blake's mind as he spoke. He usually preferred to keep quiet about it, but he had an unusual gift that could perhaps help Morgan in her quest for knowledge. Some called it clairvoyance, others psychometry. In his darkest moments, Blake knew it for the curse that it was. Whatever its name, Blake could read objects through their emotional resonance. The gloves he wore protected him from accidental contact, but they also covered a patchwork of ivory scars, where his religious father had tried to beat the visions from him.

A babble of voices came from the main exhibition room, breaking their quiet study. Blake could hear the curator speaking loudly, his excitement at sharing his work causing his words to run into one another.

"The ship was built after 1025 AD and from stem to stern it's thirty-six meters, which makes it the longest Viking ship ever discovered. We have calculated that there would have been thirty-nine pairs of oars, with seventy-eight rowers to serve them."

Blake couldn't help smiling at how bored the group must be with all the facts and figures, but it wasn't often that the curator got to hold forth to so many. Most people just wanted to see the longswords, and the bones of the decapitated Vikings held in the central exhibit, clearly the result of a massacre. British pride perhaps, fighting back against the widely held belief that Vikings raped and plundered with no defiance from the local population.

Morgan was still examining the iron staff, so Blake pulled open the side door a crack, trying to catch a glimpse of the Neo-Viking group that the curator was escorting. There were several groups of other tourists in the exhibition hall, but the Neo-Vikings weren't hard to spot. There were five men wearing rough-spun tunics over long trousers, wrapped round the middle with leather belts. They had fur skins over their shoulders, real ones by the look of them. Their faces were expressionless, even as they were shown the case of the Norse helmet and jawbone. One of the men wore a close-fitting tunic that revealed muscular arms, his left bicep tattooed with a raven in flight, its feathers entwined with rune letters. The man's eyes darted around the room, taking in everyone's position. He seemed strangely dissociated with what they were supposedly here to view.

The group shifted as they moved to the next case, revealing a woman in their midst. She could have been anywhere between fifty and seventy, her features wrinkled but her skin glowing with an inner radiance. Her dark eyes were sharply focused on the curator, as if sucking his words into a bottomless pool. Her long gray hair was wound into a plait that hung down her back, with one blue streak that ran through it like the lapis lazuli jewelry held in the Egyptian rooms next door.

"The Neo-Vikings are here," Blake said, turning back to Morgan with a smile. "They look pretty convincing, actually."

She looked up at him just as an explosion shook the building and the high-pitched shriek of the emergency alarms filled the air.

CHAPTER 3

THE EXPLOSION WAS COMPLETELY unexpected in this hall of ancient knowledge, but Morgan's military training kicked in and she pulled Blake to the floor, under the protection of the broad table while the alarm shrieked around them. In these old buildings, the threat of falling plaster and stone could be worse than any initial damage. Part of her expected more explosions.

"I've got to go and help with the evacuation," Blake shouted above the wail of the alarm and the screaming voices from the exhibition hall. "We've got to get everyone out of here."

He tried to get up, but Morgan pulled him back down.

"Wait," she said. "In Israel, this kind of thing is part of our daily drill. You don't run yet, because you could be running into something worse."

Her mind flashed to her days in the IDF: the bomb attacks she had experienced, the soldiers she had treated for PTSD … her father's body blown apart by a suicide bomber, a sack of oranges spilled on the road amongst severed limbs.

There was something very wrong here. She checked her phone – no reception. Then she heard it. In between the rhythmic siren noise, it was quiet. The screams had been silenced.

"Listen," she whispered. "Next door."

Blake cocked his head sideways. "Maybe the people have been evacuated?"

"Stay there. I'm going to have a look."

Morgan scooted out from under the table and went to the door, pulling it open a tiny crack as Blake had done minutes before.

People lay on the floor, hands on their heads, while around the room, the Neo-Vikings stood with handguns drawn. The alarm suddenly stopped and the sound of smashing glass filled the room. There was a gasp from the floor.

"You can't!"

A cry of pain followed as one of the men kicked the curator into silence.

Across the room, Morgan saw an older woman reach into a glass case. She lifted out one of the iron staffs and examined the surface before flinging it to the floor. The crash brought another collective gasp from the hostages. The woman took out the second staff, examining it with jerky movements, like an addict desperate for a fix.

"Where is it?" she said, quietly at first, her voice a Scottish lilt. "Where is the real staff?"

The woman spun around and Morgan saw burning fury in her eyes, her hands clenched into claws.

"Bring the curator here."

As two of the big men dragged the curator from the floor, Morgan knew she only had seconds to make a decision. The woman wanted the staff of Skara Brae, but once she had it, what would she be able to do with it? Not so long ago, Morgan would have given up the lump of iron with no question. She would save these people from harm and the witch would leave with her staff. But Morgan's perception of the world had changed after what she had seen with ARKANE. Sometimes darker things were at stake.

The men pushed the curator to his knees before the woman.

"The staff of power isn't here," she whispered. "Where is it?"

"How dare you come in here and threaten these people!" the curator blustered, straightening his spine, words infused with the pride of the British Empire. "This is the British Museum, a place for everybody to see these wonders, not your private shopping center."

Morgan's heart thumped in her chest at his foolhardy words. Couldn't he see the intent in the old woman's eyes? Could he only see a group he had laughed at with his colleagues this morning? With her military training, Morgan could probably stop some initial harm coming to the man, but there were too many of the Neo-Vikings and no backup. She was powerless to stop whatever might happen. She felt movement behind her and breath on her neck. Blake was at her side, watching through the gap over her shoulder. Adrenalin surging and senses heightened, Morgan felt the heat of him standing close to her, and smelled a hint of clean soap on his skin.

The old woman laughed and then began to chant, her voice morphing into that of the *völva*, the shamanic priestess. Her fingers wove in the air, spinning and dancing, as she spoke words of power that had long lay dormant. The Neo-Viking men looked at the floor as if scared to watch, but the others in the room were captivated, staring at the woman. She looked mad, unhinged. Then, the rattle of bones filled the air and a gasp of horror rippled around the room.

From the pit of the slaughtered Vikings, the bones rose into the air, disjointed skeletons spinning above the hollow Viking ship, beginning to knit back together before their eyes. Morgan heard Blake's sharp intake of breath next to her ear.

"I am the Valkyrie," the woman said. "I am the Corpse Goddess who decides who lives and who dies, who comes to feast in Valhalla until Ragnarok."

Some of the skeletons were missing heads, but they began to move in the air regardless, flexing bony joints, as if just waking up. Morgan blinked and rubbed her eyes. Part of her understood that the priestesses were fabled experts of illusion, but she could smell the decay; she could see the hacked ends of the men's fingers, where they had tried to defend themselves against the slaughter so long ago.

"Your security has been overpowered," the Valkyrie said. "All visitors and employees have been evacuated except for you, and my men will be spreading out through the museum. You're all my hostages until I get that staff. Give it to me now, old man, and perhaps I won't release the *einherjar* amongst you all."

The curator's eyes widened at this, and Morgan remembered from her research that the *einherjar* were a band of warriors who had died in battle and awaited the day of Ragnarok to herald the final war cry. Were these skeletal figures truly the vanguard of the woman's ghostly army, or was it all just illusion?

Morgan pushed the door shut. There was no time to wait any longer. The curator would give them up any second.

"We have to go now," she whispered, grabbing the staff from the table. "They want this and I'm afraid if we give it to them, things will get a whole lot worse."

Blake's face was a mask of confusion and wonder. Morgan saw the flicker of indecision in his eyes before he seemed to settle on trusting her.

"The emergency exit leads out to the back of the building onto Montague Place," he said, pushing the exit door. "This way."

They walked quickly away from the room to another

door that led out to a main exit. Morgan pushed the door slightly and peeked through the gap. One of the Neo-Vikings stood guard there, one hand on the pommel of a broadsword and the other holding a gun.

Morgan pushed the door closed again. "We can't get out this way."

"Then we have to go up and over, across to the exits on the other side of the building," Blake whispered.

The crash of a slamming door echoed through the corridor, followed by a roar of disappointment.

"Find them!" The Valkyrie's words were followed by several sets of footsteps heading in their direction.

"This way," Blake said, running up a staircase on light feet. Morgan ran after him, past mosaics from Halicarnassus and Carthage, the once-bright colors now dull with age. There were spiraling vines, dolphins leaping through the waves and Roman nobles feasting, crowned with laurel wreaths. Celebrate, Morgan thought, for tomorrow we die.

At the top of the stairs they turned into the upper galleries, where Egyptian death and afterlife were displayed and explained. The dead were bound in linen and laid in wooden cases, the inner caskets painted with the gods and symbols of prosperity in the everlasting. Their skin was burnished leather, features shrunken but still visible, even down to perfectly preserved eyelashes. Morgan shuddered. Skeletons were one thing, but she didn't want these bodies coming to a semblance of life again.

The heavy footsteps were almost behind them now. There was no way they would get out without being caught.

"Down," Morgan said, pushing Blake behind one of the display cases so he wouldn't be seen. She spun around to stand just inside the door to the next room, next to an exhibit of *shabti* figures – servants for the afterlife in blue-glazed faience and serpentine. She held the iron staff high like a baseball bat ready to strike. If the old witch wanted it for death, maybe they should start with some of her own men.

The adrenalin pumped now and Morgan's heart pounded. Once upon a time she had called it fear, but her years in the IDF had trained that out of her. Now, she called it anticipation. She itched to hit something, craving the rush that only violence could soothe. Life was simple when it came down to survival; movement into battle felt like a meditation. In a flash, she understood why the Vikings had roamed the world, raiding and exploring new places, and why perhaps these men craved the same existence.

A footstep came from just outside the doorway. As the first man walked through, Morgan swung the iron staff at his face, aiming behind his head. He leaned back in reaction, but the metal bar slammed into his nose anyway, the crunch of bone resounding in the empty hall. The man reeled, clutching his face, blood streaming through his fingers as he fell to his knees groaning.

A second Neo-Viking stood behind him, over six foot, a meaty man with piggy eyes who squinted at the staff as if he could barely see it.

"You defile the sacred," he rasped. "Give it to me, bitch, and I may let you live."

Morgan stood to face him, slamming the iron staff into her opposite palm. She smiled, her eyes cold.

"Come and get it."

CHAPTER 4

As the man lunged for her, Morgan stepped back and used the staff to smash the exhibition case next to her, sending shards of glass flying. Momentarily blinded, he raised his hands to his face. Morgan used the rounded end of the staff to thrust at his throat with a lightning-fast movement. She forced herself to hold back at the last moment, with the realization that she didn't want to kill the man, only leave him incapacitated.

The man's face was a mix of surprise and terror, his eyes wide. He gasped for breath, one hand clutching at the broken edges of the display case, blood staining the ancient artifacts. His throat was already visibly swelling and bruising. Morgan waited with the staff raised, ready to knock him down, but he slumped to the floor, chest heaving as he tried to draw breath. The other man still clutched his broken nose, moaning against the wall in the other room. The edges of her rage bubbled, the righteous anger that emerged when she or those she loved were threatened. But she was learning to hold it back, and these men weren't the true enemy.

Blake stepped out warily from behind the display case.

"You're no academic, Dr. Sierra." His voice had an edge of respect and a whole lot of curiosity in it.

"And these are no Viking warriors," Morgan said, considering the men on the ground. "This should have been harder. But we should move, in case they send backup. These guys will be up and about, wanting some retribution soon enough."

"This way." Blake hurried off down the gallery, turning several times, past bearded warriors in sculptures from Mesopotamia and artifacts from the walls of Babylon. Morgan couldn't help but look into the cases as they passed, glimpses of cuneiform engraved on tablets documenting the lives of those thousands of years ago. The academic in her wanted to look closer, but she would have to linger another time. Blake pulled out a bunch of keys as they approached a gallery that was closed for maintenance.

"We can go through here, and I'll lock it behind us. Might hold them off for a while when the next lot come looking. There's an archive storeroom that we can at least stop to think in."

On the other side of the door, Morgan followed Blake through another gallery and up a little staircase to a door with multiple locks. She raised an eyebrow at the additional security while Blake fiddled with his keys, looking for the right ones.

"I got the keys a few months ago from one of the curators. It's a great place to come and think when I need some space."

***

Blake pushed open the door to the musty room, an archive of some of the less popular exhibits. Or those that they don't want people to know about, Blake thought. He came here for silence and solitude, but also to read in private. Not books, but the objects themselves, losing himself in a world of past lives as a way to bring his own research alive. There were some who commented that his research papers were too fanciful, too full of character and possible scenarios for the objects he studied, but the grant money kept coming, so no one questioned his methods. So far, he had managed to keep his gift almost secret.

"They'll struggle to find us here," Blake said. "This room isn't even on the plans."

"It will be good to stop for a minute." Morgan looked down at her phone, frowning in frustration. "Damn. There's still no reception. They must have a signal jammer for the whole building."

"The evacuation and alarms would have tipped off the police, so I'm sure there's a host of emergency services and reporters outside." He paused. "But you want ARKANE, right? Can they do something more than the police?"

Morgan sighed. "There's more to ARKANE than just academics and conferences."

"I got that from your ability to wield a metal club back there," Blake grinned. "Most impressive. And to be honest, I'm far more interested in what ARKANE does now. Can you tell me anything about it?"

Morgan went silent for a moment, her eyes focusing on a faraway point. She shook her head.

"Not much, sorry. Only that we investigate supernatural mysteries, many of them around religious or cult objects like this one." She held up the staff. "Most of what I'm involved in, you would struggle to believe."

"Is it harder to believe that a Neo-Viking priestess caused long-dead bones to spin in the air, calling warriors from their Valhalla feast?"

Morgan smiled. "Fair point. When I identified this staff as something to be looked into further, I had no idea that others would be seeking it, too. It seems this Valkyrie priestess could possibly wield its power, whereas I can only use it as a blunt club. We need to know more about it."

Blake's heart thumped as he summoned the strength to speak of that which he kept secret. He rubbed his gloved hands together, the bumps of the scars familiar lines through the fabric. Part of him wanted to wait and see what Morgan would come up with, as he was sure she would get them out of here. But another part wanted to read the staff, a curiosity that made his hands tingle in anticipation.

He pulled the gloves off, revealing his scarred hands, the cinnamon skin marred with criss-crossed ropes of ivory.

"Oh Blake, I'm so sorry," Morgan said, her eyes widening as she took in his extensive injuries.

"My father tried to beat the gift out of me," he said. "He tried to bleed it from my skin, but it always came back."

"What gift?" The violet slash in Morgan's right eye seemed to darken to indigo as she focused on his words. Blake could see no judgment there, only sincere interest.

"I can read objects," he said, although it was hard to put into words the maelstrom of vision that consumed him when he read. "Some call it psychometry, or a form of clairvoyance. Whatever you want to call it, when I touch an object, I can enter into its emotional history. I can see the people and places it touched and feel the emotions that surrounded it. Sometimes it's hazy, but the strongest emotions also bring the most powerful visions."

"So you see violence and murder more often than happiness?"

Blake nodded. "Exactly." That was the curse, along with the flashbacks he experienced of what he witnessed. He drowned his nightmares in tequila most nights, but Morgan didn't need to know about his nocturnal vice. "I've helped the police on a couple of cases, not that they would admit that to anyone, but that has helped me reframe the gift as useful at least." Blake thought of Detective Jamie Brooke and what he had seen of the murder at the Hunterian – the grotesque specimens in jars that revealed the heart of the crime. "Perhaps if I read the staff, we might find out something more about why the Neo-Vikings want it?"

Morgan hesitated. Blake saw uncertainty in her eyes, but only for a second. She held out the staff.

"What can I do to help?"

"Can you just put it down here on the floor?" Blake sat down cross-legged. Morgan put the staff in front of him, sitting down opposite him. Her proximity made him uneasy, aware that she would be watching him, assessing what he was doing. But apparently she had seen stranger things, and to be honest, he was interested to see what was so special about this staff.

"So, how does this work?" Morgan asked. "Do you go into some kind of trance state?"

"I guess you could say that, but if you remove my hands from the staff, I'll come out of it. Sometimes I go pretty deep, and can have physical reactions to what I'm experiencing. If you're worried, just pull the staff away."

Blake laid his hands on the iron rod and closed his eyes, sensing the waves of past experience waiting to wash over him. He dreaded this moment, but also craved it. For as much as he drank to oblivion to forget some of the things he had seen, he also experienced moments of beauty that stood out like diamond stars in the night sky, a precious glimpse into the lives of those long dead.

The veil of consciousness shifted, and Blake reached back with his mind. There was a long period of dark, dormant power that throbbed and hummed, perhaps the time in the grave where the staff had been found. He heard his own pulse before it morphed into the beating of drums and his vision began to clear.

***

They came from the sea in longboats filled with men in heat for battle, the staff of Skara Brae at their head, clutched in the hands of the only woman with them, the *völva* seeress. She wasn't like the women they had left behind, those who served and bore children, subject to their menfolk. There was power in this one – a sense that she was at one with the ferocity of nature, and her will drove the men who followed her, even into death. The drums beat faster as the boats landed on the shore of an island. A priory loomed above them, carved into the rocks, its arches built to the glory of the God these monks served. The green hill slopes wound up to the priory, and the figures of people running could be seen, trying to escape the oncoming raiders.

Blake sensed the excitement of the Viking horde, their blood calling for plunder and slaughter, but under it all a resonance of pure joy. It was the first time he had truly felt it when reading. These men knew happiness in these moments. Perhaps this is what men are truly made for, Blake thought, as the rumble of the drums filled him.

"*Fyllisk fjörvi feigra manna, rýðr ragna sjöt rauðum dreyra.*"

The men shouted Norse words as they spilled out of the boats, their voices a rough chant, evoking the frenzy and hunger of the god Odin as they charged. They called for the gods to feed on the flesh of the dead, and redden this land with gore.

"*Skeggjöld, skálmöld, vindöld, vargöld,*" they chanted as they ran. "Axe-time, sword-time, wind-time, wolf-time."

Many were tattooed with the beasts that would stand with them in spirit during battle, and some wore wolf-skin pelts, the heads with teeth bared, adding to the ferocity of their appearance. With longswords and great axes held high, they ran in packs for the villages at the base of the priory, but Blake lost sight of them as he could only remain with the staff. He could hear the screams though, the wailing that soon filled the air, of women raped and men murdered, the village plundered as they died.

The seeress made for the inner rooms of the priory, and her focus thrummed through Blake's core. She wanted something from here, something very specific. He could sense her seeking it out. Two huge men flanked her, swords drawn. They pushed through the heavy wooden double doors into the sanctuary of the priory chapel, where a group of monks huddled near the altar, protecting the relics of the saint. One of them broke away carrying a heavy book, with two others flanking him. The Vikings ignored the group, for there was so much gold here, in the chalices and reliquaries, the wealth of a church that had not yet gone through the pains of the Reformation. The Viking guards stepped forward to begin piling it up for plunder.

One reached for a candlestick topped with an ornate carved eagle as a monk rushed toward them, hands raised in supplication.

"Stop," he cried. "This is the Lord's house."

The Viking backhanded him casually, swatting the man to the floor.

"The punishment of God has come upon us," the monk cried, rising to his knees, hands raised in worship. "Forgive …"

His words were silenced by the thrust of a longsword, the tip of the blade emerging through his back, dripping with blood. The monk's eyes reflected surprise as they glazed over, his mouth open in his last prayer. The Viking withdrew the sword and wiped it on the monk's habit before sheathing it again, turning his attention back to the gold.

"I want the bones of the saint and one of you for my sacrifice to Odin," the seeress said, in the local tongue. "If you give me that now, along with gold for my men, the rest of you will live to rebuild your community. Otherwise, you all die."

CHAPTER 5

Blake watched as the monks stood in mute silence for a moment, and then one whispered. The others turned. There was a flurry of gesticulation and heated argument. The eldest monk finally stepped forward, his steps faltering, his blue eyes misty with age or the fear of what was to come.

"Take me, but let my brothers leave. I will go soon to meet the Lord anyway."

The seeress nodded, and the other monks hurried away, only one looking back at the brother they had left behind, regret and shame on his face.

"Make it quick, I beg of you," the old monk said, using one of the altar rails to lower himself down, beginning to pray.

"I can't give you that, old man, but perhaps your own god will hear your screams and your place in paradise will be assured." She gestured to the two Viking guards. "Hold him."

The monk struggled as they forced him to bend forward, his back to the *völva,* his prayers spoken in halting Latin, interspersed with panicked breath.

"Sed et si ambulavero in valle mortis non timebo …"

One of the Vikings ripped the monk's habit, pulling it down to reveal thin, sagging skin on old bones. Tucking the staff into her belt, the seeress withdrew a long knife, its blade wickedly sharp with serrated edges.

"... malum quoniam tu mecum es virga tua ... et baculus tuus ipsa consolabuntur me."

With surprising strength, she thrust the knife into the monk's back and began to wrench it up and down. The man screamed and writhed, but the Vikings held him as the seeress continued cutting, sawing his ribs away from his spine. Blake felt the pulse of the monk's blood, his agony like a wave. He recoiled from the scene, sinking toward darkness into the tunnel that led back to the present day. The vision of the monk faded and his screams became little more than a whisper. But Blake knew he needed to know more, he had to see what came next in order to understand why the staff was so important. He pushed back along the tug of the staff, and emerged again into the chapel.

The stink of blood and feces filled the air, sweat and fear overlaying them. The monk's body was laid on the floor by the altar now, his ribs splayed out from his spine revealing a bloody cavity where the seeress pulled his viscera out. Blood covered her hands, her fingers curled into talons with fingernails stained crimson.

"Get me a bone from the relic of their saint," she rasped, her voice almost bestial. One of the Vikings went to the altar and opened the reliquary of St Cuthbert, taking the small finger bones out.

The seeress laid the bones on the floor, squatting next to them and crushing them with the blunt end of the staff. She scattered the powder and slivers of bone over the bloody corpse of the monk, muttering words as she waved the iron staff over it. On the final word, she thrust the staff into the raw cavity of the still-steaming body, coating the iron with gore and clots of blood. She stood again and lifted the dripping staff toward the heavens, calling in a language that resonated with power.

"Great Odin, All-Father, give me your vision."

Her eyes rolled back in her head, showing the whites, and she began to convulse. The whole chapel began to shake. The Viking men held onto the walls as the vibrations grew stronger. A great crack filled the air and the flagstones ruptured beneath their feet, steam pouring out and engulfing the seeress in its hot breath. Blake felt the heat in her transmuted through the staff, but she screamed in ecstasy, not pain, as the visions filled her.

"*Alt veit ek, Óðinn! hvar þú auga falt: í inum mæra Mímis brunni,*" she chanted, her eyes opening wider as she spoke, as if surprised by the words that came out of her mouth.

Blake felt her exhilaration as her mind filled with the knowledge of the gods, but only a fraction of what was possible.

"I know where Odin's eye is hidden," she called, "deep in the wide-famed well of Mimir."

Blake saw that the Eye of Odin would bring what she truly sought, knowledge and power that few could stand against. The monk's broken body fell through the gap in the earth as the seeress stood astride it, head thrown back, shaking as she received the gift of prophecy from the other side of the veil.

***

Blake's visions tunneled and he gasped, his eyes flickering open to find Morgan shaking him.

"Blake, are you OK?" she asked, her eyes concerned and questioning.

"Yes," he whispered. "Just give me a minute."

It took a moment to reorientate himself after reading, like putting on a pair of glasses for the first time and finding the world sharpen in focus to detail never seen before. Every time he read, Blake wondered if this time he would find himself lost somewhere, his mind trapped in another realm, another time, even though his body remained in the modern world. He always set an alarm when he was on his own.

His pulse calmed as he breathed in and out, consciously feeling his physical body on the floor of this room, where he had read so many times.

"There was a Viking raid on a monastery, on an island, a long time ago." He told Morgan of what he had seen, describing the ritual murder of the monk and the words of the seeress in her trance.

"The Eye of Odin," Morgan said, shaking her head. "I've read of this and the story gets stranger indeed. Odin always sought more knowledge, and the legend goes that he visited the Well of Mimir, the Rememberer, in the roots of the world tree, Yggdrasil. The waters revealed the wisdom of the cosmos, and when Odin asked for a drink, Mimir asked for his eye in return. Odin plucked one eye out – which one is unclear – and cast it into the well. In return, Odin drank from the waters. His eye still lies there."

Blake rubbed his temples, the pressure easing him back into his physicality.

"The feeling I got from the seeress was that this Eye is an actual object that can channel prophetic visions from the gods."

Morgan nodded. "The words she spoke have been passed down in the Poetic Edda *Völuspá,* known as the Prophecy of the Seeress. If this Valkyrie wants the Eye too, then the staff can perhaps give her the same visions as the woman you saw."

Blake grimaced. "It seems a sacrifice is needed to activate the staff somehow before the visions come." He described the injuries to the dead monk's body.

"It sounds like the Blood Eagle," Morgan said. "A horrific method of torture and execution where the victim eventually died of blood loss and shock, or through suffocation when the lungs were pulled out through the back. The wings of the splayed ribs represent the eagle, the corpse-gulper, the war-bringer and the bird of Odin."

Blake paled again, knowing that the images would emerge in his nightmares. More bloody bodies to haunt his nights.

"Could you tell where they were?" Morgan asked.

Blake shook his head. "I looked east to the sea as the Vikings ran into the priory. It was certainly an island near the coast, because I could see the land."

"It sounds like Lindisfarne," Morgan said, eyes narrowing as she tried to recall the details. "There were other monastery attacks, but the geographic features sound like the Holy Island. In 793 AD it was the site of the first Viking raid in Britain, a ferocious, surprise attack that left monks dead and much of the treasure from the monastery stolen. They repeated these raids at monasteries on other islands along the Scottish coast, because the sites were so rich."

"There was something else," Blake said, frowning at the memory. "One monk scurried away carrying a heavy book, flanked by several of the others, so it must have been important. Maybe they wrote about the raid in that?"

"The Lindisfarne Gospels are in the British Library," Morgan said. "It's an illuminated manuscript written in the century prior to the invasion. But I seem to remember that there's a page of notes added at the end. It's worth checking out when we get out of here."

An alarm bell rang out suddenly, and both covered their ears to shield them from the high-pitched shriek. When it stopped, an announcement came over the loudspeaker system in the voice of the Valkyrie.

"Bring the staff to the Great Court in the next ten minutes, or I'll start killing hostages."

CHAPTER 6

THERE WAS NO HESITATION in the woman's voice, no room for negotiation, and Morgan knew that their only choice was to go down to the Great Court. She couldn't contact ARKANE – even if she did, a team of agents wouldn't make it here in time to save anyone. She couldn't be sure that the iron staff would even do anything, and besides, once the Valkyrie had it, there was no way for the Neo-Vikings to get out of the museum.

Morgan wished she could go back to this morning, when she had left the ARKANE base under Trafalgar Square ready for a purely civilian research trip. She would have put better procedures in place, brought some kind of weapon with her, and she definitely would have brought backup. Her partner Jake was out on the firing range in the woods of Kent, finally recovered from his injuries, but she should have brought someone else. There was no point in regrets now, though. She could only go forward and take action. Morgan stood.

"We need to go," she said. "I'm not risking lives, and these Neo-Vikings are deadly serious."

Blake stood up, a little unsteady on his feet after the visions. His chiseled features looked pained and his caramel skin was still a shade lighter. Morgan wondered how he coped with the things he saw, how he reconciled it with the physical world of the here and now. She thought back to the demon creature in the bone crypt of Sedlec, how her own worlds had collided then, how her beliefs in what was truly real had been warped and twisted. They had something in common, for sure.

Blake put his gloves back on, covering the ugly scars on his hands. Part of Morgan wanted to touch them, to stroke the lines of years of pain. But if she touched him, could he read her past? Could he see part of her shot to pieces with her husband Elian on the Golan Heights, or blown apart on the streets of Beersheba with her father? She wasn't ready to let anyone come that close.

"We can go through the Mesopotamian Gallery and out by the restaurant," he said, brushing the dust from his jeans. "The stairs lead directly down into the Great Court, but we'll be easily spotted soon enough."

Morgan nodded. "Good, I want them to see us coming. We can't let them harm hostages. Are you OK now?"

Blake rubbed his eyes, blinking. "Yes, sorry. It's a bit of an adjustment coming back." His eyes fell to the staff she held. "Are you sure we should give it to them?"

The staff was cold iron in Morgan's hand, chill metal that only spoke of the dead.

"From what you've said, the real prize is the Eye of Odin, and this staff needs some kind of activation to work its particular magic. Plus, I don't think we have a choice at this stage."

They walked together back through the hall of galleries, emerging through the columns of the classical temple facade that flanked the upper entrance to the Mesopotamian and Egyptian displays. The museum restaurant was empty, nestled in the shadow of the huge round exhibition hall that dominated the central space of the Great Court. White marble steps led down to the ground level entrance.

At the top stood one of the Neo-Vikings, his hand on a modern Glock 26 pistol that looked out of place with his authentic clothing. The man gestured with his gun for them to walk down ahead of him.

Morgan had only been here when the Great Court was packed with tourists, their chatter a hubbub of life in the wide marble space. Now, it was silent except for the sobbing of those below. Their footsteps were loud as they descended the steps, rounding the corner to look down on the forecourt.

"Raise your arms," Morgan whispered as she lifted her own, indicating their surrender, holding the staff high so it could be seen. Blake held his gloved hands up too, his eyes darting to the armed Neo-Vikings that looked up at them.

The hostages were bunched together in a group near the tourist information stand, only a few meters from the front entrance of the museum. Above them, the paneled glass ceiling of the Great Court arched across the space, sun dappling the marble floor with light. Morgan counted five men below with the Valkyrie, and one behind them on the stairs. They were all armed and also held shields now, great metal roundels that made Morgan wonder what they were needed for. She wouldn't expect the British police or military to be storming in here any time soon, not without some negotiation, and even if they did, these shields wouldn't be much use in the face of modern weaponry. But whatever this group had planned, they were surely near the end of it now.

Amongst the faces of the hostages that stared up at them, a few children huddled against their parents. Morgan could see a touch of Gemma in one little girl, and she was thankful that her niece was safe in Oxfordshire. After the sacrifices of Pentecost, she had sworn to make sure her family was never involved in her missions again.

When they reached the bottom of the staircase, two

of the Neo-Vikings flanked them as the Valkyrie stepped forward. Morgan held out the staff and the woman took it, her hands mottled with age but her grip as strong as the iron staff itself.

"Why did you take it?" the Valkyrie asked, her eyes piercing.

Morgan stood with shoulders slumped, her head dropped as if she struggled to meet the woman's eyes. "We were scared," she said, her voice humble. "Please ... I'm just an academic and I'm doing a paper on the staff. We didn't know you wanted it. We just happened to be there. Truly."

A moment's silence, then the Valkyrie whipped the staff up, smashing it against Blake's cheek. He didn't have time to react, his head snapping sideways. He stumbled and dropped to his knees, clutching his face. A collective gasp came from the hostages.

"No," Morgan cried. Her military instincts kicked in as she moved to take the Valkyrie down, but the big man behind grabbed her, forcing her arm up behind her back in a grip that told Morgan he knew what he was doing. He would not be as easy to defeat as the men upstairs.

"Stay still, or I'll break your arm, bitch," the man whispered.

"It's OK, Morgan. I'm OK. Do what they want, please." Blake was standing again. A cut had opened up high on his cheekbone, and blood began to soak through his gloves as he held his face. Rage bubbled inside Morgan. She longed for a weapon so she could deal with these people, but it wasn't just her life that was at stake here.

"You're clearly not just an academic," the Valkyrie spat. "You sent two of my men back bruised and bloody. They will beat your friend here until you tell the truth, then I'll move on to the children if you continue to lie."

The Neo-Viking pushed Morgan's arm higher, to the edge of breaking it.

"Alright," she said. "I'm Dr. Morgan Sierra, from the Arcane Religious Knowledge And Numinous Experience Institute. I am a researcher, but I'm also ex-Israeli Defense Force. When the aurora borealis was seen across England and the prophecies about the date of Ragnarok came up in my research, I found a link to this staff. I came to see it for myself."

The Valkyrie nodded. "Then you have seen the days ahead. A storm is coming and you will be a witness for the truth of it, Morgan Sierra. I know of ARKANE. They will be the ones to validate the power of what is to come. And for your truth, I will spare your friend." She turned to her men. "Secure them."

The Neo-Vikings put plastic cuffs on Morgan and Blake, tugging their wrists behind their backs.

"Be a good girl now," the one behind Morgan whispered as he ratcheted the cuffs tight. He licked her ear, his tongue wet and probing. "Or I'll come back and teach you a lesson."

Morgan exhaled deeply, forcing down her natural reaction to turn and teach him a bloody lesson. He would be screaming soon enough, but Blake and the other hostages would pay a price for her anger. She calmed herself.

The men pushed the pair to the floor and put plastic cuffs around their ankles, too. The hostages around them cast surreptitious glances, not wanting to draw attention to themselves. Morgan had seen this reaction before: the urge to keep quiet and avoid the captor's wrath. But she had also seen it in photos, on the faces of those on the train cars, the Jews who had never come home again.

Blake's cheek was swelling, and bruising had already appeared around the cut.

"Are you OK?" Morgan whispered, shuffling closer to him.

He nodded, but she could see he was still reeling from

the blow and shocked by the sudden pain. "I'm doing better than him."

Morgan turned to see two of the Neo-Vikings drag the curator out to the front of the hostage group, and push him to kneel in front of the Valkyrie. He stumbled. Morgan could see he was bleeding too, clearly having taken a beating for his insolence in the exhibition hall.

The Valkyrie raised her arms, holding the staff in a tight grip, pointing it to the sky above. It seemed like an extension of her arm and the way she held the heavy metal made it appear lighter … As if it belonged there. In the moment of silence, Morgan heard the faint thrum of a helicopter in the skies above.

"You're witnesses to the beginning of a new age," the Valkyrie said, her voice echoing in the marble hall. "Those of you who are left will report to your media and they will know that Ragnarok is upon us, that I will usher in the final battle by calling up the souls of the dead to vanquish this land like our ancestors did. Too long have we been pathetic in the eyes of the world. Too long have we concerned ourselves with unimportant things. But when the moment of death comes, that is when we realize the triviality of our existence. You will know this soon enough, for a storm is coming."

The helicopter was louder now. Morgan thought perhaps it was the military finally come to free them, or a press helicopter capturing what must be a crazy scene outside.

The Valkyrie began to chant, using the iron staff to spin her words into the air around them. The wind began to blow, lightly at first, as if the doors had been opened to the world outside. It whirled about her as she chanted, the men joining for parts of the incantation, a response to her lead.

"*Nú er blóðugr örn breiðum hjörvi,*" she called, her eyes

filled with a dread darkness. "Now comes the Blood Eagle with the broadsword."

The curator's head came up, his eyes wild as he clearly understood what she said. He struggled against those who held him.

"No," he screamed. "Not that, please."

He was dragged by two of the men in front of the Valkyrie. They forced him to his knees and held his mouth open while the seeress poured a dark liquid into his mouth, chanting ancient words of sacrifice. The man slumped into silence within a minute, his eyes glazed over, mouth drooling. The men turned him so his back was to the Valkyrie and ripped his clothes away to reveal his naked torso. The Valkyrie pulled an obsidian knife from her belt, tucking the staff in its place. The light reflected off the surface of the knife. In the glitter, Morgan saw the man's death.

"Great Odin, accept this sacrifice as a herald of the New Age. The Blood Eagle will honor you," the Valkyrie said, her words in English so all could hear. "Hold him tight now."

Two of the men held the curator down as the Valkyrie plunged the knife into his back next to his spine. He screamed despite the sedation and his voice echoed through the Great Court, an animal cry of agony. The Valkyrie began to saw through his ribs and Morgan struggled in her bonds, desperate to stop the atrocity. One of the Viking men backhanded her, making her head ring. She lay stunned on the floor as the Valkyrie carved the curator's body in the ancient way. The hostages around her wept, some frozen with terror, hiding behind each other, desperate not to be next for the slaughter.

As the Valkyrie finished separating a rib she pulled it out and away from the man's body, her hands and arms coated with blood, the men on either side spattered with gore. The curator fell silent and slumped forward, shock shutting down his body, or perhaps dead already from the wounds. But the woman didn't stop. She kept carving and pulling until the ribs formed hideous wings on either side of the man's torso – the wings of the Blood Eagle. Finally, she reached in and pulled the man's lungs from his chest, cutting them from him and offering the chunk of meat to the heavens.

"See this, Odin, and bless our final steps toward glory. Give me your vision now."

The Valkyrie pulled a vial from a pouch at her belt, and sprinkled powder onto the bloody mess of the curator's back. From Blake's description of the Lindisfarne ritual, Morgan thought it must be some kind of powdered relic. The Valkyrie thrust the staff into the wound, coating the iron with fresh blood and powdered bone until it ran red, soaking the sleeves of her tunic.

She held the staff aloft again, spinning around and around, her robes flying out from her. She called out in Norse, a frenzy of blood and power upon her. Her eyes rolled back in her head and she spoke strings of words that Morgan couldn't understand. The Valkyrie was in a shamanic ecstasy, seeing into realms beyond the physical. Could she see where the Eye of Odin lay?

"It is beginning," the Valkyrie called. A vortex of winds seemed to be drawn in, spinning with her, sweeping the dust of the ancient place into the air until it spiraled upwards toward the glass roof. The hostages huddled together, shielding their eyes from the dust that whirled about them, but Morgan needed to see. The Neo-Vikings lifted their shields up over their heads, looking towards the roof as they did so. In that moment, Morgan knew what was going to happen.

CHAPTER 7

THE VALKYRIE THRUST HER staff upward with a shout of triumph. The spiral of wind hit the glass roof with incredible force, smashing the panels, sending a rain of glass down on those below. With a last reserve of energy, Morgan flipped her body and with both feet, sprang for cover as the first shards of glass fell. Blake had the sense to follow her, using his bound feet to push himself along the floor. They made it under the shelter of the tourist information booth before the glass exploded on the marble floor.

Several of the hostages crammed themselves under the overhang along with them, and Morgan pulled one of the children tightly toward her, shielding the little girl's head. Huge shards of glass fractured on the flagstones and the wind whipped the pieces like razors through the crowd as screams echoed through the Great Court. The Valkyrie stood unharmed in the eye of the storm as shards spun around her, while her men were shielded from the large pieces by their shields but were cut by the exploded fragments.

Morgan couldn't take her eyes off the Valkyrie, as she thrust the staff upward again and again. The screams of the captives were peppered with groans as people were cut down while running for cover. It was chaos in the Great Court, but the Neo-Vikings were no longer concerned with the captives.

The vortex smashed against the roof until the metal struts between the glass panes began to warp and bend. A part of Morgan screamed that this must be an illusion – how could the staff hold the power to do this? But the evidence was before her eyes. She could only imagine what it must look like from outside. The sound of smashing glass and howling wind must be heard by the press and police, who were surely now escalating their plans to storm the museum.

When the hole in the roof had stretched across half of the widest part of the Great Court, the Valkyrie stopped her spinning. The wind died down. The sound of a helicopter grew louder, and then it appeared, a shadow against the blue sky above. It was a Black Hawk, the open door revealing two men inside as well as the pilot. Hovering directly above, they lowered a winch basket that descended to the floor of the museum. The Valkyrie didn't even look back at the hostages. She entered the basket and two of the Neo-Vikings entered with her, all three holding tight to the mesh sides.

They can't possibly get away, Morgan thought. A helicopter this low over London would have the military out after them. They weren't so far from Parliament and Buckingham Palace, after all. Concern flashed through her mind, for this group was clearly well funded. This was not the work of a two-bit cult in furs. Everything in Morgan wished for a weapon to stop them, to punish them for what they had done. Instead, she lay with Blake under the overhang, unable to do anything to stop the escape.

"Your sacrifice has earned you a place in Valhalla," the Valkyrie said to the men who would be left behind. Two nodded, watching as the basket was winched up to the helicopter above the museum.

"No, take me too," one of the men shouted, his eyes wide with fear of what would befall him if left behind. He ran wildly for the cage, which was now just six feet from the ground. The man jumped and caught hold of the bottom, his fingers protruding into the cage. The winch shuddered and inched up more slowly.

"Let go," the men in the basket shouted, stamping at his fingers. "It's too heavy."

The cage inched higher and the man still held on.

"Please," he screamed. "Don't leave me."

As the cage reached the upper third of the open space, the Valkyrie bent and slashed at the man's fingers with her knife. When he still didn't let go, she began to saw at them.

"No," he screamed as blood ran down his arm. Finally, he couldn't hold on anymore. He let go, his scream silenced as he smashed into the flagstones, his blood running into the words of Tennyson carved in the marble floor of the Great Court.

The cage was winched up the final meters and the Valkyrie and her men pulled into the helicopter as it banked away out of sight, the noise of the blades fading as it flew off. Morgan's resolve was steel, refined by the heat of her rage at the murder of the curator, the injuries to the hostages and the despoiling of this great museum. She would hunt down this Valkyrie and get the staff back, and she would find the Eye of Odin.

The Neo-Vikings left behind threw their shields down. Without looking at the hostages, they ran toward the back of the museum. The hostages, many cut and bleeding, sat in stunned silence for a moment. Then one man stood up and walked toward the entrance, his steps halting as if he couldn't believe he was free to go.

There was a crash from the museum's front entrance and a team of armed police and medics swarmed in, one wrapping the man in a blanket as they passed to triage those huddled on the marble floor. A policeman called for body bags and soon the hall was alive with activity, processing the crime scene and helping those with injuries to waiting ambulances. Several of the armed police headed toward the back of the building, but Morgan considered that this was so well planned, the Neo-Vikings may well have got away unseen.

In the group of medics that entered, Morgan saw Peter Lovell, one of the ARKANE London support team. With fifteen years as a military doctor, Peter's buzz cut, upright posture and confident bearing made him stand out, and he was definitely overqualified for this type of first aid care. He came straight to her, ignoring all the others, leaving them to the official emergency services.

"Morgan, are you OK?" Peter asked. "Where are you hurt?"

"Just get these cuffs off," she said, holding her wrists out as he reached into his bag for a scalpel. "This is Blake." Morgan nodded to the side, where Blake sat staring up at the hole in the magnificent glass roof. "He has a head wound that needs to be dealt with before you look at me properly."

"Director Marietti wants you back at base ASAP, if you're OK," Peter said. "I'll take you back now and leave this lot to the crime scene techs. ARKANE will help the police coordinate the search with expert help on where the Neo-Vikings might have gone."

"Let me guess," Morgan's mouth twisted in a wry smile as he finished cutting her cuffs. "I'm the expert help."

Once Morgan's wrists were free, Peter cut away the restraints on her feet and then did the same for Blake.

"I'm going to find them," Morgan said, her hand resting on Blake's upper arm, feeling the tension under his skin. "I'll get the staff back and they'll pay for what they did to the curator."

Blake looked over to where the body of the mutilated man was being lifted onto a stretcher.

"He was a cantankerous old bastard sometimes, but he was a respected colleague and pretty fun at Christmas parties."

He smiled painfully at the memory and turned to Morgan, his blue eyes meeting hers, and she saw that his resolve matched hers.

"I want to help. You know what I can do, and if we want to find them quickly, I think we need to check out The Lindisfarne Gospels. They might have a clue as to what happened to the original Valkyrie." He turned his head so Peter could clean his wound, wincing with the sting of the antiseptic on his bruised skin and open cut.

Morgan knew that Director Marietti wouldn't like involving a civilian, but the London ARKANE office didn't have anyone with psychometric ability – not that she knew of, anyway.

Her only hesitation was that she had a bad habit of involving other people who ended up getting hurt. Morgan thought of Dr. Khal el-Souid, badly beaten in the caves of Mount Nebo as they searched for the Ark of the Covenant. He'd been lucky to escape with only minor concussion. She blushed a little as she remembered the night that followed. Khal's dark eyes meeting hers in the light of the early morning as the muezzin called the dawn prayers … How his arms had felt around her. She and Khal had shared something in the desert, but Morgan knew a relationship was never going to work, so she had left him behind and they hadn't spoken since. Blake reminded her a little of Khal, a smart man with gorgeous skin, his blue eyes the ocean to Khal's deep brown. She pushed aside her concerns. Blake was involved now, whether she liked it or not, and she needed his help for just a little longer.

"I'm sorry, Peter. I'll call Marietti en route, but we need to go to the British Library before I head back."

CHAPTER 8

MORGAN AND BLAKE JUMPED in a black cab and headed for the British Library, only a few blocks northeast toward St Pancras station. Morgan finally had reception to make a call and dialed Director Marietti's personal phone.

"Morgan, are you all right?" The gruff voice of the Director was tempered by concern. "I'm viewing some of the security camera footage now, and it's brutal stuff."

"Yes, I'm fine sir, and I'll report in full soon, but right now we have a lead that may help us locate where the Neo-Viking group are heading. Were the police able to track the helicopter?"

"The Neo-Vikings used the same type of Black Hawk helicopter as the Americans allegedly used for the raid on Bin Laden. It doesn't show up on radar, but we're tracking physical sightings right now. They flew east, then must have landed either on a boat or transferred to land transport."

Morgan frowned. "It suggests some serious funding behind the group."

"Exactly." Marietti's voice held the promise of further investigation. "There was also a vicious wind that surrounded the helicopter as they headed east, low over the river toward the sea. Nothing could get close to it. I want you back here to work on what the hell is going on."

"The leader of the group was a woman calling herself the Valkyrie, and she said some things that reminded one of the academics at the museum of The Lindisfarne Gospels." Morgan didn't want to try and explain Blake's unique ability right now, especially as she knew that Marietti might try to recruit him or at least want to know a lot more than she had time for. "The researcher is with me now, and we're going to check the Gospels out. Can you call ahead and get that cleared so we have access?"

Morgan heard the hesitation in Marietti's voice.

"All right, go check the Gospels, but then you've got to get back here, Morgan. The press are having a field day with this. While the police work on the crime angle, we need to get that staff back. Based on the footage of the Valkyrie and the wind she generated, there are plenty of people who are going to want it."

Morgan knew that there was an underground network of organizations and individuals who collected such objects. Most of them kept to the shadows, but others emerged with their plans to impact the wider world. The staff of Skara Brae, resonating with ancient power, would draw them all when the footage was inevitably released on YouTube. Some would dismiss it as fake special effects, the conspiracy theorists would turn it into the start of some global plot, but some would know the truth and seek it out. The staff was powerful in the right hands, and Morgan knew she had to get it back. If they could locate the Eye of Odin as well, then all the better.

***

The taxi pulled up in front of the British Library on the Euston Road. Morgan and Blake walked into the forecourt, past the huge bronze statue of Newton, bent to measure the world with his calipers, frowning with concentration. The British Library was a modern building, red brick on two sides of the piazza square, with the gothic spires of St Pancras station towering behind it. Three flagpoles stood in the middle of the square, the Union Jack fluttering in the breeze, while readers streamed in the doors or drank coffee in patches of sun, fingers flicking through books. Despite the modern exterior, this library was a treasure store of the written word, a nirvana for any bibliophile. Morgan loved to come here, to feel a part of the grand heritage that was England.

"I'm not sure we can just walk in and demand to see The Lindisfarne Gospels," Blake said, as they walked across the square.

"We won't have to," Morgan said. "ARKANE has phoned ahead."

Blake chuckled. "I envy you. My research is usually a combination of my own psychometric reading and then a period of begging for access to get it verified through official sources."

The entrance to the library was flanked by security guards who nodded them through, and they stepped into the spacious atrium. Sun streamed down from skylights high above the central light well, and three levels of reading rooms could be seen, with readers bustling between them carrying the clear plastic bags that were mandatory in the Reading Rooms. The sense was of open space, not crammed stacks, a portal to the information housed here in so many forms, much of it now digitized.

"The Gospels are in the Ritblat Gallery, alongside the other Treasures of the Library," Morgan said. "This way."

Up a short flight of stairs, the entrance to the Ritblat Gallery was dark, the light dimmed to preserve the precious objects within. Each glass case held priceless documents, from pages of Leonardo da Vinci's notebooks to an eleventh-century manuscript of *Beowulf*, the handwritten pages damaged by fire. Thomas Hardy's original manuscript of *Tess of the D'Urbervilles* was here, his fine cross-hatched edits still evident, as well as more modern treasures like the lyrics to The Beatles' "Yesterday."

A huge globe dominated one area of the room, a baroque vision of the heavens painted with ancient constellation figures. Pegasus, the winged horse, galloped next to the Great Bear, paws uplifted to stride across the globe. Nearby stood the collection of Christian manuscripts, most illuminated by the hands of monks long dead.

Morgan couldn't help but look into the case holding the Codex Sinaiticus, her thoughts going back to St Catherine's Monastery in the Sinai, where it had originally been kept. Written over 1600 years ago, the handwritten manuscript with heavily corrected text was the Christian Bible in Greek, containing the oldest complete copy of the New Testament. Pages of the text had been sewn into other book bindings, and a fragment had pointed her and Khal to a new location for the Ark of the Covenant not so long ago. Despite the dangers of ARKANE, Morgan lived on the edge of the boundary between the ancient world and the modern, and there was nowhere else she would rather work.

A librarian waved at them from a side door.

"Are you from ARKANE?" the woman asked. Morgan nodded. "The Lindisfarne Gospels are normally kept on display here, but they're currently resting."

"Resting?" Blake asked.

The librarian gave him a smile as she touched her hair, her eyes twinkling more as she addressed him directly. Blake's injuries only seemed to heighten his good looks.

"Even though the lights are dimmed in here, the manuscripts are still affected so we like to give them a rest in the dark now and then. Our aim at the British Library is to make sure these treasures last another thousand years for everyone to enjoy. Normally we wouldn't allow anything to disturb them, but you seem to have a special pass. We've just retrieved the Gospels from their resting place and they're ready for you to view. Follow me."

The woman pushed open a door leading away from the Ritblat Gallery, and walked ahead of them down a short corridor. At a doorway, she turned, pulling two pairs of white gloves wrapped in plastic from her pocket.

"These are mandatory for you to wear when handling the manuscript." She frowned, noticing Blake's own gloves for the first time. He turned his hands so she couldn't see the blood stains.

"Of course," Morgan said, taking them and handing a pair to Blake.

They pulled off the plastic and put the gloves on, Blake hiding his own stained pair in his pocket for the meantime. When she was satisfied they were appropriately attired, the librarian pushed open the door.

"I've been told to leave you to it, but I'll just be down the hall if you need anything."

Morgan and Blake stepped into the room, a stark white cube containing nothing but a white table with a bookrest, and on it, The Lindisfarne Gospels. The book was illuminated with artistic calligraphy and painted scenes, interweaving the cultures that influenced England at the time it was written. There were Egyptian Coptic cross-carpet pages, exotic iconography from the Eastern Mediterranean, Celtic spiral patterns, Greek Byzantine lettering and even the angular shapes of Germanic runes. Created in the late seventh century at Lindisfarne Priory, the book was considered to be one of the nation's leading artistic treasures, as well as an icon of faith.

"It's beautiful," Blake said, bending to look at the cover more closely. Gold and silver strips formed a border around the edge, each with a precious stone in the middle. The center panel was a deep crimson inlaid with Celtic woven patterns in precious metal, a fitting cover for such a holy book.

Morgan opened the first page with gloved fingers, revealing a richly colored tapestry of red and sunset-yellow tiles around the shape of a cross. The Coptic carpet style was reminiscent of Islamic prayer rugs, and miniature birds lay around the edge, beaks clutching each other's feet in a never-ending spiral. The letters at the beginning of the Gospels were illuminated in the colors of turquoise, ochre and plum, each one a world of fantastical beasts and swirling heraldic devices.

"It looks like there is other writing under the main text," Blake said.

"It's a translation," Morgan pointed, careful not to touch the page. "Old English was added between the lines of Latin, which makes it one of the oldest surviving translations of the Gospels into English. I wish we had time to study it properly, but we should really just check the back page. A colophon was added after the Viking invasion."

She slowly turned the pages, glimpsing paintings of the gospel writers transcribing the words of the Lord while angels trumpeted behind them, until finally, the last page was revealed. After the glorious extravagance and riot of color throughout the book, the colophon was an anticlimax, a page of black text, with the translation underneath and a column of text in a more casual hand, almost running off the edge of the page.

"It's a list of who helped in the making of the Gospels, but there's some text that scholars have struggled to translate." She pointed. "Right here. It's only a few lines."

"Perhaps if I try my kind of reading, I'll be able to get a sense of what the scribe was getting at." Blake pulled one of the white gloves off. "Although to be honest, I've not had much luck reading manuscripts, as they usually have so many people involved in making them."

"This one is different," Morgan said. "It's supposed to be the work of one man, attributed to Bishop Eadfrith of Lindisfarne."

"We might have a chance then. Keep an eye on the door, will you? I don't want to suffer the wrath of the librarian if I'm caught touching this book. I've had quite enough violence for one day."

Blake laid his bare fingers lightly on the edge of the handwritten text and closed his eyes.

CHAPTER 9

THE CRY OF SEAGULLS pierced the veil of Blake's consciousness and the smell of the sea made him long for ocean winds. He opened his eyes to see the ruins of Lindisfarne Priory. Cottages still burned and the remains of slaughtered animals and men lay in the streets, in the direct aftermath of the Viking attack. Blake felt the outrage of the monk who held the Gospels tightly to his breast, and the grief that washed over his soul at what must surely be the loss of what he called family.

"Come, brother." The words were rough and cut with emotion. "We can do no more here. We must get word to Eilean Idhe, for that witch and her pagan protectors were searching for something and I'm afraid what they seek has been long hidden there. If we hurry, we can make the tidal crossing and begin our long journey before the waters get too high."

Blake turned to see another monk by his side, pulling the cowl up over his tonsured head to keep the wind from his weathered face, or perhaps to hide his tears. The land had been etched in his visage and his eyes were a deep brown, like the earth beneath their feet. He strode off, and Blake lengthened his stride to keep up, feeling a strange sense of the physical body he inhabited albeit briefly. The man who clutched the Gospels to his chest was muscular yet wiry, with strength in his limbs and a clarity of purpose that made every step a statement of survival despite persecution.

As dusk began to fall, they emerged at a headland and Blake saw the crossing. A narrow strip of land ran from the island to the shore while the ocean lapped on either side, each minute reclaiming the wet ground for the sea. Lindisfarne was cut off from the mainland for all but a short time every day, a separate community of those who served God. Blake felt a sense of trepidation well up within him as he looked at the thin sliver of land left. They would be wading soon, and the waters would continue to rise, the current strong against their legs. Could he dare take the precious package of the Gospels from this place?

The other monk turned.

"We must hurry, brother. Come quickly, or the waters will be too high." He reached out his hand. "I will help you."

At his kind words, Blake felt the monk relax and his faith in God calming him. The terrors of the day faded as the two men walked into the rising waters and Blake's grip on the moment began to fade, the intense emotions around the book dissipating.

He sifted through layers of consciousness, searching for another strand to grab onto, desperate to find out where the monks were heading and learn of the mysterious reference to what was hidden at this other place. In the layers between time, he found a glimmer of revelation and pulled himself back into the monk's awareness.

***

The two monks stepped off a little boat onto a beach of pale sand. Blake could sense their exhaustion after a long and dangerous journey. He had his back to a stretch of water, and the sun was setting directly ahead behind verdant green hills. A small village of low huts with a wooden church at its center loomed ahead in silhouette.

The monk, still carrying the Gospels, fell to his knees.

"Blessed St Columba, we thank you for your protection on this journey." His prayers were fervent, cut short as a welcoming shout came from the monastery and brothers came to meet them.

***

Blake was jolted out of the trance as Morgan removed his hand from the book.

"Quick," she said. "Put the glove back on. Someone's coming."

Blake pulled the white glove on, his head reeling from the shift in perspective. How strange to be on an island one moment and then here in this surgically clean space in central London. Vertigo made his head spin and he clutched the edge of the table as the door opened.

"Are you all right in here?" the librarian asked, her eyes narrowing as she saw Blake sagging a little. He stood up straighter, giving her his best rakish smile, an implied invitation that made her blush and avert her eyes quickly.

"Yes, of course," Morgan said. "We just need a few more minutes."

"Sure," the librarian said, giving Blake a smile before she left again, the door closing behind her.

"What did you do to her?" Morgan asked, grinning at Blake. "I might invite you to be my sidekick again if you charm all the ladies that way."

Blake thought of the nights he spent under the wicked spell of tequila, the casual sexual conquests on the London nightlife scene, the practice that lay under his easy sexuality. Where once those ephemeral pleasures had satisfied him, he now began to sense the emptiness in his life choices, but Morgan didn't need to know about that side of his life.

"Just my inimitable charm," he said. "Before you pulled me back, I did discover a couple of things that might help us. The Gospels were carried away from Lindisfarne by two monks, heading for another place where the sun set behind the hills and a strip of ocean was to my back, the reverse of Lindisfarne."

"Another island, but on the west coast, you think?"

Blake nodded. "Yes, and they said something about needing to warn a community about the raids, that the thing the Vikings sought was buried there … they called it Eilean Idhe, but I'm sure I'm massacring the pronunciation."

Morgan smiled, recognition dawning on her face.

"The island is called Iona now. It's still a spiritual community, rich in the Christian tradition. The Bishop of Lindisfarne, St Cuthbert, originally came from Iona, so it makes sense there were ties between the two. The Vikings also raided the island in 794 and for many years afterwards, so perhaps they never found what they sought that day. Perhaps the monks warned them in time."

Blake heard the curiosity in her voice. "You're going there, aren't you?"

Morgan nodded. "If you think that's where the Valkyrie is heading, then yes, I'll go … but with some backup this time."

Blake knew this was probably the end of his time with Morgan, but his experiences with Jamie Brooke on the Hunterian murder and now this were helping him to see that his gift could be useful. Perhaps there could be a way to use it to help, rather than just to see visions that haunted his nightmares.

"Need a sidekick?" Blake asked, turning on his most charming smile. Morgan laughed, and he chuckled along with her, for there was no entrancing this woman. She was smart as well as attractive and saw right through his attempts. Morgan put her hand on his arm, suddenly serious.

"Thank you for your help with this, Blake. Now I can use this information to go after the Valkyrie."

"Will I … see you again?" he asked, not wanting this to be the end. "I want to know what you find, and I doubt that I'll find any kind of truth in the media. At least our kind of truth anyway."

Morgan hesitated, then nodded. "I'll find you afterwards, I promise. Why don't you stay and look at the Gospels for a bit longer. I'm sure the librarian would be happy to take you on a personal tour."

As they both laughed, Morgan leaned forward and kissed Blake on the cheek. He looked into her blue eyes, like cobalt from the illuminated script, the slash of violet in her right darker now, almost indigo. He wanted to read her, wanted to know her emotions, and her past. She intrigued him.

"This is goodbye for now," she said, turning to the door and walking out, without looking back.

***

Morgan pulled out her phone in the atrium of the library. Marietti answered on the first ring.

"Did you find anything?" he asked, his voice tense. She could hear talking in the background, and a news bulletin that still looped on the museum hostage crisis.

"I think they might be heading to Iona," Morgan said. "The Scottish island also had a famous monastery that was raided by the Vikings, and it could be that they were looking for the same thing the Valkyrie is. She called it the Eye of Odin, and the staff was just a step on that journey. The museum wasn't the end game."

"Hmm. Interesting, but things look a little different from here. We've had a report of a suspicious murder in the Orkney Islands, a man ritually killed in the Ring of Brodgar, a Neolithic stone circle. The local police say there's a group who follow the ways of the Vikings in the islands, expected back later tonight. Harmless, or so they thought." Marietti laughed bitterly. "I'm sending a team there to investigate and intercept the return of the Valkyrie."

It was over 200 miles from Orkney to Iona across land and sea, Morgan thought. If she was wrong, then she would miss out on dispensing the justice she so desperately wanted. Betting on Blake's visions over hard evidence was crazy, but she thought of how he had been in the trance. It was as if he had left his physical body, and working for ARKANE had eroded the skepticism she used to have about the inexplicable.

"I'd like to go to Iona," she said. "Then we'll be covering both angles."

"Hold on a minute." Morgan heard Marietti barking commands to those in his office before returning to the phone. "Alright, get to Iona. But if you insist on investigating there, I can't spare anyone to come with you. We're stretched as it is, and you might find nothing. We can send backup if you do get a lead. Still want to go?"

Morgan's rage about the murder in the museum was still simmering, and she didn't want to continue this fight back in the depths of the ARKANE offices. Her preference was always for action, if she had the choice. Of course, Blake's unusual talent could be completely useless, his visions merely the product of an unhinged mind. But she had seen him read, and there had been no trace of the crazy there, only a man who was tortured by what he saw.

"Yes, I want to go. But can you at least get me a weapon?"

"Head for London City Airport and we'll sort out a flight to Glasgow, and a helicopter from there. There'll be a box waiting for you. Stay in touch, Morgan."

Marietti hung up and Morgan stood in the busy atrium of the library, surrounded by the bustle of the readers, wondering whether this was the right decision. She appreciated Marietti's trust, his lack of micromanagement of his team, but she also felt a little alone without her partner, or without even Blake at her side. Then, she remembered the grotesque death of the curator, the violence of the Valkyrie in her quest. She pushed open the doors and headed for the taxi rank.

CHAPTER 10

MORGAN STEPPED OFF THE charter boat onto the white sandy shores of Iona, turning back to take her bag from the charter boat skipper. One of the Inner Hebrides, Iona was situated off the southwest tip of the Isle of Mull. West from the island was the broad Atlantic, all the way to Newfoundland. The charter flight to Glasgow, the helicopter to Mull, and finally the boat to Iona had only taken a couple of hours, but this place was another world compared to the teeming city she'd left behind.

The light was beginning to fade as Morgan looked around at the little village of Baile Mòr, its stone houses staring back toward the mainland. This was a hardy land, with a small population who preferred isolation and solitude to the bustle of the city. Morgan could only imagine the hell London would be for these people, for here time was measured by the tides, the shifting wind and the cry of the skylark.

A little way from the village streets, the mottled stone walls of the Iona Abbey stood proud, built on the site of the monastery founded by St Columba in the mid-sixth century. It had been a beacon for early Christianity, influencing the spread of faith amongst the Picts and the Scots. Although she had been brought up in Israel, her father Jewish, Morgan felt a momentary longing to find a bed in one of the Christian retreat centers and just close her eyes. The intensity of her missions with ARKANE had taken their toll, and she had the sense that things were only speeding up, that the world was spiraling toward some kind of terrifying end. The glimpses she had experienced were only one piece of the information, but she knew that Marietti understood some of the bigger picture. The ARKANE director had become haggard of late, his beard whitening in recent months. Perhaps it was almost time to ask him to share what he knew.

"Can I help you, lassie?" The broad Scottish accent was welcoming. "I saw you coming from the boat there." The man wore just a t-shirt despite the chilling wind, his bare arms roped with muscle as he carried a box wrapped in brown paper toward the charter boat that was preparing to leave again. His face was rugged, with deep laughter lines. "Are you with those others?"

It had to be the Valkyrie's group, Morgan thought. They had a head start on her, but they couldn't have been here too long.

"Yes, I'm with them," she smiled as she spoke, "but I missed a connection. Do you know where they went?"

"They're up at the abbey, all dressed up it seems. But we get all sorts here, to be sure."

The man shook his head. So many pilgrims came here to worship and pay homage to history, to find their sense of God in this wide open space, that Morgan guessed he witnessed a lot of strange people coming through.

"Thank you for your help."

The man walked toward the boat, calling to the others to wait up for his package. Morgan bent to her small pack, and with her body shielding the view from the boat, she checked to ensure the Barak SP-21 pistol was loaded.

A rumble of thunder made her lift her head to the sky.

Toward the west, dark clouds were gathering and the wind was picking up. Fat drops of rain began to splatter down and a chill pierced the air. Morgan thought of the vortex the Valkyrie had commanded back at the museum, and looked up towards the Benedictine abbey. The light was dim now, but she could just make out figures in front of the twelfth-century stone building.

Morgan pulled her hood up and tugged the thick coat closer around her as she walked quickly up the main street toward the abbey. It was known as the *Reilig Odhráin*, Road of the Dead, where the funeral procession would walk with the body of Christian dead to be buried in the abbey grounds. Early Kings of Scotland were buried here, including *Mac Bethad mac Findlaích*, known to history as Macbeth.

The darkness grew thicker now as clouds billowed above in shades of violet, shot through with flickering lightning. The few people remaining outside in the streets ran for cover, closing windows and preparing for the storm. They were used to the vagaries of the weather on this peninsula by the Atlantic, with nothing to shield them from the elements. Now, Morgan was counting on it to disguise her approach to the abbey as she crept to the edge of the great medieval building.

As she drew closer, Morgan saw the Valkyrie standing in the rain, a fur wrap covering her gray tunic, her hair plastered to her head as the drops ran unheeded down her face. There was steel in the old woman's posture, a hardness in her features and a new knowledge that darkened her eyes. She held the staff of Skara Brae in front of her, gnarled fingers clutching it tightly.

Three of the Neo-Vikings were digging under the base of the eighth-century St Martin's Cross. The ring behind the medieval cross symbolized eternity and the presence of a halo, and the stone was carved with scenes from the

Bible. Even from a short distance away, Morgan recognized Daniel in the lion's den, Abraham with sword raised to sacrifice Isaac, and writhing serpents around circular bosses. One of the men pushed against the heavy stone, rocking his body back and forth to try to move it.

"No," a voice cried. A man ran out from the cover of the abbey doorway, clearly one of the clergy. "That cross has stood by the grace of God for over 1200 years on that spot. You can't just knock it down."

He grabbed the arm of the Neo-Viking, who laughed, a deep rumbling sound, and reached around the back of the man's head, yanking it forward to smash against the stone. The clergyman groaned in pain and slumped a little, but the Neo-Viking pulled him forward again, driving his skull onto the arm of the cross, blood now oozing from the wound, staining the ancient stone.

"Enough," the Valkyrie said, her Scottish lilt a direct order. "Finish digging. The Eye is under there, I've seen it in my visions. It calls to the staff now. Dig harder."

The Neo-Viking threw the clergyman to the ground, where he lay clutching his head as the rain slammed down upon his prone body. Morgan willed him to stay still and just wait. Even with a weapon, she couldn't stop all of them, and with people in the abbey, she didn't want to risk making a move. She pulled back around the edge of the building and texted Marietti at ARKANE, informing him that the group was there, though she knew that backup wouldn't get here in time to stop the Neo-Vikings recovering the Eye of Odin. If she was honest, part of Morgan wanted to see what happened when the Eye was recovered. She was drawn to the edge of darkness, for the glimpses she had seen into the realm of miracle had given her a taste of something beyond the mundane world.

A loud rumble of thunder echoed across the bay, followed quickly by a crack of lightning. The storm was almost upon them. Morgan peered around again to see the Neo-Vikings pushing the stone cross to the ground, its granite pedestal split open. The Valkyrie knelt before it, her hands thrust into the earth. She pulled out a slim metal box and held it to the sky, rain hammering down upon her uplifted arms.

"For you, Odin. *Skelfr Yggdrasils askr standandi, ymr it aldna tré, en jötunn losnar*," she called to the heavens. "Yggdrasil shakes, shiver on high the ancient limbs, and the giant is loose."

The triumph in her voice sent a shiver down Morgan's spine. The words the Valkyrie spoke were from the *Völuspá*, a prophecy of the end times, heralding the battle known to the Vikings as Ragnarok.

The Valkyrie opened the box and her men gathered close behind her to look inside. The expression on their faces was one of wonder, and more than that, of visceral desire. Morgan had seen that look before, on the faces of those who saw the huge gems of the Jewel House in the Tower of London and coveted them. The Valkyrie lifted the object from the box and turned to the men, the lump of yellow rock in her hands. There was a fire inside the precious stone, a burning that turned its facets to gold even in the darkened world around. The raindrops seemed to bring it alive. Odin's Eye was said to shine like the sun, and this rock looked to be a huge piece of rare yellow diamond, worth many millions. Morgan knew it would serve a darker purpose tonight.

"We must go to the west for the summoning," the Valkyrie said, looking up into the swirling clouds, eyes unblinking in the heavy rain. She indicated the injured man on the ground. "Bring him."

CHAPTER 11

Morgan stepped back quietly to hide in the shadow of the abbey as the Valkyrie and her men passed close by, dragging the moaning clergyman between them. The group entered a car and drove away into the rainy night. Morgan had checked the maps and seen the famous Bay at the Back of the Ocean, a wide west-facing sweep of white sand looking out across the sea to North America. It was just over the other side of the island, but too far to walk or run. She looked around the car park, spotting a mountain bike alongside a low fence. It wasn't locked, as these islands hadn't been a crime hotspot. Until tonight.

Grabbing the bike, Morgan pedaled hard after the car toward the west of the island. The rain lashed down upon her, but she soon warmed as her breath came hard, heart beating fast with the exertion and apprehension of what was to come. Could the Valkyrie really summon the final destiny of the gods with the Eye of Odin?

As she pedaled faster, rising to her feet to push hard up the hill, Morgan smiled, an almost manic excitement rising within her. In one sense, she had never felt so alone, with no backup, her partner Jake at the other end of the country, her family not even knowing what she was doing or where she was. But she also recognized that the thrill of the edge was what she constantly sought. It made her feel alive. If she should die here today, it would be with the grin of the berserker on her face, going to meet her fate laughing at the gods.

At the crest of the hill, Morgan paused to catch her breath and, through the rain, saw the headlights of the car near the rocky headland. A mist was rising from the earth: the smell of wild thyme and the salty tang of the ocean spray hung fresh in the air. The sound of the waves on the beach could be heard beneath the thump of the rain, and the crackle of lightning burst through the charged air, the forked silver striking the rocks below.

She let the bike freewheel down the hill and then left it so she could continue on foot, creeping through the rocks at the edge of the bay, hiding behind one to peer through at the tableau.

One of the Neo-Vikings pushed the clergyman to his knees on the rocks as the Valkyrie began to spin the staff, holding the Eye of Odin in her other hand. A shrill cawing filled the air. Morgan looked up to see a flock of dark birds, the ravens of the island, begin to fly in a circle in an eerie reflection of the movements below. The Valkyrie whirled the staff, weaving patterns in the air, chanting in a voice that grated against something in Morgan's very soul.

"*Snýsk jörmungandr í jötunmóði,*" the Valkyrie called into the spinning vortex that materialized around her. "In giant-wrath does the serpent writhe."

With those words, she pointed the staff at the kneeling clergyman. The Neo-Viking behind him pulled the man's head back and sliced his throat with a heavy knife. Arterial blood sprayed into the whirling tornado around the Valkyrie, the droplets whipped into the spiraling air until it was as if she stood within a wall of blood that the rain could no longer penetrate. The Eye of Odin glowed in her hand, its light illuminating her face, a prophet of long-dead gods.

The Valkyrie turned to face the vast expanse of the Atlantic.

"*Ormr knýr unnir, en ari hlakkar, slítr nái niðfölr.*" Her voice was a shriek now, rising above the rumble of thunder that echoed around the bay. "Over the waves he twists, and the tawny eagle gnaws corpses screaming."

She stretched out the staff and held the Eye of Odin close to it. Through the veil of blood, the golden light from the stone looked like a ray of the sun as it shot out into the boiling sea below. It seemed to carve a path in the water, some kind of bioluminescence revealing the depths below.

One of the Neo-Vikings lifted a great curved horn to his lips and blew it, the deep sound a sonorous vibration that shook the rocks they stood upon. The other two Neo-Vikings dropped to their knees, as the waters boiled and in the distance, Morgan thought she saw coils of some great creature arching from the deep. The legends of Ragnarok told of *Jörmungandr*, the Midgard serpent that encircles the earth holding his tail in his mouth until the day he lets go and the world ends.

Morgan tried to focus on what she thought she had seen, but between flashes of lightning, it could have been nothing more than waves. The Neo-Vikings were transfixed by the sight of the golden ray, and she knew she needed to finish this. She pulled the gun from her pack. The power of this staff, the Eye of Odin … It all needed to end here.

The Valkyrie stood with arms pointed toward the deep, the wall of spinning blood around her, and it seemed to Morgan that she began to lift from the rock to hang in the air. The ravens flew faster around the top of the vortex, a dark host crowing the victory of those who worshipped the ancient gods, calling for their return.

Aiming for the Valkyrie's back, Morgan fired once, twice, but the bullets ricocheted off the vortex, one hitting a Neo-Viking in the eye on rebound. He slumped to the ground without a sound, but the other two men jumped to their feet, roaring with anger. The Valkyrie turned her head at the noise and her hands faltered, the light from the staff and the Eye wobbling in the water. She refocused, chanting louder with darker words, her eyes rolling back in her head as she floated upward. The boiling in the ocean seemed to double in intensity and lightning strikes hit the waters with a hiss, the clouds above whirling in a tornado. Something was coming, something from the other side.

Morgan left her hiding place, leaping across the rocks sideways to the Valkyrie. One of the men moved to shield his mistress and the other pursued. Morgan turned and shot again. A double tap and the man went down, his bulk falling between the rocks.

Only one man stood between her and the witch now. Holding the gun out, Morgan stepped across the rocks, hyper-alert as the man held his arms wide, inviting her to him. She aimed at his mid-section, finger squeezing the trigger. The moment she fired, a sharp tug on her ankle pulled her down and pain exploded as Morgan's knee cracked on the sharp rocks. The man she had shot first reached up to grab her, his face a mess of blood where his head had hit the rocks, the chest wound bleeding but not fatal. Losing her grip, the gun went clattering down the side of the rocks.

Morgan kicked backward, ignoring the pain as she smashed her boot into the man's face. Her Krav Maga military training took over, and she put every ounce of force into her kick. The man's head flicked back, and he lost his grip on her ankle. Morgan turned, using her momentum to push herself up from the rocks and kicked at the man's head, connecting with his temple with a sickening crunch. Breathing hard now, Morgan's vision narrowed. Her senses heightened, she heard the sound of the ocean boiling, the crows cawing, the Valkyrie chanting, and felt an electricity in the air as the veil of reality shifted.

Aware of danger from behind, she turned to see the other Neo-Viking almost upon her, his eyes wild. The gun was out of reach now and Morgan bent her knees, her palms outstretched in the waiting Krav Maga stance. The man lumbered toward her, over six feet of muscle, his face tattooed with Norse runes, a mark of devotion to his gods. He grimaced. Morgan saw his teeth were filed and marked with black.

"I will rip your throat out," he taunted, "and the Valkyrie will feed your corpse to great *Jörmungandr.*"

He ran at her, leaping over the rocks, hands outstretched. Morgan waited for him to get close, willing him to attack so she could hurt him. The blood lust was high within her now. She wanted to beat this man into the earth and leave his bones to rot.

The man led with a punch. Morgan brushed his hand aside with an open palm, using the other arm to slam her elbow into his temple as she shouted her rage, her voice coming from a primal place of survival. She followed through with hammerfist strikes that made the man reel. But he kept coming, head lower now, swaying a little. Morgan didn't relent. She went toward him again and as he tried to grab her waist to pull her to the floor, she grabbed his ears, twisting them with a savage yell. She used all her strength to spring from the rocks with one knee lifted and slammed it into his face, once, twice, as fast as the lightning strikes above. The man went down and Morgan leaned in, using her bent knuckles to slam into his throat.

Leaving the man gurgling for breath, Morgan turned back to the Valkyrie. Either side of the golden ray of light, the ocean was forming a wall of white water and violent waves, a path for whatever was summoned. Morgan felt the world hum in the pulsing throb of the golden light, the pounding of the waves and the triumphant chant of the

Valkyrie, her thin body transformed into power.

The gun was useless now, but there was still a chance to disrupt whatever was coming. Morgan ran at the vortex, pushing off the rocks to leap through the wall of blood, her rage exploding in a primordial roar. She slammed into the Valkyrie and the witch shrieked as the vortex began to crumple and the blood dropped to the rocks, covering them both in gore. Morgan wrestled with the woman, and the golden Eye slipped from the Valkyrie's grasp into the gap between the ocean walls, the golden light somehow holding the waves back.

"No," the Valkyrie cried, scrambling away from Morgan, still grasping the staff. The witch leaped from the rocks down into the gap of the ocean. Morgan didn't hesitate, jumping after her and knocking the woman to the ground. Above them, the walls of water loomed, the edges faltered as the power of the light pulsed in and out. The witch scrambled for the Eye of Odin, and Morgan grabbed for the staff, pulling it from the woman's grip, the iron hot in her hands. She felt the spray from the ocean around her, the droplets thicker than the rain, power on the edge of collapse.

Morgan turned and ran, clutching the staff to her as the Valkyrie laid hands on the golden Eye, screaming Norse curses, but the power had gone from the gem. Morgan leaped from the exposed sand as the walls of water came crashing down, the cries of the Valkyrie buried under the boiling ocean. Morgan looked out to the sea as the thunder rolled further off, and the lightning lessened. In the distance, she thought she saw the coils of an ancient creature rise once more and then sink below the depths.

CHAPTER 12

THE NEXT DAY, MORGAN stood at the window in Director Marietti's office, looking out over the tourists in Trafalgar Square as he wound up his phone call. This was the public section of ARKANE, where meetings with outsiders happened, but most of the complex lay under the Square, people walking above, unaware of the secrets kept below. It was a long way from the Bay at the Back of the Ocean and what Morgan had seen in the whirling vortex of blood and boiling waves. The Valkyrie's body had been found washed up on the beach at dawn, her hair bleached completely white, her face frozen in a rictus of horror. Had she glimpsed the realm of Ragnarok at the end, Morgan wondered? Had she seen the warriors waiting to storm back onto the earth for the final battle?

ARKANE had a team of divers searching for the Eye of Odin beneath the waves of the rocky headland. It was dangerous work, hampered by wild ocean currents and inclement weather, and they might never recover it. Perhaps it was better that way.

Marietti put down the phone, turning with a worried expression. He stroked his short gray beard, shot through with white to match his salt-and-pepper hair.

"Martin has traced the funding for the helicopter and

the Neo-Vikings' organization to a front of companies. Behind them sits a group called Tempest." Marietti frowned. "They're new to us, Morgan, but they worry me. The tempest represents upheaval and chaos, a force of nature that can't be stopped. I fear we haven't seen the last of this group."

Morgan heard the words of the Valkyrie in her head, *a storm is coming*, and knew that this was just the beginning.

"I'll have Martin start to research them," Marietti said. "I know you want to work on the package sent from your father next." He picked up the iron staff from the desk, the dull metal giving no sign of the havoc it could wreak when wielded by the right hands. "This will have to go down in the vaults. It can't go back to the British Museum now. Can you explain?"

Morgan nodded. "Of course. There's someone I need to see over there anyway."

***

Crowds outside the British Museum took pictures of the giant cranes repairing the glass roof. The national treasure would be open to the public again soon, and the news reports had inevitably moved onto the next disaster. The Neo-Vikings had been dismissed as a crazy religious group, and any murmurings of the supernatural had been quashed with evidence that the videos of the vortex had been tampered with. No hint of what had occurred on Iona had reached the mainstream news, and ARKANE would make sure it never would.

"Morgan, I'm so glad you could come." Morgan turned to see Blake standing by a coffee cart, two steaming cups in his hands. "I took the liberty …" He raised one of the cups.

She took it smiling, checking the dark liquid inside before taking a sip.

"Just how I like it," Morgan said, wondering if Blake had read something of her in their brief time together, and whether that would be an altogether bad thing.

The cut on the side of his face was a raw pink, the eye socket swollen and bruised in a palette of purple. The color against his darker skin only served to emphasize his piercing blue eyes, and Morgan wondered if this man ever looked really rough. They sat on the low stone wall as tourists milled around them and the hammer of construction rang throughout the square.

"Your curator friend is avenged," Morgan said. "But I'm afraid the museum won't be getting the staff of Skara Brae back."

Blake sighed. "Probably for the best. I'm not sure people here want to remember, anyway." He turned to look into her eyes, searching for the truth. "Did you see what it could do on Iona?"

In a flash of memory, Morgan saw the Valkyrie, floating within the spinning wall of blood, the ray of gold summoning something from the depths. Part of her wanted to share that with Blake. If he touched the staff and read it with his gift, he would see it, too. But he was not ARKANE, and it was time she returned to working with her own team.

"I saw nothing more than we both witnessed here," Morgan said, watching disappointment cloud his eyes. "But the Neo-Vikings won't be back, for sure."

"And will I see you again?" Blake reached for her hand with his gloved one.

Morgan squeezed it as she stood up. "I never say goodbye." She smiled. "I've found that life has too many surprises in store."

She walked away without looking back into the tourist throng, just another face in the crowd.

AUTHOR'S NOTE

THIS NOVELLA IS MEANT to be a rollicking fun read! Although I did research the Vikings, this is a work of fiction and I have embellished for dramatic license. The Norse quotes are from the Poetic Edda poem *Völuspá*, where a *völva*, a witch or shaman, tells Odin the story of the creation of the world. You will find the places, manuscripts and objects in 'real' life, but I have turned them into a story of my own construction. All mistakes in research are my own.

You can see associated pictures on Pinterest:
www.pinterest.com/jfpenn/ragnarok

Inspiration for the story

My own fascination with *Game of Thrones* and its Viking mythology of wolves, ravens and dragons first inspired this story. Couple that with the Northern Lights being seen across the UK early in 2014 (http://bit.ly/1jsqbtE) and the Viking Ragnarok proclaimed for Feb 2014 (http://dailym.ai/1aTiTXq) and I had an inkling for the story I would write.

The British Museum had a special exhibition about the Vikings, which I attended in early March 2014. The longboat and decapitated skeletons were there, as were the other objects described. I love the supernatural so I was struck by the staffs of the *völva* and the information on Viking magic. As I started to research afterwards, I discovered the Poetic Edda and the story took shape.

The British Museum also features in my book *Prophecy*, which was based on an exhibition on religious relics. I foresee many more exhibitions there forming an integral part of my work! I've used artistic license for the floor plan and the exits.

Orkney

The Ring of Brodgar is within the Neolithic heritage site in the Orkney Islands in the far north of Scotland, closer to Norway than London. You can see the aurora borealis there in the winter months.

Lindisfarne

The Viking raid of Lindisfarne is a historical fact. *The Anglo-Saxon Chronicle* records:

"In this year fierce, foreboding omens came over the land of the Northumbrians, and the wretched people shook; there were excessive whirlwinds, lightning, and fiery dragons were seen flying in the sky. These signs were followed by great famine, and a little after those, that same year on 6th ides of January, the ravaging of wretched heathen people destroyed God's church at Lindisfarne."

The Lindisfarne Gospels are in the British Library and can be visited there when not 'resting.' The location of the relics of St Cuthbert are a secret known only to a few monks, although the records show it as intact when the Vikings raided, so my use in pagan ritual is fictionalized. You can look at the Gospels online here: http://www.bl.uk/onlinegallery/sacredtexts/lindisfarne.html. The colophon in the back page of the Gospels is actually a list of who contributed to the creation of the book, but perhaps my version is more interesting!

Iona

The description of Iona is as exact as possible, and its early importance to Christianity is fact.

GATES OF HELL

AN ARKANE THRILLER
J.F. PENN

"A depth of beginning, a depth of end;
a depth of good, a depth of evil."

Sefer Yetzirah 1:5

"I ... have the keys of hell and of death."

Revelation 1:18, King James Version

PROLOGUE

SANTIAGO PEREIRA STUMBLED AS he ran through the park, dropping to one knee as he gasped for breath, heart pounding. He glanced behind, his eyes darting around the empty streets. Yesterday's newspaper blew across the road, the rustle making him start as the cool wind blew in from the sea. He tasted salt in the air, a scent of pine from the hills above the city, and in the moment of stillness, hope rose within him. Perhaps somehow he had lost the man who shadowed him.

A footfall and then measured steps echoed through the square, striding towards him with no rush. Tears welled and Santiago's heart swelled in his chest. There was still so much to do, too much at stake for this to end here. He was an old man now, though, and he couldn't fight alone. He thought of Sofia, her deep brown eyes crinkled with laughter as she danced. His many mistakes had kept her from him, but maybe their distance would protect his granddaughter now.

Santiago looked up at the Sagrada Familia basilica before him, its facade a mosaic of eclectic architectural styles that his own hands had played a part in creating. A flock of sparrows rose from the spire, their song a hymn to the Creator. He rose to his feet and forced his body into an exhausted half jog, over the quiet street towards the holy place as the footsteps behind him grew ever closer. Santiago slipped through the turnstile gates and hurried towards the Passion facade, the oversize statue of the bound and whipped Christ before him, thorn-crowned head bowed in exhaustion.

"It's time to give it up, Rabbi." The voice was close, barely raised, the authority clear. "Your watch-keeping is finished, and now I will finish what your Remnant could not."

Santiago turned slowly, his back straightening as he faced the man who brought judgement – a man he had never thought to see again. Adam Kadmon had the physique of a boxer in his prime, his face strong and angular, his brow heavy. Santiago almost flinched to see the scar that bisected Adam's right eye leaving it white and sightless.

"You will bring destruction if you pursue this course, Adam. The Key is not for this generation. We are not ready as a people for what it could unleash."

Adam shook his head. "You were the one who inspired me with a passion for the Kabbalah. You were the one who told me of the Key, and now it is time." He ran his hand through his thick hair, an almost nervous gesture. "It is over time. You lack the strength to finish this, but I can bear this burden. I will bring an end to this earthly corruption, and we will no longer be the Remnant. We will be *Los Devoradores*."

Santiago backed away at his words. His hands rested against the pillar where Christ was tied, his fingers seeking out the striations of the stone. As his workman's calloused hands caressed the stone, Santiago tried to draw strength from the carpenter the Christians believed to have given himself for those he loved. The old man sighed, sagging as he leaned back against the rock.

"Perhaps you're right. Besides, I'm too tired to stand in your way anymore." He bent his head, looking at the ground. "I'll tell you the final piece of what you seek – but let us go to the roof together, as we used to do when you were young. I'll tell you there."

Adam stepped forwards, a curious smile playing around his mouth.

"I know you, Rabbi. I know you're not constrained by this physical flesh. But I will come with you to the roof, and we'll finish this together."

Adam walked to the great double doors of the basilica, the words of the Lord's Prayer etched into them, the raised letters a testament to the faith that inhabited this place. He pushed them open with a slight creak.

Santiago paused inside the doorway, breathing in the air that lay within the hallowed walls. This was not his faith, and yet the basilica had been under construction for the whole of his lifetime; it had become his stability. Its progress had marked the days of his own life. Like the scriptures, there were layers of meaning within each of the stones in the basilica, and craftsmen had always been the mouthpiece of God.

Adam pulled apart the doors of the workman's lift that would take them to the top of the Tower of the Passion. Santiago followed him inside and felt the younger man take his elbow, as he used to do in his youth. Once, Adam Kadmon – as he now called himself – had been his star pupil, back in the days when the Remnant had still been a vibrant force. Then, that touch had been one of respect; now, those fingers were tight and pinched his skin. The hands he had watched carve discarded stone into magical shapes were now instruments of harm. Santiago flushed, shame washing his cheeks. He was responsible for teaching Adam the knowledge that could now be used to usher in the Final Days. Part of him didn't believe the Key was real but if it was, the time was nearly upon them when the Gates could be opened ... Santiago sent up a silent prayer to his God.

The lift cranked its way upwards, the mechanical grind of chains resounding in the stone tower. It was cold, the chill of the morning amplified by the dark stone interior, as the light of the sun wouldn't pierce this tower until the afternoon. Finally the lift stopped, and Adam pulled apart the latticed screen, waving his hand forward.

"After you, Rabbi."

Santiago stepped out into the narrow walkway. The top of the towers were still under construction and there were two more facades to be built. This was a project that would last generations, the pride of Catholic Spain, perhaps the only great basilica of the modern era. Scaffolding surrounded the back part of the tower, and Santiago stood for a moment, looking out across Barcelona. His mind teemed with possibilities, like the letters of the Torah spinning before him, a kaleidoscope of universes. He sensed Adam standing close behind and Santiago could smell the residual smoke from the distinctive Gitanes cigarettes his pupil smoked.

"The Key," Adam whispered. "Where is it?"

Santiago thought of the manuscript he had sent to London a few days before, after the dream of darkness had come again. The Misshapen and the Polluted of God had come creeping from the Gates of Hell, their black bodies dark upon the earth, leaving a trail of ash behind them and laying waste to humanity. The ancient book was the hope of deliverance in the face of evil, and the only other knowledge was with the Remnant, handed down from the descendants of Jews who had kept the secret for generations. When Sofia had rejected her heritage, Santiago had become the last of his line to keep the secret. He could only hope that the daughter of his old friend would rise to the challenge he had sent her.

Looking at Adam, Santiago saw the shadow of the young man he had taught. Perhaps he might have handed the responsibility of the Remnant to Adam once. But then that one incident had changed everything, and Adam still wore the scars. A line bisected his right eye, cutting deep into his cheek, the scar tissue white against his darker Mediterranean skin.

Santiago reached out a hand and touched Adam's face, overcome with remorse.

"I failed you back then. I'm so sorry."

Adam grunted and waved his hand, dismissing the sentiment. "My scars have shaped me, Rabbi, and gave me reason to seek the Key. The Gates of Hell must be opened so judgement can fall upon those who have persecuted us all for generations." His gaze fixed on Santiago. "So tell me now, where is it? We don't have much time before the workers arrive."

Down on the street the sound of traffic had begun as the city awoke. Time had run out. Santiago breathed in deeply, tasting the air once more, inhaling the cold smell of stone.

"I'll show you," he said. "Come."

The old man shuffled around the perimeter of the tower towards an opening that led out onto a walkway between the towers. Warning signs and yellow hazard tape were stuck to the walls. Tarpaulin stretched over the opening, the edges flapping in the wind.

"I know where Sofia is," Adam said. "So don't try anything."

Santiago froze. He closed his eyes, seeing his granddaughter's face, hearing her laugh. Adam had loved her mother once, and back then Santiago had hoped they might be bound together as family. But would Adam harm Sofia now? Could he take that chance? Santiago's heart beat hard in his chest, his pulse so loud it surely echoed around the tower. He put his hand to his head, suddenly dizzy with fear, but the memory of his dream, the Misshapen turning the world to ash, made him more afraid than anything Adam could do. Sofia would be caught up in this whatever he did, and he had to trust that this next generation could finish what his own could not. He opened his eyes, resolve strengthening his voice.

"You know the Sagrada Familia is crowded with symbols – I have taught you this since you were a boy. But there is one symbol I have never shown you. It is on the head of the risen Christ. Come."

Shuffling to the tarpaulin, Santiago pulled the edge up, ducking under and emerging on edge of the roof, overlooking the gigantic statue of the risen Christ affixed to the middle of the basilica. Behind him, the spire of the Passion Tower rose into the sky, streaks of cirrus cloud above it, like scars across the blue. In front of him, the Tower of the Nativity rose above another uncompleted facade. Santiago smiled. For a moment, he was a young sculptor again, the sound of chisel on stone echoing through years of memory. For all his failures, at least he had left his mark here.

Adam stepped out behind him onto the narrow ledge, one hand gripping the low stone wall, the only barrier between them and the hundreds of feet to the courtyard below. This was the domain of angels, their words of praise to the divine carved into stone roundels at either side of the facade. And here in the center, God's risen son triumphant in glory. As a Jew, Santiago had never understood the portrayal of a physical manifestation of God, this worship of graven images that his scripture forbade. But over the years, the stone effigies had been a constant, emerging from the rock even as his own life had been carved away.

Santiago gazed out over his city, his Barcelona. He looked south, casting his mind towards Sofia, sending his granddaughter the love he had been unable to truly show her. He shuffled further out, away from the shelter of the tower. He could feel the wind now as it buffeted him, and he instinctively leaned into it as the ledge narrowed and the wall sloped lower, tapering off to nothing but a sheer drop.

"That's far enough," Adam shouted above the wind. "Where's the symbol?"

Santiago pointed across to the gigantic head of Christ, as he continued to inch towards the edge. His voice was strong now, his bearing proud.

"There is a code in this facade, if you know how to read it. You knew once, Adam, but now you've forgotten the true path. In your rage, you have betrayed your ancestors. I thought I could show you the way when you were young, but now, it's too late."

As if in slow motion, Santiago saw Adam's good eye flicker in realization of what was to come. His hand lifted from the ledge and began to reach for his Rabbi, fingers grasping for purchase. But this was the only possible end, the only way to keep the Key from Adam's dark purpose.

He would have to trust that the book would get to the last daughter of the Remnant, that she would be the right person to find the Key before Adam: that she would keep the Gates of Hell closed. With a last burst of strength, Santiago threw himself away from Adam's grasping fingers, using his momentum to leap into the air. For a moment, there was stillness. He thought the angels might catch him and bear him to safety, but then time caught up. Santiago plummeted to the ground below, his last whispered word the secret name of his God.

From the spire above, Adam looked down on the body of his Rabbi, the old man's blood running down to the feet of the bound and whipped Christ.

CHAPTER 1

THERE WERE SEVERAL SECRET entrances to the Arcane Religious Knowledge And Numinous Experience Institute, known as ARKANE. Dr Morgan Sierra preferred the one beneath St Martin-in-the-Fields church because she could grab a really good cup of black coffee on her way in. As she walked down the steps into the crypt, Morgan wondered briefly what the staff thought she did within the church hierarchy, but luckily the polite restraint of the British kept all inquiries confined to a raised eyebrow now and then.

Her steps were slow and tentative this morning, her body still recovering from the ordeal at the British Museum, when Neo-Vikings had used ritual murder in their hunt for the staff of Skara Brae. Morgan knew that she should probably take a few days off to rest, but she wanted to see the manuscript as soon as possible. Thoughts of it had been haunting her, and now she finally had time to pay attention. She had also heard that Jake Timber was finally cleared to return to active service. Morgan's stomach fluttered with anticipation at seeing him and she smiled, shaking her head at the teenage sensibility. Jake was her

ARKANE partner, but they hadn't worked together since he had been crushed by a demon in the bone church of Sedlec, his injuries putting him in a medically induced coma. She knew he would be desperate to get to work now, and she was certainly pleased to have him back.

After grabbing her coffee, Morgan ducked down a tiny side corridor in the crypt. It was filled with large metal plates with images of saints etched in their surfaces, used in the brass rubbing classes so peculiar to English school trips. Boxes of postcards were piled high towards the end of the corridor, next to what looked like a store cupboard. But the keypad and discreet retinal scanner were indications of what really lay behind.

The public face of ARKANE was academic, commenting in the media on the rise of religious fundamentalism as well as funding conservation of historical artifacts. But under Trafalgar Square, the real ARKANE had its state-of-the-art labs, a secret research center for investigating supernatural and religious mysteries across the world. London was the global hub, but most ARKANE agents worked in the field, on the trail of ancient sacred objects – working on the edge of what most would even question as reality.

Morgan swiped her identity card and bent her eye to the scanner, hearing the faint click as the door released after a few seconds. She stepped into another short corridor, the plain white walls hiding the array of equipment that verified her identity, ensuring that no unauthorized person ever breached the inner halls of ARKANE.

As she entered the elevator at the end, Morgan reflected on the first time she had come down here. Her beliefs had certainly changed since then. In her old life as a psychologist for the Israeli Defense Force and then Oxford University, she'd investigated religion from a scientific viewpoint. As an ARKANE agent, she had experienced a darker reality – a world where ancient power was used to summon the unseen, to call on evil to murder and destroy, and science played a secondary role. ARKANE stood between humanity and the abyss, and the fight was never ending. The feeling within the Institute right now was that events were escalating but then, Morgan knew that humanity had always considered itself on the edge of the End Times. Was this age truly any different?

At the bottom of the lift, Morgan walked briskly through the glass-walled corridors, heading for a private office away from the main research area. She glanced into one room as she passed, where language experts analyzed a stone tablet depicting a demon holding a sacred plant. It was from a cache of objects ARKANE had acquired on a rescue mission to the Shrine of Jonah near the occupied city of Mosul in Iraq. The academic in her longed to go and join the team working on the Assyrian artifacts from Nineveh. Access to these objects was part of the reason she had joined ARKANE, but the mysterious manuscript called to her now and she turned back down the corridor.

As she sipped the final inch of her coffee, Morgan reached the office of Martin Klein, ARKANE's Head Librarian. As the unofficial Brain of the Institute, Martin was more comfortable in the world of data and knowledge than personal interaction. He found patterns in the chaos of overwhelming information, seeing things that those more tied to traditional thinking would miss, and Morgan knew how important he was to ARKANE. He had become a friend to her and Jake as well, although she was careful to respect his need for physical distance. She knocked.

The door burst open and Martin's beaming face greeted her, a sure sign that he had discovered something interesting. His enthusiasm brimmed over and he stood bouncing on the soles of his feet like a puppy waiting to play, his roughly chopped mop of blonde hair falling into his eyes.

He pushed it away with a gesture of impatience as he waved her in.

"Come in, come in. You're going to find this manuscript fascinating."

The walls of the little office were dense with images: fantastical creatures and mathematical symbols next to formations of galaxies and calligraphic quotes from philosophers. The walls acted as a kind of working memory, a way to distract one part of Martin's brain while he delved into the deeper realms of his subconscious. The walls were repainted regularly and it seemed such a waste to lose the workings each time, but Morgan knew that Martin didn't even see them anymore, assimilating whatever he needed to learn. She could only wonder at what went on in his mind, and she was grateful that she could borrow his brain for her own personal project this time.

She walked to a white table by Martin's desk, where a leather-bound book lay propped on a wooden stand to keep the pages from bending back too far. She took the pair of thin white gloves Martin handed her so she could touch it without damaging the fragile pages. Stepping closer, Morgan opened the book randomly, the gold edges flashing in the light as she examined the diagrams, symbols and Hebrew words.

"It's a *Sefer Yetzirah*," Martin said with triumph. "The Book of Creation or Formation, supposedly written by Abraham, or more likely by the great Rabbi Akiva. It's not exactly easy reading, but it's considered to be one of the earliest extant books on Jewish esotericism. It's very exciting to have one here, I must say."

Morgan nodded, a frown on her face as she bent to the manuscript, pushing back the dark brown curls from her face in order to see more clearly. She touched a finger lightly on one page.

"There's a stain here," she murmured, pointing out a russet blotch on the edge of one page.

"Um, yes, yes," Martin was hesitant. "I have some ideas about what that might be – I've sent a sample to be tested."

Visions of the bloody murders she had witnessed in the last few days came to Morgan's mind, and she closed her eyes for a second, pushing the images away.

Opening her eyes again, she picked up a letter from the table beside the book. It had arrived in the package with the manuscript and was still unopened. Her name was on the front. The handwriting was her father's, but Leon Sierra had been dead for three years, blown apart by a suicide bomber on the number twelve bus in downtown Beersheba, Israel. Another pointless death in a struggle that most thought would never end. The letter was curious, as this package had only arrived a few days ago, even though it had been written before he died. Morgan's heart beat faster at the prospect of reading her father's words.

Martin interrupted her thoughts.

"The book is from Amsterdam, where many Jews from Spain ended up over time. It became an early center for Hebrew printing and publishing, as well as a hotbed of Kabbalism." He pushed his thin wire glasses back into place. "This particular manuscript is notable for the illustration in the front. Look."

Pulling on his own thin white gloves, Martin carefully turned the pages until the frontispiece was shown.

"This is an amulet for protection against Lilith, the Night Specter, one of the impure demons of Jewish Kabbalism. She belongs to Gamaliel, called the Polluted of God, and she kills young children unless this amulet is displayed. It's rare to see this, dare I say, superstition – in a *Sefer Yetzirah*. I wonder why it's here?" He turned a few more pages. "This is odd, too. This one page was loose, removed from the bindings but left within the book alongside your father's letter."

The page was covered in strange symbols and what

looked like a form of Hebrew prayer, but she had never seen anything like it before. Morgan's frown deepened. She picked up the brown paper wrapping that the book had come in. Her name was inked on the front in her father's sloped handwriting, but the address had been written in a different style and had clearly been added more recently.

"Where was the package sent from?"

Martin looked up from the book. "I tracked it back to a central post box in Barcelona, near El Call, the Jewish quarter of the old city. Or at least where the Jews used to live …"

His voice tailed off and his eyes flicked nervously to Morgan. Since a fire at the Grand Lodge of England when they had both narrowly avoided being burned alive, Martin had been more protective of her. Morgan appreciated the gesture, but the history of Spain's Jewish population was nothing new, repeated around Europe in those dark centuries. Based on her recent trip to Budapest, the story wasn't over yet.

"My father, Leon, was a Sephardic Jew," she explained. "The Sierras originally came from the south of Spain near Granada and left during the expulsion in 1492, when Spain united under Ferdinand and Isabella and they forced conversion, death or expulsion." She tilted her head to one side, trying to remember the details of the north-eastern area of Spain. "I think that Barcelona was mostly cleared of the Jewish population in 1391, with pogroms wiping out many of them, and then the expulsion finished off the rest. But I've heard that there's an active synagogue there, small but growing once again. Whoever posted the package must be part of that community, so they shouldn't be too hard to find."

Martin nodded. "I was able to lift a couple of partial fingerprints from the package, and I've set a search on them. Shouldn't be too long before we have some leads."

Morgan's fingers brushed the faded blue ink on the envelope, imagining her father inscribing the words years ago at his desk in Safed. His head would have been bent to the desk, his hand flowing over the page as he whispered words from the Torah or sang snatches of the Hebrew songs he loved so much. He had been a secular archaeologist earlier in life, but after she had joined the Israeli Defense Force as a psychologist, Leon had discovered his faith in the scriptural analysis of Kabbalah, a form of Jewish mysticism. Leon had practiced gematria, a way of analyzing the numeric value of words to divine meaning in their numeric equivalents. Morgan remembered him telling a story of Rabbi Ishmael from the Talmud, who watched a scribe writing sacred words on a Torah scroll:

"My son, be meticulous in your work," the Rabbi said, "for it is the work of Heaven. Should you omit one single letter, or add one too many, you would thereby destroy the whole world."

The precision of words was of primary importance to the Kabbalists, so on one level Morgan was desperate to know what the letter said. On a deeper, emotional level, the thought of opening it frightened her – knowing these would be the final words she would ever hear from her father. She took a deep breath and reached for the letter.

CHAPTER 2

Morgan opened the envelope carefully, trying not to damage the letter within. Inside, there was a single page of cream paper with her father's message on one side.

Morgan, my daughter,
I hope you never have to read this, for if you do, then you are the last of the Remnant. We have protected the location of the Key, but now we are threatened and it is in jeopardy.
It falls to you now.
Those who seek the Gates of Hell must not find the Key. It is not for us to open, for to do so will usher in the Last Days.
I love you.
Papa

As she read the words, Morgan could hear her father's voice in her ear, his breath in the air around her sweetened with the honey cake he'd loved so much. Her tears dropped onto the page, making the blue ink run a little. She wiped her eyes and dabbed at the smudge with her sleeve, not wanting to mar his precious words.

"I don't know what it means," she said, shaking her

head as she handed the letter to Martin. "He believed in the spiritual realms, but I've never heard of this Remnant, or a Key – or even the Gates of Hell, in this context. What do you think?"

Martin examined the words, his forehead creased in concentration. "Hmmm ... The Gates of Hell are usually mentioned in association with the Christian Church, not the Jewish tradition. Jesus addressed the apostle Peter, calling him the Rock on which the church would be built and the Gates of Hell would not prevail against it. But your father being Jewish, it's definitely odd. Give me some time and I'll find out about this Remnant for you."

He handed the letter back to Morgan and she laid it gently on the table. Martin was not one to shrink from a challenge. His life's work was to build the most complete database of human knowledge – not the easy stuff that Google archived, but the secrets and mysteries, the conspiracies and truths that most did not even want to know.

"He was a Kabbalist scholar in the last years of his life," Morgan said, her voice wavering as she fought back the tears that threatened.

She remembered standing in her father's little house in Safed, north of the Sea of Galilee, the last time she had seen him. Her husband Elian had been killed on the Golan Heights during a skirmish with Hezbollah, and she had traveled up there for her father's combination of love and fatalistic acceptance of God's will; his sense that nothing happened without a reason, even if that reason didn't benefit the individual directly. Morgan could never bring herself to believe as he did, but given what she had seen with ARKANE in the last few months, perhaps she was now beginning to witness that supernatural side for herself. She was aware that beneath her, in the very lowest levels of the ARKANE vault, lay the Pentecost stones and the Devil's Bible alongside other artifacts of great power. Why not add the Key to the Gates of Hell?

Morgan found herself smiling at the thought, so far from the beliefs she had entered ARKANE with not so long ago.

"Glad to see you smiling again, Morgan."

The voice was deep, with a hint of South African heritage, and Morgan turned to see Jake Timber in the doorway. He wore a blue tailored shirt that fitted his muscular body, noticeably leaner after his convalescence. Despite his recent injuries, he still moved like a powerful jungle cat as he entered the room, a beautiful predator Morgan was undeniably drawn to. She wanted to go to him, touch the corkscrew scar just above his left eyebrow, tell him how scared she had been and how glad she was to have him back. All she could do was smile more broadly.

"How you doing, Spooky?" Jake said.

Martin flushed a little at the term of endearment, the nickname Jake had bestowed upon him based on his uncanny ability to discover hidden things that no one else would have considered. Morgan knew how much Martin looked up to Jake, and that he would do anything for his friend. The three of them had made a good team in previous missions, with her and Jake out in the world, and Martin and his hacking skills their secret weapon back at base. Morgan let herself revel in the moment, three friends reunited in a brief span of calm – a rare situation and one she didn't take for granted.

"Jake, I'm so glad you're back," Martin said, a trifle stiffly. He put out a tentative hand, as if he'd learned that's what you should do when you see a male friend. Jake skillfully ignored the gesture, understanding that Martin hated physical contact. Instead, he produced a pack of colored paint markers from behind his back and put them in Martin's outstretched hand.

"These are for your wall. I found them in the therapy ward at the hospital, and thought you'd do a better job than me at using them."

Morgan's smile widened at the pleasure in Martin's face as he accepted the unusual gift. For a man with so many PhDs, he liked coloring as much as Morgan's little niece, Gemma.

"I don't have anything for you," Jake said, turning to Morgan. "Sorry about that, but perhaps I can keep you company on your next mission. It sounds like you've been having way too much fun without me."

His amber eyes darkened and Morgan recognized the undercurrent in his words.

"You didn't miss much, to be honest," she said. "And it's been no fun without you."

But her words hid reality, for if Morgan was honest, Jake had missed a lot and she had definitely changed while he had been in hospital. She thought of her hunt across Egypt for the Ark of the Covenant, the labyrinth under Budapest, and the extraordinary abilities of Blake Daniel in the halls of the British Museum as Neo-Vikings wreaked havoc in central London. Would she and Jake be able to return to the trust they had previously established as partners since he had missed so much? Had she become too independent in his absence, too used to working alone?

"What's this book then?" Jake asked, breaking the tension. "New mission?" He walked to the table. "It's always a manuscript, isn't it? I wonder if in the future, ARKANE agents will find old tablets or laptops and regard them as we do these objects."

Morgan handed him her father's letter. "It's not a mission," she said. "It's more of a personal investigation right now. The book was sent by my father along with this note."

Jake raised his eyebrow, the corkscrew scar twisting with his surprise.

"But your father is …"

"Dead, yes, no need to step lightly around that fact."

Morgan turned back to the pages of the book. "I can read some of the text, but the meaning is obscure although it must be something to do with the Gates of Hell."

Jake shook his head in mock resignation. "Gates of Hell? You really take me to the most fun places."

Morgan smiled again, and she realized that she had missed this. Jake's sense of humor was part of what she loved about working at ARKANE. He made life-threatening situations far more attractive.

Martin's computer chimed, a complex bell fragment that left the listener wondering what the missing note was, like a question mark in the air.

"Must be the fingerprints from the package." Martin bent to the computer screen. "I'm surprised they're back so quickly."

He scanned the screen, eyes widening, his already pale face becoming whiter as he read what was there.

CHAPTER 3

MARTIN STRAIGHTENED, HIS FACE stricken.

"What is it?" Morgan asked as she and Jake moved to join him by the screen. Martin instinctively moved away from them as he explained.

"The fingerprints on the package belong to a man found dead this morning at the base of the Sagrada Familia basilica in Barcelona. The police report indicates suicide. It seems that he jumped from one of the towers."

Morgan looked down at the face of Santiago Pereira, a stonemason, sculptor and a Jew of Barcelona. She grasped her father's letter tightly in her hand.

"Jumped, perhaps," she said. "Or maybe he was pushed. It's too much of a coincidence. Either way, I have to go there. Martin, can you call Marietti and say I'm on my way up? I need some time out for a personal trip."

Jake reached out a hand as Morgan turned towards the doorway. His fingers were warm on her bare skin, his latent strength evident in just this one touch.

"Want some company?" he asked, and there was a deeper question in his amber eyes.

Morgan hesitated, part of her wanting to keep her

father, her family, partitioned away from ARKANE. After all, they had been willing to risk her sister and niece during the fires of Pentecost. She thought of the end of that day, of watching the ashes smolder alongside Jake, how their fingers had entwined in the sunrise.

She nodded. "I could use some help with Marietti actually. I'm pretty sure he has us earmarked for something else."

Jake chuckled. "Yeah, right. A mysterious Jewish manuscript that might lead us to the Gates of Hell? Marietti won't be able to resist this."

Morgan turned back at the doorway. "Actually Martin, I'll take the letter and that extra page of the manuscript. It must have been kept separate for a reason. I'll try to figure it out en route to Spain."

Martin carefully folded the page and put it into the envelope with the letter, handing it to her.

"You two go safe now," he said.

***

Director Elias Marietti's office was in the public-facing building of ARKANE, several stories above ground with a window that looked across Trafalgar Square to Nelson's Column and the Fourth Plinth, an art space currently hosting a bright blue cockerel. Marietti was staring out towards the National Gallery as Morgan and Jake entered the office, his back slightly hunched, shoulders tight with strain.

As he turned, the light from the window illuminated the white in his hair and Morgan noticed that he seemed to have aged recently. The creases in his forehead had deepened and his eyes were heavy lidded, bags of purple under them like bruises as the shadows played across his strong features. She knew that Marietti had protected the secrets of ARKANE for many years, but she wondered whether something new had caused this recent change in the Director's features. Now, however, was not the time to ask.

"Martin told me about the book and the letter, Morgan." Marietti was always gruff and to the point; today was no different. "What do you hope to find if you go to Barcelona? We have too much to do here right now. I need you both." His eyes flicked to Jake. "There are things I haven't told either of you yet. Things that concern all of us."

There was a challenge in Marietti's eyes, as if he wanted to hammer the world into submission and the members of his team were his blunt instruments. Morgan strode into the center of the room, leaving Jake in the doorway. This was her fight, and she knew Jake's allegiance would be tested. After all, Marietti was his mentor, the man who had recruited him into ARKANE years ago.

"There will always be something going on," she said. "You told me yourself that our fight will never end, and I left the manuscript alone to investigate the staff of Skara Brae because you were concerned about the threat of Ragnarok. I almost died on that island, you know that." She hesitated, unsure of the tone she wanted to use. "Whatever you say, I'm going to Barcelona. My father wrote that letter to me and I need to know why Santiago Pereira sent the book and why he died. The Gates of Hell are probably just a metaphor, an old man's fantasy, so I might only be a few days. But I *am* going."

Marietti was silent, turning to look at the oil painting on the wall, his face in momentary contemplation. Every time Morgan had been in the office, there was a different painting on the wall, courtesy of Marietti's love of art and his special relationship with the creative establishment in London. This painting showed the corpse of a young girl laid out upon flagstones in the snow, surrounded by doves and pigeons. Her dark hair was spread like a nimbus around her face, her red skirt entangled with her legs. Her breasts were bare and ropes were wrapped around her wrists, as she lay at the foot of the cross she had been crucified on. It should have been a violent image, evoking horror at the girl's murder, but the snow lent it a peaceful aura, drawing the viewer into a moment of calm.

"It's St Eulalia," Marietti said, "as portrayed by John William Waterhouse in the Pre-Raphaelite style. She was a saint of Barcelona, tortured and crucified for her beliefs during the persecution of Christians under Diocletian in the third century." He turned, his eyes boring into Morgan's. "The Jews have not been the only ones to suffer in that city, so be careful what you search for, Morgan. You might just find it."

Morgan stood unmoving, meeting his gaze. Her heart pounded as she challenged his authority, but she would not back down. After a moment, Marietti sat down heavily at his desk with a sigh.

"Alright, then. But you only have three days to get the answers you want. Jake, you go too and make sure you're both back next week."

Morgan nodded and turned back towards the door. Jake walked out in front of her, heading for the elevator. As she reached the doorway, she thought she heard another whisper.

"Because we're running out of time."

She turned briefly to see Marietti with his eyes closed, a look of agony on his face. A jolt of concern made her wonder if they were doing the right thing; if perhaps they should stay and work on whatever was worrying the Director. But then she thought of her father's handwriting, his desperate note and the crime scene photos of Santiago Pereira. Resolve hardening, she left Marietti to his contemplation.

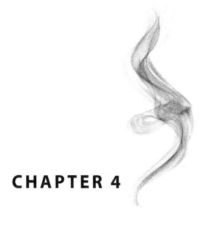

CHAPTER 4

PACING UP AND DOWN the length of his library, Adam Kadmon whispered prayers under his breath, entreating the divine to show him the next step. It had seemed as if his quest had been close to completion only a few days before, but the old man had been stronger than expected. Santiago's death had left questions unanswered and Adam no longer had any hope of finding the Key unless he followed the path of the coded numbers left by the Remnant. It would take longer, but there was still time before the alignment of planets brought the dark world closer to this one, the veil between them thin enough to pierce with the Key.

He heard a laugh outside, and a splash of water in the pool below. Adam went to the window and looked down to see one of his men by the fountain, flirting with a girl from the kitchen. Their faces reflected an age-old courtship dance that had been repeated here for generations. His family's ancestral home in Seville was nestled in the midst of the old town, a tiny entranceway hiding the palatial interior. Modeled in the Moorish style, the pool in the center of the house was open to the sky. The rest of the building surrounded it, protecting this peaceful heart in the bustling city.

Adam's fingers touched his own face as he looked down unseen on the flirting couple. He had loved but once, and still wore the scar. The girl below laughed and Adam heard his past echo in the sound. He hardened his heart – there were more satisfying things than earthly love. He slammed the shutters of the library, banging them closed. Outside he heard the couple silence and imagined them walking swiftly away from the courtyard, never daring to look back.

He paused by wooden shelves that stretched to the ceiling, full of books on the history of Spain and manuscripts of Kabbalah wisdom. Knowledge had no inherent morality, and Adam had learned that good and evil were in the eye of the beholder. He had been collecting these books for years, gorging himself on the pain and suffering of the people of this land. Now, it was time to act.

Adam pulled down the book that had led him to this quest so many years ago. It was a handbook of the Inquisition, a documentation of the torture that had been inflicted on his ancestors, the *Conversos*, the Jews who had been forcibly converted to Christianity and then persecuted anyway. Tortured on the rack, broken on the wheel and burned at the stake at the orders of an empire whose end must come. Some might say that Spain was secular now, that religion was secondary to the pursuit of money and pleasure, but religion still lay at its heart. This world needed cleansing. It was past time.

Santiago's pity still jarred him, and he remembered the old man's face as he'd jumped. There had been peace in his eyes, as there had been when he had taught so many years ago. In those early days, Santiago had taught Adam the ways of Kabbalah mysticism that were approved and sanctioned, aimed at a higher purpose. But as Adam had dabbled at the edges, where the white-hot truth of the Torah melted into ivory and then in shades towards black, he had discovered Jewish demonology and caught a glimpse of the other side.

The black ink of the Torah letters had appeared as a deep well against the white page. In his mind, he had tipped over and fallen into the pool of pitch. As a teenager he had been mocked for his slight frame and bookish ways, but all of that had fallen away when he perceived this other realm. It became an addictive retreat as the bullying intensified. He remembered Santiago's face when he spoke of what he saw, the Rabbi shaking his head as he listened. Adam's voice had faltered, doubt flooding him as his mentor had spoken of the thin line that a righteous man must walk. He told of Jacob's ladder, and the different worlds that existed closer to God, where the air was thin and angels could walk the earth. But there were also darker realms, where the body was heavy and dense and where demons roamed. Those who could see through the veil could perceive both extremes, but the true Kabbalist must gather up the fragments of light from the broken vessels and restore them to God, leaving the darkness behind. He had made a decision then to follow Santiago's path of light … until the day the other boys had come for him.

Adam pulled his Gitanes cigarettes from his pocket with slightly shaking hands. He lit one and inhaled deeply, allowing the smoke to permeate his lungs as he regained control. He walked to the oversize table where he had laid out the astronomical maps, the pages of calculations he had pored over for years now. In just over two days' time, at exactly 1:02 a.m., Mars, Earth and the Sun would align. Although this event was relatively regular, happening every 778 years, this occasion would be followed by four dark red "blood moon" lunar eclipses, a highly unusual Tetrad that had coincided with extraordinary religious events throughout history. One had occurred as the Jews were expelled from Spain in the fifteenth century, and Adam was determined that this event would rectify that injustice and avenge his ancestors.

"The sun shall be turned into darkness, and the moon into blood, before the great and the terrible day of the Lord comes," Adam whispered, quoting the words from the book of Joel.

He gathered up one of the maps, rolling it into a tight cylinder, and walked to the end of the great hall, his footsteps echoing on the polished marble. He paused in front of a wooden table with a large square box set upon it, carved with symbols of the occult. Above it was his most precious possession, a painting of Blanca Pereira, capturing the beauty of her youth.

When he had first met the Rabbi's only daughter, he had been an awkward teenager with a devout love of the Torah. He had thought to win her through her father's favor, but she had fallen for the handsome, guitar-playing Javier Rueda. Javier had played on his good looks and charm, a mean bully with the face of an angel and the smile of an innocent. Adam remembered the night when Javier and his gang of local boys had cornered him in a ruined building site, back when he had been called Luis – a name he rejected as stigmatized now.

The boys had taunted him, pushing him between them, their blows becoming rougher until he lay on the floor, hands wrapped around his head as they kicked him. He could still feel the pain and the cold of the stone beneath, as he wet himself in fear. The years fell away and he was back there, reliving the shame of it.

"Look at the little son of a *puta*," Javier spat at him. "How pathetic."

The other boys were drawn in by the taunting, wanting to bloody their hands. Wanting to be men. The stink of piss filled the air and Luis felt shame wash over him, his fear amplified by humiliation.

Javier drew a knife, hefting it from hand to hand, his eyes flashing with desire to see blood welling. He gestured to two of the bigger boys.

"Hold him down," he said, advancing.

"No, please," Luis cried. "I'll do whatever you want."

"I want you to stop coveting what you can never have." Two boys held an arm each, kneeling down and pressing Luis' body into the dirt. Another sat on his legs, pinioning him. "Stop ogling my girl," Javier said. "You're not worthy to look at her, and as punishment, I'll make sure you never look again."

The knife had a polished silver blade. It reflected the hate in Javier's eyes as he slashed it down, once, twice and then again. A white-hot, burning pain seared across the side of Luis' face, and it was as if his eyeball exploded. He screamed, thrashing against the boys who held him down. With his other eye, Luis could see the excitement in Javier's face, the almost sexual arousal at the sight of blood and broken flesh.

Javier raised the knife once more, but shouts from the perimeter of the building stayed his hand. The boys looked towards the noise and their demeanor changed. Javier bent closer.

"Keep that other eye away from my girl."

"We've gotta go," one of the boys whispered urgently. "There's someone coming."

Javier nodded and they ran off, leaving Luis curled up on the ground, his hands over his ruined eye. The demolition man who had disturbed the attack took Luis to hospital, but they hadn't been able to save his eye. As the pain-relief drugs had taken him into a realm of visions and swirling mist, Luis had made a decision. He would say nothing of the boys who had done this. No one would believe his word against the favored sons of the town anyway, but he would have his revenge on Javier in the promise of the Misshapen, the Devourers and the dark Kabbalah.

That night, as he lay in a drug-fueled dream, Luis had wrestled with the angel as Jacob once had. The dark angel was powerfully muscled, with burning skin and horns. It forced his head towards a pit, twisting his arm until Luis' face was near the edge.

"Open this gate and the world will be devoured," the dark angel had rasped. "Creation will be remade. The one you love will be returned to you and those you despise will be torn asunder."

He had glimpsed a whirl of oblivion in the pit, a riot of crawling things that made him both shiver and marvel at the power he might hold one day. Luis couldn't forget those words. His quest since that day had been to open the gate and let whatever was beneath into this realm.

He had drawn the dark angel, sketching its misshapen features, its mouth dripping with the blood of innocents. A thrill of the forbidden had sparked in his mind, a way to better his teacher, a way to avenge his pain. A way to finally win the heart of the girl he loved. He had become Adam Kadmon after that – a new man with purpose.

***

Emerging from the memories of the past, Adam looked up at Blanca's painting, her captured perfection unmarred. She had been despoiled by the man he most hated, Javier Rueda, who married her and became Santiago's favored pupil. Her eyes looked out at him from inside the painting.

"I'm sorry," he whispered, guilt twisting his guts, a punishment for his own failure. Adam reached out a hand and gently caressed her cheek, the blush pink a terrible reminder of what he had lost.

"I will not fail this time, Blanca. I will find the Key, open the gate and you will be returned to me, as the dark one promised."

Adam reached out and caressed the top of the wooden

box, tracing the symbols. A smile danced upon his lips as he considered what was inside and how the world turned again in the circle of his revenge. There had been a daughter of the union between Blanca and Javier – Santiago's granddaughter, Sofia. Those beyond the Gates of Hell required a sacrifice, starved as they were of blood to sustain them, and her death would also finish the line of Rueda.

Footsteps echoed in the hall beyond the library and then one of Adam's bodyguards entered, his heavily tattooed features sinister in the half light.

"We're ready for you, sir."

Adam rose to his feet, his face grim with determination.

"Take this box to the plane, and send someone to clean up the Sagrada Familia. We have much to do tonight."

CHAPTER 5

THE PRIVATE PLANE FLEW down the east coast of northern Spain and then banked towards the west on the approach to Barcelona. Morgan looked out the window at the sparkling Balearic Sea, the water a deep blue in the afternoon sun. She could almost feel the cool touch of salt waves on her skin and it reminded her of trips with her father to the Israeli coast, on the opposite side of the Mediterranean. He had loved the water, spending hours swimming with her in the waves, ducking under and throwing her up so she could do somersaults before landing in the blue. He had chosen to live away from the ocean as his love of Kabbalah had grown, moving to the hillside town of Safed, a place of scholars. After that, Morgan had barely gone swimming, shunning the swagger of the Tel Aviv strip and with no time to escape further afield. She and Elian had always worked so hard, never realizing how short their time would be together. He would have loved this ocean too.

"Have you been here before?" Jake asked, interrupting her thoughts. He leaned over to look out her window at the city, and Morgan was acutely aware of this living man, forcing aside the memories of her dead husband.

"Only for a conference years ago," she said, relishing the feel of Jake pressed against her. "I didn't see much of the city then, but I did devour the guidebook." She pointed down to the port area. "That long strip of sand north of the port is Barceloneta Beach, popular with locals and tourists alike. I had some marvelous paella there once …"

"Not sure we'll get much time for the beach on this trip," Jake grinned wickedly. "Maybe another time. I could use a tan after way too long in hospital."

The thought brought to Morgan's mind the physical scars he must have from the multitude of operations. Unwillingly, she found herself led then to the scars she could never see – mental scars he must still carry. Could she trust Jake if it came to another physical threat?

"What's that area?" Jake asked, pointing down to a hill with a number of large buildings nestled upon it and a cable car that slanted down towards the beach.

"Montjuïc – home to many of the city's great art collections. They hosted the 1992 Olympics there, which was also when they revamped the whole city. Not sure we'll get there either, though."

***

The plane banked around and down to the airport and they were soon in a taxi heading for the Sagrada Familia basilica.

"I love these old buildings," Jake said, as the taxi lurched around the Barcelona streets, winding its way in and out of tall blocks, dodging the motorcyclists. "Check out those balconies."

He pointed up and Morgan leaned across to see classical caryatid figures carved into stone pillars supporting a green-edged balcony above. Red flowers spilled over from a tiny garden and a tabby cat lay trapped in a sunbeam, licking its paws. This close, Morgan could smell Jake's skin, clean and fresh with a hint of dark spice; she wanted to bury her head against his chest. She pulled back quickly at the thought.

"We have nothing like these in South Africa," Jake continued, oblivious to her reaction. "I'd love to live in one of these flats overlooking the ocean, up where the breeze is fresh, but still in the heart of it all."

A moment of silence passed before Morgan spoke.

"I have a little house in Oxford," she said. "It's more of an occasional sun trap than breezy, but that's more appropriate for the British weather." Jake said nothing, waiting for her to continue. "I have a cat too. Shmi is totally spoiled by my neighbor, who looks after him most of the time. I shouldn't really have him anymore – I suppose I should find him another home, but he's independent enough. When I'm back he makes me feel as if I should just stop all this running around and adventuring. Do you ever feel like that?"

Jake sighed softly, his expression serious. "I didn't stop thinking about it lying in that hospital bed. I knew that I had a choice. I could leave ARKANE with plenty of benefits and buy myself a place somewhere, retire from this crazy life." He turned and looked at Morgan. "But I'd be so bored in about a week, and so would you."

She laughed. "Damn it, but you're right. Maybe we just need a weekend off."

"Maybe you do," Jake said, "but I'm itching to get into your mystery."

The taxi turned into the square in front of the basilica and they caught their first glimpse of the Temple Expiatori de la Sagrada Família.

"Wow," Jake said, as he got out of the car. Morgan followed and looked up at the four towering spires of the Passion facade that stretched into the blue sky above them. Imagined and begun by the obsessive genius architect and sculptor Antoni Gaudí in 1883, the basilica was still under construction after more than a hundred years. The towers swelled with organic grace, betraying Gaudí's disdain for straight lines, finding none in nature. Instead, he combined the Gothic and curvilinear Art Nouveau forms in his creation, directing the gaze towards Heaven but also tinged with a sense of fun. The four spires, representing four of the apostles, were topped with starbursts outlined in bobbles of gold. Words from the liturgy burst from the stone high above them – words that were almost out of sight of the crowd below, where only the angels could see them. Morgan wondered what it would be like to fall so far.

Beneath the spires, a gigantic sloping portico was tethered to the ground with stone pillars like the trunks of sequoia trees stretching to meet at the center. Beneath it was the Passion facade, inspired by Gaudí, but decorated by Josep Subirachs in the mid-twentieth century. The angular sculptures portrayed the story of Christ's passion in a tableau of torture and death, watched over by a man with Gaudí's face, a tribute from Subirachs to the master who had breathed life into this glorious work.

There were cranes on both sides of the building, and the cacophony of an active building site. The metallic thunk of tools on scaffolding, the sound of drills and the tap of chisels on stone. It was exhilarating to see something with so grand a vision, driven by a belief that spanned several lifetimes to completion.

Morgan followed Jake into the forecourt before the Passion facade, and spotted a *policía* from the Guàrdia Urbana de Barcelona scanning the crowds, as if he was waiting for someone. Martin had arranged for them to meet a police officer here in order to get a briefing on the case, so she caught the man's eye as they walked over.

"*Bienvenidos* to Barcelona," the man said, hand outstretched, as they approached. "I'm Inspector Ramon Perez. Your colleague told me of your interest in this case, and of course, I'm happy to share our information with you." Morgan caught a flash of concern in Ramon's expression as he spoke. She wondered briefly what strings Martin had pulled to get them in here. Being with ARKANE certainly had its benefits in terms of access.

"Where was the victim found?" Morgan asked, after the customary introductions.

Ramon pointed a meter away from them, just outside the overarching stone portico. A dark stain could still be seen on the ground, and Morgan shuddered a little as she remembered the crime scene photos of Santiago's smashed body on the gravel path.

"We think he jumped," Ramon said. "There's no evidence of anyone else being here. We've also discovered that Pereira had been forcibly retired from the basilica team a few months ago due to his age. Understandably, after so many years working in and around the basilica, he was depressed. His wife and daughter died years ago, he was estranged from his granddaughter and alone. So, it's not surprising really."

Morgan nodded as she turned to consider the detail of the facade, with the huge statue of the bound and whipped Christ at its center. Above the post of torture, there were several levels portraying aspects of the Passion story. The Last Supper was being eaten alongside Christ dragging his cross, watched impassively by muscled soldiers in armor, the crucifixion in its central position. She noticed a four-by-four square chart, like a Sudoku puzzle, carved into the stone next to the betrayal of Christ by Judas.

Her father had always made a game of adding up the numbers on license plates whenever they drove anywhere, and as he became obsessed with gematria and numerology, the results had taken on new meaning. Morgan quickly added up the first line: 33. Then the next, which was the same again. She realized that all the rows, columns and diagonals added up to 33, the age of Christ when he was executed. There were also two numbers repeated twice: 10 and 14. When the four were added together, the total was 48. According to the numerical order of the Roman alphabet, it was the gematria for INRI, Iesus Nazarenus Rex Iudaeorum, the text inscribed upon the cross of the crucifixion. Morgan wondered what other codes were hidden in this magnificent house of God.

"Did Santiago work on this part of the basilica?" She squinted up at the details of the building in the rays of the afternoon sun, noting the inverted face of Christ with his vicious crown of thorns.

Ramon nodded. "He apparently worked here for most his life, only taking a year or so off to help with reconstruction work at the Mezquita in Córdoba. He worked alongside the sculptor Subirachs in the late 1960s, so perhaps he wanted to die here by his life's work."

"Perhaps …" Morgan said, walking closer to the side of the building, where Jake bent to examine a low metal door. He turned on her approach.

"It's fascinating," he said quietly. Morgan took in the riot of symbolism displayed there, words that scattered across the door in shades of green and purple. With curves and patterns, medals and roundels, it seemed to be so jam-packed with meaning, there was no room for understanding.

"I hope it's not for us to fathom," Morgan said under her breath so Ramon couldn't hear. "We only have the weekend."

"We should go inside now," Ramon said, interrupting them, clearly aware of the late hour of the day. The Catalan were renowned for their acute sense of work/life balance and the focus on what was really important. "I've halted the tourists so we can go up the tower alone, and of course, you need to have a quick look inside the nave." A sense of pride echoed through his last words, and his back straightened. Morgan appreciated Ramon's love for the basilica and his city, recognizing that it was how she felt about Jerusalem.

"Of course," she said. "Please show us around."

Ramon led the way through a great pair of double doors, words from the Bible in Spanish crammed into the space, some words picked out in greater relief. Above them, Morgan noticed the Greek letters for alpha and omega, the first and the last. She traced the letters on the door, the lines so familiar to her. She had been brought up in Israel as a secular Jew, but because her mother was a Christian, Morgan was not actually Jewish and had never converted. She felt at home in the plain synagogues her father frequented, but the depth of beauty in these graven images struck her here. She turned from the door to see Jake a few steps ahead with Ramon. As he entered the main nave of the church, Jake looked up and Morgan saw his jaw drop.

CHAPTER 6

Jake turned and beckoned, his eyes wide with wonder. Morgan followed them through and walked into the main nave of the church, a wide smile dawning on her face as she gazed up at the fantastical architecture. An elvish kingdom, a fantasy forest of marble pillars rose from the floor separating into branches that supported the high coffered ceiling in Gaudí's unique design. The impression was organic, as if the earth had grown up into this space, reaching to meet high above them in a forest canopy. It was light and airy and Morgan could imagine Cirque du Soleil performers in here, leaping and twisting in praise to the Creator. It was a far cry from the austerity of Gothic architecture and somber darkness of most great European cathedrals. This was all light and pattern, rippling in the evening sun. The palette of color moved across gentle pinks and blues from the Montjuïc stone to darker granite and the almost burgundy of Iranian porphyry. Light streamed in through multi-hued windows of rainbow glass, all circles and curves, caressing the flagstones as light would ripple through the forest leaves.

Those who worshipped the pagan gods of nature would

feel at home here, Morgan thought. The only obvious nod to Christianity was the figure of Christ on the cross under a parachute above the simple altar. But it was dwarfed by the sheer overwhelming beauty of the stone trunks and intricate design of the basilica, lifting the worshippers' spirits above their earthly pain.

Morgan remembered sitting with Jake in the darkness of St Mark's Basilica in Venice just a few months ago. He had asked about her beliefs then, and the shadows had given her permission to share. She had told him of glimpsing God under the waters when scuba diving, looking up at sunbeams through waving fronds of giant kelp, floating in her own natural cathedral. This place made her feel the same way, a buoyancy of spirit, and she could see why Santiago Pereira could have worked here even as a Jew. It wasn't God who created these distinctions between religions, only man, and the sense of something truly ineffable could certainly be found here.

Jake turned back to her, grinning like a schoolboy, his delight evident. It was as if the demon-inflicted wounds had disappeared and he was whole again. Morgan captured the moment in her mind, grateful that the appreciation of beauty could still punctuate life in surprising moments, though the wonder never lasted long.

"Come then," Ramon said, walking towards a side door. "This way and we can ascend the tower."

***

The lift clunked its way to the summit and soon they stood looking out over the city from on high. It brought to mind the biblical story of Jesus tested in the wilderness by the devil, taken to the summit of a mountain and offered all the kingdoms of the world if only he would bow his head to worship. He had been encouraged to throw himself from the highest point of the temple, to demonstrate that he truly was God's son and that the angels would come and lift him up. Morgan looked down over the wall of the tower, feeling a little dizzy, on the edge of vertigo. Sweat prickled under her arms. Behind her natural fear there was a compulsion to feel the sensation of flying, of falling.

"We live in such a beautiful world," Jake whispered, his amber eyes reflecting the dying rays of the sun. It seemed his near-death experience had given him a new love of life and Morgan was grateful for his enthusiasm. It was counterpoint to her dread at possibly discovering something about her father that would tarnish his image in her mind. He had been her hero, and there was nothing that he could do wrong in her eyes. But would this trip alter the memories she had of him?

Ramon pulled aside a tarpaulin and pointed to a shallow ledge beyond.

"We think he jumped from there. There would have been no reason to go out otherwise and the tarpaulin was found flapping in the wind, when it should have been tethered shut."

"Is there any security camera footage?" Jake asked.

"No." Ramon shook his head. "Not here, but cameras show Pereira entering the main gate not long before his death was reported. There are places where the cameras don't monitor parts of the perimeter, so just because he came in alone doesn't mean there wasn't anyone else here. But the body showed no signs of a struggle, only injuries from the impact." Ramon crossed himself. "He would have died quickly."

Morgan looked out at the stone walkway. There was nothing to indicate what had happened, nothing that might direct them to why Santiago Pereira went off that ledge. She stepped out and walked towards the end, where the wall sloped off towards the air of the city.

"Careful," Ramon said, his voice tinged with concern.

Morgan stopped only inches from the edge. She understood the pull of oblivion, the attraction of finality. The rays of the sun illuminated the gold on the statue of the risen Christ below her and the reflection glinted, as if there was something offsetting the smooth surface. She squinted a little and saw a symbol carved on the back of the statue's head. It looked like a similar grid to the Subirachs square below, but she couldn't be sure.

As Morgan bent towards it to look closer, she heard a whisper on the wind, a sound she recognized from her days in the Israeli military, distinctly out of place in the cooling air of the Barcelona evening. Her eyes flicked up and away from the cathedral, widening as she saw in a split second what would happen next.

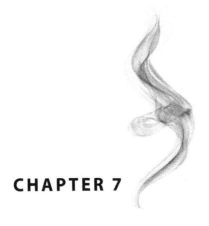

CHAPTER 7

MORGAN TURNED AND TOOK one more quick step before leaping towards Jake and Ramon, pushing them to the hard stone floor as she rolled inside the tower. The air exploded behind her with a whoosh of hot air. Debris showered down as the tower shook from the impact and chunks of rock crashed from the tower onto the forecourt as masonry and sculpture collapsed. A chorus of screams and shouts rose from below as injured tourists ran for cover.

Ramon pulled his radio from his belt, crouching on the floor of the tower as he spoke rapidly in Spanish, his police-issued Walther P99 pistol in his hand.

Morgan sat up, her ears ringing.

"RPG?" Jake coughed his question as debris settled around them.

Morgan nodded, her face grave. She stood up, brushed the stone dust from her clothes, and went to the ruined doorway, tentatively peeking out in case of further attack. The statue had been obliterated, the impact precise and the surrounding damage substantial enough to add several more years to Gaudí's multigenerational schedule. The symbol so briefly glimpsed had been thoroughly erased.

She looked out towards the direction that the rocket had come from. The area was dense with housing and it could have been fired from any of those rooftops or high windows. Whoever had fired it would be long gone by the time the address could be triangulated. Morgan was sure that the statue had been the target, the rocket small enough not to do truly extensive damage. This was not terrorism. It was intended to cover up whatever symbol Santiago Pereira had carved up here, and it made Morgan even more curious to follow his trail.

"Santiago's death couldn't have been a suicide if someone is cleaning up," she said. "We need to get to his flat quickly, in case there's more evidence to destroy."

It took only minutes to get down from the tower, and Ramon radioed for a car to meet them by the gate. The ground floor of the basilica was chaos, with injured tourists triaged on site by medical staff and a full-scale evacuation of the area underway. Some people were silent, eyes wide as they clutched their children's hands, walking as fast as possible away from the building. Others chattered nervously in Spanish, eyes darting around at backpacks as if they suspected who was responsible. The ever-present threat of terrorism fed the panic, memories of the Madrid 2004 bombings coming to the fore, when simultaneous explosions on the train system had killed 191 people and wounded 1800. The panic was almost palpable in the air and it would only take another loud bang for this crowd to stampede.

In the midst of the throng, Morgan caught sight of an old woman standing absolutely still in the forecourt, her gaze fixed on the crucified figure of Jesus above. Her lips moved in swift prayer, her fingers clicking through the rosary beads as she called out to her God.

The click of cameras and whirr of cell phones could

be heard as the wail of sirens grew ever louder. Police and security shouted directions as they tried to evacuate people away from the area where masonry might fall. The usual building-site noise had stopped, to be replaced by the sounds of an explosion aftermath, a cacophony that Morgan knew only too well from Israel. Back in her own country, she would have expected a second bomb, one that targeted those who came to help the injured. But this was different. This was a very specific attack. The question was whether they had already finished cleaning up the rest of Santiago's life.

***

With the siren wailing and tires screeching around corners, it was only a few minutes' drive through the back streets of Barcelona to the Plaça Nova, where vibrant shopping streets merged into the Barri Gòtic, the heart of the medieval city. Ramon pulled the police car over at the edge of the square, overlooked by the towering cathedral – slightly disappointing after the eccentric grandeur of the Sagrada Familia basilica. Ramon spoke with the officer who had accompanied them, and the man nodded, getting out and joining the group.

"This is as close as we can get with a car," Ramon said. "We have to walk into El Call. The word means alleyway, and you'll see why in just a minute."

Ramon walked swiftly into the maze of tightly wound streets, so narrow that most of the area was pedestrianized. Morgan began to jog and Jake loped next to her, his long legs striding to keep up. The buildings surrounding them made a labyrinth of little shops, doorways that opened into secret courtyards, and tiny flats that clung to the edges of history. Restaurants and bars opened late here, and Morgan glanced into a tea shop as they passed, the smell of jasmine dispersing into the streets.

It was darker now, and the looming buildings prevented the last rays of sun from penetrating the tiny lanes. Morgan thought of the persecuted Jews, hunted down and massacred here, their blood mingling with the rain. Civilization was only a thin veneer over man's more animal nature.

Round another corner, Ramon stopped in front of a metal door with four call bells for the flats above. A mezuzah was hammered into the wall next to it, a simple ivory box containing a piece of parchment inscribed with verses from Deuteronomy, the prayer of *Shema Yisrael*. Ramon pointed down another side street.

"The synagogue of Barcelona is just over there. It's actually tiny but it's at least functional these days. It was bought in the 1990s after extensive research and opened to the public in 2002, six hundred years after the last Jews had been emptied from the city." Ramon shook his head as he pulled out a key. "Amazing to think of its restoration after all this time. Apparently, Santiago Pereira helped with the conservation, bringing his stonemason skills back into the local community."

Ramon opened the little door, indicating in rapid Spanish that the other officer remain at the street entrance to the flat. The officer nodded and took out his radio, finger ready on the emergency call button.

Morgan and Jake followed Ramon up several flights of stairs into a tiny one-bedroom flat nestled in the eaves of the building, with skylights that made the place seem bigger than it really was. As Morgan stepped inside, she had a flash of sensory memory. The air smelled of cedar wood and old scrolls, like her father's place in Safed. This was a scholar's abode, belonging to a Rabbi, a teacher of the Torah. The main room was plain with a tiny kitchenette and a single bed that doubled as a sofa. There was a cupboard with a few clothes and a hanging tool stand with pockets for the implements of a sculptor. She quickly realized that this room held no real interest for someone consumed with mysticism. It was the hub for his physical body, but the real Santiago, the Rabbi obsessed with symbols, was elsewhere.

Morgan walked through into the room beyond. It was here she found a deeper sense of the man who had sent her the *Sefer Yetzirah*. Shelves lined the walls with the Torah, Talmud and Rabbinic teachings stacked neatly. On a plain wooden desk, there was a scroll rolled out to display several columns of Hebrew text. A notebook lay open next to it, with the handwritten etchings of a man obsessed by the words of his God. Morgan could sense echoes of her father here in the familiar setup of the Torah scholar. Santiago would have sat here for hours, deepening his consciousness and sinking into a trance state through the repetition of prayer and meditation on the words of God, for in each of those words lay a world within a world.

"The scene has been processed already," Ramon said. He walked in behind her and pulled a couple of pairs of sterile gloves from his bag. "You can wear these and go ahead and look through his things. Pereira's wife and daughter were killed in a car accident several years ago. Santiago was in the car too, but he was thrown free. There's a granddaughter, Sofia, a flamenco dancer in Granada, but there's no indication of any contact with her for at least a year. We're still trying to track her down to notify her of his death."

Morgan pulled on the gloves and leafed through the notebook on the desk. Santiago's Hebrew scrawl consisted of musings on the meaning of verses, and gematria equivalents for a section of Ezekiel, the vision of the living creatures emerging from a fiery whirlwind. There were doodles on some pages, stylized letters but nothing specific about the *Sefer Yetzirah*. At the back of the book, there was another sketch. It was a black pencil drawing of a skeleton, its mouth open in a scream, its body shaped into a key design. Morgan frowned. Could this represent the Key they sought? Was it real, or figurative? There was another four-by-four square grid beneath it, the numbers different from the ones on Subirachs' square. Had this been the carving on the back of the statue?

A hoarse shout came from downstairs and then a single gunshot. Morgan started, turning her head at the noise. Ramon whipped his pistol out, pointing it at the entrance to the flat, his face stricken at the fate of his fellow officer. He pulled his police baton from his belt, hands shaking a little, and passed it to Jake. They waited on either side of the front door for whoever might emerge from the stairwell.

"Hurry, Morgan," Jake whispered.

She tucked the notebook into the inside pocket of her jacket, looking around quickly for anything else that could indicate what the symbol on the statue had been. On a little table close to the ark where Santiago kept his Torah scroll, Morgan noticed a silver photo frame. In it were three generations of Pereiras, snapped in one happy moment several years ago. Santiago himself was in the center, surrounded by the women he loved: his wife and daughter standing with their hands on his shoulders. His granddaughter, Sofia, stood in a classic flamenco pose, one arm raised, her face dramatically serious but the fire in her eyes still evident. Santiago smiled in pride, a moment captured before tragedy had befallen the family.

A volley of gunshots peppered the front door and Ramon fired a couple of shots back through the splintered wood. Enough to hold them off momentarily, but Morgan knew he would be out of ammunition soon. An eruption of shots came from the street below, followed by screams, the smash of glass and running feet.

"Morgan, we really need to get out of here," Jake called

softly from the other room. "There are more of them than we thought. We can't stay any longer."

His voice was calm with an edge of excitement. Morgan knew he would be feeling the adrenalin rush, heart pumping, ready for action. The addiction of what they did meant these moments were both danger and lust, a heady attraction.

Morgan grabbed the frame and pulled the back off to extract the photo. She found two more square-numbered grids carved into the inner back side of the frame. At a swift glance, it looked like the numbers were the same on each. Morgan refastened the frame and put it inside the other jacket pocket. She went back into the main room, looking around for escape options, her senses heightened.

Another shot came from the stairwell and Ramon fired back again, two shots, enough to halt them for just a few seconds. Morgan dragged a chest of drawers below the largest skylight and clambered up on it. She pushed the glass until it tilted away from her enough to reveal the tiled rooftops beyond.

"We can get out this way," she said. "Quick, Jake, give me a boost up and I can help you from outside."

A flurry of gunfire came from below and the wood of the door completely splintered, the lock exploding. Ramon stepped back quickly.

"You go," he said. "I'll keep them occupied."

"No way," Jake said, determination in his expression. "These guys want the flat, not us. If we get out of their way, they might not follow. You need to come with us."

He turned and boosted Morgan upwards. She climbed out, pulling herself onto the rooftop, and then reached down to help Ramon, tugging his arm as Jake pushed him from below.

The sound of feet hammered up the stairs and the door burst open just as Jake reached up, gunfire filling the room.

CHAPTER 8

Morgan and Ramon yanked Jake up and he pulled his legs through the skylight a split second before gunfire shredded the room below. The three of them didn't stop to look back, but ran across the maze of rooftops away from the scene. The light was fading fast and the gloom would hopefully hide their escape.

A clattering came behind them and Morgan looked back to see one man clambering out of the skylight.

"Down!" she shouted, pushing Ramon sideways and ducking behind a buttress separating two properties. A ping and a chip of stone exploded near her shoulder. She looked sideways to see Jake sheltering a little further away. His eyes reflected her own thoughts. If only they had some weapons, this might be going differently. He grinned suddenly and she couldn't help but smile back, reading his thoughts. It was good to be out here together.

Another shot shattered a window behind them, this time at closer range. It was time to get out of here.

Scooting to the edge of the building, Morgan looked over to see a large balcony and an open window below.

"This way," she whispered, slipping over the edge and

dropping down onto the wide stone terrace. White curtains billowed around them as Ramon and Jake followed.

Morgan stepped inside to find a beautiful apartment, the table set for dinner. A woman in a short pink dress walked into the room, a gin and tonic in her hand. She clutched at the wall as she saw them, dropping the glass in alarm.

"It's OK," Morgan said, her hands out in the international gesture of reassurance. Ramon started speaking in Spanish, pulling his police ID out even as he got on the radio to call for backup. A shout came from the rooftop above, and the woman retreated into her bedroom.

"We have to get out of here," Jake said. "It doesn't look like they're giving up. We need to get out onto the street and lose them in the maze of the old city."

They hurried out into the streets below, ducking under porticos and bar umbrellas to stay out of sight from above until they were far enough away to be sure they were safe. A police car eventually picked them up near the port and Ramon escorted them to a hotel, checking them in under assumed names and assigning them police protection.

"I'll come by in the morning and we can go through everything we know about the case," Ramon said as they walked towards the lifts. Morgan shot Jake a quick glance before she nodded.

"Of course. We have a lot to discuss."

Jake reached out his hand. "Thank you, Ramon. I know you lost a man tonight. It's going to be a tough time ahead."

Ramon shook Jake's hand with a strong grip, resolve in his expression. "Eduardo was a good man and he had a little son … We'll get the bastards."

He turned and walked off, leaving Morgan and Jake alone.

***

On the fifth floor, they paused outside Morgan's room.

"How long do you need?" she asked.

"Give me an hour," Jake said. "I really need a shower, and I'll get the plane on standby. It's only a couple of hours' flight to Granada. We could even catch the late flamenco show and talk to Santiago's granddaughter."

***

In her room, Morgan pulled out Santiago's notebook and photo frame. The numbers on the checkerboard sketched in the back of the book and etched in the frame were the same, but different to Subirachs' square. The latter totaled 33 in any direction but these numbers added up to 70. Morgan tried to recall what she had seen on the back of the statue's head on top of the tower. Had it been the same as this, or were they a series of squares that together would add up to a clue? She took a couple of pictures with her smart phone and emailed them to Martin Klein back at ARKANE. The art of gematria was such that it could be used for a specific message, but it could also result in gibberish, the numbers translated into words that meant nothing. If Martin could sift through the myriad options, it might help them figure out what the numbers meant.

Morgan lay back on the stiff bedcovers, relaxing for a moment as she replayed the events of earlier today. She heard the rush of water next door as Jake started his shower. He hadn't shown any signs of being affected by his injuries, so maybe he really was fully recovered. She imagined how his scarred body must look under the water spray, and a smile played at the corner of her mouth as she allowed herself that brief fantasy. *Post-action adrenalin*, she thought, *always devastating for the libido*. She wondered if Jake was thinking along the same lines and went to the connecting door between their rooms, her palm on the handle. She only had to enter to see if he felt the same way. After a moment, she turned and headed into the shower in her own bathroom.

***

A few hours later, just after eleven p.m., the plane taxied to a halt at a small private airfield near the city of Granada. To the British, the hour might be considered late, but to the Spanish, the night was still young. Morgan was used to the later hours, as Tel Aviv ran on a similar clock. She let her hair down as they headed into the city, brushing out the dark curls and putting on some darker makeup.

"Might as well play the part of a tourist after some nightlife," she said, catching Jake's sideways glance at her ministrations. There was an appreciation behind his raised eyebrow; it seemed that the chemistry that had sparked in the fires of Pentecost was still alive and well.

Jake's phone buzzed.

"It's Martin," he said. "Santiago's granddaughter, Sofia, is performing at the Alhambra in some kind of flamenco extravaganza sound-and-light show. It's already started, but the festivities go on well into the early hours. She'll be in several sets so she should be there for most of the night with her band."

The taxi sped through the city and Morgan gazed out at the streets, busy even at this late hour. Granada sat at the foot of the Sierra Nevada Mountains, and Morgan was thrilled to be back. Her father had brought her many years ago, a teenager keen on discovering more about her roots. Her name came from this area, and her ancestors had roamed these craggy mountains, only an hour from the ocean in the southeast corner of Spain. This was Andalucia; the word conjured its past, the soft fullness of the Arabic *Al-Andalus*, a melting pot of influences from ancient Greeks, Romans and Byzantines through to Muslims, Sephardic Jews and the Catholic Church that still dominated here.

Morgan thought for a moment of her sister, Faye, back home in England. A twin in blood, but so different in looks and personality. Faye's daughter, Gemma, looked like a Sierra, with darker skin and almost black hair, more like Morgan's child than her blonde sister's. Her own family was so mixed in origin that this multicultural area of Spain would always feel like home.

They rounded a corner and caught sight of the Alhambra, the fortress on the hill a forbidding welcome to new arrivals. The eleventh-century palace had been constructed by a Moorish emir, and even though the Reconquista of Spanish Christendom had taken the city, the Islamic architecture still remained.

They pulled up to the gates and bought tickets for the flamenco event, heading in through the wide entrance.

"Where's the dancing?" Morgan asked the ticket seller.

"In the Court of the Lions," he said, glancing down at his watch. "The last set has just started, so you'll have to hurry."

Morgan led Jake quickly through the terrace of the western-style palace towards the Moorish buildings beyond. The mournful sound of flamenco guitar floated on the balmy night air, and Morgan breathed in the scent of flowers from the extensive gardens. She could see across the valley to the narrow winding streets of Albaicín, where she had stayed with her father so long ago. She heard his voice telling her stories of how the cave dwellings of Sacramonte had sheltered their ancestors as blood was spilled on these streets.

They reached the Court of the Lions, surrounded by the stunning arabesque architecture of the ancient Moorish kingdom. Slim pillars in cool ivory-colored marble led towards soaring archways intricately designed with filigree geometric shapes and Arabic calligraphy. The overwhelming sensation was light and delicate, as if the stone palace was constructed of magically spun air. The Court of the Lions was open to the night air, a courtyard surrounded by one hundred and twenty-four white columns topped with decorated archways. In the center of the courtyard, a great alabaster fountain supported by twelve marble lions spouted water, sparkling in the subtle lighting that only seemed to enhance the otherworldly atmosphere. The courtyard was filled with people, eyes riveted on the scene before them.

A young man sat on the edge of the fountain, plucking his guitar while next to him stood two older men and a woman, singing a song of the *gitanos*, the Romani people of Spain. In front of them, a young woman danced with the proud stamps and hand claps of flamenco. Her scarlet dress with full ruffled skirt accentuated her dark skin and her full eyebrows arched as she turned, arms raised.

Morgan saw her face in profile and recognized the young girl in the picture in Santiago's room, the granddaughter he was estranged from. Her dance mesmerized those watching, the embodiment of *duende*, the soul of Andalucia that undulated through her hips and the arch of her back. Morgan had heard that true *duende* resonated with a heightened awareness of death and a dash of the diabolical, and there was truly an edge of darkness as Sofia moved. The shadows at her feet were almost living things that she stamped back into the depths of the earth. The wail of the older woman's song grew louder, a desperate lament for the loss of their homeland. Sofia whirled, her steps faster and faster until she stood motionless at the crescendo, the guitar silenced by the applause.

She held the pose as the noise died down, waiting for

quiet again. She turned and gestured to the guitar player, and Morgan caught the look that sparked between them, recognizing an intimate knowledge. This was Sofia's boyfriend, perhaps the cause of the rift with her family. He had the look of a Moroccan-Spanish Arab, his long dark hair worn loose about his face – a Muslim, perhaps, or a *gitano*, a man Santiago may have considered beneath his pure-blood Jewish granddaughter. The young man began to pluck the strings and one of the other men from the group stepped forward to dance with Sofia, stamping with fast heels.

A figure stepped from the crowd, standing poised on the edge of the open ring. He wore the black shirt and tight trousers of flamenco and his strong features brought to mind a toreador, a bullfighter in his prime. He had been wounded in battle, his right eye scarred and sightless, but Morgan's gaze was drawn to his wide chest, muscled arms, and his posture of dominance. She tensed at his entrance, aware of the imminent danger Sofia was in, but perhaps this man was just a member of the troupe, a plant for dramatic effect.

The man stepped forward, raising his arms, commanding attention as he stamped rhythmically towards Sofia. She turned in the dance, away from the man in her troupe, indicating her acceptance of his challenge. The man began the dance of the bullfighter, and they circled around each other as the music soared. There was a chemistry between them, and even though the man was old enough to be her father, he was attractive, a dark intensity in his gaze as he danced closer to Sofia, calling his *olé* as he clapped. She spun in his circle, tilting her body towards his. Morgan saw the guitar player's eyes narrow at this rival. The taut strings of attraction held the pair at arm's length, but as the music reached a crescendo and the song ended, the man reached out and pulled Sofia to him.

The young woman's eyes widened, her mouth opened in a gasp. Morgan stepped forward, suddenly realizing the threat. Then the spotlights flicked off and the fire alarm rang out, its piercing shriek echoing around the Court of the Lions as the whole area was plunged into darkness.

CHAPTER 9

Morgan froze as the shrill alarm filled the courtyard and darkness sparked a panic amongst the hundreds of people crammed into the tiny space. Someone screamed and shouts erupted as the mass of bodies began to surge for the exits. Morgan felt Jake's hand on her arm and they pushed sideways to stand against one of the marble columns as the tide of panicked humanity swept around them.

"We need to go in the opposite direction," Jake said close to her ear. "Away from this emergency exit."

Morgan pressed back against the pillar, feeling the cool weight of the gun against her back. They had made the decision to carry weapons after Barcelona, but the Barak SP-21 pistol was next to useless in this crowd in the dark. She thought of the man's face, his ruined eye that did nothing to diminish his proud bearing. Was he responsible for Santiago's death? And if so, why did he want Sofia?

The pressure of the crowd lessened a little and Morgan started to push through the oncoming horde, heading back into the square, Jake following behind. The flash of torches illuminated the delicate archways above, flickering across the names of God inscribed on the walls. Beneath the cries of the crowd, Morgan heard running feet heading towards the gardens, the sound echoing on the marble of the hallways inside the palace.

"This way," she whispered. She pulled her gun out as they found themselves alone in a high vaulted room, shafts of moonlight catching the trellis windows and turning the tiles around them to spun silver.

The cry of a woman came from a little way ahead, swiftly muted.

Morgan ran around the room to the other side, weapon held angled down and in front of her. Jake flanked her, going the other way, until they were both at the entrance to the next room. A flash of torchlight came from the corridor beyond. Morgan carefully peered round the column.

A crack of stone and a gunshot echoed. Morgan pulled back quickly as another round blasted the centuries-old palace wall. Jake took the chance to fire back. A shout of pain came from the room beyond.

"They're taking Sofia," Jake said, firing again into the room, pulling away as the men returned fire.

"There's no point us engaging here," Morgan said. "This way." She turned and ran for one of the vaulted windows, tucking her weapon back in her jeans before climbing out. She shimmied down, using the intricate decoration for finger-holds, into the gardens below. She heard Jake get off a couple more shots and then he clambered out the window to join her. The darkness was complete out here, the scent of flowers overladen with smoke from the gunfire. The sound of a helicopter carried on the night breeze.

"That's how they're planning to leave," Morgan said. "I seem to remember that there's a more open area by the pool. They could be using that." She ran swift and low, keeping close to the wall of the palace until they emerged next to a pool surrounded by palm trees.

A shot whizzed by Morgan's ear and they took cover again, only able to watch as the man with the scarred eye was pulled up into the helicopter, a limp Sofia in his arms.

As the helicopter banked away to the west, the armed men faded into the night, no longer needed and eager to escape the growing police presence at the hilltop palace.

"We need to get out of here," Morgan said. "We can't be found with weapons. They'll hold us for too long." She walked to the parapet at the edge of the pool, looking down into the dark green below. "You up for a climb?"

Jake smiled, his teeth white in the dark. "I'll take that challenge. Race you to the bottom."

Together, they slipped over the wall and disappeared into the darkness below, hand over hand into the woods below the citadel.

***

Morgan beat Jake to the bottom by a few minutes and she watched him finish the difficult clamber down. He clearly favored one side and she could see the stiffness in his body. When he finally reached her, there was sweat on his brow. That wouldn't have been there prior to the devastating injuries he had sustained. Morgan felt a flicker of concern for his health – wondering at the same time whether she could really trust her partner to have her back if they bumped into another shooting party.

"You OK?" she asked.

Jake nodded, leaning against a tree. "Give me just a minute." His breathing was uneven and Morgan saw pain in his expression, both physical and from his own frustration at not being at full health. He had been signed off for active duty and she knew he'd been in training since discharge from hospital, but his weakness made her uneasy. One part of her wanted to fold him in her arms, to let him take strength from her own. But there was another part, the soldier with a mission, who knew she should request another partner and let Jake go home.

She pulled out her phone and texted Martin Klein, describing the man with the scarred eye who had taken Sofia. She knew he would come up with something in the next few hours, but where should they go in the meantime? They had no way of knowing where the scarred man might have taken Sofia, or even why she was important to the hunt for the Key.

Morgan slipped Santiago's notebook out of her jacket and, using the light filtering through the trees from the Alhambra, she counted the numbers in the grid. The photo frame had a different set of numerals carved into the back and Morgan had copied them into the notebook too. So now they had three different grids, if Subirachs' was to be included, and one that had been blown apart on the statue of the Sagrada Familia. Martin was working on the possible gematria answers, so there was nothing to do but wait. She stood up. Jake's color was returning and he breathed more easily now.

"Let's head back to the plane," Morgan said. "It's late and if we give Martin some time to work on the info, I bet he'll have something for us soon."

They walked together through the trees, eventually emerging on a residential street. They walked towards traffic noise and soon caught a taxi back to the airfield.

Back in the plane, Morgan immediately grabbed a blanket, curled up in one of the large chairs and fell asleep. Her years in the military had taught her to take advantage of any lull, however brief, repairing the body and mind with unconsciousness.

***

Jake watched Morgan's face relax as she slept, but her curled body still seemed to hold its tension. His own muscles still spasmed from the effort of the climb down the Alhambra wall. Before the injuries, he could have beaten Morgan down, and he was angry – really angry that he wasn't able to even match her. He had spent years in the British military honing his physical fitness and combat skills, and the ARKANE missions had kept him fresh. He'd passed the last battery of tests with top marks, yet he couldn't even get down a simple wall climb without feeling nauseous. He had wanted to throw up at the bottom, his legs and arms shaking with the effort, and the pain in his chest excruciating. It had to be more than physical. The demon in Sedlec had crushed his bones, but had it also crushed his love of the game?

Jake glanced over at Morgan once more. She was made for this work, and she looked glorious as she did it. Moving through the dark of the Alhambra, weapon in hand, she had been stunning to watch. Her slight curves did nothing to hide the hard edge of her resolve, and he knew she respected strength. Would she turn from him now he had shown weakness? They were friends, for sure, and after what they had been through together, they were more than just work partners. There had even been moments when they could have taken it further, for the spark of attraction remained. But now, Jake thought he glimpsed doubt in her eyes.

Morgan sighed in her sleep and a dark curl slipped down to cover her cheek. Jake ached to touch her, but instead, he closed his eyes, willing the darkness to come.

CHAPTER 10

Sofia heard voices as her consciousness returned, men speaking in rapid Spanish arguing over a football game. She tried to open her eyes, but a dark scarf prevented her from seeing too much. It smelled of apple tobacco smoke from the hookah pipe bars and for a moment she was transported back to the warm Granada evening, laughing at something Alejandro had said without a care in the world. Then she remembered the lights going out in the Court of the Lions, the men who had taken her and their rough handling before oblivion.

Though blindfolded, Sofia could sense that she was lying sideways on a reclinable chair, a safety belt snapped tightly shut and pulled across her hips. Her hands were cuffed behind her back, her throat was dry and a bitter aftertaste lingered. Her head throbbed and from the sound of engines, she was on an aircraft. Where was she? Why had she been taken? Sofia recalled Alejandro's face as the lights had gone out, his fingers frozen on the guitar strings. Had anything happened to him?

The men's conversation stopped suddenly and Sofia was aware of someone sitting down in the chair next to hers as the air shifted. Her heart thumped and she closed her eyes again, unwilling to face what was coming. A moment later, her blindfold was removed.

"I know you're awake, Sofia." The man's voice was smooth and deep, rich like molasses. "Come, have coffee with me. I'll take the cuffs off if you promise to at least hear me out."

Sofia took a deep breath and opened her eyes. She shifted on her seat and turned her head to see who spoke. It was the man from the flamenco dance, as she had known it would be. When he had stepped forward last night, his bearing proud, she had sensed danger in him, but she had been drawn to it. For when Sofia danced flamenco, she became someone else. No longer the independent woman she was in the daylight hours, Sofia became the archetype of femininity; and as the music transformed her, she had responded to this man's dominance. The slash of scar tissue over his eye only served to give him gravitas, his thick hair and muscled limbs exuding a masculine presence she couldn't help but respond to, despite their obvious age difference.

She looked around, trying to get her bearings. They were in a small private plane with luxurious seats, fully equipped galley and entertainment space. Four men sat intently watching a football game, their neck muscles taut in the effort not to turn and see what was going on. The man noticed her look, stood up and pulled a curtain across, giving them a modicum of privacy.

"What do you want?" Sofia said softly, meeting his gaze. His one good eye was sensual, the color of winter spices, offering a trace of dark pleasure.

The man lifted his fingers to her cheek. Sofia froze, willing him away, but he gently caressed the side of her face, tracing her fine bone structure.

"You look so like your mother." His voice was wistful.

Sofia frowned. "You knew her?"

He pulled a knife with a short blade from his belt. Sofia jerked back instinctively, pressing herself against the wall of the plane, her heart thumping in a rhythm of fear.

"It's OK," the man said, his tone gentle. "Turn and I'll cut your cuffs off. They were just temporary – you're my guest now."

After a moment, Sofia relented, turning in her seat. She felt a brief tightening around her wrists and heard the sawing of the blade, then her hands were released. She rubbed her skin, restoring circulation as the man poured black coffee into two espresso cups, carefully placing one of them in front of her with a spoon and two sugar cubes. He was precise in his movements, deliberate and practiced.

"Who are you?" she asked, as he poured a glass of water and set it down next to the coffee.

"Drink," he said, lifting his own cup to full lips, his big hands dwarfing the crockery. His mouth was generous and sensual, his tongue licking the *crema* from his mustache after drinking. Sofia drank the glass of water straight down and then took a sip of her coffee, beginning to feel better already. She felt his gaze on her, watching her throat as she swallowed.

"How did you know my mother?" she began again. "Why am I here?"

He smiled, his dark eye glinting a little in remembrance. "Blanca was just as curious and impatient as you." His gaze flicked to hers. "And I loved her for it."

Sofia heard a dark promise in his voice, something that made her gut twist. She realized that his kind of love wasn't something she wanted to experience. She waited for him to continue.

"My name is Adam," he said finally. "I knew your mother when she was young and I ... had dealings ... with your father. I also studied with your grandfather a long time ago, so my life has been entwined with your family for many years."

Sofia looked out the plane window, down at the fields of Spain far below.

"Then you'll know both my parents are dead, and I haven't seen my grandpa for years now. He disapproves of the way I live, my dancing and my boyfriend. It's not proper for a Jewish girl, according to his outdated rules of life." She snapped her head back around. "What happened to Alejandro?"

"He's fine," Adam said, waving his hand dismissively. "He's not my concern, for now at least. We left him behind in Granada." His eye flicked again to Sofia's. "But I came to tell you something, as a friend of your family."

He reached forward and took her hand. Sofia wanted to pull away, but there was something hypnotic about his gaze. She understood what a rabbit must feel like as it faced the devouring eyes of a wolf.

"Your grandfather is dead."

His words were hard and unyielding. Sofia gasped and tried to pull away but Adam gripped her hands tightly, forcing her to face him.

"He killed himself yesterday by jumping from the top of the Sagrada Familia." Tears ran down Sofia's face as Adam compelled her to listen. "His body smashed on the stone in front of the basilica."

"No, no." Sofia wept openly now and Adam pulled her towards him, embracing her and holding her head tight against his chest. She wanted to pull away, to run far from this stranger, but as his hands stroked her hair, she relaxed into his arms. He smelled of coffee roasting and cinnamon cologne, and as her tears soaked his shirt, she sobbed harder, remembering times past.

Her grandfather had been a stubborn old man, trapped in a previous generation's way of doing things, but he had loved her. Sofia knew that. Guilt rose, a crushing pain in her chest at the thought of him dying without knowing that she had loved him, too. He had mourned the death of his daughter, her mother, for many years and really, Sofia had been all he had left. But she had denied him that relationship out of stubborn pride.

The tears rose again until at last her emptiness was complete. Adam handed her a tissue and she blew her nose as she pulled herself together.

"Are you taking me to the funeral?" she asked. "Are we going to Barcelona?"

Adam shook his head. "Not yet. The funeral will be in a few days, the local Rabbi is organizing it. You don't need to worry about anything. But before he died, Santiago told me of a Key that he sought, something precious … but he was so depressed at the end, so distraught that he wasn't able to finish what he started." Sofia's chest tightened and the prick of tears threatened again at his words. "He told me that you could help with this quest, that you knew something of its whereabouts."

Sofia frowned, confusion transforming her face. "I don't know about any Key. Grandfather wouldn't talk to me about his Kabbalah knowledge. After all, I'm just a woman." Her voice was bitter. "And way too young. I think perhaps he would have told me later on, as my mother was taught after my father disappeared … but now it's too late."

Adam's face darkened at her words, his expression evoking storm clouds, his mouth taut. He reached out and clutched her wrist tightly, his fingers crushing, turning her skin white beneath his grip.

"You must know something. Think, girl."

There was no trace of familial concern in his voice now. Sofia straightened her back, meeting his gaze.

"Take your hands off," she whispered. "You're clearly no friend of my grandfather if you would hurt me."

A range of emotion swept over Adam's face as he looked at her. A flash of something like love flickered in his expression again and for a moment, Sofia thought he might pull her back into his arms and comfort her again.

Instead, his hand pulled back and, with an open palm, Adam slapped her face hard. Sofia's head snapped sideways and she gasped in shock at the sudden pain.

"You spoiled little bitch," Adam said. "You don't know what hurt is, pretty one. Shall I give you to my men back there and you can find out?" His gaze raked down her body, lingering on her curves. "I've seen you dance, and I like what I see." He leaned closer, his voice tinged with spite. "Perhaps I'll use you myself."

Adam stood up and with one hand, he grabbed her hair and yanked her towards him. Sofia grabbed at his hands, fighting him as he roughly grabbed her breast, squeezing it tight, making her wince with pain. He laughed at her distress.

"How I wish that bastard Santiago could see this. He would have given me anything to spare you, perhaps even the Key itself. But it's too late now." He reached down and lifted her skirt, his hand rough on the skin of her thighs. "If you don't know anything, there's only one more use I have for you." He stopped suddenly, a dark smile on his lips, and Sofia saw madness in his gaze. "But before we proceed, I think we need an audience."

He thrust her away from him. Sofia fell hard, knocking her cup to the floor, the spoon falling underneath her. Her fingers crawled to it, clutching the makeshift weapon. She looked around the cabin, searching for any way to escape, desperation rising within her.

Adam walked over to a square wooden box on the floor, its rough panels carved with occult symbols.

"I keep this with me as a reminder of what drives my quest, and how I deal with those who stand in my way."

He opened the lid and lifted out a large glass jar, his hands obscuring the interior. The preservative liquid inside was yellowish and something round and heavy moved inside the jar as the plane rocked with turbulence. A dark foreboding rose within Sofia's chest. She didn't want to know what was inside.

Adam lifted it higher to examine what was within.

"Your father took my eye many years ago. Then he took your mother." His smile was wolfish. "Years later, I repaid the debt."

Adam bent and thrust the jar in Sofia's face as she drew back in horror. The eyes of the severed head were wide and staring, the mouth fixed in an agonized scream. Sofia couldn't look away. For a moment, she thought that it couldn't possibly be her father. This fleshy specimen didn't look like him, but then the features coalesced and beneath the grimace of death, she saw the man who had danced with her, teaching her the steps of flamenco as a girl.

No," she gasped, her hand lifting to her mouth. A moan escaped her, a keening animal sound as she reached out to touch the jar. Adam pulled it away.

"Your family has always been a thorn in my side," he said. "Even in death, they plague me. I would know of this Key or your precious Alejandro's head will be next in a jar."

"Please," Sofia said, her voice weak. "I'll tell you all I know. I promise. Please don't hurt Alejandro." Adam nodded for her to continue. "Grandfather would always talk about how the Sagrada Familia was his lifelong passion, but his heart would always belong to the Córdoba Mezquita. It was there he met my grandmother, you see. Please, whatever you seek. It must be there. That's all I know."

Adam paused for a moment, then thrust open the door to the cockpit.

"Change of plan. We're heading to Córdoba."

He turned back to Sofia. "And you, my dear, I will keep pristine for the final day. Your sacrifice to the Devourers will complete the circle your mother and I began so many years ago. Your father took what I loved most – now I will return the favor."

CHAPTER 11

THE BUZZ OF HER phone woke Morgan and she felt around for it on the chair next to her.

"I know where you need to go next." Martin's enthusiastic bounce was evident even at this early hour. Morgan pulled up the blind on the window of the plane, squinting a little. It was just after dawn. Fingers of pink touched the skyline of the city and thin clouds were highlighted with the golden glow of morning.

She sat up, pulling the blanket off. Jake was still sleeping in the chair next to her, his handsome face marred with a little frown, as if he was solving impossible problems in his dreams. She nudged his chair with her hip as she stood up and his eyes flicked open, his hands coming up in automatic defense. He relaxed as he saw her.

"Go ahead, Martin," she said, switching to speakerphone and then moving to the little galley to put coffee on.

"The man you saw at the flamenco is Luis De Medina, but he's known to his followers as Adam Kadmon, a name used for primordial man in Kabbalah teaching. The spiritual realm of Adam Kadmon is said to represent the *sephirah*, or divine attribute of the crown, the specific divine will and plan for creation. He wants to return the earth to this perfect state, cleansing it of those who despoil its perfection."

"Not egotistical at all then," Jake said with a chuckle.

"Exactly," Martin said. "It seems that Kadmon was a student of Santiago's, thrown out many years ago over a fight. He courted Santiago's daughter, wanted to marry her but she chose another man."

Morgan thought of the way Kadmon's gaze had devoured Sofia's body when he stepped into the flamenco circle. Was he obsessing over the daughter as he had the mother?

"He also has a small militia group, well-funded and armed. It seems their plans are escalating, so whatever Kadmon wants to do, he intends to do it soon."

Martin hesitated and Morgan sensed he was holding something back.

"What is it, Martin?" she said, her voice sharp.

"He's … ummm … known to ARKANE, actually. I don't know how much I should tell you, Morgan. This file is marked for top level security only. I haven't cleared it with Marietti."

Morgan could hear uncertainty in his voice.

"We could be running into this man and his organization again soon," Jake said, his voice gentle. "We need to know what they're capable of. I'll sort anything out with Marietti, I promise."

A moment of silence and then Martin started speaking, his words running into each other as he hurried to get them out.

"ARKANE has always monitored the Kabbalistic community, as it does with any religious group, and Santiago was one of an international group of Rabbis called the Remnant, who met in secret once a year in different locations. They were known to protect the Key to the Gates of

Hell, although this was always assumed to be something metaphorical, based on the symbols of their faith. This man, Adam Kadmon, was originally groomed to join that group but it seems that he dabbled in the dark side of Kabbalah, obsessed with demonology."

Morgan poured black coffee into two cups, handing one to Jake. She wanted to hear what Martin had to say but there was a flutter in her gut, a pressure in her head. Somehow, she knew he was going to say something that would change everything.

"There were always ten of them, a minyan, the number required for public prayer. But then, about five years ago, the Rabbis started dying. Two from heart attacks, and one under anesthetic in routine surgery. One was beaten to death in his own home – the one who had convinced the others to shut Kadmon out." Martin hesitated again.

"Then there was your father, Morgan," he said slowly.

She took a deep breath. "What about him?"

"Although his death was recorded as part of a suicide bombing, we believe it was to cover up his assassination. His … umm, body parts were recovered from the hospital and tested positive for a fatal drug overdose. It's more than likely that he was already dead before the bomb that killed the rest of the bus."

Morgan's hand flew to her mouth and she closed her eyes, resisting the tears that threatened. Jake put out a hand to comfort her, and she thrust her arm out, holding him away, her eyes flashing a warning.

"Why wasn't I told before?" she asked, her voice deadly calm.

"I didn't know," Martin said. "Truly Morgan, I only just came across this information."

Morgan remembered how her mentor and friend, Father Ben Costanza, had warned her about ARKANE. She could never fathom the layers of secrets they held – even about her own family, it seemed. Her chest was bursting, her heart pounding as she tried to reconcile this information, tried to hold back her anger.

"So just to be clear: this Adam Kadmon was responsible for my father's death? It wasn't a random suicide bomber."

Her voice was frost now.

"It would seem so," Martin said.

Morgan's world shifted ever so slightly, as the ramifications of the truth sank in. Her fingers clutched the edge of her seat so hard that her knuckles were white with pressure. She had spent so long working on forgiveness, arguing with fellow Israelis that despite her own loss, she still believed that the two states could one day live side by side in relative peace. She had spent years trying to build something positive from her father's death, but she had also spent those years not knowing the truth, not knowing that actually, her father had been murdered by one of their own.

A Jew of Spain had killed Leon Sierra, and now he would pay. This was no longer a hunt for the Key to the Gates of Hell.

This would be her bloody revenge.

"Where is Kadmon now?" she asked.

"I'm still working on that."

"He wants the Key more than anything," Jake said quietly, his amber eyes a pool of concern. "If we find that, he'll come to us, and then he's yours, Morgan."

She relaxed her clenched fists and took a deep breath, exhaling slowly. "You're right. That's the best way to get to him. Martin, have you been able to work out the possible options for the gematria on Santiago's numbered squares?"

"This numerology is an interesting thing," he said, turning professorial. "There is never one final true answer. The codes in each square add up to 70 which has many meanings in the biblical tradition. It is made up of two perfect numbers: seven, representing perfection, and ten, representing completeness and God's law."

Morgan remembered her father teaching her of these things during lazy summer days in the hills of Safed, his face alive with passion as he described the wisdom of the Torah.

"It can represent a period of judgement," Martin continued, "as ancient Israel spent seventy years in captivity in Babylon, and it is especially connected with Jerusalem as seventy times seven years were mentioned in the book of Daniel as necessary for the city to end its sin and enter into everlasting righteousness."

"So we must go to Jerusalem then?" Jake cut in. They had traveled there together during the hunt for the Pentecost stones, and Morgan felt a moment of hope that she could return to the city she loved.

"I don't think so," Martin said. "The art of gematria is also about finding the equivalent meaning from the codes, and the number 70 can also mean *malakh* – an angel or messenger from God. In simple gematria, it can stand for the word Vatican."

"My father and those like him would never have used simple gematria," Morgan said. "It must be Jewish and based on the Hebrew letters."

"Hmm," Martin mused, and they heard tapping as he worked. "In that case, you might be closer than you think. I considered that perhaps the two squares could be added together. Why else would you etch two of the same in the back of the photo frame? They are an exact match and two lots of 70 make 140. I wrote a little program that calculates place names based on gematria and narrows down results based on resonance with Jewish history. Only one name popped up."

CHAPTER 12

IT WAS ONLY A short flight to Córdoba, northwest of Granada over the flat agricultural plains. Morgan gazed out the small window at the panels of gleaming color below, the fields a patchwork of gold and green. She saw her father's formative early years in the landscape, working in the fields alongside grandparents she had never known. He had left his family to pursue his love of archaeology in faraway places, as he had later left her own mother to return to Israel. Perhaps there were distant cousins here, remnants of a family Morgan had never known. Her family had been fractured, but perhaps broken was the new normal in this world, where the phrase 'nuclear family' evoked images of war, not cozy perfection.

Morgan thought of her twin sister, Faye, who had never really known their father, brought up instead by their mother in England. Faye had a right to know how Leon had died, but Morgan questioned whether it would even bring tears to her eyes. After all, she had never known a life with him in it.

Her sister lived in an ordered world, where being a wife and a mother were the pillars of her faith and service to the

Christian God she believed in. Some days, Morgan craved the normality that Faye lived within, a cocoon of baking and book groups, playing with little Gemma and church outings led by her pastor husband, David. But as much as that life attracted her, it repelled with its lack of excitement, its absence of the edge that Morgan craved. It was a dark addiction that she knew Jake understood, and the moments where life hung in the balance brought meaning in the aftermath. Without risk, life was far too dull. Her father had indeed raised the right twin, and Morgan knew that only she could honor his memory. She would tell Faye later, but this was her responsibility now.

***

The private airstrip was just outside the city limits and a taxi was waiting for them on arrival, sweeping them through the streets towards the ancient center. Córdoba had been a hub of learning during the Caliphate over a thousand years ago, famous for the books collected by its knowledge-hungry rulers. Baghdad and the East were far in advance of Europe then, inventing the Arabic numerals and algebra still used today, along with decimal notation and the zero. As they drove into town, Morgan wondered if those in the mess of modern Iraq even knew how great their nation once had been. It was the curse of great empires perhaps that someday they must fall, as the British Empire had done, and the American reach had begun to crumble as the East rose again. The great cycles of civilization were an unstoppable force on the face of the earth, building and growing and then falling prey to entropy, the disorder and collapse that devours us all in time.

Morgan and Jake exited the taxi on the edge of the river Guadalquivir near the cathedral.

"Where are we heading?" Jake said, as Morgan strode off ahead of him into the narrow streets of the old city.

"The synagogue first, it's the most obvious place for Santiago to have frequented," she said, walking faster, as if she could outrun her residual anger. Her words were curt and she could see that Jake struggled with how to break the tension as they walked. High white walls flanked the narrow streets, with doorways marked by blue numbered tiles and shops hunkered into the stone. There were no brand-name stores here, just individual shops specializing in different wares, the same as it had been for generations.

"We don't need to talk about what happened to my father," Morgan said a moment later, as they walked down the Calle de los Judíos and emerged into a tiny square in front of the synagogue. "I'm not upset over his death anymore, I've come to terms with that. But I'm livid at Marietti for not telling me what he knew when he recruited me." She took a step away and then turned back, eyes blazing. "And I *will* have a reckoning with this Adam Kadmon. He's mine, Jake. Remember that."

Jake raised his hands in mock surrender. "Of course. You're the avenging angel and I'm your slightly broken sidekick." His mocking smile twisted the corkscrew scar at the edge of his left eyebrow, but Morgan could see truth in his eyes. There was fear in the amber depths. Not of whoever they might meet, but of letting her down. She softened.

"I still need you, Jake," she said, reaching one hand out to touch his arm. "What you did in the crypt of Sedlec saved us both. Your scars are mine too. Stay with me for this ... please."

She couldn't say any more, couldn't put into words what having him back as her partner meant now this emotional bombshell had shattered her objectivity. This trip had been a search for something in her father's past, and now it was all-consuming revenge. She needed someone who would stop her if she went too far. After all they had been through, she trusted Jake – and there was almost no one else she could say that of. His eyes darkened and she knew that he felt it, too; the bond between them went beyond just ARKANE partners now. He nodded.

"We'd better get on with it then," he said. "I know you want to move fast. I'll work hard to keep up."

His joking tone broke the intensity of the moment, and Morgan wiped the prick of tears from her eyes, turning towards the synagogue.

They entered the low door, stepping back to a simpler time, when there was nothing between the faithful and their God. Built in 1315, the building was of basic design, the prayer room almost square, overlooked by a gallery for the women. The walls were decorated in Hebrew script, geometric patterns and decorative arches drawing the eyes upwards. The air was cool in the shadowy space, the high windows letting in some light but protecting the interior from the harsh Mediterranean sun. It was a refuge, and Morgan sensed an ancient peace, as if the generations of faithful had impregnated the walls with their prayers.

After the expulsion in 1492, the synagogue had become a hospital, a school and a chapel, finally reopening as a synagogue in 1985. The story of repressed centuries had been repeated across Spain, the efficacy of ethnic cleansing demonstrated in how long it had taken for Jews to find a place here again. Morgan felt a pull of allegiance, a sense of wanting to stay and help rebuild this community. It was the same feeling that had driven her in Budapest, where the rise of anti-Semitism was once again staining the political landscape. Her people, yet not her people. She was Israeli, not Jewish; British and yet not Christian; a woman without a place – except for ARKANE, a sanctuary for misfits.

"There's nothing here," she said suddenly. "This is not

where Santiago would hide a code. This place was sacred to him, and he wouldn't have carved into these walls."

Jake nodded, looking around the open space. "And there's really no place to hide it, no way to keep a grid of numbers secret here. It would be too obvious. So what's next?"

Morgan ran her fingers across the Hebrew script on the wall, thinking for a moment.

"When we were at the Sagrada Familia, Ramon mentioned that Santiago had worked on the Mezquita here. It's a church built by the Visigoths around 600 AD and then turned into a mosque during the Caliphate, rededicated as a Catholic cathedral in the thirteenth century. There's been a lot of restoration work, and from what I remember from my visit here long ago, it's seriously ornate. It would be a far better place to hide a code and it's not far from here."

Morgan and Jake headed back out into the sun, dodging the tourist groups as they walked the short distance to the Central World Heritage Site of the Mezquita. They emerged from the crowded streets into the Patio de los Naranjos, an Islamic-style ablutions court with fountains for ritual purification before prayer. The orange trees were welcome shade from the baking sun, and the sound of splashing water made this an oasis of calm. Jake walked to the fountain and plunged his hands in, scooping water up his arms and onto his face. Droplets sparkled in the sunlight and Morgan imagined the faithful repeating this action over the last thousand years, an unchanging ritual that bound generations.

"This is glorious," Jake said, his tousled dark hair wet around his temples. Morgan watched a drop of water trickle down his neck and into his shirt, and she itched to trace its path with her fingertip. She turned quickly to the archways that led into the church.

They walked in and gazed through the riot of pillars

that filled the grand space, linked by archways of red brick and white marble, the striped design repeated throughout the distinctive building. The pillars were all different sizes and types, some reused from the old Visigoth cathedral and others shipped from all over the empire in porphyry, marble and jasper.

As a mosque, the columned interior had once been open to the air at each side, a continuation of the forest of trees outside. As a church, it was more enclosed, the dim light enhanced by candles at the myriad altars. It was early so there were still only a few worshippers kneeling around the place, and a calm silence gave the atmosphere solemnity. The ornate decoration was exhausting to look at, with a combination of elaborate arabesques and detailed Arabic script in gold, rust-red and turquoise, surrounded by the Catholic icons and shrines around the walls. Morgan appreciated the incredible architectural beauty of the place, but she felt nothing of God here. The air was thick, every breath heavy with incense and candle smoke, cloying in the back of her throat.

"Santiago could definitely have carved his numeric code somewhere here," she said. "This place wouldn't have been sacred to him."

Jake turned around, stretching his arms wide as he indicated the sheer volume of space. "But where would it be? This place is huge."

Morgan gazed deeper into the forest of pillars. "I've heard that there are 856 columns here, and given his passion for numerology, it would make sense for Santiago to have carved on one of them. The question is, where to start counting?"

She began walking slowly, skirting the edge of the heart of the cathedral and heading for the *mihrab*, a semi-circular niche indicating the *qibla*, the direction of Mecca. Jake walked alongside her as they both tried to get a sense for the perspective of the place. The *mihrab* was at the opposite end from the Patio de los Naranjos and the Puerta de las Palmas, where they had entered. An extension in 960 AD had enlarged the mosque, adding even more pillars in the southerly corner.

"Hebrew is read right to left," Morgan said, walking to the furthest corner. "So I would start here for my count."

"What number are we counting to?" Jake asked, staring into the maze of columns.

Morgan grinned. "Now that really is the question. We should try all the numbers we have come across so far: 33 and 48, 70 and 140. While we're doing that, I'll have a think about the other possibilities."

They began to walk through the forest of stone, counting silently until they reached the thirty-third pillar. Morgan crouched to examine the base and Jake stretched up to look at the carved capital, its tendrils of leaves indicating it originally came from a Roman temple.

"Nothing," he whispered.

Morgan straightened. "Nothing here either. Let's try forty-eight."

A dull clang echoed through the church as they stepped away from the pillar, as if something heavy had been dropped. Morgan started, hand automatically going for her weapon. The sound of shouting voices followed, a flurry of Spanish and then what sounded like a gunshot and finally, silence. The few worshippers in sight turned their heads instinctively to the noise. One woman crossed herself and headed for a side door.

"What do you think?" Jake whispered, his hand hovering near his concealed weapon.

"Let's hurry," Morgan said, stepping quickly around the pillars to count further. As they reached forty-eight, the great doors of the Puerta de las Palmas swung open, the squeak of the hinges echoing through the cathedral. Morgan peered round the column to see a number of men entering, each armed with an assault weapon.

CHAPTER 13

Morgan counted ten of them, far too many for her and Jake to take on. The distance and the gloom would obscure them for the moment, but they had to hurry. Adam Kadmon must have worked out the last code, or perhaps Sofia had told him of this place. Morgan thought of the stunning young woman, wondering what Kadmon wanted her for, whether she even knew her grandfather was dead by this man's hand. Her heart pounded. If Kadmon was here, she would have a chance to reach him soon. Her hand curled around the grip of her gun.

She felt the whisper of Jake's breath on her neck, his hand over hers, staying her motion.

"There are too many of them. We need to find the code and get out of here. You take seventy, I'll take 140 and I'll meet you by the Puerta de San Esteban."

He slipped away, walking softly on the cool stone floor, his lips moving as he counted silently. Morgan took a deep breath and followed him, trying to ignore the men at the other end as they spread out slowly amongst the worshippers. They didn't know her or Jake by sight – they hadn't been clearly visible in the dark of the Alhambra, and Kadmon's men had no reason to suspect anyone else was here looking for the code.

She counted to pillar 70 and searched it, her fingers running over the smooth marble. Nothing. She closed her eyes for a second, considering Santiago's state of mind. What would he have been thinking as he tried to hide his tracks?

Slow footsteps echoed in the row of columns nearby, and Morgan turned to face the nearest shrine, walking quickly to kneel before the candlelit image of Saint Eulogius, one of the martyrs of Córdoba. She bent her head as if in prayer as the figure passed close behind her. The polished metal of a giant candelabra caught a glimpse of his profile and she saw that it was Adam Kadmon, his face concentrated on counting as she had done. Her hand snaked to her gun in the small of her back. All she had to do was turn. She had a clear shot.

She stood and quietly moved behind one of the pillars, heart pounding as images of her father's face came to mind. Kadmon was still clearly in view. She pulled her Barak SP-21 pistol, sighting on his head, finger tightening on the trigger.

At the last moment, she sensed someone behind her. As she began to turn in defense, he pulled her against his body, her back against his chest, his strong hands holding hers over the gun. She struggled, arching away from him, ready to fight.

"Morgan," Jake whispered next to her ear, her name a caress. "You can't do it here. There are too many men with him. What good is killing Kadmon to revenge your father if you're gone as well? He wouldn't have wanted that."

Morgan relaxed a little, letting Jake hold her tight for a moment. She could feel his heartbeat thud and the strong length of him against her back. The rage within her wanted to throw his arms off and finish Kadmon, whatever the consequences. A darker need, an edge of the forbidden, made her want to press back against him, tease him until he groaned, but this was really not the time for such distraction.

She took a deep breath and exhaled slowly. Jake was right, Kadmon would keep. They were both hunting for the Key to the Gates of Hell, after all, so there would be another time. Jake relaxed his arms and Morgan reluctantly pulled away from him, putting her gun back and hiding it within her jacket. The footsteps of Kadmon and his men were moving towards the back of the cathedral now, perhaps beginning a new count.

She looked towards the paintings of the saints around them, noting the scenes of judgement and remembering her father's teaching. For Christians, Hell was the place the wicked were sent but for Jews, that place was known as something else. Santiago might have used the same word for his coded reference to Hell. Pulling out her smart phone, Morgan quickly calculated the gematria for Gehenna, a site outside of ancient Jerusalem where followers of Moloch had sacrificed children to their gods millennia ago. It was worth a try.

"Pillar 106," she whispered, pointing. "Back that way."

They stole through the forest of columns, their movements economical, using the dense pillars as shields. There were still a few faithful worshippers within the church, but most had hurried away at the threat of violence so there was more chance of being spotted.

Counting backwards through the church, they made their way to 106 and almost immediately, Morgan found the coded square chiseled near the bottom of the column. She frowned. The square also added up to 106 in all directions, numbering the pillar the same as the position it stood in. Strange. She had been expecting a different code, one that would direct them to the next location, but this was all they had. Morgan took a picture with her smart phone and together, she and Jake slipped from the cathedral, leaving

Kadmon's men behind. Even if they had to search each pillar individually, they would have the code themselves within a few hours. Morgan tapped on her phone as they walked through the corridors, sending the photo to Martin Klein back at ARKANE. They only had a short window of opportunity to get ahead of Kadmon.

Once outside, Morgan and Jake slipped into a tourist group heading for the Alcázar de los Reyes Cristianos, the royal palace and one of the primary residences of Ferdinand II of Aragon and Isabella I of Castille, architects of the Reconquista. Morgan knew the Alcázar had also been used as the headquarters of the Inquisition in this area. Its Arab baths, designed for sensual pleasure, had been turned into chambers for torture and interrogation. Morgan definitely didn't want to go in there, and once they were far enough away from the Mezquita, she ducked into a little cafe in a side street. Jake followed, buying two cups of strong black coffee and waiting until Morgan had taken a sip before speaking.

"I'm not sorry for stopping you back there," he said. "We wouldn't have made it out of the church even if you had killed him. There were too many men."

Morgan took another sip and looked at him, the violet slash of color in her right eye a vibrant glow. She knew Jake was right, but the lust for revenge still burned in her.

"Don't stop me again." Her voice was cold steel.

Jake nodded, taking a sip of his coffee.

"What's the code this time?" he asked, after a moment's silence.

Morgan pulled out her phone, opening the picture of the carved square grid. "The number 106 represents Gehenna, the Jewish equivalent to Hell, which is how I worked out where the code was. But look, the numbers in the square also add up to 106." She held the phone up for Jake to see.

"Maybe it's a double again?" he said. "So it's 212, rather than 106."

Morgan shrugged. "It could be that, or so many other variations on a theme. I never understood the logic my father applied to his Kabbalah studies, but Martin can plug all the options into the gematria matrix and see what he comes up with." She took a longer sip of her coffee. "I've been thinking about this Key, trying to work out what it could be. A physical object, or maybe just another code?"

"Or a person?" Jake mused. "Someone who knows something that Santiago and your father wanted to protect."

Morgan's phone buzzed with a text. "Wow, that was quick. Martin must have optimized the gematria search."

She scrolled through the page of options. "Using 212, our destination could be Hong Kong or Canberra in Australia."

"Neither is particularly Jewish," Jake commented, his eyebrows lifting.

Morgan smiled. "And to be honest, I never want to visit Canberra again. It's one of those constructed cities with no soul, just bureaucrats and fake water features. It might be a version of Hell, but I don't think the Key to the Gates would be there. It doesn't have enough history. Hong Kong is a different matter though – it's one of those cosmopolitan places where you can find anything."

A second text came in and Morgan's face paled as she looked at it.

CHAPTER 14

"WHAT IS IT?" JAKE asked, reaching his hand out to touch Morgan's arm.

"Safed," she whispered, her eyes wide. "The gematria number for where my father used to live in Israel is 106. The town of Safed is also the center of Jewish Kabbalah, one of the four holiest cities to Jews. It must be the right place."

Jake pushed back his chair. "We need to get going then. Kadmon will eventually find that code and he won't be far behind us."

Morgan sat motionless in the chair, her gaze fixed on a point in the distance, her mind whirling as she considered facing the city again. She still owned the tiny flat that her father had lived in at the time of his death. *His murder*, she corrected herself, rage burning again within her. She had left the flat in the care of the Rabbi who had officiated the funeral, and he occasionally emailed to ask what she wanted to do with the rent he collected on her behalf. She always donated it to whatever cause he suggested, and really, she had never thought she would return to the little town in the hills of Galilee. But it seemed that Israel kept pulling her back.

Jake held his hand out to help her up, his dark eyes concerned. "I'll be with you. It's going to be OK."

She smiled and accepted his hand, feeling the squeeze of pressure, the reassurance of his presence. But as she stood, she thought of Kadmon's face in the Mezquita, his determination matching her own. She didn't want to bring his brand of destruction to her father's beloved town, and yet, it seemed, she had no choice but to pursue the Key there.

***

Five hours later, the pilot announced that they had crossed into Israeli air space and would soon be landing on a private airstrip near Safed. Morgan had spent the journey in turmoil, memories of her father bringing tears to her eyes even as rage bubbled within at the years of her father's life Adam Kadmon had stolen. Now she took a deep breath, readying herself to face the past. Her father had sent the letter knowing this day would come – she had to trust that he would have left clues she could follow.

They landed and jumped into a taxi, driving towards the town. Morgan looked north to where flat white Mediterranean buildings reflected the sun, the green hills bringing the city into relief. Her father liked to say that Safed was a city on a hill, like Jerusalem, one of the high places closest to God. She caught glimpses of the narrow cobblestone streets winding around the dwellings, and imagined his footsteps walking there years ago.

Eventually, Jake broke the silence.

"I've never been here, Morgan. Maybe you could tell me a bit about it?"

She shook her head, sighing a little. "Sorry, I know I'm distracted. This place brings back memories and I'm trying to think where the Key might be. Perhaps talking about the city will help, and it does have a hell of a history. Legend says that Safed was founded by a son of Noah after the great flood. The book of Judges recounts that the tribe of Naphtali dwelled here, and the city was mentioned in the writings of Josephus at the turn of the first century." She pointed out the window. "You can see some of the remainder of the ancient walls up there. It was a fortified city during the Crusades, taken first by the Christians, who were later wiped out by the Mamluk Sultanate, who turned it into a Muslim city. It's been fought over ever since, becoming primarily Jewish over time, but even now it's discussed in heated tones, like so many holy sites. It doesn't help that the president of the Palestinian National Authority, Mahmoud Abbas, was born here, evicted with his family during the war." She smiled, shaking her head a little. "I don't think this land will ever be at peace. People have been fighting over it for millennia."

Jake looked over at her, his eyes soft. "Because people love it … like you do. This land inspires passion that too easily spills into bloodshed, and there's both a blessing and a curse in that."

Morgan nodded, silent for a second before she continued.

"After the expulsion of the Jews from Spain in 1492, some of the prominent Rabbis came here and Safed became a global center for Jewish learning. It had a printing press to spread the teachings and a vibrant community of synagogues. My father was part of the school of Lurianic Kabbalah, started by Isaac Luria in the sixteenth century. Luria is buried in the cemetery here, one of the tightly packed graves, all painted bright blue. It's a strange place …"

Her voice trailed off as she visualized her father's grave in the corner of that same cemetery. The day she had buried him was the day she had sworn to end her life in Israel and begin again, an academic in Oxford far away from the blood and mayhem of this land. She had seen too much death in those years. Her husband, Elian, had died in a hail of bullets on the Golan Heights and other friends had perished in the unending conflict that Israel couldn't seem to escape. She had chosen another way and taken the path of academia – so why was it she was back here once more, ensconced in conflict, surrounded by death? Morgan imagined the ghosts that clung to her, the darkness that hid in her shadow. She pushed the thoughts aside.

"Luria was known as Ha'Ari, the Lion," she continued. "His disciples wrote down his teaching so it could be passed on. He's probably one of the most well-known Jewish mystics, considered to have spoken with the prophet Elijah." Jake raised an eyebrow at that and Morgan smiled. "Yes, well, he was an ascetic with plenty of secrets known only to his disciples. He was called to deliver Israel from the *klipot*, the husks of evil, and help souls to find *tikkun* – the restoration of the divine sparks of God scattered throughout the earth. Like any spiritual system, it has its quirks, but my father believed it as truth."

The taxi pulled up at the end of the steep cobbled path, wide enough for pedestrians, thin carts pulled by donkeys, and the inevitable scooters. Morgan and Jake began to walk up past little shops with shutters painted in hues of the ocean. The colors were picked out of a palette made from the sky and the Sea of Galilee, across the hills to the southeast. They passed a pottery shop and then a painter's studio, where abstract canvases with Hebrew lettering hung on the white walls. The smell of turpentine wafted from the shop, pointing the way to a working artist's haven. The stone walls and streets around them were clean and fresh, cafes interspersed with green plants and blooming flowers.

It was an oasis of calm directly opposed to the craziness of Jerusalem that they had visited together not so long ago on the hunt for the Pentecost stones.

"The city has always attracted artists," Morgan said. "Particularly those with a spiritual side." They rounded a corner to find a crossroads with a little path that snaked steeply up the hill. "My father's place is just up here. Martin called the Rabbi who looks after it, and we're allowed in to have a look while the tenant is out for a while."

They walked up a few hundred meters and Morgan paused in front of the door, her hand poised with the key in the lock. The door was painted in the same shade as her own blue eyes, the same as her twin sister and their English mother. The color had faded a little but she still remembered her father painting it when he had first moved here. He had been very much in love with her mother once, but had chosen Israel and archaeology over a stable family life in the wet winters of England. Leon Sierra had chosen independence and his own way of life, and perhaps Morgan had learned that from him. In a parallel universe, she would be happily married to Elian with a brood of children, her parents growing old together, her twin sister and niece by her side. Some of the Kabbalists believed in the multiverse, worlds between the light and darkness, shades of good and evil where events had turned out in a different way. But this was her only world, Morgan thought, and the choices her family had made were now her own.

Morgan turned the key and pushed the door open, pausing on the threshold. For a moment, she expected the smell of her father's cooking to greet her. He had always baked when she visited on temporary leave from the Israeli Defense Force military base further south. It was just an excuse for him to enjoy *rugelach*, the rolled pastries of Ashkenazi origin filled with chocolate and nuts. She would nibble while her father tucked in, his eyes lively as she told stories of her latest work. But the scent in the air was only fresh with a hint of salt, the wind from the south blowing in through an open window.

Jake walked in after her, and Morgan looked around the room. It was a humble space with a foldaway table for eating, a little kitchenette to the side and a bedroom one level above. Under the stairs was a study area where her father had probed the mysteries of the Torah and the Zohar, the Book of Splendor, as the letters of revelation spun before him. Morgan had never seen him engrossed in study, as he had always worked in private, but she had imagined him there. His spirituality had deepened over the years and the mysticism of the Kabbalists had become his obsession, as if somehow he could stop time and step into the space where the divine touched the earth. Regret welled up within her. Perhaps if she had insisted on knowing more about his quest, whatever this Key was, he would have told her of the Remnant. Perhaps she could have protected him, even saved his life.

"It's a hell of a view," Jake said, looking out the window over the white rooftops to the rolling hills of Galilee and its inland sea beyond.

Morgan came to stand next to him, so close she could feel the fiber of his shirt on her arms. Leon would have liked Jake, a man of action whom he would have trusted to protect his daughter. She smiled then, for her father had never really believed that she could look after herself physically, even when she had won national Krav Maga competitions. The Israeli martial art was only part of her skills these days, and she wondered what Leon would have thought of ARKANE and her role there now. He certainly would have understood the metaphysical side of what she had experienced.

"Are you OK?" Jake said, turning to look at her. "You're quiet."

All she needed to do was take a half step closer and she would be in his arms.

"I'm just thinking," Morgan whispered. "It's been a long time since I was here." She stepped away, back into the center of the room. "None of this is my father's stuff though. It's like a new place with the old one beneath. I'm trying to put myself back into how it was when he was here."

She turned towards the kitchenette, pointing to a space on the wall.

"He always had a picture of me there, changing it every year as my career progressed." She touched the wall where the image had once hung, no trace of it now under the newer paint. "In the corner of the frame, he would tuck the latest picture of Faye that my mother sent annually. He used to send one back to her as I grew."

"I don't think anyone would allow twins to be split up and raised separately these days," Jake said. "Didn't you find it strange without your sister?"

Morgan shook her head. "Not really. My parents were unorthodox in their child-rearing, for sure, but you've met Faye. You know how different we are and our parents differed in the same way. Maybe they saw the same in us when we were young. I could never regret my childhood, the times I had with my father growing up. Faye had our mother and England and we were both loved. We had different lives, but like many broken families, something new was able to grow from the wreckage and create beauty in its wake."

The sound of a plane flew low overhead and Morgan instinctively looked up.

"If none of your father's things are here, how are we meant to find whatever the next code is?" Jake asked.

"I didn't say they weren't here, just that there was nothing on show that was his." She headed towards the stairs leading up to the bedroom. "His stuff is in the attic."

The sudden sound of footsteps outside made Morgan freeze. Jake turned at the noise and as the key in the lock rattled, they both drew their weapons, training them on the door as it opened.

CHAPTER 15

THE DOOR OPENED SLOWLY and a man stepped through, awkwardly juggling his keys and two bags of shopping. His eyes widened as he saw Morgan and Jake, his gaze dropping to the two weapons pointed at him. There was a split second when Morgan saw him consider his options, an echo of how she would have behaved in the same situation. Then he gently put the bags on the floor, dropped his keys to the mat and raised his hands to show they were empty. He was tall, with black curly hair; his two-day stubble emphasized a prominent jaw. Morgan saw military experience in the ready stance of his fit, well-muscled body. He wasn't afraid of them, just curious.

"I'm Mikael Levy and this is my home," he said, in Hebrew and then again in English with a slight accent, as he registered Jake's confusion.

As Morgan covered him with her weapon, Jake moved forward and searched Mikael, patting him down swiftly. Mikael's eyes fixed on Morgan's and she felt a prick of recognition as she matched his gaze. Had she met him before? He was definitely younger than she was, but not by too many years. She struggled to think where it might have been.

"He's clean," Jake said, and Morgan lowered her gun.

"Of course I am," Mikael said. "I just went to the market." He bent to pick up the bags. "There was a text from the Rabbi, but I wasn't expecting you so soon. I presume you're here about Leon's things?"

He walked slowly to the kitchen, still wary of them. "I have *rugelach* and coffee. Let me make you some." His dark eyes flicked to Morgan again and he smiled. "Your father told me all about you … I'm opening the drawer now." He pulled it open slowly and brought out a tiny photo frame. "He always had this with him, and so I keep it here as he would have wanted me to." Mikael handed it to Morgan and she saw her own face in the frame, frozen in a moment of happiness. She remembered the day it had been taken, at a wedding of a friend when she and Elian had danced into the small hours and Leon had laughed along with them. She placed the photo back down on the countertop.

"Have we met before?" she asked, stepping closer as Mikael switched the kettle on.

"A long time ago, but I was a new recruit and you were with Elian in those days." A hint of a smile danced at the corners of his mouth. "He was a hero to us younger men. The way he died …" He broke off, shaking his head. "I'm sorry. You lost your husband that day. But you should know that his leadership and bravery are still held up as exemplary. He is remembered."

In the moment of silence that followed, Jake stepped forward, holding out his hand. Morgan could feel him bristling at this younger man's intimate knowledge of her past.

"I'm Jake Timber, Morgan's professional partner." Mikael took the proffered hand and they shook with a firm grip. So firm that Jake's knuckles turned white.

"How come you knew my father?" Morgan asked, breaking the tension of their masculine posturing.

Mikael continued making coffee, putting the little pastries on a plate as he talked.

"Like you, I did my time in the military but I became disillusioned with the never-ending spiral of violence. My wife …" He sighed. "She died after complications in childbirth and my son died soon after."

"I'm so sorry," Morgan said, acknowledging his pain. Mikael nodded in unspoken thanks.

"I came up to Galilee to hike, spending a lot of time alone during that time. I had no patience with religion, much to my parents' distress. I think they hoped I would find solace in the *shul*." Morgan smiled at that, understanding the Jewish parental pressure to attend the synagogue. "I met Leon in the hills behind Safed one day and there was something in his demeanor, a peace that I craved. I was angry with the world, but he began to teach me another way." Morgan felt a flash of jealousy that Mikael had been able to access a side of her father she had not been privy to. "After I left the military I moved up here to be closer to the Kabbalist community. I only had a few months with your father before he was killed."

The grief on his face was raw and in a flash, Morgan remembered where she had seen him before.

"You were at his funeral," she said. "You stood at the back, away from those who gathered close."

Mikael nodded. "I didn't know enough people at that point and I didn't feel as if I belonged. I knew how devastated you were, how much you had been through, first Elian and then Leon. I understand why you had to leave."

"But why do you live here now?" Jake asked, a hint of suspicion in his voice at this man's familiarity. Morgan put a hand on his arm, feeling the tension there, trying to calm him. Mikael's eyes followed her gesture, noted the caution as he continued.

"As I learned Kabbalah mysticism from Leon, he began

to speak of a Remnant, an exclusive group of Rabbis from around the worldwide Kabbalist community who met once a year to meditate on the darkness in the world. They believed it was growing, spreading, taking root, and they worried that the balance was tipping away from the light. They were also getting old and I think that perhaps Leon wanted me to become a part of it." Mikael shook his head. "Some days I think I was wrong about that, but now I'll never know. After his death, I found no written trace of the Remnant, and I can't find anyone who will even acknowledge their existence."

"That's why we're here," Morgan said softly. "The Remnant are gone, murdered, as my father was, by a man who hunts what they protected." There was no surprise in Mikael's eyes at her words. "You knew he wasn't killed by a suicide bomber?"

Mikael nodded. "I suspected. He was frenetic in those last days, spending hours in study, reciting verses until he reached an almost shamanic state, an alternate realm of consciousness. He was truly a practitioner of the highest art. There are pages in the attic, reams and reams of notes he made while in trance, meditating on the letters of the Torah or the words of the Zohar. Most make no sense at all, but there are hints of what the Remnant were protecting."

"I want to see them," Morgan said.

Mikael nodded. "Of course." He poured coffee into three mugs, putting out non-dairy creamer and sugar on a plate next to the pastries. "I'll go and get the boxes."

"Do you need help?" Jake asked. Mikael hesitated a moment and then nodded. The men went upstairs into the bedroom above and then into the loft space further up. Morgan could hear their muffled conversation, sounding each other out in their attempt to build a bridge. They both had military backgrounds but she knew that Mikael's spiritual side would make Jake uneasy. Together, they had seen things that would make the most eminent skeptic believe in something beyond the physical, but Jake had no patience with organized religion. Even many Jews would consider Kabbalism to be on the edge, however, a mystical dimension far from the confines of strict Hasidic law. Mikael seemed to blend the spiritual with the physical, and perhaps that was what they needed in their quest.

Mikael and Jake soon came back down, each carrying two boxes that Morgan vaguely recognized from what had been left in the little house after her father's death. The local Rabbi had organized her father's effects, leaving her to mourn without the terrible process of sorting through his things. She had promised to come back when the immediacy of grief had receded, but of course, she had not returned. Was it now too late?

"I helped the Rabbi pack Leon's work away," Mikael said. "His memory has been honored, Morgan."

His dark eyes were kind and Morgan saw that Mikael had loved her father in his own way. Part of her wished she could have known him properly back then, maybe talked to him at the funeral. What would her life have been like if she had stayed here, made her home in this hillside town?

"All the boxes contain fascinating insights, but this particular one has some of the last pages Leon worked on in the days before he died."

Mikael pulled a sheaf of loose paper sheets from the box. They were dense with drawings and Hebrew writing in black pen. There were faces in the margins, contorted figures, some human and some clearly demonic. Morgan reached for one of the pages, where a spiral vortex spun, misshapen figures crawling from a central pit, their claws reaching for the world above, jaws open to devour those who stood in the way.

"His drawings got darker in the days before his death," Mikael said. "He was researching the demonology of Kabbalah and the *klipot*, the husks of evil in this world ... Then there's this."

He pulled a page from a clear plastic envelope that protected it from damage. It showed a Key, made of a skeleton lifting its bony hands to plead with the Heavens above. The etching was rough around the edges and there were Hebrew letters and symbols inscribed around it. The whole drawing was surrounded by a circle, as if the line could contain its dark presence. Morgan shivered as she gazed at the skeletal figure, interceding for a doomed mankind, a more detailed rendition than the rough sketch in Santiago's notebook.

She took the page, the paper smooth on her fingers, and tried to imagine her father drawing something like this. Had he actually seen the Key? Or did he draw this while in one of his mystical trances?

"My father wrote a letter to me," she said. "I don't know when it was originally written, but it was sent recently by another man, one of the Remnant." Mikael's eyes widened with hope. Morgan shook her head. "He was killed a few days ago, but in the letter, my father mentioned a Key. Perhaps this is it. Are there any indications of where it might be or what it opens in his papers?"

Mikael shuffled through the pages.

"I've been through them all, over and over. I can't find anything that points to where it might be, and it's certainly not here. Apparently the Remnant didn't actually have it, they only protected its location. I'm not even sure they wanted it found." Mikael paused and stood up, striding to the window to look out over Galilee. "I've been trying to follow Leon's path into Kabbalah mysticism, and I've seen glimpses of this Key in my own trance states."

Jake's rapid exhalation made Mikael spin around.

"Do you doubt the physicist who studies elementary particles in order to understand the cosmos?" he said, repressed anger in his tone. "Or the biologist who examines cellular DNA to fathom how the body works? DNA is just a code that makes up the sum of human life and in the same way, the Kabbalist uses letters of the Torah to understand the spiritual heart of the world. Don't judge what you don't understand."

Jake raised an eyebrow at Mikael's outburst. "Oh, don't mind me, I'm ever the skeptic. What do you think, Morgan?"

Morgan knew he wanted her to back him up, to make some flippant comment that would put her on his side against Mikael. But as she looked at the man her father had trusted, his pupil in the mystic arts, she found herself with a glimmer of hope that he might be able to help in their quest.

"I'm not writing anything off at this point. We should consider all the angles."

Jake looked back down at the papers, his shoulders slumping as he ignored them and began to read again.

"I think we need to –"

Morgan's words were cut off as a blast of hot air and the cracking sound of an explosion shook the flat, the low rumble of collapsing buildings following swiftly after.

CHAPTER 16

MIKAEL AND MORGAN DROPPED to the floor next to Jake and all three of them crawled quickly under the large dining table, sheltering in case of falling debris. Another explosion came from nearby and they could hear shouts of people in the street, along with running footsteps. A lone woman wailed, her cries of grief a sound that this land knew only too well.

"Rockets from the north?" Morgan said, as it became clear the attack was over.

Mikael shook his head. "I doubt it. It's been quiet here for a long time now, and it's too much of a coincidence that this would happen on the day you arrive." He crept to the window, peering out across the town. "There's smoke coming from the airfield, and more around the area of the synagogue Leon used to attend."

"We need to get out of here," Jake said. "I should have let you finish that bastard Kadmon in Córdoba."

Morgan checked her weapon and then tucked it into the back of her jeans. "There's still time for that," she promised with a dark smile. "But for now, we need to move. They'll come here next, for sure." She picked up the sheaf of her father's papers, the skeletal Key prominent on the top of the pile, then turned to Mikael. "Should we take anything else?"

"Just a minute." Mikael went into the study and returned with her father's books of the Torah and the Zohar, the Book of Splendor. He put them in a holdall, along with a smaller bag he pulled from a cupboard under the sink, the familiar outline of a weapon inside. "OK, let's go. I've got a car parked at the bottom of the hill."

Jake eased the front door open, and signaled the all-clear. Mikael sprinted out into the street, Morgan and Jake following right behind him. The sound of sirens filled the air and the scent of smoke blew on the breeze. There was a deadly calm about the people who moved through the streets. This was a city that understood the threat of attack. The people here had survived so much over the years that it didn't surprise them when their world was threatened again. Many expected it, retaining the perspective of living each day as their last, relishing each moment they could live on this precious land. *I'm sorry, Papa*, Morgan thought. *I'm sorry for bringing this on your town.*

At the bottom of the hill, they reached a covered car park for the residents of the pedestrianized streets further up the slope. Mikael clicked a button on his keys as they jogged through the rows of cars, and a dusty green Jeep Wrangler flashed its lights. They pulled open the doors and jumped in, Morgan hopping in the back as Jake jumped in the passenger side.

Mikael drove out of the car park, wheels screeching as they turned onto the main road, heading away from the city and south towards the Sea of Galilee. Morgan gazed out the back window, searching for any sign that they were being followed. It looked like they were free and clear, but then two 4WD vehicles zoomed out of the side streets, several men with weapons visible in each.

"I see them," Mikael said, teeth clenched as he stepped on the accelerator. He wrenched the wheel to the right and headed into the scrubland. "We can't stay on the main road. They'll catch up and there are more towns up ahead." The Jeep bumped over the stony ground, hurtling Morgan sideways in the back. She struggled back to her seat and pulled on the safety belt just as the Jeep took some air. It flew over a bump and down into the ditch beyond. The jolt on landing slammed through her body and she glanced at Jake, wondering how his injuries were holding up to this rough treatment. His face was a little pale, but he showed no sign of pain.

"They're flanking us," Jake said, his weapon ready. "I hope you know what you're doing, Levy."

A volley of bullets flew at them from one of the vehicles and Mikael pulled the wheel sideways, but it was too late. The passenger side windows blasted apart, the safety glass collapsing inwards. Morgan pulled her sleeve up to protect her face. She saw blood on Jake's face as some of the glass cut him, but he fired back and the other vehicle pulled away. As it did so, the driver hit a large stone and the vehicle tipped sideways, its speed suddenly halted. It overturned, smoke pouring out the side as the men scrambled out, still firing after their escaping prey.

Morgan turned her head to look at the other vehicle as they sped alongside it on a parallel track, navigating the scrubland on the outskirts of the city.

"These guys look pretty upset about their friends," she said. "What's the plan?"

"We might be able to lose them in the Limonim Forest," Mikael shouted above the din. He shifted gears and changed direction, pulling away from the other vehicle. "I know the tracks in there."

Ahead of them was a patch of green, with some oak and pine areas interspersed with new plantings. As the other driver turned into an intercept pattern, Mikael pulled off the track and drove straight into the forest. The muscles in his forearms stood out as he struggled to keep control of the wheel across the rutted forest floor.

Morgan spun round in her seat as they entered, the dense trees now shielding the other vehicle from view. Mikael knew this area so they would have an advantage in here, but would the other vehicle even try to come in after them, or remain to ambush them on the routes out of the area?

"It would be good to have a chat with one of these guys," Morgan said, as their speed slowed and Mikael guided them through the trees. The car engine was brutally loud in the calm of the natural surroundings. "I'd like to know where Kadmon has his base, what he's planning. What do you think?"

Jake nodded, rubbing the blood from his head with his shirt sleeve. "I'd definitely like to have a few choice words with them."

"There's an area up ahead where we could wait," Mikael said. "If they come in here, they'll have to pass us."

"Just stop a minute," Morgan said. "Let's see if they're even following anymore."

Mikael slowed and shut down the engine. For a moment, all Morgan could hear was their breathing, calmer now the immediate threat was over. Then she heard the sound of another vehicle revving as it tried to navigate the forest, the crunch of gears as the driver downshifted.

"They're coming," she said, her voice determined. "Let's get to your spot quickly."

They drove on a little way until they reached a clearing in the wood, a temporary shed standing in the corner.

"There are tools in there," Mikael said. "Rope, axes, that kind of thing."

"Park the Jeep next to it," Morgan said. "I've got an idea."

***

Ten minutes later, the remaining 4WD vehicle rolled into the clearing, three men inside with guns at the ready. They stopped when they saw the empty Jeep next to the hut, parked carefully at the far side of the clearing. The man in the passenger seat spoke into a short wave radio, waited a second and then signaled for the two others to get out.

The men exited the vehicle and walked towards the hut, guns in outstretched hands before them. They covered each other with sweeping movements, scanning the forest around them. One had a submachine gun slung across his shoulder and as they reached the hut, he lowered his pistol and holstered it. His meaty hands gripped the stock of the submachine gun and without warning, he peppered the hut with bullets.

Strips of wood flew off the structure. The metallic sound echoed through the clearing, smoke dissipating on the breeze. The other man walked towards the hut, his own pistol at the ready. Just as he stepped forward to open the door, his head rocked sideways and he dropped to the ground, blood flowing from a wound on the side of his neck. He clutched at it, writhing in pain. The other man sprinted for cover behind the hut, on the opposite side from where the attack had come. Another shot rang out and he went down too, hand clutching at his chest. He turned towards the woods and shot off the remaining bullets into the green before collapsing.

The remaining man in the vehicle scooted across into the driver's seat, scrambling for the keys, trying to get away. Morgan pushed her gun against the side of his head, leaning forward from the backseat, which she had slipped into as the gunshots rang out.

"Put the keys down," she said, her voice molten steel.

The man raised his hands, his eyes wide in the mirror.

His face was heavily tattooed, marking him out as one of Kadmon's men. As his gaze met hers, she saw something else in him, a flash of fear, not of her, but of what would happen to him because of this. She knew an instant before he took action, that he would not give up so easily.

Sure enough, he thrust open the door and threw himself out, scrambling to his feet and running towards the woods. Morgan jumped from the backseat, sighting on the man as he ran. She aimed and fired once. He dropped to the ground, clutching his leg, then pulled himself up again, dragging his injured limb, trying to get into the forest.

Mikael and Jake emerged from the woods behind and to the side of the hut. As Jake checked the bodies of the other two, Mikael joined Morgan as she walked after the injured man.

"I'm not going to kill you," she said. "I just need to talk."

He turned, his expression desperate as he shouted at her, a stream of Spanish she could just understand.

"They'll kill me anyway. Please, finish it."

The man fell to the ground, his hands clutching the bloody wound. Morgan kept her gun trained on him and approached cautiously.

"Where is Kadmon's base?"

The man moaned, his eyes watching Morgan, but she knew the fear was not of her, or of dying here. There was no time for hesitation, and she saw Adam Kadmon's face as she shot into the man's other leg and he howled in agony.

"Where are you going next?" Morgan moved closer, her aim now clearly between his legs. Her eyes were fixed on the wounded man's face, her face a sculpted portrayal of fury.

Mikael raised an eyebrow. "Remind me not to piss you off," he said.

This time the man wouldn't shut up, a torrent of words spilling from him, his breath ragged as he clutched at both legs, blood oozing out onto the pine needles.

"What did he say?" Mikael asked.

"Kadmon wants the Key, and when they find it, they will take the girl to the Gates. He doesn't know where the Gates are exactly, but it's a castle, and not here or in Spain. Sofia is with them, and they call her a daughter of the Remnant." Morgan felt a kinship with the young woman, hunted for what her grandfather had started, and what Morgan's own father had protected.

Jake came over and stood next to Morgan, wiping blood from his hands.

"Those other two had no identity papers, nothing to trace them. But clearly others from the group will be coming through the forest to find them. We need to make a move." He gently touched Morgan's arm. "There are too many of them to try and get Sofia back now. We have to trust that he's keeping her alive for a reason."

Morgan nodded.

"Alright, we'll retreat for now but we're not leaving Israel until we know where to find the Key. And I know just the person to help us."

CHAPTER 17

Pushing the blue door open, Adam Kadmon stepped into the modest home that had once been Leon Sierra's haven. He had never met the man, but he had paid the bomber who had blown the bus up that day, promising extravagant reward for the martyr's family. In a land scarred by such killings, it was a less noticeable method of ridding the world of another member of the Remnant.

There were a couple of boxes on the floor. The contents of one lay strewn across the carpet, a man's handwriting on the pages of jumbled notes. Adam bent to pick up a couple of the pages, scanning the stream of consciousness. He frowned. Were these just the ravings of a man deep in a spiritual trance, or was there a truth hidden in Leon's papers? Those who had been here before the attack must have taken anything of real worth, but who were they and why did they also seek the Key?

Adam walked into the area where Leon Sierra had studied. The air felt rarefied and Adam was aware of a tingling sensation, as if something shimmered just outside his vision. A rush of doubt flooded through him. He had assumed that the Remnant were corrupt, inflated with a sense of their own importance, unwilling to commit to the grander goal. But had he actually destroyed the man who could have led him to the Key?

Sweat broke out on his brow, prickled under his arms as a sense of anger and frustration rose within. Adam began to systematically search the room, emptying drawers, lifting papers, looking for clues to where he should go next. He strode into the kitchen, pulling open drawers and cupboards.

A radio crackled from outside. The door creaked open and Carlos, his tattooed bodyguard, put his great head around the corner. His expression was downcast, his eyes not meeting Adam's.

"They've escaped, sir. One of the vehicles was disabled in the scrublands and when the men got inside the nearby forest, they found three of our men dead and the targets missing." He fell silent, waiting for the explosion to come.

Adam slammed his fist down on the kitchen countertop, the sound reverberating through the apartment.

"Bastards," he said, his face contorted with anger. "Get access to the satellite surveillance. I want to know where they're going next." His gaze dropped to the counter and he noticed a small photo lying there. A woman looked out at him, dark curls around a striking face, her eyes a brilliant blue with a violet slash through the right.

Adam picked it up, looking more closely at the image. She would be older now, but this was definitely Leon Sierra's daughter. He had not intended revenge on the children for the sins of their fathers, but if this Morgan was intent on beating him to the Key, he would have to deal with her as he would with Sofia. The daughters of the Remnant would be a sacrifice to the dark power that drove him onwards.

CHAPTER 18

FATHER BEN COSTANZA FOUND his breath a little short as he walked up the stone steps to his office on the first floor. He stood at the window as his pulse calmed, watching the students lazing on the grass below in the quad of Blackfriars Hall in the heart of Oxford. He smiled a little. They were so young, these students, their faces lit with hope and the possibility of a bright future ahead. He still taught some tutorials in theology, but his mind was often elsewhere these days.

Ben knew the students saw him as another creature, utterly removed and invisible to their worldview, his wrinkled, shrunken old flesh anathema to their young lives. Had he once looked at his own tutors that same way? A flash of memory and Ben remembered that one amazing summer when he had fallen in love. As a Catholic priest who had taken his vows, he could only ever dream of her, and Marianne Sierra had belonged to another anyway. At least he could honor her memory and watch over her twin girls as their lives progressed.

Pulling his smart phone from the folds of his black Dominican cloak, Ben checked the text again. It had been a while since he had heard from Morgan, and yet here was a message from her halfway across the world asking to speak with him. He worried about her involvement with ARKANE, but equally, he recognized a spirit of adventure in her, a wild creature who could not be tamed. That kind of spirit must be allowed to roam, and he would be here as long as possible to help her.

Would he want to be young again now, in this crazy fast-paced world? Ben looked out the window once more. It seemed as if the rate of change kept increasing. He had just come from a meeting to discuss how they would turn the precious library area on the ground floor into a more usable space. Right now, it was filled with shelves containing oversize physical books, some beautifully illustrated, many of them containing precious wisdom from the history of the Church. The young librarian had told the gathered monks that the students had petitioned for more desks with super-fast Wifi connection, and proposed removing the old shelving, retaining just a few of the old books for display and decoration purposes. Ben shook his head. Times had changed indeed, but he supposed that even Oxford must move with those times.

He sighed and turned to put his little kettle on: his daily cups of blended chai were at least one way to stay in control of his world. He turned on the computer and poured his tea, sitting down carefully, the chair creaking under the weight of his old bones. He signed into Skype and called Morgan.

Ben smiled as he saw her lovely face on the screen, the dark brown curls hanging loose about her face, her blue eyes vibrant and the slash of violet almost glowing on the screen. Ben saw the fire in her and knew she must be on a mission again. He had seen that look on her face before, when he had helped her track down the Ark of the Covenant. It had almost ended them both in smoke and flames, but here they were once again.

"Hi, Ben," Morgan said. "You look well. Are you OK?"

Ben smiled. "As well as can be, although the autumn turns and my old bones start to protest at the rigors of the Order."

Morgan laughed. "I've never envied you those crack of dawn masses, but I know you love it really."

"When are you coming home again?" Ben asked.

Morgan's Oxford house was only a few streets away from Blackfriars, but she was rarely there these days. Ben sometimes popped in for a cup of tea with her neighbor to visit Morgan's sometime cat, Shmi.

A shadow crossed her face and Ben noticed the strain in the muscles around her eyes. "I can't say exactly, but once again I need your help with something. Do you have time?"

"For you, anything, my dear. You know that."

Morgan pulled out a sheaf of paper and held it up to the camera. "Can you see this?"

It was blurry at first, and then the focus shifted. The drawing showed a kind of key, with a skeleton on top pleading with Heaven. It was haunting, as if the bones communicated a desperate need for salvation. It was surrounded by symbols and Hebrew words, written in a shaky hand. As Ben stared at it, the sun went behind the clouds outside and a cold wind blew through the old window frame in front of the desk. He shivered and pulled his cloak more closely around him.

"What is it?" Ben asked. "Is that what you're looking for?"

Morgan pulled the image away again, but the picture was seared into Ben's mind, the bony limbs imprinted on his consciousness. He knew that he would see the Key when he closed his eyes tonight.

"We think it's meant to be the Key to the Gates of Hell," Morgan said, raising her eyebrows and giving a wry smile.

"I know it sounds a little crazy, and we don't actually know whether it's real or what it's supposed to do, but my father was trying to protect its location before he died." Ben heard the pain in her voice, and although he had no love lost for Leon Sierra, his heart ached for Morgan.

"And you want to find it now," Ben finished for her.

"There's more." Morgan paused, her eyes flashing with anger and Ben knew he would never want to stand against this fierce woman. "Someone else is looking for it, as well. Someone who is capable of great violence, someone who wants to open these Gates and let whatever is in there out into the world." She shook her head. "It sounds crazy but what I've seen with ARKANE makes me wonder … What do you think, Ben? I'm at a loss as to where to go next. We need to find the Key, but I don't know where to start. The clues have stopped in Safed."

"Email me a copy of the image," Ben said, "and I'll have a look in the archives here. There are still a few favors I can call in with the theologians of Oxford if necessary. I suppose it's urgent as ever?"

Morgan smiled, her eyes lighting up at his acquiescence. "Of course, but I know you love the chase. I'll bring you back some chai spice when I come for tea next time, I promise."

"Make that soon." Ben turned serious. "You be careful now, Morgan. Your family wants you home again, as do I."

Morgan looked wistful, her voice tinged with guilt. "Have you seen Faye and Gemma?"

"They came to a fundraising event the college put on last week. Gemma was such a sweetheart, until she ate too much ice cream and ran around like a little hellion." Ben laughed, his eyes crinkling in pleasure at the memory. "It's so good to have the laughter of children around the college. We old men take ourselves far too seriously otherwise."

"I wish I could have been there with you all, Ben." A

frown deepened in Morgan's forehead. "I want to be home more, but this is something that I have to see through, something about my father's death. I don't want to tell Faye until it's all over so please don't mention I called, but I miss you all."

Ben nodded. "Give me a few hours to work on this Key and I'll get back to you. Get some rest, you look tired."

Morgan smiled and signed off, her face disappearing with the connection. Ben's office was quiet and lonely once more as the warmth of her voice faded. The computer dinged a moment later as an email arrived and Ben steeled himself to look again at the image of the Key. Something about it made his skin itch, as if tiny creatures burrowed into him with jagged teeth.

He opened the file, noting the fine detail of the skeleton, the intricacy of the edges of the Key. He forced his gaze away from the image and looked at the words and symbols etched around the edge, translating from the Hebrew, allowing the mesh of his mind to start making connections.

Ben sat back in his chair, staring out into the quad. The sounds of Oxford faded away as his mind roamed the stores of memory, years of theology and philosophy swirling about him as he tried to sift through the patterns. Sometimes the truth was not one specific thing but an amalgam of many. He had learned with age that the truths of his own Church were built upon the beliefs of other faiths, even the superstitions of pagans, whose gods had been assimilated into the Christian faith over millennia. For Ben, this layering was like a rich silt where new shoots could grow and the compost of ancient faith allowed new life to rise. It was into these layers that his mind now wandered, for even though Ben was surrounded by books and papers, his computer tapped into the vast storehouse of the Bodleian Library, the trick was knowing where to start looking.

After a moment, Ben refocused. He took a sip of his chai, the spicy tea now cool in the ceramic mug. He pulled himself up from the chair and went to his bookshelf, which took up the length of his study, encompassing the entire back wall. *Even if they digitized the whole of Blackfriars Library*, he thought, *I will keep my physical books here until they cart me out in a box.* His joints creaked as he stooped a little. *That may be sooner than I would wish*, he mused.

Ben reached for his King James Bible, one of several versions he kept for study along with the scriptures in Hebrew and ancient Greek. The only way to truly fathom the words was to read in the original, but for this, the King James Version would suffice. He lifted the heavy tome and rested it on the back of a chair, his fingers skipping through the thin pages, familiar verses leaping out at him as he thumbed his way to the back. Here it was, Revelation 1:18: *I am he that liveth, and was dead; and behold, I am alive for evermore, Amen; and have the keys of hell and of death.* But this was Jesus speaking in a New Testament text, not a Jewish scripture. Why would the Kabbalists refer to something Christian?

He flicked back through the Bible to Isaiah, a book sacred to both Jews and Christians, and after a few moments, found what he sought. *I said in the cutting off of my days, I shall go to the gates of the grave: I am deprived of the residue of my years.* The pages rustled as a draft blew in from the windows and Ben shivered a little, feeling the cold deep in his bones. He prayed that it would not be Morgan who was cut off and deprived of years. *Take my old bones, Lord*, he prayed. *But not hers.*

The Hebrew version used Sheol for the grave, an abode for the dead, a dark place cut off from God where shades dwelled. Sheol was a neutral place, whereas the term Gehenna was truly the destination of the wicked, the biblical Valley of Hinnom where pagans had sacrificed their children to Moloch. Was this Key to a dark underworld or a true Hell, Ben wondered? The pleading skeletal Key flashed through his mind. It was surely from a place of torment, a place of the dead.

Ben sighed, and reveled in his breath. At this stage in his life, each moment was a blessing, each inhalation a miracle. He turned back to the bookshelf and pulled an oversize tome on biblical art history down, the exertion making him wheeze a little. He laid the book on his desk and opened it to the sculptures of Rodin, flicking over until he saw what he was looking for.

The Gates of Hell were fifteenth-century bronze doors depicting scenes from the Bible, influenced by Dante's *Inferno* and the inspiration for Rodin's more famous works. The original figure of *The Thinker* sat at the top of the doors, looking down at the suffering below. The couple from *The Kiss* had been portrayed in the panel originally, but were removed as they didn't fit the scene of suffering. The effect was chaotic and movement seemed to shudder from the images on the page, the detail of the sculpture depicting sinners writhing in torment, trying to escape the cloying embrace of the bronze sea. Ben stared into the picture, the juxtaposition of so much history of speculation about what Hell could be. But again, it was the Christian Hell, a place of active suffering.

Ben slammed the book shut, his mind on the simpler world of the early Jews. What was hell when you lived in the desert? It wasn't fiery torment. It was ... of course, it could only be. Ben smiled and turned to the computer to call Morgan back.

CHAPTER 19

"The more I think about it, I'm convinced that this whole thing resonates with salt."

"What do you mean?" Morgan asked, frowning at the screen as Ben's image crackled a little over the Skype connection. Jake and Mikael stood behind her, both listening closely to the conversation.

"Bear with me," Ben said, his voice lively, the excitement of his realization driving him on. "The idea of Hell for the ancient Hebrews was a place of emptiness, a land where nothing would grow, a place of death where you couldn't even drink the water. Salt seasoned their food and was an integral part of sacrifice, as well as being used to preserve the dead in many cultures at that time. It's a powerful symbol of both life and death. Now look at the image again," Ben continued. "See, the chemical symbol for salt, NaCl, is scribbled on the edge of the page. The calligraphy makes it hard to understand but once I started looking, there were other things too. On the opposite side, you can just make out the word *melekh*, or King. It has the same gematria number as salt, which is 78. It's all there. Do you see?"

"OK," Morgan said, a trace of doubt in her voice. "I can see those things in the text surrounding the Key, but how does that help us find where it is?"

Ben hesitated. "This is where we have to extrapolate a little and I'll admit, I may be wrong about the location. But for the ancient Israelites and modern Jews, the Dead Sea is also called the Salt Sea. There are even some who believe that the site of Sodom and Gomorrah lies beneath those waters. Scripture tells us that Lot's wife was turned into a pillar of salt there, and now, similar salt pillars rise from the depths. Of course, the exact location of Sodom and Gomorrah has never been officially acknowledged so this is where you'll need the restricted archaeological surveys that I know have been done on the Dead Sea. I'm sure your ARKANE contacts can get those for you."

Morgan turned to Jake and he nodded, pulling out his smart phone to send details to Martin Klein. Ben continued.

"Did your father ever mention the Dead Sea, Morgan? Did he ever take you down there?"

Morgan nodded. "Of course, we did the tourist trip to Ein Gedi and on to Masada, but there wasn't anything that particularly stands out from what I remember."

"He was in Beersheba when he was killed," Mikael said, his voice flat. "We don't know why he was so far south in the Negev desert, but perhaps it was something related to the Key."

Ben frowned at the unfamiliar voice.

"This is Mikael Levy," Morgan explained, as Mikael ducked into the frame and waved a hand. "He worked with my father. He's helping us search for the Key."

Ben smiled, and Morgan saw his relief that she had friends to help her.

"Well, I think you should investigate the Dead Sea," he said. "From the drawing, we assumed the Key was made of bone, but perhaps it could actually be fashioned from salt?" He paused. "Go safely, Morgan."

***

A few hours later, they were parked up near the water's edge on the western bank of the Dead Sea, a few kilometers south of the resorts that had grown up around Ein Gedi. During the drive down along the west bank of the Jordan River, Martin had sent them a GPS location based on classified sub-aqua archaeology and Mikael had called in some favors to get them appropriate scuba gear for the environment. Once again, Morgan was grateful for the access and connections that ARKANE provided.

"I didn't even think you could dive the Dead Sea," Jake said, as they started to pull the gear from the back of the Jeep.

"It's considered extreme and only for highly experienced divers," Mikael said, as together they hefted down a chest. He flipped open the lid, revealing kilos of lead. "You also need a lot of extra weight to get down. At over nine times the saltiness of the ocean, we'll be super buoyant." His eyes glinted. "Oh yes, and you'll need to wear a full face mask so you can't accidentally swallow any water while you're down there. The salt concentrate can swell the larynx and lead to near-instant asphyxiation."

Morgan almost laughed out loud at Jake's deep frown, but she knew he wouldn't lose face by voicing his concerns. Mikael was right about the dangers in what they were attempting, but she knew that they were all experienced divers so it wouldn't be a problem – if they remained calm, of course. She looked back to the north. And if they didn't have to deal with any company.

The guys began to strip, Mikael revealing a tightly

muscled torso with just the right amount of dark hair. Morgan averted her eyes before he noticed her gaze. Jake kept his t-shirt on, and she felt a rush of concern. Would his injured body deal with the gear? Would his scars hurt in the salt?

"Maybe one of us should stay up here?" she said. "Just in case Kadmon's guys find us."

"You volunteering?" Jake said, his eyes blazing as he pulled on his wetsuit, the challenge obvious. Morgan shook her head.

"Guess one of us wouldn't be much use against them anyway." She smiled innocently. "And who would want to miss out on the chance to dive this place?"

She stretched out her arms and spun around to encompass the landscape in her reach. The low hills were shades of dust, an arid brown strewn with rocks and boulders. On the border of Jordan, Palestine and Israel, the Dead Sea was also the lowest place on earth, lower even than sea level. Salt encrusted the shoreline where the waters lapped, a languid blue that belied the hyper salination of its depths. It was a harsh environment, an eerie place that people drove through as fast as possible, fleeing the desert where nothing lived. The spirits that haunted here were withered and desiccated, their corpses mummified by the dry heat, their souls seeking a place to rest in this parched land.

Seeing the two men were almost ready, Morgan pulled on her shorty wetsuit quickly, tugging the neoprene over her skin. The water temperature was like a warm bath all year round and with the additional gear, it was good to have at least some freedom of movement in her lower half. They dragged the weights to the water's edge, putting them on in the water, using its buoyancy to aid the completion of gearing up. They each buddy-checked the other, silent as they made sure they would all be safe. Mikael carefully inspected the seals on their face masks, and Jake checked his in return as Mikael attached a catch bag full of extra gear to his jacket with a carabiner clip.

Finally, it seemed they were ready. Mikael took the lead, pointing his thumb down, indicating descent. Morgan dumped the air from her BCD jacket, exhaling as she let the weight pull her under, relaxing her lungs so she became negatively buoyant, sinking beneath the gentle waves. Under the water, Morgan breathed more easily, the rhythmic sound of her regulator lulling her into the relaxed state that diving aroused. The combination of long deep breaths, physical ease and a sense of wonder brought her alive down here. The world beneath made her excruciatingly aware of her physicality, the shortness of life and her tiny span upon the earth. Strangely, that insignificance brought her comfort, for when her bones were dust, this place would just carry on. The peace she experienced when diving was addictive and Morgan craved the depths, understanding those who chose to keep descending until narcosis made them uncaring of ever surfacing again. Down here, life could turn on an exhalation, when the diver sank past the ability to return.

The weight that had been so constricting above water now enabled her to sink into the welcoming green, the buoyancy of the salt lifting the weight from her chest. Morgan tilted her body so she could sink further down. The pressure forced her mask against her face and she equalized instinctively. Her movements were natural, but this was unlike any other dive she had ever done. Whereas usually she would expect to be surrounded by ocean life, this environment was empty, at least to the human eye. In fact, there was a vital microbial and bacterial population here, thriving in the severe environment of the lake.

A crystalline pillar loomed suddenly from the murky water and Morgan kicked her fins gently, gliding towards it, keeping her arms folded against her chest so as not to touch anything by accident. Through her mask she could see the individual salt crystals that had coalesced over time into these giant columns, reminiscent of ice sculptures. The nodules looked like a strange form of coral, clumped together in cauliflower shapes to rise up through the cloudy water. There were other natural sculptures sticking up from the bottom, some like boulders and others with fingers pointing towards the blue sky above. Morgan spun in the water and looked behind her, the two figures of Jake and Mikael following behind. With the identical masks and tanks, it was hard to tell them apart.

The turbulence from her fins lifted a coating of dust from the salt, clouding the water. For a moment, she lost sight of her companions and Morgan hung motionless, her senses alert. The skeletal figure flashed into her mind, its limbs outstretched, begging for salvation.

A ping echoed through the water, a distinctive metallic sound. Mikael had attached an elasticated ball to his tank and by flicking it, he could at least communicate a little. Morgan swam towards the noise and the long forms of the two men were soon visible again. She gave the OK signal and Mikael turned to fin deeper, checking the compass heading on his computer console.

They swam past freshwater vents that jetted into the bottom of the Dead Sea, the less saline water appearing as coils and eddies like smoke twirling up to the surface. After a few minutes, Mikael slowed as they reached a particularly dense area of salt structures. He hung, neutrally buoyant, in the water on the edge, checking his compass. Morgan glanced at her computer, noting depth and time. They would have to do longer decompression stops at this point, but they still had time left. Mikael pointed into the maze of salt pillars and then swam in, Morgan following with Jake behind.

They finned between the pillars, and Morgan looked up

and around her at the towering structures. So few people had even seen this place, it was pristine, untouched. There was a sense of the primitive, that perhaps these were ancient gods turned to salt, destined to lie forgotten here in the silence of millennia. There was a touch of the sinister as well; if it had been Sodom and Gomorrah, the tales told of this city would indeed haunt the depths. Morgan remembered a story told by her father from the *midrash*, where a young girl had taken pity on a beggar and given him bread. The people of Sodom were so corrupted that when they discovered her good deed, they coated her in honey and hung her from the city walls until she was stung to death by bees. The story had stuck in Morgan's mind and she could never eat honey without thinking of the girl on the walls. The Talmud said that the girl's dying screams had heralded the city's destruction, for they had driven God to obliterate the place where no righteous man could be found.

Mikael stopped finning and hovered in mid-water by a thick pillar. He examined his dive computer carefully and then pointed at the nearby column. Jake glided closer and Morgan followed suit, peering through the murky water at the surface of the salt structure. At first glance it was like any of the others, a combination of glossy surface nodules and grey silt covering. But then Morgan saw what Mikael was pointing at. Engraved into the salt was the six-pointed Seal of Solomon, the image from the fabled ring that had given the King of Israel the power to command demons, a protective amulet against evil. The two interlocked triangles symbolized the impact of the spiritual on the physical realm – that as above, so below. It signified the mingling of opposites, the good and the evil natures, beginning and end, each as necessary to the world as the other. Morgan remembered her father teaching her this symbol, so resonant to Jews as the Star of David. She finned closer and lightly ran her fingers around the edge of the star, looking for what it might signify here.

The swirling silt from the water had encrusted the engraving but as she brushed it away, she saw something else, an indentation where a hole had been plugged. Morgan's heart thudded with excitement and she began to brush away the silt. Jake came closer and with his spare regulator he released a spurt of air, revealing what was underneath.

CHAPTER 20

A HOLE RAN HORIZONTALLY into the rock, and there was clearly something metal within it. Jake turned and beckoned, moving away from the pillar to allow Mikael access with his catch bag of extra gear. Mikael's scuba diving contacts had recommended bringing down a special type of pump which super-heated water and used a nozzle to direct the flow, causing the solidified salt to melt under the high pressure. Now Mikael took it from his bag and, bracing himself against the next pillar, he directed the nozzle towards the metallic glint. The salt dissolved and swirled in the water like milk.

After another minute, Mikael shut off the flow and they waited a second for the cloudy water to dissipate before finning back to look at the pillar. The shape of a small metal box could clearly be seen. Morgan met Mikael's gaze, matching his excited smile with her own and then turned to give an enthusiastic OK signal to Jake. Mikael blasted more of the salt away, until finally Jake was able to lift the metal box from the pillar and place it into the catch bag.

Morgan could hardly wait to get back up to the surface, but they did the required safety stops as they ascended, ensuring correct decompression but taking longer than she would have wanted. As she hung mid-water, she caught Jake's eye and smiled at him. His grin matched hers. This was why Morgan loved ARKANE. It wasn't just the illicit knowledge, the sense of being on the edge of the unknowable. It was also the thrill of what they could do in the world, and she was glad Jake was back to enjoy it with her.

Finally, the three of them broke the surface of the water and the weight of the lead hung heavy on them again. Morgan tugged off her jacket and weight belt, dragging them to shore, her legs trembling at being subject to gravity again, the freedom of weightlessness lost. Jake spluttered as he pulled off his mask too fast, getting water into his mouth. He spat and hawked his throat, grimacing at the violent taste. Mikael grinned, turning away quickly so Jake didn't see his amusement, and carried the catch bag up to the Jeep along with the gear.

Morgan grabbed a towel and opened a can of Coke, handing another to Jake to wash out his mouth. The cool sweetness was refreshing and she began to feel connected to her body again as the post-dive headiness wore off. She tapped the catch bag.

"What do you think? Should we open the box here, or wait until we can get it to a controlled environment?"

"I'm sure we can get access to a lab at one of the universities," Jake said. "It would only delay us a couple of hours."

Mikael opened the bag and pulled out the box, placing it on the edge of the Jeep. It was a camouflage dark green metal. Jake bent closer to examine it.

"It looks like a World War II ammunition box," he said. "It should have kept the contents dry." He turned to Morgan. "Do you think your father put it there?"

"I really don't know," she said. "But it seems there was a lot I didn't know about his life." She reached for the box and lifted it slightly with both hands. It was heavy and the contents shifted slightly.

"I think we should open it now," Morgan said. "The Key looks pretty robust in the diagrams."

Jake raised an eyebrow. "Uh huh," he said with a grin. "Not that you're impatient or anything. And if Marietti asks, I wasn't here for this part."

Morgan smiled back, rebellion in her eyes, as Mikael grabbed a screwdriver from the back of the Jeep.

"Here," he said, handing it to Morgan. "It's all yours."

She put the tip of the screwdriver into the gap where the lid was tight against the rest of the box and began to lever it, going around the edges, shifting a millimeter at a time. Had her father sealed this years ago? If he hadn't left it there, he must have at least known of its existence. His drawings of the Key were so intricate that he must have seen it for himself. Morgan thought of him diving down into those murky depths, precious cargo in hand. Maybe he'd been running from something back then, too. Before that bastard Kadmon caught up with him.

After levering slowly for a couple of minutes, finally something gave and the pressure relaxed. The seal broke and the lid popped up. Morgan examined the contents as Jake and Mikael leaned around to look at it too.

"Well, that's disappointing," Jake said, voicing everyone's thoughts.

The box contained a milky white sludge with lumps of solidified salt within it. Clearly, water had gotten into the box over the years, dissolving whatever had been there. Morgan poked the screwdriver into the contents, testing to see if there was anything underneath the viscous gunk. The tip just kept touching the metal container on the opposite side. A flood of disappointment made Morgan's heart sink. All this way for nothing. If the Key had been salt, then it was gone.

Jake pulled out his phone, his expression serious. "I'll see what Martin can find out. There must be other options."

Morgan walked to the water's edge and stood looking out towards Jordan on the opposite bank. She imagined her father standing here. What would he have been thinking back then? Had he been desperate to hide the Key, aware of its potential power?

"I don't believe Leon would have put the Key down there," Mikael's voice was soft, as he came to stand next to her. "If he had wanted to destroy it, there would have been easier ways. I knew your father, Morgan. He was a smart man. This is just another test, I'm sure of it."

She nodded. "I feel that way too, but where do we go now?"

The sound of engines in the distance made them both look up and to the north. The noise carried on the still air and the vehicles were a while away, but Morgan sensed a wariness in Mikael's stance. She felt the same.

"How about we think on this while driving south?" Morgan said, heading back to the Jeep. "I'd like to visit Beersheba anyway. Perhaps my father left something there before his death."

Mikael nodded. "It's worth a shot."

As they approached the Jeep, Jake finished putting the rest of the gear into the back and they hopped into the vehicle. They drove south in silence and Morgan gazed out at the harsh landscape, a deathly beauty that put life in perspective. Out here, it all became very simple: find fresh water or die. It was easier to be close to God, because civilization had been stripped away. In the cities, humanity found endless ways to divert attention from the bigger questions, but out here, with no distraction, you could only face stark truth. For a moment, Morgan wanted to stride across this hard place and mourn her father, alone but for the wide expanse of the sky above.

Jake's phone buzzed.

"It's Martin," he said after a moment. "There are salt

caves a little further south, alongside the southern basin of the Dead Sea." He turned in his seat, hope in his eyes. "They're located underneath Mount Sodom, which is entirely made of halite or rock salt. Most unusual apparently."

"A dry environment, too," Mikael said. He stepped on the accelerator and Morgan noticed him glance in the mirror, his concern evident. "It's got to be worth a look, and it's not far from here."

***

Within half an hour, they had reached a more industrial part of the Dead Sea, where the water was a collection of shallow pools processed to extract minerals. It had a desolate air, as if this ecosystem sensed the end was near and each day another inch evaporated into the atmosphere. Electricity pylons stood across the sandbanks, their shadows like stakes into the heart of the land.

Jake pointed up to the hills on the right side of the road.

"You see that separate pillar up there. It's called Lot's Wife."

"The Lord rained down burning sulfur on Sodom and Gomorrah … destroying all those living in the cities and also the vegetation in the land. But Lot's wife looked back, and she became a pillar of salt," Morgan said, quoting from the book of Genesis. "I never thought that was quite fair. She always seemed quite blameless in the whole sordid tale."

"Not much in scripture is fair," Mikael said, no trace of amusement in his voice. As his eyes flicked to meet Morgan's in the mirror, she caught a flash of something off to the side of the road. She turned her head to see a huge truck barreling out from behind one of the works' buildings. She shouted a warning. But it was too late.

CHAPTER 21

MIKAEL SLAMMED THE WHEEL sideways in evasive maneuvers but the truck smashed into the driver's side, the sound echoing through the desolate salt valley. Mikael threw his arm up to protect his face, his body thrown violently sideways by the impact. Jake's head whipped back and smashed into the glass on the passenger side. He grunted and his head dropped to his chest, unmoving. Morgan slammed into the side door, the pain of impact rocking through her.

But the attack wasn't over, as they were pushed towards the steep edge of the road.

"We have to get out of here!" she shouted at the two men, smacking her fists against the seats in front of her, but Jake was still and Mikael's responses were sluggish as he shook his head slowly in a daze.

The truck revved again and the Jeep slid off the side of the narrow road. Morgan braced herself in the seat as the vehicle rolled down the embankment towards the water. They were strapped in, but it didn't lessen the impact as the Jeep landed upside down in the shallow water. Scree and rocks tumbled down with them, pelting the upturned vehicle. The saltwater began to seep into the vehicle immediately. Jake's unconscious body lay face down, his mouth open, the trickle close to his face.

Morgan could hear shouts from men on the road above and the slip-sliding of coarse rocks as they began to descend the slope. This was not an accident, and she had a feeling these men weren't intending to help. She undid her safety belt and drop-rolled into the body of the vehicle, then reached down to undo Jake's belt and drag him up so his face was at least out of the intense salty water. Blood dribbled from a deep cut on his temple, pooling in the corkscrew scar. She slapped his face and he groaned.

"Jake, you bastard, wake up," she said, shaking him. "I need you."

Mikael coughed in the seat next to them, rubbing his chest. "Is he OK?" he whispered, his voice hoarse.

Morgan turned to see Mikael's handsome face frowning with concern. Jake rolled his head suddenly and groaned, just as a hail of rocks announced the arrival of the men outside.

Morgan reached for her gun. Mikael put out his hand to stop her.

"There's no point," he said. "There's too many of them. You know that, but if we can give Kadmon the box, maybe he'll be satisfied with that."

"Get out of the vehicle," a rough voice shouted in a coarse Spanish accent. "Don't even think about any weapons."

Mikael reached out a hand to Morgan and took hers, squeezing a little.

"We're going to be OK, I promise." He smiled and Morgan saw her father's confidence in his expression, a certainty about the world. It was a confidence that spoke of a knowledge that went deeper than this physical realm. Was there something Mikael hadn't told her?

He undid his belt and slithered out of the car sideways.

"I'm not armed," he called, putting his hands out first as he was roughly pulled out and dragged up. "My friend is hurt in there. Please be careful."

Faces appeared at the windows and several men bent to drag Jake out the side window. Morgan crawled out after him. As she stood up, she couldn't help but stare at the mountain of a man who led this group, his face tattooed.

"Where's Kadmon?" Morgan asked, wiping the blood from her hands onto her jeans. "Didn't he want to get his hands dirty?"

The man jerked his thumb towards the salt mountain.

"He's up there, which is where you're going, too."

He pulled out a bottle of water and tipped it over Jake's face, the cold making Jake splutter and cough but bringing him round. He shook his head, looking dazed.

"Morgan?" His first word was of concern for her, and Morgan couldn't help but smile.

"Bring them," the big man said to the group. Two of them lifted Jake under his arms, propelling him forward, and the others prodded Morgan and Mikael with their guns, herding them up the embankment back to the road. A tiny path wound up the cliff in front of them.

"Walk," the big man said, forcing them ahead. "It's not far from the top."

Panting and wheezing, clutching their injuries, they stumbled up the slope. Morgan was hyper aware of every difficult breath that Jake took, cursing her idiocy in letting him come on this mission. He had barely recovered from his last lot of injuries and she should have known that this wouldn't be a basic search-and-rescue trip. Once more she had put someone she cared about in danger.

She glanced over at Mikael, his eyes focused, darting around the men, assessing their strengths. At least he seemed to be alright and his wounds were healing fast, the cut on his head almost gone. Perhaps the dry heat and the salty air really were the restorative tonic they sold to the tourists.

At the top of the hill, Jake fell to his knees, coughing as Morgan clutched him tightly. One of the men thrust a bottle of water at them.

"Drink this. We can't have you dying … just yet," he laughed.

Morgan lifted the bottle to Jake's mouth. "Sip it," she whispered. "Not too fast."

Her eyes met Mikael's, her rage barely suppressed, his own reflected back at her. He shook his head, barely perceptible, but she understood. This was no place to attempt any kind of escape. There were too many of them. Besides, she was ready to face Adam Kadmon now – for her father, for Santiago and Sofia, and since none of them had the Key, there was still everything to play for.

When Jake had recovered a little, the group marched on, trudging through the salt hills towards a cave entrance, a slant of jagged rock. A sign clearly noted that this entrance to the caves was forbidden, with danger of collapse. Where once these caverns had been open to the public, rockslides and cave-ins had now made them unsafe to explore. The tattooed man pulled aside the sign and walked into the crack in the rock, fitting a head torch to his thick skull. The guards that followed pushed Morgan, Jake and Mikael onwards, following with their flashlights, shining the way ahead.

It was cool inside, a pleasant temperature, and the air smelled fresh, as if filtered through the salty rock and purified on the descent. Beyond the noise of their footsteps, Morgan could hear dripping. Water that had formed the caves still trickled through here, creating new pathways one droplet after the next. Torchlight illuminated glimpses of the cave walls as they walked, layers of salt like rings of bark belying the age of this place, lines laid down over millennia by the inexorable waters. The path wound around sculptural formations in the salt, reminiscent of the landscape beneath the waters further north. Time mattered little here and whatever happened on the outside, these caves would outlast the horrors of men.

The darkness began to lighten as they came to a wider section of the tunnels, finally emerging into a large cavern. It was open at the top, where white clouds scudded across a blue sky, oblivious to the human drama below. A thick salt pillar rose from the center of the space, pockmarked with gaping dark holes around its outer edge. Adam Kadmon stood in front of the pillar. Morgan had to restrain her desire to rush him, envisioning how many times she could smash his head into the salt rock before his men took her down.

"Welcome," Kadmon said, turning to look at them. "And apologies for calling such a dramatic halt to your progress on the road."

The tattooed man stepped forward and handed Kadmon the green metal box.

"Of course, I know the Key is not in here." He tossed it aside, the clang as it dropped absorbed by the thick cave walls. "I took my research a little further than your ARKANE friend." He nodded at Morgan's widened eyes. "Oh yes, I know all about you now, Morgan Sierra. I knew your father, of course. His death was one of the easiest of the Remnant to arrange."

"You bastard," Morgan shouted, lunging forward, intent on reaching him as her rage erupted. The tattooed man turned as she moved, backhanding her across the face and knocking her to the floor. Another man held a gun to her head, the muzzle pushed hard against her temple. Morgan froze, her breathing fast as she tried to hold herself back, suppressing her fury.

Kadmon's smile was amused at her attempt, and Morgan

swore silently that she would see him dead before the end of this.

"Now I have two daughters of the Remnant," he said. "A potent sacrifice for the Gates of Hell, but we still need the Key. When we hacked your communications to Ben Costanza, we took the research deeper, accessing the records of this area. It seems your father was here once before, Morgan; he knew people who had sheltered here during the war." He turned to look at the pillar. "But it seems they left more than the Key in this place. Listen."

In the hush of the cave there was a muffled sibilance, the hissing of serpents and a rustle of scales as they slid over one another. "They writhe through the pillar, a nest of them, protecting what's inside." Kadmon pointed to a man lying prone towards the side of the cave, his body still curled up in agony. "They're quite testy as well, as he discovered. I don't want to waste any more of my men, so I thought perhaps you might have more luck. All you need to do is crawl in through one of the holes and get the box from inside the pillar."

"How do you even know the box is in there?" Mikael asked.

Kadmon pointed at the prone man.

"He saw it, and told us before his throat closed and he couldn't speak anymore. The box looks to be bone or ivory, carved with symbols of the dead. But enough talking – I want this done before the sun goes down and we lose the light." He gestured to the two men holding Jake up. "That one looks half dead already, he can go first."

"No," Morgan said. "Leave him. I'll do it."

Kadmon laughed. "I love the sentiment, but I need you for later. Your sacrifice can wait, but he's expendable now."

He nodded at two guards and they dragged Jake towards the pillar. He dropped to his knees as they stopped supporting his weight, his head drooping. Kadmon stepped closer.

"If you –"

Jake exploded from the floor, pushing himself up fast, propelling his body forward. He ducked his head at the last millisecond, his thick skull crunching against Kadmon's face.

"Arrghhh!" Kadmon bellowed in pain, blood streaming from his broken nose.

Before Jake could continue his fight, two of the guards jumped on him, tackling him to the ground, beating at his body with their fists and boots. Several of the men around Morgan moved to join in and she took her chance, praying Mikael would do the same. She lashed out at one of the men and pulled him forward, slamming her knee into his solar plexus, and whipping her elbow down onto his neck, leaving him gasping on his knees. Behind her, she heard the grunts of men fighting. Morgan bent and picked up a rock from the floor, ready to finish her guard off.

A gunshot rang out, echoing around the chamber.

Morgan instinctively ducked, using the man she had beaten as a shield.

"Stop this," Kadmon's voice was ragged and nasal, his face bloody and broken. Morgan peered round to see that he held a gun to Jake's head. "The next bullet ends him if you so much as twitch."

CHAPTER 22

"FINISH IT, MORGAN." JAKE'S voice was unwavering as he pressed his head into the gun, teeth gritted, eyes blazing. "Take this bastard out for me."

Kadmon laughed. "You're still outnumbered, and you have no weapons. I admire your spirit, all of you, but it does you no good. If you help me get the box, I'll leave you alive. How about that for a deal?"

Morgan stood up, hands raised in surrender. "Don't shoot him, please."

Kadmon gestured with his free hand. "Tell your friend."

She turned to see Mikael with one of the guards in a neck lock, the man's face bright red as he struggled for breath. Mikael met her gaze, and she could see that he would continue the fight if she allowed it.

"Please," she said softly. After a split second, Mikael relaxed his grip and released the man, who collapsed, panting. Immediately, the rest of the guards swarmed them, tugging their arms behind their backs, forcing them to their knees again.

Kadmon used his gun to lift Jake's chin.

"Now, since you seem to have made such a dramatic recovery, why don't you get me the box?" He nodded and the men behind forced Jake to his feet. "Which entrance do you want to take?"

Morgan watched in dismay, her heart thumping with anxiety. Growing up in Israel, she knew there were several kinds of deadly poisonous snake, and the worst of them, the Israeli Mole Viper, lived in these desert parts. If there truly was a nest in there and Jake was bitten with no help at hand, survival was unlikely. There was no anti-venom and they were a long way from any medical help, even if they could get away. Morgan struggled to come up with another plan, but she could only watch as her partner considered his next move.

***

Jake could taste blood in his mouth as he walked slowly around the pillar, peering into each hole. He stalled for time, each second that passed forcing him closer to a darkness from his childhood in South Africa. His head thumped with pain and he reached out a hand to brace against the rock. The rhythmic sound of sibilant hissing pulled him back into memory.

His father's hand clutched his arm, dragging him down to one of the worker's huts on the farm as a boy. In the shadows of a meager dwelling, a man lay on a low bed curled up in agony, his body swollen from a snake bite. Jake met the man's eyes and saw terror there, a level of suffering that went beyond the fear of death. His father had made him stay to watch the man die in pain, a vital lesson of the bushland. Jake had carried a *sjambok*, a heavy leather whip, after that day and had beaten many snakes into the dirt until their bodies lay smashed and broken. But the man's expression haunted him and that childhood horror still left him shaken.

Jake looked over at Morgan, on her knees and held captive because of his inability to protect her. He couldn't fail her again.

He took a deep breath, exhaling sharply before crawling into one of the widest holes. His heart hammered in his chest but he pushed inside. His muscled shoulders almost spanned the width, but he wiggled down, pulling his feet up behind him. Jake paused as his eyes adjusted to the dark, the light sandstone walls close around him. He pushed away thoughts of their collapse, aware of the tons of rock above him. His breath came fast and his vision narrowed as the dizziness of panic threatened to overwhelm him. Sweat prickled on his skin, his palms slick with it. *Breathe*, he told himself, *there's still a chance you can do this.*

After a moment, he crawled forward slowly and the hissing sound grew louder and more violent. Jake held himself totally still, willing the creatures to quiet. He could see a turning in the tunneled rock ahead, perhaps the opening to the chamber that held the box. It was only a few meters. He pictured Morgan behind him, determined that she would not have to crawl in here. He moved forward again, reaching out with tentative hands to pull himself onwards.

The hissing intensified and a sinuous shadow darted from the tunnel, striking Jake's outstretched hand. He cried out as a burning pain shot up his arm. He pulled it away, instinctively shuffling back as the snake threatened to strike again. His dizziness escalated and Jake knew that panic would overwhelm him if he stayed in the tunnel. He would die here, entombed in rock, snakes slithering over his rotting corpse.

Jake backed out of the tunnel, drenched in sweat, his arm a searing pain. As he emerged into the light, he saw the double puncture marks, the skin already swelling as his heart pumped venom through his body.

"Get back in there, you idiot," Kadmon shouted, pushing Jake towards the hole again. "You've got time before the poison affects you. Keep crawling and you might just save your friends."

Jake stood by the hole without moving, his head hanging down, a sense of his own failure welling within. His breath was fast, the panic all-consuming. Tears pricked his eyes as he sought to hold onto his composure, but the base phobic reaction was too much. He fell to his knees by the pillar, limbs weak and shaking.

"I ... can't go back in there." He turned his head towards Morgan. "I'm so sorry."

***

Morgan saw the desolation on Jake's face, something that went much deeper than the pain of a snake bite. She realized that she knew too little about his past – and that she dearly wanted to learn more when they made it out of here.

She stepped forward. "I'll go instead," she said. "I'll get the box. You don't need me when you have Sofia."

"No." The voice was commanding, and Mikael pushed Morgan aside, his eyes fixed on Kadmon's. "I'll go in. Leave them be."

"So be it." Kadmon gestured and the guards dragged Jake to the edge of the cave. Morgan ran to him, kneeling at his side. She cradled his head, desperation welling up as each ragged breath tore from his chest, his heart beating erratically, his expression betraying his devastation. Morgan felt as helpless as she had in the bone church of Sedlec. Her friend was dying and it looked like Mikael would go the same way. How could it be any different when he crawled within the pillar?

But something had changed.

As she calmed herself, Morgan noticed that the atmosphere in the chamber had turned, the air somehow growing thicker. Mikael was chanting, at first in a whisper. Then his words grew stronger. He spoke Hebrew prayers, the words somehow familiar, and yet their phrasing was foreign – as though spoken with an accent she had never heard before. Kadmon must have recognized something because he held out his gun, hand shaking as he pointed it at Mikael, his eyes wide with something like fear.

Mikael squatted down by the pillar and drew in the dust with a slim finger. Morgan could just make out a circle with symbols etched inside and around it, as Mikael continued to chant, his voice echoing in the chamber. His tone was powerful, commanding, and it transformed him. Was this what her father had taught? Was this the Kabbalah magic that was only spoken of in whispers?

Mikael completed the symbol and then clutched the air above it, pulling it into him and inhaling some of the dust. The symbol disappeared in a rush of air as he finished, going silent for a moment. He stood up; he seemed taller now.

"You speak of things …" Kadmon's voice wavered and trailed off. "How do you know these words of power?"

Mikael ignored him and bent silently to one of the wide openings in the side of the pillar, crawling inside. Morgan waited to hear the hissing grow louder, but there was nothing more than a shuffling as Mikael crawled deeper. The sibilant hissing seemed more of a welcoming chorus this time, unconcerned by the intruder in their midst.

A few minutes later, Mikael emerged with a small ivory box in his hand, carved with symbols of power representing the Kabbalah tree of life and words in Hebrew script. Kadmon reached for the box, but Mikael held it just out of reach, his confidence unshakeable.

"We leave now," he said. "My friends stay here and you give them a mobile phone to call for help. I'll come as your sacrifice, but they stay here."

Morgan's forehead creased with confusion. What was Mikael doing?

Jake coughed and shuddered a little. Morgan stroked his thick hair, one hand on his chest, his heartbeat weaker now, its rhythm skipping. Whatever Mikael planned, Morgan knew she needed to make sure Jake was safe and for that, they needed to get out of here soon.

A moment of indecision and then Kadmon nodded.

"Whatever you want." He smiled. "You'll be an even more appropriate sacrifice to the Misshapen Ones."

Mikael handed the box over and turned back to Morgan. He moved towards her and Jake, the guards backing away from his advance, allowing him to kneel by Jake's side. He began to trace another circle in the dust.

Across the cavern, Kadmon stroked the box, his good eye gleaming with lust for the powerful object which must surely lie inside. He walked away from the group of guards, his back turned to shield what was within from their view.

Mikael's chanting was different now, a sing-song prayer as he finished drawing on the ground. He turned Jake's head, opening his mouth a little. Then he pulled the symbol from the dust and blew on his upturned palms. Morgan thought she saw something shimmer in the air, something that Jake inhaled, coughing as he did so. His eyes drooped closed and his head relaxed against Morgan's arm, his heartbeat becoming steady again.

"Look after him," Mikael whispered, his dark eyes glowing with some otherworldly power. "I've given him more time, but he still needs medical attention."

"What – " Morgan's words were cut off by Kadmon's audible gasp. He spun around in triumph, holding a white object aloft in his hand.

"It's here," he cried, a childish delight in his voice.

Morgan laid Jake's head on the ground gently and rose with Mikael as Kadmon walked over with triumph. He held out the Key for his men to see, his palm slightly curled so he could close his fist if any tried to snatch it. Morgan couldn't help but look at it; its presence seemed to suck the life from this dry place. The handle, or bow, of the Key was intricately carved into a skeleton figure, its bony hands lifted towards Heaven, pleading for release, its jaw open in a tortured scream. The knobs of its vertebrae became the blade, with a tangle of bone that surely wouldn't fit any normal lock.

"Legend tells that the Key is made from the bone of one of the dark angels, one of those who guard the Gates of Hell." Kadmon's voice was reverent. "The lock will open when this bone fuses with the rest of its remains and the eternal circle is completed." He looked at Mikael. "You know this – you have clearly sought it too. So come with me now, and we'll finish this together. You will see it open before you are torn apart by the Devourers."

"I do not serve the one you do," Mikael said, his body taut. Morgan could almost hear a powerful hum coming from him, like a generator storing energy, readying itself for some final event. "But I will see this ended." He held out his hand. "You promised a mobile phone."

Kadmon's eyes narrowed as he closed his fist around the Key. Then he nodded at one of the men.

"Give them yours," he said. "Then cuff this one and gag him. Blindfold him after we're out of the caves. I wouldn't want any kind of mishap on the way to the Gates."

The guard tossed a mobile phone on the ground near Morgan, as two others cuffed Mikael, moving quickly, clearly concerned about his powers. He looked at Morgan just before they placed the blindfold. His gaze was piercing and in his eyes, she saw a promise. He would finish what her father had wanted to. He was the last of the Remnant – she knew it without question, in that moment. He hadn't told her everything before, but she knew that Mikael would stand side by side with Leon's memory; that he would act as her father would have wanted. Her heart went out to him, and she took a step forward, wanting to touch his hand. A guard pushed her away and they marched from the cave, pushing Mikael before them.

Morgan turned and picked up the phone as they left, checking the bars to find there was no reception. She cursed and began to jog towards where the men had exited. Maybe Mikael could get them to at least let her and Jake out of the cave first.

A boom resounded through the cave and a shockwave lifted her off her feet, slamming her back onto the salt-rock floor of the cavern. Her ears rang as she lay stunned, realizing too late what had happened: Kadmon's men had set an explosion at the entrance to the cave, causing it to collapse. They were trapped down here, with Jake on borrowed time.

CHAPTER 23

FROM WHERE SHE LAY on the floor, Morgan could see all the way to the hole in the roof of the cave. The sun had dropped in the blue sky, but the harsh desert light still cast shadows within. The vast central pillar stretched almost to the top, only a few feet from open air. Perhaps it was close enough for her to climb out, or at least get a signal on the phone.

Morgan took a deep breath, feeling the ache in her chest from the fall as well as the earlier accident, the exhaustion in her body from the scuba dive and the adrenalin hangover from the rush of the day. In her twenties, she could have shrugged off the physical pain, but now … perhaps she was getting too old for all this. Perhaps she should have stayed at Oxford University and followed the academic route after leaving Israel.

She laughed softly, shaking her head as she got to her knees and then pulled herself up, using the wall of the cave for support. This was where she belonged, out in the field for real-time adventure, not studying artifacts that were the end result of someone else's experience.

Jake coughed from where he lay, his face pale once

again, his eyes closed in pain. Morgan went to him, lying down by his side and pulling him into her arms. It was the first time they'd been this close, and Morgan wished it could have been under different circumstances. He whispered something in Afrikaans, a language she'd never heard him speak, a timbre of pleading and desperation as if he was locked in a terrifying memory. She cradled his head, rocking him back and forth.

"It's alright," she murmured. "I'm here. You're going to be fine, I promise."

His eyes fluttered open, the amber-brown meeting her gaze.

"Morgan." Jake's voice was hoarse, but the way he said her name made her smile.

"Shhh." She put a finger on his lips. "Save your strength. We'll make it out of here. We always do."

His lips twitched a little as if to smile, and then he grimaced, fists clenching in pain. Morgan pulled him closer as his muscles spasmed, his stubble rough against her neck. As the convulsion passed, he moved his head away slightly.

"There are some benefits to dying," he said, voice muffled against her skin.

"You're not dying if you can make comments like that," she said, pulling away slightly, just enough to look into his eyes again. His skin was paler now, and his joking words weren't enough to hide his pain. He raised his hand and cupped her cheek.

"Morgan … if you go after Kadmon and I can't be with you, please be careful. Your father wouldn't have wanted you to die in his memory and I …"

"Your scars are mine, remember," Morgan said, her voice soft. "You're always with me, Jake. But this isn't over and you're not dying here. Promise me."

He nodded, but Morgan could see his eyes were unfocused now, his forehead clammy with sweat. There wasn't much time.

She untangled herself from him and laid his head down gently, turning him onto his side in the recovery position in case he lost consciousness entirely. She stroked his hair one last time and then stood to assess their options.

Walking slowly to the rock fall that blocked the exit, Morgan checked the area, looking for any way they could dig themselves out. But the cave-in had been well-orchestrated, the charges at several places along the tunnel. The salt rock had spilled out, many of the chunks too big for her to lift on her own. The faint cry of a desert eagle broke the silence, the call of a hunter. Morgan looked up at the opening and saw the bird silhouetted against the blue. That's where she needed to be.

She turned and studied the thick pillar, the round openings an easy foothold to get her started. Her eyes narrowed as she followed the contours up to the smoother surface nearer the top, the salt rock polished by the rain. It was a long fall.

Morgan put the phone in her inner jacket pocket and walked to the pillar. The sibilant hiss of the nest of snakes had calmed, but she still placed her foot gently into the large entrance hole. No need to goad them into emerging to check their territory. She began to climb, her body remembering the instinctive moves that she had once practiced with Elian in the Judean desert, exploring the Ein Farah canyon. The muscles in her legs ached but she pushed them to the limit, reaching for the handholds above her and propelling herself up.

Her breathing was labored as she reached the halfway mark. *Don't look down*, she thought, wedging herself into a crack and pulling out the cell phone with one shaking hand. There was half a bar showing. She dialed Martin Klein's number, but the phone just beeped with no service. She had to go higher.

Morgan's leg muscles and forearms burned with pain,

but she knew Jake didn't have much time before the venom began to shut his system down. Despite her concern, it was Adam Kadmon's face she saw at the top of the climb. He would pay for her father's murder, would pay for Jake's pain, and she would be the one to take him down.

Taking a couple of deep breaths, Morgan began to climb again, her eyes fixed on the opening above, imagining herself out there in the open. To keep her mind from the pain, she thought of Mikael, the near-glow on his face as he had chanted prayers she didn't recognize. After what she had seen with ARKANE, his powers seemed only surprising because he hadn't revealed them sooner, but she wondered what his angle was on the Gates of Hell. Did he even care about Kadmon's agenda, or was he intending to wrest some kind of power for himself?

Finally, Morgan could go no further. Her heart hammered in her chest, her leg muscles burned, her arms shaking with the effort of the climb. Sweat soaked the back of her t-shirt. The rock had smoothed out and there were no further handholds, no way to boost herself up higher without the certainty of falling. She pulled out the phone again. Three bars.

She dialed Martin's number, heard the ringing tone and breathed a sigh of relief. *Please answer*, she thought, exhaling a long breath, trying to calm her heart rate. It kept ringing and then finally clicked into voicemail. Tears of frustration welled up and pricked her eyelids. There were other ARKANE numbers she could call, but Martin had a unique way of shortcutting how things were done, oblivious to politics and people's feelings. He was their best hope for organizing the quickest response.

She closed her eyes, hung up and dialed again, willing him to be there. This time the phone was picked up.

"Hello." Martin's familiar voice was curt, as if he had been deeply engaged in something and resented the intrusion. Morgan imagined him pushing his glasses up his nose, pulling his attention from whatever held his interest.

"Martin, it's Morgan, we need help and I haven't got long."

"Of course, of course." She had his attention now. "Go ahead, give me the details."

"Trace this signal and get a helicopter medevac here as fast as possible. We're in a salt cave under Mount Sodom. Jake's hurt and …" Morgan looked down at the cave floor far below, realizing that she had no plan for the descent. "I'm stuck up a very high pillar."

"Um, OK." Martin's voice was bemused, but Morgan could hear his fingers tapping fast on the keyboard at his desk. "I'll mobilize out of Dimona, the closest military base. It shouldn't take too long. Can you hang on in there?"

Morgan felt the strain in her arms, her legs still shaking. She'd been run off the road and nearly blown up today, not to mention diving the crushing depths of the Dead Sea.

"I guess I'll have to," she said. "Tell them to hurry, though. The light's fading."

Martin cut the line and Morgan started counting, her whole being concentrated on clutching the pillar, focusing as the seconds ticked away.

***

The sound of chopper blades overhead stopped Morgan at number 1806 and she managed a faint smile, hoping they would find the hole quickly. Once the light faded, there would be little hope of being found, and no way of descending, either. The silhouette of a helicopter soon appeared above the hole and a safety ladder descended. Morgan looked up to see a soldier leaning out the door, gesturing for her to grab the swinging end.

With one shaking arm, she reached for it on the next pass, clutching it to her chest, feeling it tug upwards. She let go of the pillar and wrapped her legs around the rope, winding her body into the space between the rungs. The helicopter winched her up, and she ducked her face against the wind that buffeted the air around her. Strong arms pulled her up into the body of the chopper, strapping her into one of the seats with practiced movements. There were two soldiers in the back and another upfront with the pilot. One of the men put a headset on her.

"Are you alright?" he said in Hebrew. "We were told you're IDF but we have no record of any teams out here."

"I was in the Israeli Defense Force a number of years back," Morgan replied in Hebrew. "Thank you for coming to get us but my friend is still down in the cave. He's been badly bitten. We need to get him out."

Morgan explained about the cave-in and the soldiers had a brief conversation, still hovering over the hole. A minute later, one geared up with a harness and extra safety ropes.

"It's too narrow for a stretcher," he said. "So I'm going to go in and get your friend. Will he be conscious?"

Morgan shook her head. "I don't think so. Please hurry."

The soldier roped up and leaned out of the helicopter as the other man did a final check of the equipment. One last nod and the soldier jumped backwards, letting out his rope and abseiling from the chopper, down towards the hole. He slowed at the entrance, maneuvering inside and then letting out more rope. Morgan watched him descend into the darkness alongside the great pillar.

Inside of two minutes later, the winch began to engage and wind back up, pulling the soldier and his unconscious passenger out. Morgan watched the men ascend, anxiety for Jake and her own exhaustion making her head ache. Jake's body slumped in the harness, his head lolling against the soldier he was strapped to. He would get the best medical treatment now, and somehow she knew he would be OK. She should probably get some medical help herself, she should rest, but Morgan heard Adam Kadmon's name in the beat of her heart, and she knew she couldn't stop now. Once Jake was in medical custody, she needed to find out where Kadmon's team had gone … because she was going after them.

Morgan helped pull the other soldier and Jake into the helicopter and soon they were flying southwest to the Dimona military base in the Negev desert. Morgan used the helicopter's communication channel to get back in touch with Martin at ARKANE.

"Can you track the group who left the caves before us?" she asked, struggling to be heard above the din of the helicopter blades. "Then I need transport out of here to wherever they've gone. They must be heading for the Gates now. I have to be there."

"Give me some time to hack the satellites, but I'll be able to find that information easily enough." Martin's fingers tapped a staccato rhythm. "The transport links and airspace for Israel are so heavily monitored, I'll be able to discern a heading soon. How's Jake?"

Morgan looked down at her partner's pale face, his lips pursed together in pain. She stretched out her fingertips and touched the heartbeat in his neck, feeling the strength of the pulse. Whatever Mikael had done, it had definitely given Jake more time than Kadmon's man back in the caves.

"I think he'll be alright," she said. "But you'll want to get him home as soon as he's stabilized."

"Do you want me to mobilize an agent to take his place?"

A beat of silence. Morgan thought of the wounds Jake had suffered by her side; the deaths of the men in the desert of Tunisia. She remembered the groans of Khal El-Souid, beaten in the caves of Mount Nebo while on her quest. She brought suffering to those who worked alongside her, and she couldn't face the thought of putting anyone else in danger.

"I … won't be on my own. Mikael Levy worked with my father, he's a Kabbalist but also ex-military. Don't worry, Martin, I have my backup, so please don't send anyone else."

There was a hesitation. "If you're sure, but Morgan, please be careful. I can't have all my friends in hospital."

Morgan smiled a little. "I certainly don't want to end up there." Although she wondered if perhaps hospitalization was on the more positive end of the equation when it came to the Gates of Hell. "Can you get back to me with travel details ASAP? I'll sort out comms when I land."

"Of course, back soon."

The chopper landed at Dimona military base, and a pair of medical staff ran towards the helicopter with a stretcher. The two soldiers helped lift Jake out, strapped him down and then wheeled him off towards the medical building, as the helicopter's blades stopped spinning and relative quiet descended. The military base was busy, always alert and in motion, as all bases in Israel were. The threat was constant, the training continual, and this was a world Morgan knew – that all Israelis understood.

"Your friend is in good hands," one of the soldiers said, his dark eyes kind. "I know others who've been bitten round these parts and they've made a full recovery when treated quickly."

"Thank you," Morgan said. "Your help saved his life, and mine."

"He who saves one soul, it is as if he saves a whole world." The young soldier blushed, as he recited the motto of the Israeli Medical Corps.

***

Morgan climbed out of the helicopter as another soldier came running up, a cell phone in his hand.

"This is for you," he said, handing it to Morgan. "There's someone on the line and the phone is yours when you're done." Morgan could see deference in his eyes, and she wondered what strings Martin had pulled this time, what story he'd spun to get this kind of attention. Whatever it was, she was grateful.

She put the phone to her ear and her eyes widened as she heard what Martin had discovered.

CHAPTER 24

"Seriously?" Morgan said. "I'm going back to the Czech Republic?"

As Martin explained where she was headed, dark memories resurfaced from the night when she and Jake had confronted a demon in the bone crypt of Sedlec chapel. The scar throbbed in her left side where its claws had ripped through her skin, and her hand instinctively rubbed at the old wound. She barely heard Martin's words now, her frown deepening as foreboding rose within her. They had barely escaped with their lives that night and now it seemed she was going back to that area, as Martin had traced Kadmon's group to Houska Castle, just a few hours north of Sedlec.

"The military are going to transport you back to Tel Aviv," Martin explained. "Then I've arranged a private charter plane from there. I'll send the details of the castle to your phone and you can read it en route. It's only around four hours' flight and because of the one-hour time difference, you'll be there before midnight." His words brought visions of torchlight and evil swirling through her mind. "Let me know when you get there and what else you need," he continued. "There'll be a care package in the hire car when you get to Prague. Be safe, Morgan."

As she hung up, the helicopter's blades began to spin again. She ducked and ran back, hoisting herself into the belly of the chopper. They ascended into the darkening evening, and Morgan gazed out across the Negev desert. The shadows on the dunes seemed to move, twisted figures emerging from the rocks, a promise of desolation in the way they slunk across the barren earth. The Key had been hidden in the caves of Sodom, a place legend said God had destroyed because of human depravity. It made her wonder what it could possibly unlock.

***

Morgan dozed on the short transfer to Tel Aviv and managed to go through the motions of necessary paperwork to leave the country. She had a brief thought of calling her friend Dinah, who worked near Jerusalem – of sleeping in a real bed and laughing about old times. It seemed that whenever she came to Israel, Morgan found herself dashing about on a mission for ARKANE, but perhaps she could just forget all this for one night. She soon dismissed the thought, however; memories of her father lingered, his scribbled last words urging her onwards. Kadmon was within reach, and he didn't know she was coming.

Once on the private plane, their heading locked in for the Czech Republic, Morgan finally allowed exhaustion to catch up with her. The flight would be a few hours, so she pulled on an eye mask, set the alarm and sank into a deep sleep.

***

The alarm woke her too soon, and Morgan sat bolt upright in the cabin, the darkness broken only by flashing lights on the wings outside the window and the green cabin safety strips. For a moment, she thought she was back home in her little Oxford house, but then the roar of the plane brought her back to reality. She shook her head, clearing the fog, and went to the galley area to make the thick dark coffee that was her addiction.

Returning with a steaming cup, the aroma stimulating her senses, Morgan checked her phone, opened the file that Martin had provided and devoured the information.

A hundred kilometers north of Prague, Houska Castle had been supposedly haunted since the ninth century and was now in private hands. Martin had traced the ownership to a shell company owned by Luis De Medina, the man they knew as Adam Kadmon. Morgan flicked through pictures of the castle, mostly older shots with unclear images of the place. It didn't look like anything special, just another crumbling Eastern European estate. Morgan thought of Trafalgar Square in London, and the levels of ARKANE's secret base underneath that few knew of. Appearances could be deceiving indeed.

Records of previous building plans showed a level under the structure that was rarely seen, a series of secret caves only accessible by those who knew how to find them. Martin had noted that the castle's defenses were considered strange, as they didn't face the outside to protect those within. Instead, they faced inward towards a central courtyard, as if trying to prevent something inside from getting out.

The report detailed that the chapel was built over a bottomless well, claimed by locals to be the gateway to Hell. All kinds of ghosts had been sighted there, from headless horses to chains of tortured men and black-winged creatures that threatened those who tried to investigate further.

Its lore was so powerful that during the late 1930s the Nazis had taken over the castle and carried out experiments on dimensional portals and other fringe occult practices. Rumors had also circulated that it was where they kept women of pure blood to service officers and multiply the master race. Now it seemed that Adam Kadmon was trying to open whatever dark gate lay beneath the castle.

Morgan laid the smart phone down and gazed out the window, the dull roar of the plane almost hypnotic as she stared into the shifting black shapes of the clouds outside. The clash of her belief systems jarred her, as it seemed to in every ARKANE mission. The scientist in her, the psychologist who believed in the empiricism of observable truth, knew that there could be no gate to Hell, that Kadmon's quest was just a fantasy, and the Key purely an artifact of curiosity with no real power. That part remembered her father as a man who had found his God in Kabbalah, his spirituality in the letters of the Torah and friendship with the men of the Remnant.

But that side of her had been squeezed into a smaller box by what Morgan had seen with ARKANE and the powers she now knew worked in the world. The Pentecost stones, the Devil's Bible, the Ark of the Covenant, and more recently the staff of Skara Brae – these were experiences she could not explain in any scientific manner. This interpretation made her father into the practitioner of a powerful mysticism, murdered for his ability to commune with the infinite.

Morgan sipped her coffee, the turbulence of the plane reflecting her inner state. Kadmon was just a man, but did the Key make him more than that? Would Mikael stand with her when it came down to confronting whatever dark power lay beneath Houska Castle? Her father had trusted him, or at least that's what Mikael had said. She had no way of knowing if he spoke the truth. *Help me, Papa, wherever you are,* Morgan thought, as the seatbelt light came on and the plane began to descend.

***

Morgan drove out of the Prague city limits, the care package Martin had left next to her on the seat. Knowing her penchant for speed, Martin had managed to get her an Audi R8 Spyder convertible. With the top down, the night air was chill but it made her skin glow and her eyes sparkle with pleasure. She darted through the empty streets, heading north and east, the roads narrowing as she approached a more rural area. Morgan reveled in the power of the vehicle, shifting gears to speed around corners, her body barely moving, foot pressed down on the accelerator. The euphoria made her smile, tasting the exhilaration of movement, truly alive in these moments where risk edged closer to oblivion. She glanced at her watch. Just over two hours until the dawning of the day of reckoning, when many believed the veil to the other worlds was thinner, more permeable.

Finally, she rounded a corner and saw Houska Castle, lit from below to emphasize its imposing presence. It perched on the edge of a rocky sandstone cliff, its Gothic hall hugging the side of the mountain. The dense forest encroached as far as it dared, leaving a distance between the edge of nature and the domain of man. Morgan had read in Martin's notes that the castle was never meant to be inhabited. There were no kitchens, no water source, no proper fortifications and it had been nowhere near trade routes when it was built in the thirteenth century. It was only constructed to keep the demons from escaping the Gates of Hell and the chapel was built directly on top of the pit, in the hope that the power of the faithful could keep them from ascending.

From this distance, the lights in the castle seemed to be concentrated in only one section, far from the tourist entrance. Morgan didn't have enough time to approach with care and she wasn't expected, so she drove right up to the car park. The area was dark and there were no guards, no sign that anyone was here at all. She parked and slid out of the car, tucking the gun from Martin's package into her jacket pocket alongside the page from the *Sefer Yetzirah*. She pulled the head torch out as well, but didn't turn it on, spending a moment absorbing the atmosphere.

The night was still and quiet. Morgan took a deep breath, inhaling the scent of the pine forest below the escarpment. The stars were brighter away from the city – some of them seemed to throb, pulsing with power. A chill wind picked up dust from the ground and whirled it around in a mini tornado. As Morgan blinked and rubbed her eyes, she heard the nicker of a horse and the sound of hooves on the tarmac beneath the wind. She whirled around, her vision still blurred. There behind her, standing proud, was a huge black stallion. Its mane hung in dark waves, its eyes wide with terror. It pawed the ground, whinnying, its gaze fixed on the air behind her.

Morgan put a hand out.

"There boy, it's OK," she said, wondering where it had come from, how it could have appeared from nowhere so quietly. It seemed spooked by something behind her. She turned to look and the wind picked up, further whirling the dust around them with violent force. Pieces of stone and glass began to surge into the air. She put up her hands to protect her face as the particles bit into her skin. She pulled her sleeves over her hands and watched in horror as the sharp objects cut into the horse's flesh.

As blood began to drip from his skin, he reared up, lips curled back in fear. Morgan stepped away from the powerful hooves. She couldn't stand to hear his pain, wanting to help but knowing she couldn't do anything. The cuts deepened on the horse's neck, dark blood pulsing from the wounds. He crashed down and galloped past Morgan, rushing headlong towards the cliff edge, drops of thick blood falling to the ground as he thundered to the brink.

"No!" Morgan couldn't help but shout, her hands outstretched as the horse leapt out into the void. But as she watched, expecting to hear the dying scream as it fell, the horse disappeared into the black – not falling but just fading away.

The wicked wind gained in ferocity and Morgan pulled her jacket closer about her, watching as the drops of horse's blood faded on the ground beneath her feet until it was as if they had never been.

A moment later, she heard a huffing sound behind her and turned to see the same magnificent black stallion pawing at the ground. His eyes were tortured, intelligent, as if he knew that he was doomed to repeat this painful end into eternity.

"I'm so sorry," Morgan whispered, understanding now that this was just some replay of a long-ago event, a glitch in the environment of this dark place. She stepped towards the main doors into the castle, her heart hammering in her chest. What else was trapped here on the edge of reality?

CHAPTER 25

SOFIA STUMBLED AS THE men dragged her down the stairs and into the stone chamber below the castle. It was cold and damp with a chill that penetrated her bones, every breath a freezing inhalation. Her mind was foggy with the drugs they had given her over the last few days, but she was aware of the space around her, the sound of their voices. There was an excitement in the air, anticipation of something, and she forced the giddy nausea down as she tried to make sense of what was happening.

Adam Kadmon knelt by a gigantic round trapdoor set in the middle of the room. He reached out with one hand and placed it gently on the surface, whispering a prayer of some kind. His back was bent as if a heavy load pressed down upon him. For a moment, Sofia saw beyond the lunatic he had become to the man of faith he had once been. He rose and turned, walking towards her, and she straightened her back, standing proudly to face her captor. She was a Rueda, and she would not back down, even now.

"Sofia." Adam's voice was soft, a caress on his lips. He reached out to stroke her cheek and she froze, unflinching as he touched her. "You should have been my child, but your mother was deceived. She loved Javier when she should have chosen me." His face contorted, a glimmer of suffering from years of obsession. "I tried to win her, but he held her heart until death." Adam closed his eyes for a second, and when he opened them, Sofia saw tears in his unscarred eye. "Her death was a mistake, you have to know that. The car bomb was only meant for Javier …"

He shook his head and turned back towards the trapdoor. Through the haze of drugs, Sofia felt the impact of his words ricochet in her mind. This man had killed her whole family, threatened the man she loved and now held her captive for some unseen purpose. Sofia tugged her arms out of her captors' grip, her energy taking them by surprise as she lunged for Adam.

"Bastardo," she screamed at him as she raked at his face with her nails. She drove him back onto the trapdoor as she attacked, her grief and rage exploding into violence. The guards rushed forward to restrain her, but Adam grabbed her arms, pinning them behind her back and pulling Sofia against his body.

She struggled violently in his grip, trying to bite his face, desperate to draw blood. He grabbed her hair and pulled her head back, his strength pinioning her.

"Shhh," he whispered. "You can't win. This is how it must be."

With one last burst of strength, Sofia twisted in his arms but he held her tight until she could struggle no more, collapsing in his embrace.

"My father was a good man," she sobbed. "My mother loved him because he was everything you could never be."

Adam's grip tightened in her hair at the words, pulling until Sofia winced in pain. He bent to her neck and inhaled the scent from her skin.

"You have no idea what –"

His words were cut off as the trapdoor under their feet vibrated and a deep boom resounded in the chamber.

"It begins," Adam said, his voice triumphant. He pushed

Sofia away, back towards the guards. "Secure her."

Two of the men dragged her to the other side of the chamber, lifting her onto a gigantic sarcophagus. Sofia fought them with every last ounce of energy, screaming as they tied her down onto the cold stone. Across the room, she could see another captive being secured to a pillar, his mouth gagged, hands bound. His gaze met hers, and Sofia felt a moment of hope that he was there to save her.

The boom came again from below the castle, echoing through the chamber and resounding through the stone at her back. Adam leaned over her, a cloth in his hand. Sofia caught the scent of chloroform and she twisted in her bonds, turning her head away from the drug that would take her back into oblivion.

"I'm sorry." Adam closed his eyes as he brought the soaked cloth to her mouth, holding it there as her struggles subsided. "I'm sorry Blanca, my love."

CHAPTER 26

THE GREAT DOOR TO Houska Castle was carved with the writhing bodies of demons as they climbed over the damned, pricking them with great pitchforks. In the daytime, Morgan might have smiled at the appeal to tourist dollars by emphasizing the supernatural vibe. But with the bleeding horse galloping endlessly towards the cliff edge behind her, the door had a more sinister quality, a promise perhaps of what lay within. She pushed against it and the door swung open on silent hinges, revealing a dark corridor stretching inwards.

Morgan pulled her head torch out and the light flared, casting a bright path onwards. She stepped inside to find paintings upon stone walls, plinths for sculptures before them. There was no one inside, no sense that a presence was waiting in the dark, no sound other than the wind and the thump of her own rapid pulse. Morgan stepped inside and the door swung back behind her. She reached a hand to stop it, but the door was too heavy; it clunked shut. Nausea rose and her heart hammered, her mind screaming to get out while she still could. She shut her eyes, summoning her father's calm face. He had sent the book to her to stop the

Gates of Hell being opened. She couldn't turn back now.

At the end of the corridor, Morgan could see a faint light from an open courtyard. Her footsteps echoing in the old hall, she walked towards the light and looked to either side, the head torch illuminating artwork on the walls. One picture portrayed fantastical beasts of mythology devouring human sacrifices; in another, a mob of demons fought against a group of angels. It looked as if the balance of the battle favored the dark side, as the angels' wings were torn and bloody, their faces scarred. One looked to Heaven with desperation in his eyes, hands raised in prayer as a demon sank its teeth into the angel's neck. These were not the popular religious paintings of Europe's churches, where good always vanquished evil. Here, a different truth was celebrated.

A rattling of chains and the rhythmic stomp of feet came from ahead. Morgan looked up, directing the head torch towards the sound, but the light couldn't pierce the darkness that far away. As she walked towards the noise, the lamp flickered and then died just as she reached the threshold to the inner courtyard.

Clouds scudded across the sky and patchy moonlight illuminated the scene. Morgan stood on the step, trying to work out what she was seeing. A long line of men were chained together, dragging themselves around the central quadrangle, their voices a cacophony of moans and the discordant notes of an ancient chant. They stamped their feet onto the stone beneath, leaving marks of bloody filth behind them. The stink of unwashed bodies, rotten flesh and decay filled the air. Morgan clutched at the stone walls either side of her, rooted in the doorway, anchoring herself to what she could feel with her fingertips. These men must surely be another of the dark hallucinations, a ghostly chain gang destined to suffer here night after night.

She looked more intently at the group, forcing herself

to witness their pain. Several of the men were decapitated, their necks a bloody mess with white bone peeking through, but their legs still walked on. One of them carried his own head, the eyes fixed and staring in a rictus of horror, the mouth still moving in desperate prayer. There were men with missing limbs, some partially torn off, dragging their remains in endless circles.

A frenzied barking came from one corner of the courtyard and the men nearest that area screamed in terror, pulling away as far as their chains would take them. One of them disappeared, dragged away from those around him; the sounds of ripping and tearing could be heard above the panic as his screams died away. Morgan put her hands over her ears at the awful noise of flesh devoured, the crunching of jaws.

A massive black dog stalked from behind the men, its mouth dripping with dark blood, spittle flecked around its muzzle, eyes wide with bloodlust. The chain gang froze, quiet now, their dead eyes following the dog's path as its huge head swung back and forth, looking for the next victim. Morgan watched the tableau, waiting for it to stop and repeat itself as the horse had done outside.

The dog's gaze shifted to her, growling as its lips pulled back over sharp teeth and Morgan was sure it could see her physical form. Suddenly she wasn't so certain this was all a hallucination. It stepped towards her, nails clicking on the flagstones.

Morgan slowly reached inside her jacket and pulled out her gun, sighting on the dog's muzzle.

"Don't even think about it," she whispered.

The feel of the weapon made her confidence surge and she stepped down into the courtyard. The dog took another pace towards her, snarling now, the growl in the back of its throat a rumbling that echoed around the stone walls. She saw its back legs flex as it prepared to jump. Time slowed as her logical brain insisted this wasn't real, but the most base part of her animal nature recognized a mortal threat. Saliva and blood dripped from the dog's mouth. As the slime pooled on the ground, its eyes narrowed and it sprang at her.

Morgan shot once, twice.

The bullets had no impact on the beast as it leapt with powerful legs extended, its jaws open to snap shut on her flesh. Morgan continued to fire and then flinched, ducking against the wall, head turned away as she anticipated the snap of its jaws, heart almost bursting in her chest.

Suddenly it was silent again, and she opened her eyes to find the beast gone, the chained men disappeared. But across the courtyard was the gigantic figure of Adam Kadmon's tattooed bodyguard, flanked by two other men with guns pointed at her. For one crazy moment, Morgan was glad they were there, grateful to see those she knew as physically real. The man began to clap, as if celebrating her performance.

"I see you met the resident courtyard ghosts," he said. "Our intruder alarm, if you like."

"What … were they?" Morgan said, her voice shaking. She put her gun down on the ground and stood up straight, hands wide in surrender. There was no point in trying to overcome these three, and besides, she wanted to be where Kadmon was now.

The tattooed man shrugged. "There have been many legends of this place over the years, and it's said that the layers of the dead built up until they thrust into the physical realm. We know this place is built over a bottomless pit, and the castle draws those who would use blood magic to open the void beneath."

"And you – why are you here?" Morgan asked. "Why join Kadmon?"

He pointed to the sky. "You don't understand our true

purpose or you wouldn't stand in our way. Tonight, the stars align, and the dark gods are ready to join us. This is the first chance in generations to open the gate." He looked at his watch. "Come now, we must hurry back. Adam will be grateful that he has another daughter of the Remnant for the occasion." He gestured to the other men. "Bring her."

Morgan went with them, unresisting, following the man down another winding corridor to a chapel lit by candlelight. A huge painting of the Archangel Michael dominated the wall facing the altar, the leader of God's army attacking the hordes of Hell. He looked every inch the Teutonic warrior. In another painting, Michael pulled his great sword from the neck of a dragon, his shield burning as the beast spewed a rain of hellfire over him.

"This way," the tattooed man said, striding through the chapel towards the altar. He stepped behind it and then began to descend into the depths that ran below what Morgan remembered from the blueprints of the castle. The man behind prodded her forward and Morgan walked on.

Beside the altar, she noticed a strange painting for a Christian place of worship: a female centaur – a pagan creature, half woman half horse – her arrow nocked and aimed at a human figure tied to a stake. Morgan noted that the woman was left-handed, for which the Latin word was *sinister*. To be so marked was to be associated with Satan and the reverse of everything good. A strange image for a chapel, but then the legends of this place told of half-human creatures emerging from the depths of Hell beneath. As she stepped down into the darkness behind the altar, Morgan wondered what would be waiting below.

She followed the men as the stairwell wound down, lit by torches of flame placed in metal brackets, a touch of the medieval in this Gothic place. The smoke from the fires whirled in the air, an incense note to the woody scent. Morgan tried not to breathe too much in, keeping her breath shallow. The smoke clouded their view and she stepped carefully on the slippery stone. In the distance they could hear a rhythmic booming noise, a thumping, and she thought of the dog in the courtyard, the sound it would make if locked up. This sounded more powerful, more determined. More calculating.

The cold was piercing as they descended, making Morgan think of the icy Hell of Dante, not the fiery pit portrayed in most Hellish vistas. The walls were wet in parts, as if water seeped through the cracks. As her fingers brushed against a patch, they came away bloody, the thick viscous liquid clinging to her skin. She shivered and rubbed her fingers on her jeans, not wanting to think about the bodies behind these walls, the twisted minds that had created this place. Finally, they emerged into a round room at the bottom of the stairs.

Great torches of flame set in medieval iron brackets on the walls cast a flickering glow around the room. A gigantic round wooden trapdoor was set into the middle of the flagstones, covered with intricate carvings of occult symbols. There was a copper roundel in the middle of the door, its bronzed surface burning a deep red. Centered within the roundel was a keyhole. The booming noise echoing around the chamber came from underneath the trapdoor. Something was beating on it from the inside, trying to push its way out.

CHAPTER 27

MIKAEL WAS STRAPPED TO a stone pillar at the side of the room, his mouth gagged. He looked at Morgan with sorrow, as if he had hoped not to see her again – as if he had not wanted her to come to this dark place. Beyond the trapdoor was a sarcophagus, a giant stone coffin, and on its lid lay Sofia, tied spread-eagle, wearing the red flamenco dress she had been taken in. Her eyes were closed, her body relaxed. She moaned, clearly drugged and only partially conscious.

"Glad you could join us." Adam Kadmon stepped from the shadows to stand in front of the trapdoor. "The blood of the Remnant will strengthen the dark ones as they emerge." He looked at his watch. "The alignment approaches." His good eye was bright, almost manic, shining with the desire to see what pounded on the trapdoor. The booming reverberated around the room, and Morgan had to speak loudly to be heard.

"You really want to release whatever is down there?"

Kadmon smiled, and Morgan saw an edge of madness there.

"This is the culmination of my quest, the final step on

my journey. The Crusaders said it best: my God will know his own and spare the ones who are faithful." He turned to the men, nodding towards Mikael. "Bind her with him. The three of them will be the first for the Devourers to consume, to speed them on their way into the world."

The tattooed man pulled Morgan across the room and tied her to the pillar alongside Mikael, facing the pit. The great trapdoor seemed to bow outwards, pulsing as if whatever was beneath tested its resistance. The booming increased in tempo. Vibrations shook the ground they stood on, making Morgan's teeth rattle and her ears ache. Adam Kadmon withdrew the Key from its box.

A tapping on her hand drew her attention. Morgan looked at Mikael and realized he was trying to communicate something to her, his eyes desperate as the seconds ticked onwards, the words he spoke muffled by his gag. As she tried to work out what he was trying to say, she remembered the chanting in the salt cave. Whatever he could do, he needed the power of words to do it. She yanked against the ties that bound her, but there was no way to free her hands.

"Lean towards me," she whispered, and as Mikael pulled as far as he could to meet her, she leaned forward, using her teeth to catch the edge of his gag. She tugged and lost her grip, teeth slamming together. She tried again and this time gripped tighter, yanking her head downwards as he pulled away from her. The corner of his mouth was uncovered now and she tried one more time, her lips meeting his briefly as her teeth bit down on the gag. A shock of electricity sparked between them, the air almost crackling, and then his mouth was free.

Mikael began chanting under his breath immediately, his eyes flicking to the trapdoor as it bulged obscenely, ready to burst. Morgan saw the bonds on his wrists drop away, but he didn't charge at Kadmon as she would have done; he just bent to the ground and began to draw symbols in the dust.

Adam held the Key up, his gaze fixed on the skeletal shape which glowed in the torchlight. It pulsed, throbbing in Adam's hand as he approached the straining doors above the pit. As he stepped near it, he cried out in pain and Morgan saw vicious spiked tendrils emerge from the blade of the Key, stabbing into his hand. A slick of blood coated Adam's fingers. He grimaced but kept walking, fixed on the final goal.

As he approached, the metal of the lock piece on the door began to melt and morph, reforming itself into a pool of burning liquid. The groans and thumps under the door grew louder, as if those beneath could sense the approach of he who would release them. Adam's eye burned now, reflecting the copper liquid he stared into. His arm was pulled forward as the Key was drawn towards its home, desperate to fulfill its final destiny. Morgan could see a hint of fear in his gaze as he leaned forward, his hand so close to the liquid metal.

At the last moment, he dropped the Key and the lock accepted it, sucking it whole into a spinning vortex before releasing it back into Adam's hand. A deep clunking sound filled the room. The lock dissolved. The ancient wood began to crack, thick wounds splitting across its surface as dark pitch welled up from its surface. Adam backed away quickly.

Mikael looked up and Morgan saw recognition there, as if he had foreseen this moment. He spun and sketched in the dirt around her, enclosing her in a circle of protection, etching symbols in the dirt on the boundaries.

"This is all I can do for you," Mikael whispered to Morgan, standing up briefly next to her. "I can't release you because you won't be able to stop yourself attacking them. But this is not a physical fight and you can't win your way. These are the shades of Sheol, conjured by the terror of ages and released by a magic we hoped to control." He stroked her cheek with one finger. "I had hoped to spare you this, but now you will witness the end."

"In my pocket," Morgan said. "There's a page from the book my father sent me. It has symbols like the ones you've drawn here. Perhaps it will help."

Mikael reached inside her jacket pocket, pulling out the page from the manuscript. He unrolled it and hope dawned in his eyes.

"This might just be …"

He bent to the ground, kneeling again, his chanting louder now. No one paid them any heed as pitch from the trapdoor began to evaporate into the air, a billowing of black smoke that crept into the corners of the room, exploring the reaches of its space. Morgan could smell burnt flesh in its shadow, a sickly odor of decay overlaid with a promise of everlasting darkness. Adam's good eye began to take on the blackness of the air around him, the white darkening as shapes began to slink from the pit.

The smoke in the air shrouded the room in darkness and formed a bridge from one side of the veil into reality. Morgan watched as bat-like creatures with leathery wings pulled themselves from the pit, their muscles wasted and unused for millennia. One of them stood tall, fixing its gaze on one of Kadmon's men. It reached out a clawed hand and grabbed the man's neck, choking his screams as the thing bent to suck from his face. The man writhed in its grip, his body becoming desiccated as the wings spread out, blood pulsing through them now. When they were fully unfurled, the thing dropped the man's wasted body and flew upwards, its cry one of dark pleasure.

One visibly female form slithered close to the tattooed man, winding herself around his body, her breasts full and voluptuous as she touched him. Morgan saw conflict in the man's face as he gasped at her cold touch, arousal and fear vying for dominance as her mouth claimed his. Her tongue thrust into his throat as he tried to escape and the woman's body began to change, her full figure rotting and pulling apart. He began to choke, trying to push her from him but she was like smoke to his grasping hands. The remnants of her tattered skin pushed onto his, her bony fingers clawed into his chest, pushing through his skin and tearing open his chest. Her tongue withdrew from his mouth and she bared her teeth, lowering her head to feed on his exposed heart.

Morgan watched the unfolding scene with mounting horror, as more creatures emerged from the pit. A gigantic bulbous toad slithered out, its huge tongue flicking out to taste Sofia's skin, leaving a black residue on her perfect face. It began to waddle towards the bound girl, its black lids fixed on its prey, and Morgan knew they didn't have much time. She turned her head to Mikael, praying that he would have a way to save her – to save them all.

Mikael knelt on the ground, rolling and shaping a ball of muddy dirt as he repeatedly spat into the dust to bind more of it together. His gaze were fixed on the misshapen wraiths emerging from the pit, their diaphanous bodies becoming more substantial with every second. Under his breath, he chanted words from the *Sefer Yetzirah*, the Book of Creation that summoned divine life. Morgan watched as he picked up a shard of splintered wood from the floor, slicing into his palm.

He squeezed drops of blood out into the mud and began to shape the lump into a tiny figure of a man. The page of the book was next to him on the floor and he began to copy the Hebrew letters from it onto the stone, using his blood as ink. As Morgan watched, the letters gleamed gold and spun in the air, lifting from the ground and drawn into the muddy figure. As they were absorbed, the figure grew, first to the size of a child and then into a grown man and finally, to a giant made of mud and the blood of a righteous man, its features a mess of molded clay but its hands like clubs. The letters of power surged within like the pulses of its blood. In the swirling smoke of the dark chamber, it gleamed with a golden light.

Morgan beheld the golem, the ancient creature that had protected the Jews in times of trouble. It was animated earth, the extension of the man who had conjured it, driven by the power of the unnameable. Mikael reached up with one finger and traced a single word on its forehead: *chabal*, destroy. The golem reared up, its great meaty fists clenched as it turned towards the pit.

CHAPTER 28

THE GOLEM LUMBERED TOWARDS the toad-like creature, putting itself between the demon and the daughter of the Remnant. Morgan watched as it began to push the toad back towards the pit, its terrific strength evident as the monster gurgled its rage.

"No!" A shriek rang out and Adam Kadmon stepped forward, wraiths swirling about him, their opaque figures waiting to feed. He held the Key aloft, pointing it towards Mikael and Morgan. A cloud of the ragged Devourers flew at them, gigantic maws wide open with a depth of blackness inside that threatened endless terror.

Morgan's breath caught in her chest as she froze, expecting to feel their chill embrace, but the demons stopped inches from her, clawing at the invisible barrier Mikael had drawn about her. The fiends screamed and scratched, desperate to tear her flesh and feed so they could materialize.

Hebrew letters spun around Mikael now, his hands lifting as he spoke his chants louder and louder into the vortex of darkness that circled around him, the Devourers darting towards him, trying to penetrate his ring of power. He thrust one hand out and a golden aleph flew from him, pinning one of the demons against a wall, burning its smoking flesh, its scream an animal howl as it dissolved. With both hands now, he shaped some of the shining letters together and rolled them together to form a glowing ball. He threw it into a group of the shades. They burst apart as it struck them, shadowy tatters falling to the ground like rags, their remains dragged back towards the pit by some dark gravity.

As Mikael cast his golden letters against the horde, the golem used his thick legs to drive the giant toad back to the edge of the pit. With a final heave, it tipped the creature into the void as the winged demon swooped down from above. It sank its talons into the golem, claws ripping at the golden word that animated it. Mikael drew in the air before him, his fingers moving like golden lightning, leaving trails in the smoky air around them. Then he blew on the word and sent it to the golem to renew his strength.

Adam Kadmon screamed and launched himself at Mikael, his expression wild, teeth bared like a berzerker in the throes of bloodlust. Mikael turned too late and Kadmon knocked him to the ground, the golden letters dropping in the air, almost falling to the floor. The shades that threatened Morgan inched closer. She pulled her head back as their dripping mouths snapped at her face.

Mikael managed to get an arm free and he sent a wave of glowing letters her way, pushing the demons back. Morgan felt the bonds about her wrists relax and drop.

"Get to Sofia, take her out of here," Mikael shouted. "Go! The letters will protect –"

His words were cut off as Adam punched him, Mikael's own circle of protection weakened by his actions to help her. Morgan wanted to run to him, drag Adam off and beat him back to the pit herself. The two men grappled on the floor, surrounded by a host of dark wraiths waiting to feed and strengthen themselves to go out into the world above.

She couldn't let that happen, but somehow she knew that if she approached, if she tried to intervene, the delicate balance Mikael juggled would be lost. She thought of Jake, his words in the cave, and she made her choice.

Morgan took a deep breath and stepped out of the circle towards where Sofia lay on the sarcophagus. The wraiths drew closer. She could almost feel their icy touch, the morbid caress of tattered skin on hers. She ran around the dark vortex and began to work at the ties that bound the young woman. The golem and the winged creature still wrestled on the edge of the pit near them, and Morgan glanced over as she tried to get Sofia free, afraid that any minute the demon would come for them.

A rumble came from deep beneath, like the belching of a huge fire and a whooshing noise as something was released below. Whatever had been freed, it was coming up towards the gate and it would burst into this world within seconds.

Morgan looked up and across the room, meeting Mikael's eyes for a split second. It was as if the world stood still, and she saw eternity in his dark eyes. She saw a man her father had chosen for this task, who was powerful enough to command the letters of the Torah and accept the burden of sacrifice.

"No," she whispered, even as she understood what he must do.

With a roar, Mikael stood, thrusting Adam Kadmon away from him so the man fell to the ground. The skeleton Key skittered across the floor. Mikael raised his hands up, his voice lifting in powerful prayer as he called down the power of the unnameable into the letters and symbols he carved into the air. He pushed his hands towards the giant hole in the ground and the golden letters began to pour into it, filling it with golden light. The wraiths were sucked back down, as if the vortex had reversed.

A rumble came from below and a hideous screech of frustration as the ground shook with violence. Small bits of stone and masonry fell from the ceiling. Morgan worked faster. Sofia moaned, her eyes fluttering. Morgan pulled her from the sarcophagus, just as a huge chunk of masonry smashed down where Sofia's head had been only seconds before.

"We have to get out of here," Morgan shouted. "I need your help now." She shook her, but Sofia was looking around the chamber in catatonic horror, the shock of what she saw stunning her into unmoving silence.

Across the room, Mikael forced Adam Kadmon back towards the pit as golden letters poured from his lips and hands. It was exquisitely beautiful; Morgan tried to freeze the image in her mind as the brilliant letters illuminated the dark wraiths, burning them like airborne torches. Mikael was almost aflame, his face shining as had Moses' on the heights of the mountain when he saw God. Morgan understood how her father must have craved this kind of power, and yet, once wrought, it could only destroy.

Mikael's voice became like a rushing waterfall and he spoke the powerful curse, the *Pulsa diNura*, calling down the lashes of fire from the angels of destruction. At the edge of her vision, Morgan thought she saw a shimmer of angels' wings beating back the demons towards the pit. The sucking vortex swirled the wraiths back into it, and Morgan felt the pull of the vacuum. She pushed Sofia back behind the sarcophagus, the heavy stone preventing them from being sucked down as the dark things were hurtled back from whence they came. The golem wrapped its thick arms about the winged creature and then fell forward into the pit, its clay body dissolving as it dropped, its weight dragging the demon down with it.

Morgan could see the strain on Mikael's face as he became a conduit for whatever worked through him, the forces of the light he had sought as his life's work – just as her father had done before him. Adam Kadmon tackled him from behind, driving him forward. They toppled for a moment, hanging on the edge of the pit.

"No!" Morgan's cry was lost in the whirlwind. Mikael met her eyes, his smile a blessing, and she knew that he saw his God in that moment. He stretched out his hand and the skeleton Key flew into the air, hovering above them in the vault. With one last shouted prayer, an explosion of gold letters burst from him, illuminating every corner of the dark place, driving the remaining demons back into the pit. Mikael fell together with Adam Kadmon into the vortex and the vacuum pulled the great trapdoor shut after them. The Key dropped to the vast swirling copper lock, melting as it fused with the metal, a swirl of bone solidifying until it froze into place.

A second later it was silent in the vaulted chamber, with only the echoes of Mikael's prayers ringing in Morgan's ears. She fell to her knees on the giant trapdoor, tears flowing down her cheeks.

"Mikael," she whispered. She put the palm of her hands on the wood, hoping to feel something from below. But it was cool, dead, as if nothing had even happened. She knew that if she could lift these doors, there would be nothing beneath them but the flagstones on which they rested. Mikael was gone, his last vestiges of power used to close the portal to whatever world was beneath, perhaps this time for good.

A chunk of stone fell from the roof, crashing onto the flagstones and splintering into fragments. The structure of the castle had been weakened by the great forces that had waged here, and more of the roof began to fall. Morgan stood and grabbed Sofia, wrapping the girl's arm around her neck, half dragging her to the stairwell.

As they left the chamber behind, Sofia seemed to revive,

the fear of being buried alive taking over. Together, they ran from the depths, up into the chapel and out through the courtyard. The whole place collapsed about them as they ran, making it into the car park as an avalanche from the mountain above shook the earth, burying the castle under tons of stone.

Only minutes later, the two women stood on the edge of the destruction, gazing at the steaming pile, praying that nothing would rise again from those depths as the wail of approaching sirens came from across the valley.

CHAPTER 29: TWO DAYS LATER

MORGAN STOOD LOOKING DOWN at the grave of Mikael Levy. His body hadn't been found, of course. She knew it never would be. But he would be remembered here in Safed, surrounded by the great names of Kabbalah, the blue paint on his tomb honoring the fact that he belonged.

She placed a small stone on the edge of the grave and then her fingers touched the black ribbon pinned to her jacket. It represented the rending of clothes, the tear in the heart of the mourner. Morgan closed her eyes and sent her thoughts out to Mikael, hoping that somehow he would know he was missed, that his sacrifice had closed the Gates of Hell … for now at least. There was no other alignment of planets within this generation, and with the portal buried and the Key destroyed, Morgan couldn't see how that route to the place below could be opened again. It didn't mean others wouldn't try to break through into that other realm, but her faith was stronger now, and she knew the darkness could be beaten. No one would ever know how much Mikael had given, but she would remember his sacrifice.

A bird sang a sweet song from the trees above her, its piercing cry a lament for the man her father had chosen as a worthy successor. Morgan felt the sun on her face and the turning of the world in the beat of her heart. This was her land, but she had chosen a different path and ARKANE's mission was even more strongly written on her life now. She would sit shiva for Mikael, participate in the seven days of mourning, then she would go back to London and be ready for whatever Marietti needed. For whenever darkness encroached on the earth, there would be people of the light ready to fight it back down.

AUTHOR'S NOTE

I WANTED TO DELVE into Morgan's family history in this book, and I had always intended to do a book about Spain when I first introduced Leon Sierra's heritage in *Crypt of Bone*.

I love Spain and visited Barcelona earlier this year where I imagined the opening scene at the Sagrada Familia. It really is one of the most amazing churches in the world, a true delight to behold and my wide grin matched Jake's when I entered for the first time. I've also spent time in Granada, Córdoba and Seville and I want to go back there and spend more time in Andalucia. It's an area I can't get enough of and all the architectural details described are based on real places and history. I have also been to flamenco nights in Seville, hence the scene in the Alhambra, another amazing location.

You can see some of my own pictures of Spain, as well as other images that inspired the book here:
www.pinterest.com/jfpenn/gates-of-hell/

Kabbalah

There are many schools of Kabbalah and I discovered just how complex a belief system it is as I read more about it. It takes years of study to even begin to probe the meaning of the Torah, so although I tried to base the book on research, it would have been a complicated treatise if I had tried to include much of it. I've taken some fascinating aspects of Kabbalism, such as the power of the Hebrew letters that make up scripture, but essentially I have fictionalized it and all embellishments and mistakes in research are my own. Here are some aspects that may be interesting:

- The *Sefer Yetzirah*, or Book of Creation, does detail the creation of a golem

- You can play around with gematria at: www.gematrix.org

- Adam Kadmon is a representation of Primordial Man in Kabbalah

- The Pulsa diNura is indeed a Kabbalah curse

- The Kabbalah representation of evil, Qliphoth, does include the Devourers, the Misshapen and the Polluted of God, and there is a theory of the multiverse in Kabbalistic thought

Israel

I visited Safed many years ago and was struck by the peaceful hilly streets. I also remember the color blue as a vivid aspect of the town. I have always been drawn to visit there again, so hopefully that trip won't be far off.

Diving the Dead Sea is indeed possible, but it doesn't sound like much fun! www.deadseadivers.com

The Caves of Sodom are real, but closed to visitors.

The Gates of Hell

After using Sedlec in my book, *Prophecy*, I didn't expect to find the Gates of Hell only a few hours away! Although there are a number of places in the world that claim to be the Gates, Houska Castle seemed the most interesting. It has several centuries' worth of haunting stories, including the horse and the ghostly chain gang described, plus some architectural features and art that I wanted to include.

The planetary alignment and blood moons did occur earlier this year, in 2014 as I write, so it seemed a fitting time to write of the opening between the worlds.

ACKNOWLEDGEMENTS

For ONE DAY IN BUDAPEST

As always, my love and thanks to Jonathan, my first reader and wonderful husband. And a huge thank you to my readers, I hope that this book has both entertained you and made you think.

Thanks to my line editor, Jacqueline Penn, who keeps me on my toes with her insightful challenges. Thanks to author TJ Cooke, www.TJCooke.com for his suggestion of the Memorial Park, which turned out to be a great setting for the final scene. Thanks to Meg Tufano for her fantastically detailed beta-reading.

Thanks as ever to my cover designer, Derek Murphy from bookcovers.creativindie.com who did another fantastic job and to Liz Broomfield from Libroediting.com for proofreading the final draft. Thanks to Jane Dixon Smith www.jdsmith-design.com for the interior formatting.

For DAY OF THE VIKINGS

To my readers, thank you so much of your continued support. I hope to keep entertaining you for many years to come.

Thanks to the British Museum for the Viking exhibition, and for all the ideas I continue to have within those hallowed walls.

Thanks to Matt Prior and Joseph Keith Hannaby for providing the practicalities of a helicopter winch through the British Museum's roof. It can be done apparently!

Thanks to Jen Blood, my editor, for her fantastic work in improving the text, and to Wendy Janes for proof-reading so well.

Thanks to Derek Murphy from Creativindie for the brilliant book cover design, and to Jane Dixon Smith at JDSmith Design for the print interior.

For GATES OF HELL

Thanks to Jen Blood, my brilliant editor and first reader, as well as fantastic author of dark mysteries. And also to Wendy Janes, my proofreader, and to Marcia A. Kwiecinski for the helpful comments.

Thanks to Derek Murphy, from Creativindie, my fantastic book cover designer, and to Jane Dixon Smith at JDSmithDesign.com for the print interior design. And also to Danniel Soares, who designed the Key to the Gates of Hell, the illustration on the front of the book.

Thanks also to Paul Murphy, whose book *As I walked out through Spain in search of Laurie Lee*, inspired some of the Spanish setting.

Thanks for joining Morgan and the ARKANE team!

If you loved the book and have a moment to spare, I would really appreciate a short review where you bought the book. Your help in spreading the word is gratefully appreciated.

More books in the international bestselling ARKANE thriller series. Described by readers as 'Dan Brown meets Lara Croft.'
Available in print, ebook and audio formats at all online stores.

Stone of Fire #1
Crypt of Bone #2
Ark of Blood #3
One Day in Budapest #4
Day of the Vikings #5
Gates of Hell #6
One Day in New York #7
Destroyer of Worlds #8
End of Days #9

The London Psychic Series. Described by readers as 'the love child of Stephen King and PD James.'
Available in ebook, print and audio formats.

Desecration
Delirium
Deviance

d Fiendish Angels, short stories inspired by *erno*, on the edge of thriller and the occult.

Risen Gods
American Demon Hunters: Sacrifice

WWW.JFPENN.COM

ABOUT J.F. PENN

J.F.Penn is the New York Times and USA Today bestselling author of the ARKANE thrillers and London Psychic crime series as well as other dark fantasy stories. Her books weave together ancient artifacts, relics of power, international locations and adventure with an edge of the supernatural. Joanna lives in Bath, England and enjoys a nice G&T.

Try a free thriller at: www.JFPenn.com

Connect with Joanna online:
(e) joanna@JFPenn.com
(w) www.JFPenn.com
(t) @thecreativepenn
(f) www.facebook.com/JFPennAuthor
www.pinterest.com/jfpenn/

For writers:

Joanna Penn also writes non-fiction. Available in print, ebook and audiobook formats.

Joanna's site www.TheCreativePenn.com helps people write, publish and market their books through articles, audio, video and online products as well as live workshops. Joanna is available internationally for speaking events aimed at writers, authors and entrepreneurs. Joanna also has a popular podcast for writers on iTunes, The Creative Penn.

ABOUT J.F. PENN

J.F.Penn is the New York Times and USA Today bestselling author of the ARKANE thrillers and London Psychic crime series as well as other dark fantasy stories. Her books weave together ancient artifacts, relics of power, international locations and adventure with an edge of the supernatural. Joanna lives in Bath, England and enjoys a nice G&T. Try a free thriller at: www.JFPenn.com

Try a free thriller at: www.JFPenn.com

Connect with Joanna online:
(e) joanna@JFPenn.com
(w) www.JFPenn.com
(t) @thecreativepenn
(f) www.facebook.com/JFPennAuthor
www.pinterest.com/jfpenn/

For writers:

Joanna Penn also writes non-fiction. Available in print, ebook and audiobook formats.

Joanna's site www.TheCreativePenn.com helps people write, publish and market their books through articles, audio, video and online products as well as live workshops. Joanna is available internationally for speaking events aimed at writers, authors and entrepreneurs. Joanna also has a popular podcast for writers on iTunes, The Creative Penn.